"Why is all of this...bad?" Becca asked.

"Because they're giving what they don't have."

"Many in our community have more than enough."

"And many don't." Daniel scrubbed his hands over his face. "Many don't, and they've given part of what little they have to me. That's not right because I—"

He stopped midsentence, a pained expression on his face.

"What? You had nothing here, Daniel. People wanted to help. Now, don't ruin it by letting your pride become involved."

"It's not pride."

"What is it, then?"

"I can't... I can't explain why this is such a terrible thing, Becca. Just trust me. I should not have accepted this much help."

He seemed to be stuck on the fact that he was poor.

Men were a mystery to her, and Daniel Glick? Daniel was a paradox. For a guy who carried around a book and filled it with words of wisdom, he had a lot of learning to do.

Vannetta Chapman has published over one hundred articles in Christian family magazines and received over two dozen awards from Romance Writers of America chapter groups. She discovered her love for the Amish while researching her grandfather's birthplace of Albion, Pennsylvania. Her first novel, *A Simple Amish Christmas*, quickly became a bestseller. Chapman lives in Texas Hill Country with her husband.

Carrie Lighte lives in Massachusetts next door to a Mennonite farming family, and she frequently spots deer, foxes, fisher cats, coyotes and turkeys in her backyard. Having enjoyed traveling to several Amish communities in the eastern United States, she looks forward to visiting settlements in the western states and in Canada. When she's not reading, writing or researching, Carrie likes to hike, kayak, bake and play word games.

USA TODAY Bestselling Author

VANNETTA CHAPMAN

The Amish Christmas Secret

&

CARRIE LIGHTE

The Amish Widow's Christmas Hope

LOVE INSPIRED

INSPIRATIONAL ROMANCE

LOVE INSPIRED®
INSPIRATIONAL ROMANCE

Recycling programs for this product may not exist in your area.

ISBN-13: 978-1-335-41887-6

The Amish Christmas Secret and The Amish Widow's Christmas Hope

Copyright © 2021 by Harlequin Books S.A.

The Amish Christmas Secret
First published in 2020. This edition published in 2021.
Copyright © 2020 by Vannetta Chapman

The Amish Widow's Christmas Hope
First published in 2020. This edition published in 2021.
Copyright © 2020 by Carrie Lighte

This edition published by arrangement with Harlequin Books S.A.

For questions and comments about the quality of this book, please contact us at CustomerService@Harlequin.com.

Harlequin Enterprises ULC
22 Adelaide St. West, 40th Floor
Toronto, Ontario M5H 4E3, Canada
www.Harlequin.com

Printed in U.S.A.

CONTENTS

THE AMISH
CHRISTMAS SECRET

Vannetta Chapman

This book is dedicated to Kristy Kreymer.

But my God shall supply all your need
according to his riches in glory by Christ Jesus.
—*Philippians* 4:19

Your wealth is where your friends are.
—Plautus

Chapter One

Daniel Glick moved into his new place on the first Tuesday in October. The next day, the local bishop—an old fellow named Saul Lapp who looked to be in his eighties—gave him a ride to Tim Beiler's place. Tim was apparently the go-to guy in Shipshewana, Indiana, if one was looking to purchase a buggy horse.

Daniel didn't even attempt to negotiate down the price of the mare. Constance was dark gray along her mane and from her hindquarters to her hooves. The rest of her coat was nearly silver. She was more muscled and longer bodied than the horse he'd owned in Pennsylvania, standing fifteen hands high and weighing in at 825 pounds. An American saddle-bred, she was three years old and presented a nice gait. More important, her name perfectly matched her disposition.

He'd purchased the worst farm in Shipshewana.

His buggy looked as if it might not hold together in a good storm.

But he wouldn't skimp on the horse. The mare was fundamental to his new life in Indiana. She was the beginning of a twenty-year relationship. He'd gladly pay full price.

The bishop had dropped him off at Tim Beiler's place, assuring Daniel he had the best buggy horses in the area.

Tim Beiler looked to be in his late forties. With a salt-and-pepper beard, he was built like a fireplug and didn't even blink when he quoted a price several hundred above the high side for a good buggy horse.

"She's the best mare I have."

"I'll take her."

"*Gut.* You won't regret it." If Tim was surprised that Daniel didn't haggle the price, he hid it well.

Daniel counted out the bills, thanked the man and told him he'd ride her home. It wasn't often that he rode a horse, let alone bareback, but then again, it wasn't often in a man's life that he moved over five hundred miles to a place where he knew no one, and purchased a new horse.

He took his time on the way home, riding the horse along the side of the road, taking in the *Englisch* and Amish homes of Shipshewana, Indiana.

The October afternoon was bright with sunshine.

Fall flowers bloomed to his left and right.

Leaves crunched under Constance's hooves. She seemed to enjoy the sounds of fall and the freedom of the afternoon as much as Daniel did.

Soon the *Englisch* neighborhoods gave way to picture-perfect farms. He turned west. Here the farms became smaller and noticeably poorer, largely because there wasn't sufficient top soil for farming. Most of Shipshe was quite fertile, but this area would be a challenge for the best of farmers.

The property he'd purchased was four and a half miles from the center of town and was in a marked state of disarray. Its condition suited Daniel to a tee. He wouldn't have to worry about *Englischers* pausing in their cars to take pictures.

Seclusion.

Peace.

Quiet.

Those things had been at the top of Daniel's list as he'd sought a property far from home. The Realtor had tried to persuade him to look at more expensive properties with "livable" homes. He hadn't shown the advertisements to his parents, but he could have guessed their reaction—surprise followed by disappointment. They expected him to make something of himself, especially given *their situation*.

"Unto whomsoever much is given, of him shall much be required." His *dat* loved to quote the verse from Luke's gospel. It was amazing to Daniel that he didn't see the hypocrisy in that. The inheritance they'd received had literally destroyed their family, and yet he would dare to lecture Daniel on how he should live his life.

The inheritance was the reason he'd left.

Call it running away or deserting his family or

starting over. The name of it didn't matter so much as the fact of it. He was five hundred miles away from a life that had only yielded pain and betrayal. He hoped five hundred miles would be far enough.

He'd been looking for solitude when he purchased the place, and he had no doubt he'd find it here. As for the decrepit condition of his house and barn and fields, if there was one thing he didn't mind, it was a challenge.

Once home, he brushed down the mare, put oats in a bucket and hooked the bucket to the fence. Then he set her loose in the east pasture, which was the only portion of his farm that had a fence in good enough condition to hold her. Walking toward his barn, he nearly laughed. He shared it with a neighbor he hadn't met yet—the barn had been built directly on the property line. It was one more reason no one had been interested in the property. The structure looked as if a good wind would blow it down, and the house was no better.

He had the skill and the time to repair both.

But the horse he would keep in the pasture until the structure was sound.

He'd walked into the barn and was putting the brush on a shelf when he heard a high-pitched squeal from the other side of the wall. With every fiber of his being, he wanted to ignore it. He would meet his neighbors soon enough, but he had no desire to do so on the second night in his new place.

"Get back!"

Definitely a female voice, from the other side of

the barn. Poisonous snakes were rare in Indiana, but it was possible that his neighbor had encountered a copperhead or timber rattler. He'd never forgive himself if she was bitten while he stood on his side of the barn enjoying his solitude.

He threw one glance back toward his home, then sighed and walked around the barn. If someone had asked him to guess what he might find there, he wouldn't in a hundred years have guessed correctly.

A young Amish woman—Plain dress, apron, *kapp*—was holding a feed bucket in one hand and a rake in the other, attempting to fend off a rooster. The rooster was a beautiful Brahma, over two feet tall, with a red comb and golden cape. At the moment, the bird was strutting and crowing and occasionally jerking to the right and left, trying to peck the woman's feet.

"What did you do to him?" Daniel asked.

Her head snapped up, and her eyes widened. The rooster took advantage of her inattention and made a swipe at her left foot. The woman danced right and once again thrust the feed bucket toward the rooster. "Don't just stand there. This beast won't let me pass."

Daniel knew better than to laugh. He'd been raised with four sisters and a strong-willed mother. Laughing was not the correct response when he saw a don't-mess-with-me look in a woman's eyes. So he strode forward, snatched the rooster up from behind, pinning its wings down with his right arm, and keeping its head turned away from him with his left hand.

"Where do you want him?"

"His name is Carl, and I want him in the oven if you must know the truth." She dropped the feed bucket and swiped at the golden blond hair that was spilling out of her *kapp*. "Over there. In the pen is fine."

The pen she pointed toward looked as if it had long ago held pigs. Given its current condition— it was as dilapidated as everything else—Daniel doubted whether it would keep Carl corralled for long. He dropped the rooster inside and turned to face the woman. She was probably five and a half feet tall, neither heavy nor thin, and looked to be around twenty years old. Blue eyes the color of for-get-me-not flowers assessed him.

She was also beautiful in the way of Plain women, without the adornment of makeup or jewelry. The sight of her nearly brought a groan to his lips and reminded him of yet another reason why he'd left Pennsylvania. Why couldn't his neighbors have been an old couple in their nineties?

"You must be the new neighbor. I'm Becca Schwartz—not Rebecca, just Becca, because I was the second born and my *mamm* decided to do things alphabetically. We thought you might come over and introduce yourself, but I guess you've been busy. *Mamm* would want me to invite you to dinner, but I have to warn you, I have seven younger siblings, so it's usually a somewhat chaotic affair, and we're probably having soup same as every night this week seeing as how the price of hay has dropped again and hunting season hasn't started yet."

It was a lot of words.

As she talked, Becca not Rebecca had stepped closer. Daniel took a step back.

"Didn't catch your name."

"Daniel... Daniel Glick."

"We didn't even know the place had sold until last week. To say we were surprised would be a huge understatement. Thought Jeremiah was fooling with us—Jeremiah is my *onkel* on my *dat*'s side. He's a real prankster. So when he told us the place had sold, we didn't believe him at first. Most people are leery of farms where the fields are covered with rocks and the house is falling down. I see you haven't done anything to remedy either of those situations."

"I only moved in yesterday."

"Had time to purchase a horse, though."

They were standing outside the Schwartz side of the barn. Becca stepped past him, crossed her arms over the top of the fence and whistled twice.

Constance raised her head as if to nod and say hello, then went back to grazing.

"Nice mare."

"Ya."

"Get it from Old Tim?"

"The man didn't strike me as terribly old."

"He's older than Young Tim but not as old as Timothy." Becca shrugged as if to say, *you know how it is.* "Hope you didn't pay what he was asking. He always starts high."

The last thing Daniel wanted was to get into a conversation about how he'd overpaid for the mare.

What he wanted to do was walk away. He'd purchased eggs, bacon and bread when he was in town the day before, and his stomach was beginning to growl.

Then he glanced back at the barn.

The Realtor had explained that he owned half of it, which he hadn't taken the time to question. He stared at it now, wondering how to broach the subject or if Becca would even know the answers to his questions.

How did one own half a barn?

As if she could read his mind, she said, "The Coblentz *bruders* built it this way back when Shipshe was barely a dot on the map."

"It's barely a dot on the map now."

"They came from Ohio, purchased what they thought was two pieces of prime real estate that shared a property line. Built the barn so that each could use half and planned to build their houses in sight of one another. George Coblentz built your house, and Clarence had just begun to plan out his on what is now our side when they had their fight."

"Fight?"

"Over a woman, of course." Becca smiled broadly as if she found the whole story amusing. No doubt she'd told it a dozen times before. Her blue eyes literally twinkled.

If he were honest, she looked like an Amish woman that you might find on the cover of an *Englisch* tour brochure. Her hair was golden blond, prettier than wheat in the fields—not that he could see more than an inch of it. She had a button nose, the lightest dusting of freckles and a smile that should have been able to charm the bad-tempered rooster, Carl.

"Don't know the woman's name—"

"What woman?"

"The one the Coblentz *bruders* fought over."

"Ah."

"Don't even know if she was interested in either of the *bruders*, but the old folks will tell you that she left town before Clarence managed to lay the foundation for his house. Each *bruder* thought the other had driven her away. Clarence built the fence because he wasn't speaking to George and didn't want his cattle crossing over. The next year he built his house."

She tilted her pretty head toward a single-story home that looked as if it had been added onto with each additional child. "Neither stayed long. Clarence moved on to Wisconsin and George went back to Ohio."

"So the barn…"

"Is half yours, half ours."

"I've never owned half a barn before."

"Too bad Carl's on this half, as he's the most foultempered rooster I've ever encountered. *Gut* thing I brought him over to this barn, though. I don't believe my hens are ready to meet him yet."

"Your parents have another barn?"

"*Ya*, up past our house."

Daniel could just make out a structure that looked to be in no better shape than the one they were standing beside.

"Why are you and Carl here and not in the…uh… newer barn?"

"My parents said I could use this one for my projects."

"Projects?"

Before Becca could answer, someone stepped out onto the front porch of her house and rang the dinner bell. "Sounds like the soup's ready. Care to come and meet the folks?"

"Another time. I have some…um…unpacking to do."

Becca shrugged her shoulders as if it didn't matter to her whether he joined them or not. "Guess I'll be seeing you, then."

"Yeah, I guess."

He'd hoped for peace and solitude.

He'd hoped to be left alone.

He'd prayed that he wouldn't have to deal with women for a year or longer.

Instead, he had half a barn, a cantankerous rooster, and a pretty neighbor who didn't mind being a little nosy.

What kind of projects did she have?

And how much time did she spend in the barn they shared?

None of which was any of his business. He'd come to Indiana to forget women and to lose himself in making something good from something that was broken. He'd moved to Indiana because he wanted to be left alone.

Meeting the neighbors was way down his to-do list.

* * *

Becca barely thought about the tall, handsome and largely silent Daniel Glick for the rest of the evening. She didn't dwell on his dark brown hair, brown eyes with a hint of gray, muscular frame or serious demeanor. Instead, she spent her time trying to figure out exactly what he was doing in Shipshe.

Unfortunately, her unruly family gave her little quiet for thinking. Dinner for ten was no easy affair. Clyde, David and Eli had to be reminded to knock the mud off their shoes before coming into the kitchen. Francine was mooning over a boy at school and burned the corn bread. Georgia had her nose in a book—Georgia always had her nose in a book, even when she was supposed to be stirring the soup, which had resulted in a nice crust on the bottom where it had stuck. As for Hannah and Isabelle, they'd tried to sneak in two of the barn cats in their apron pockets.

Things were quiet for exactly thirty seconds of the meal, while the entire family joined hands and silently prayed. After that, the chaos quickly returned. Her *dat* loved to tell jokes during dinner. She couldn't imagine where he got them from, but he seemed to have an endless supply and delighted in sharing them.

"What did the baby corn ask the mama corn?" He grinned mischievously as he spread butter on Hannah's corn bread.

"I know," Hannah declared.

Isabelle shook her head, causing her *kapp* strings to bounce and nearly land in her soup. "No, you don't."

"I could guess."

"Then guess already."

"I don't know, then. I forgot."

Hannah and Isabelle were at the age where they were either arguing or sitting with their heads so close together that they appeared to be physically joined. Theirs was a tumultuous relationship, but *Mamm* declared that was normal for twins, especially five-year-old twins.

"The baby corn leaned close to the mama corn and asked…where's popcorn?" Her *dat* laughed at his own joke, oblivious to the fact that Becca had rolled her eyes, and Clyde and David had both groaned quite loudly.

The twins giggled, though, and soon her siblings were discussing what corn would say if it really could talk. Dishes were passed back and forth, three different spills were cleaned up, and in general, pandemonium was once again the word of the day.

To be honest, Becca didn't mind too much.

She'd learned to tune most everyone and everything out when she was focusing on something, and at the moment she needed time to ponder her new neighbor.

Who was Daniel Glick?

Why had he bought that tumbling-down excuse for a farm?

Assuming he couldn't afford a better farm—because who would buy something terrible if they could afford something good—how did he have enough money for the mare? The mare was a real beauty. Becca planned to go back over the next day and take a closer look.

She mulled several possible scenarios in her head through dinner. Before she knew it, everyone was darting off to finish chores or spend a few minutes outside as the sun set. She washed and dried the dishes by herself, which she preferred because it gave her time to think. Kitchen cleanup was one of the very rare quiet times in their home, since everyone scattered rather than get dragged into the chore. Becca dried the last spoon, hung the dish towel on the hook and stepped out on the front porch to enjoy the end of the day.

The sun was just beginning to set, casting long shadows across the fields. She could almost pretend that they lived on a beautiful farm, with rows of flowers surrounding their vegetable garden, a large new barn and at least three buggies.

Their farm wasn't beautiful.

They'd not been able to afford flowers again this year, and their vegetable garden had been harvested weeks ago.

As for the buggy, they had exactly one and it seemed to be on its last wheel.

Her quiet assessment of their living conditions—something her mind insisted on turning to, time and again—was interrupted all too quickly.

"You were quiet during dinner tonight." Her *mamm* was sitting in the porch rocker and hemming a dress, probably for Hannah or Isabelle, by the size of it.

Becca wasn't sure she'd ever seen her mother just rest. She always seemed to be sewing or darning or knitting or cooking or cleaning.

"I was?"

"You don't have to talk about it if you don't want to."

"Talk about what?"

"Whatever's on your mind."

"You'd think that in a family as big as ours, some things would go unnoticed."

"Is that what you want? Not to be noticed?"

Becca sighed and turned from the porch railing to face her *mamm*. "I met our neighbor today."

"Did you, now?"

"Have you met him?"

"*Nein*. Your *dat* told me he saw a young man moving in yesterday, or rather he saw Bishop Saul drop him off at the place. Apparently, the man didn't come with any furniture."

"A mystery wrapped in an enigma."

"It is hard to imagine who would have bought it—that place has been empty a very long time." She shifted the garment on her lap and continued hemming. "It will be *gut* to have neighbors again."

"Oh, I'm not sure you'll feel that way about Daniel Glick."

"And why would you say that?"

Becca walked over to the adjacent rocker and perched on the edge of the seat, lowering her voice as if to share a secret—though there was no one else on the porch and she didn't actually know any secrets about Daniel. "He's not very...how do I say this? He's not particularly friendly."

"How so?"

"Oh, I don't know. Usually, people tell you something about where they came from or why they moved to an area. I talked to the man for ten minutes, and I can't tell you anything more than his name. Oh, and he bought a mare—a beautiful mare—from Old Tim."

"I hope he didn't pay too much."

"Probably he did, because I said the same thing and he got all stiff and put-out-looking."

"Hmm."

"Also, I invited him to dinner, but he said he had unpacking to do."

"Curious."

"Where's he even staying? You know as well as I do that the house is about to fall in on itself. I'm sure there are holes in the roof, and the floor was rotten in places last time I walked through it."

"You walked through the Coblentz place?"

Becca waved away her concern. "Years ago. Abigail and I were playing hide-and-seek on that side of our property, and I thought it would be super smart to hide in the old house. I'm lucky a rat didn't bite my ankle."

"You two girls certainly did know how to get in trouble."

"The boys were just as bad."

"You're not wrong." Her *mamm* tied a knot in her thread, then snipped it with a tiny pair of scissors. "Perhaps Saul will schedule a workday."

"What would that accomplish? Unless you're saying we should pull down Daniel Glick's house and start over. Now, that might make sense."

Which seemed to sum up all they could think of to say about their new neighbor.

Becca was about to get up and check on her hens when her mother asked about the new rooster. Sighing and sinking back into the rocker, she described how the beast had tried to attack her, and how Daniel had come to her rescue.

"Now you know why the Grabers gave him away."

"Molly Graber told me as much, but I didn't believe her."

"You didn't really need a rooster. You're making *gut* money with the eggs from your hens."

"Not really, only $3.50 a dozen."

"What made you think you wanted to raise chickens?"

"Because I read this book…"

"I should have guessed that."

"The book said that *Englischers* will pay for organically raised chickens."

"Meaning what exactly?"

"You know—organic. Natural. Like pretty much everything around here." Becca tapped her fingers against the arm of the rocker, trying to remember exactly what the book had said. "Let's see…no chemicals or steroids…"

"We definitely don't have any of that."

"No GMO."

"I don't even know what that is."

"There was a bunch of other stuff." What had the book said about natural breeding and raising? She might have to check it out again because suddenly she was drawing a blank. "I do know that they said I could get $10 to $25 a chick, and that I could also sell the manure and the feathers."

"All you need is for Carl to cooperate."

"Exactly. He's a Brahma, and they're supposed to be docile."

"You don't say."

"Apparently no one has told Carl that. He's an ornery creature. I don't dare let him out of the pens in the old barn."

At that moment there was squawking and crowing, followed by Carl strutting into the yard and proceeding to chase one of the barn kittens. Hannah and Isabelle were chasing the rooster, and Cola the beagle was circling the entire group, barking with a loud voice that seemed to say, "Hey, hey, hey."

"Sounds as if your rooster escaped the old pens, dear."

Becca didn't bother to respond. She was already running down the porch steps and across the yard, wondering what she could use to catch Carl and what she was going to do with him after she did catch him.

Roosters were definitely more challenging than they'd described in the book; at least this rooster was. The book had definitely said that he'd be gentle and attentive to the hens. Ha! Her hens would lose all their feathers after one look at Carl.

Maybe the book was wrong.

Maybe the author didn't know what she was talking about.

Or maybe the author had never met a rooster quite like Carl.

Regardless, Becca's plan to make pockets full of money from selling organic chickens seemed to fade before her eyes. There had to be a way she could help her family financially. There had to be something she could do that would allow them to set a little bit of money back instead of simply getting by from week to week. That never seemed to bother her *mamm*—who stayed too busy with her daily chores to notice—or her *dat*, who would simply wink if she brought it up, and go on to tell another joke.

Becca hurried after Carl-the-bad-tempered-rooster. She thought that should be his full official name. The rooster wouldn't be her first project that didn't work out, but she wasn't going to let that stop her. She vowed for the hundredth time that she would find a way to lift her family out of abject poverty. But she might have to come up with a better idea than organic chickens.

Perhaps Daniel would be willing to go in on a project with her. By the looks of his situation, he could use additional funds as much as they could. The only problem was, he'd been quite standoffish.

She'd have to think of him as one of her projects.

All she needed to ensure his help was a good plan.

Chapter Two

Daniel spent Wednesday checking and mending the fence line in the east pasture. The last thing he needed was to see Constance trotting down the road without him. Spending time in the pasture with her also allowed him to get to know the mare. She was skittish at first, watching him out of the corner of her eye. By the end of the day, though, she was following him along the fence line—grazing within a few steps of wherever he was working.

Constance. He suspected that if he looked up the word in a dictionary, he'd find it meant steadfast or faithful. The mare seemed to be all of that and more. She was the exact opposite of the people who had been in his life up to this point. Animals could be trusted.

They didn't deceive.

Didn't pretend to feel something they didn't.

Didn't have ulterior motives.

With a determined effort, he pushed thoughts of

the past away and focused on the moment in front of him.

"We're going to get along just fine." He ran a hand down the mare's neck and felt her relax. They were becoming used to one another—him and Constance. They made a good team. He planned to spend an hour each evening with her—checking her hooves, brushing her coat and generally working to help her grow accustomed to his presence.

Much to his dismay, that same hour seemed to coincide with the time Becca puttered around in the old barn. He made a concerted point of staying in the field with the mare rather than bringing her into her stall. That didn't succeed in keeping Becca on her side of the fence. She had no problem joining him and asking intrusive questions about his day.

Was he planning to redo the house? Yes, of course.

When? Soon.

Did he miss his family? Some.

Why wasn't he married?

Yes, she'd actually asked him that. Instead of answering, he'd deftly changed the subject. "How are you doing with Carl?"

"I've renamed him."

"Have you, now?"

"He's officially Carl-the-bad-tempered-rooster."

"I take it things aren't going well, then."

If he'd thought he could aggravate her into leaving, he was sorely mistaken. She'd simply taken the horse brush out of his hand and begun stroking Constance. "Carl may not work out."

"Tell me you're not thinking of eating him." He hoped she noticed the sarcasm in his voice, but if she did, she didn't show it. In fact, her expression turned quite serious.

"Oh, I might. This is a farm, and I have no problem adding that rooster to *Mamm*'s pot. *Nein*. It's more that I hate to give up on him. I keep thinking there might be one more thing I can try that will tame his unruly spirit."

"Such as?" In spite of his vow to avoid Becca Schwartz at all costs, Daniel found himself pulled into the details of her crazy scheme. He'd already heard about organic chickens and how much money she could earn if Carl would simply settle down and cozy up with the hens.

"I've yet to teach Carl his spot in the pecking order."

"Which is?"

"Below me!" Becca squirreled up her nose. "The problem is that he sees me as a trespasser."

"In the chicken coop?"

"I can't keep him in that thing. Did you see him earlier? He was chasing me across the field."

He had seen that and couldn't have held in his laughter if he'd tried. Fortunately, Becca had been too far away to hear him.

"I visited with Irma Bontrager this morning. If you haven't met her, she's our neighbor to the north. Anyway, Irma raised some prize-winning hens and roosters in her day."

"And what advice did Irma give you?"

"Wear knee-high rubber boots."

"Do you have a pair of those?"

"Of course not." She raised the hem of her skirt enough to reveal her calves. "Kneepads—fortunately they're a bit large on me and stretch nearly to my ankles. My *bruder* David—he's easy to pick out of our brood because he's always on his bike—he used to do quite a bit of in-line skating when he was younger. Said I could have them."

She nodded toward the rake she'd been holding the day before. "Irma also said to keep a weapon handy, and I'm to stomp and stare if he attempts to attack."

His mind flashed back on her running across the field, being chased by Carl. "Has that worked?"

"Not yet. Irma also said some roosters won't train, so I shouldn't be too hard on myself."

"Are you? Too hard on yourself?" Daniel wasn't sure why he was asking. He didn't need to know every little detail of Becca's life, but at the same time he was curious about what she'd say or do next.

"I don't think I am. I want things to work out, but if they don't, I always have a next plan."

"A next plan?"

"Yup." She looked as if she was about to say more, then clamped her mouth shut and continued brushing the mare.

Which technically was Daniel's job.

Thursday he decided that work on the house could wait. He didn't really mind sleeping outside on the back porch, and he probably had a couple of weeks before the weather turned cold.

Constance, on the other hand, needed a good solid stall.

He was on top of the barn's roof, pulling off shingles and rotted boards, when a buggy pulled into his yard. A tall, middle-aged man hopped out of the buggy and stood with his head back, hand shading his eyes, assessing Daniel's work.

"Beautiful day to reroof a barn."

"It is."

"Mind if I come on up?"

Daniel was a bit surprised at the question, but he waved him toward the south side of the barn, where he'd propped the ladder. The man scampered up quick as a cat and was soon perched on the side of the roof next to him. He was tall and thin, with a brown beard that was only slightly tinted with gray. The eyes were what gave him away—blue eyes the exact same shade as Becca's.

"Name's Samuel... Samuel Schwartz. We own the other half of your barn."

Daniel simply nodded.

Three days ago, that statement would have floored him, but he'd decided to accept the situation since he couldn't change it. He was tempted to offer to buy Samuel's half so he wouldn't have to deal with chatty girls and crazed roosters, but he was supposed to be poor. It might start rumors if he waved a wad of money at his neighbor the first time he met him.

"I've been meaning to put a new roof on this barn

for years, but every time I'd get a little ahead, another *boppli* came along…not that I'm complaining. Sarah and I have nine *kinder*, and I wouldn't mind one more. There's something about holding an infant in your arms…"

Daniel knew nothing of that, so he turned the conversation back toward the barn. "I thought I'd repair the whole roof since it doesn't make much sense to patch half of it."

"But…"

"It was something I planned for when I bought the place… Financially, I mean."

"Roofing isn't cheap. You're sure you can afford this?"

He was going to have to think about how to explain things to folks without raising questions. From the look on Samuel's face, he could tell that what he was saying made no sense to the man. He'd purchased a farm that hadn't been productive in many years. The fences were falling down, pastures were overrun with thistles and weeds and rocks, and the house was plainly uninhabitable. Yet, here he was saying that he could afford to roof both halves of the barn.

When he'd first cooked up this plan to disappear, he'd promised himself that he would retain his integrity. He had vowed that he wouldn't lie to anyone, but now he understood that was going to be difficult unless he was willing to disclose how wealthy he was.

And that he was not willing to do.

He knew firsthand that such knowledge only brought trouble.

If he couldn't lie, and he couldn't tell the truth, he'd have to just stay silent on certain subjects.

Samuel had given up waiting for an answer. He reached down and pulled up a rotten board. "Doesn't seem right, though—your paying for my half."

He tossed the board onto the pile on the ground, turned to Daniel and smiled. "While I don't have any extra money lying around to help with the cost of materials, I do have two sons who are hard workers."

"Oh, I don't—"

"I'd come myself, but I told my *bruder* I'd help at his place. My boys—Clyde and David—are *gut* workers. They'll be here first thing tomorrow morning. Assuming you were planning on working on it again tomorrow."

"I'll be working on it."

"Gut!" Samuel pushed his hat down on his head and stood to go. He'd made it back to the ladder and started down when he stopped and called out again. "Almost forgot that Sarah sent me over to invite you to Sunday dinner."

Daniel managed to stifle a groan.

"I can see by your expression that you're wanting to say no, but that probably wouldn't be wise. She'd just show up on your doorstep with a basket of food. From the looks of your porch, she might fall through if she attempted to knock on your door."

"I was planning to get to that next."

"No man can do nothing and no man can do everything."

Daniel had no idea how to answer that, so he shrugged.

"We usually eat at noon on off-Sundays." With a nod, Samuel Schwartz disappeared below the roofline, only to pop back up again. "Why did the police arrest the turkey?"

"I have no idea. Why did the police arrest the turkey?"

"They suspected it of fowl play!"

Daniel could hear Becca's father laughing to himself as he walked toward his horse and buggy.

The horse was a chestnut gelding. Even as far away as he was, Daniel could see gray around his eyes and muzzle. He guessed the horse's age at fifteen or older, and he wondered why Samuel hadn't purchased a newer one. But then the man had said that he had nine *kinder* and no extra money. Daniel couldn't help but smile when Samuel pulled a piece of carrot out of his pocket and fed it to the horse before climbing back up in the buggy.

The buggy itself looked to be in as bad a shape as Daniel's—the rear driver's side had been dented in, and there was a long scrape down the passenger side, as well. Did they have another newer horse and buggy? There was no way the entire Schwartz family would all fit in the one Samuel was driving, so the family must have another. Otherwise, how would they get to church meetings?

None of which was his problem.

He wasn't going to get involved with the Schwartz family. He'd tried helping folks before, and every single time the situation had ended up worse than when he'd first become involved.

Nein.

He wouldn't be repeating that mistake here in Shipshewana.

Hadn't he come here to start over and put all of his past, including his newfound wealth—*especially* his newfound wealth—behind him?

Daniel turned his attention back to the roof, wishing with all his might he could finish it before Becca's brothers showed up to help.

It turned out that Clyde and David were excellent workers. They had their father's good nature but weren't as chatty as their older sister. Clyde was eighteen and worked on an *Englisch* farm three days a week. David was sixteen and thrilled not to be going back to school. He was happy to do anything that didn't involve a textbook. "For now I help my *dat*, but I'm hoping to find a real job this winter."

Both boys were tall and thin like their father.

They'd arrived as the sun was breaking the horizon Friday morning. Unfortunately they weren't alone. Becca was with them. At first he was afraid she planned to stay and help, but she put his mind to rest with a wave of her hand. "I'm not good on ladders."

"*Ya.* Remember the time you fell out of the tree house?" Clyde nudged David. "Thinking of one of her business plans and missed the last two steps. Had to walk in one of those boots for a month."

Becca turned away from her *bruders* and toward Daniel, thrusting a large basket in his hands.

"What's this?"

"Lunch—thick homemade bread and peanut butter spread, some oatmeal cookies and a large jug of raspberry-flavored tea. *Mamm* sent extra for you. Said you couldn't possibly have time to cook with all that needed to be done here."

Daniel felt guilty taking their food, but he couldn't think of a reason to turn it down that they'd accept.

"Tell her thanks."

"You can tell her yourself, when you come for dinner Sunday."

He closed his eyes and tried to think of a reason why he couldn't accept the invitation, which only caused Becca to laugh.

"I was surprised when *Dat* said you'd be there, knowing how much you like your privacy…"

"It was a goal when I moved here."

"And how you've avoided meeting my entire family…"

"*Avoid* is a strong word, since I've been here less than a week."

"But there you have it. You can look forward to an excellent meal, my *dat*'s jokes, and answering everyone's questions about why you moved to Shipshe."

She was definitely antagonizing him, and she was doing it on purpose. It was time he shifted the attention away from himself, so he stepped closer to her and said, "Maybe I'll hear more Becca stories. Tell me again how you fell out of the tree house."

Becca pressed her fingers to her lips, but a laugh still escaped. "You're pretty intent on keeping the focus off yourself, but that won't work with me. Maybe you'll have better luck with my parents."

She sashayed away before he could come up with a good retort. Becca Schwartz was free-spirited, excessively energetic, and irritating. She seemed bent on pulling him out of his shell. Well, good luck with that. He happened to like the shell he'd built around himself.

Then he looked up and saw Clyde and David waiting on top of his barn's roof. So much for being alone.

He'd removed a good bit of the roof the day before. Working together, the three of them were able to finish pulling off the rest of it in a couple of hours, and they started laying new cross boards before lunch. They were eating underneath the maple tree when Clyde asked him about the horse. "She's a beauty. What's her name?"

"Constance."

"*Gut* name," David said. "Our horse should be named Lazy."

David and Clyde laughed at that, though neither seemed particularly upset about the old horse or the condition of their buggy.

"We only have the one, but since it's all we've ever had we're used to it," Clyde said.

David mentioned riding his bike most places. "It's

a problem if the weather turns bad, but we make it work."

To say they were good-natured was an understatement.

Daniel tried to remember a time when he'd been as content as Becca's *bruders* seemed to be, but he couldn't. Which proved that money didn't solve every problem. If it did, he'd be the happiest man in town.

If it did, he wouldn't have needed to move.

By the time the sun had begun to set, they'd repaired all of the rotted sections and begun hammering on shingles.

"Should be able to finish this tomorrow." David swiped at the sweat running down the back of his neck.

"Good thing, too, since rain is coming next week."

"Wouldn't want Constance in the rain."

"She's going to love her new digs."

Daniel tried to tell them that they'd done enough, that they didn't need to return the next day, but David and Clyde only smiled and said they'd see him in the morning.

Daniel was so tired that his legs felt like lead and his arms actually ached. He'd turned thirty the previous spring. He didn't consider himself old, but he also hadn't replaced a roof in a long time. The truth was that if he hadn't had David and Clyde helping, it would have taken him much longer. Clyde scampered up and down the ladder like a well-trained monkey, and David toted stacks of shingles as if they weighed nothing.

It had been a long day, a *gut* day, and Daniel was satisfied with what they'd managed to accomplish.

He cared for Constance, then went to the back porch and made a supper of instant oatmeal, coffee and toast—all done over an old camp stove. He forced himself to boil more water and wash up before collapsing into his sleeping bag. The bag was rated to twenty degrees, and the evening's temperature was nowhere near that. Lying there on his back porch, looking out at the stars, Daniel was in many ways happier than he'd been in a long time.

The quiet of the evening felt like a blessing poured over his soul.

The air was clean and crisp, and he felt as if he could breathe again for the first time in a long time.

But his mind insisted on tossing around questions for which he had no answer.

How did Becca's family cope with so little?

What was behind her insatiable curiosity about his past?

Why did the Schwartz family seem so satisfied—even in their poverty?

He thought of what Samuel had said. *No man can do nothing and no man can do everything.* He wasn't sure he understood it exactly, though the words had the ring of truth to them. He fetched his backpack and pulled out the notebook he often wrote in. Copying down the line, he studied it for a moment, then sighed, closed the book and stored it back in his bag.

As he tossed and turned, his mind returned again and again to his neighbors.

What was he going to do about pretty Becca Schwartz, who found an excuse to visit the barn every day?

And how was he going to maintain a distance between himself and the rest of the community, between himself and his neighbors? Because above all else, Daniel was determined to live a private life. He didn't want to develop friendships that would cause more heartache, and he certainly didn't want anyone attempting to fix him up with one of the local girls.

Dating and friendship were fine for other people.

But Daniel had learned firsthand that they wouldn't work for him. Friends would learn of his money, and then they would expect him to help—which he was only too happy to do. The problem was that when money became part of the equation, friendships took on a false tone. Too soon, strangers would be showing up at his place asking for a handout. Reporters would come by wanting to write about the Amish millionaire.

There was no end to it.

There was no peace in it.

He was better off alone, which was the way he planned to stay. His attempts to date since receiving his inheritance had been disastrous. *Nein.* He was better off without the heartbreak, even if it meant he occasionally felt lonely. He tossed onto his left side, his hip digging into the porch floor and a part of him wondering if he could sneak a new mattress into the house.

Becca Schwartz would notice.

She'd probably tell him he'd paid too much for it.

He almost laughed aloud at that. She was a spunky one. He'd give her that. The little that he'd seen of her had convinced him she was a hard worker, and it wasn't because she wanted to buy a new handbag or an *Englisch* phone. No, all Becca had mentioned when she was talking about her problem with Carl-the-bad-tempered-rooster was earning money for Clyde to purchase a buggy or her desire to buy the twins new coats. She cared about her family, that was for sure and certain.

It seemed to him that the *gut* women were already taken, and the ones—like Becca—who were looking for a better life, he had no business becoming involved with. The last few years had taught him they were after his money and not interested in him as a person.

No, the money he'd inherited had erected a wall between him and everyone else, and he didn't know how to climb over or move around it.

But he didn't need to.

He only needed peace and quiet to live out his own life.

And if he had to pretend to be poor in order to do that, he was happy to do so.

Becca had been over to Daniel Glick's place every day, and she'd yet to have a meaningful conversation with the man. He was plainly not interested in sharing any details about his life.

Which was fine.

She'd been brushed off before, and she didn't take it personally. She did enjoy working on puzzles, though, and there was definitely a mystery surrounding Daniel. She meant to solve it. So she plied her *bruders* with questions, though they could tell her very little. You'd think they'd have paid more attention, working with the man for two full days.

He slept on his back porch.

He was using an old camping stove to cook on.

He seemed to be every bit as poor as they were—though there was the horse. The horse was a beauty. How had he been able to afford it?

Daniel had managed to avoid her when he was on the roof and she was in the pens. She'd relocated Carl inside the old barn and was attempting to introduce one of her hens to the rooster. All she'd accomplished was to receive a peck on her left ankle—directly below the borrowed kneepads. Carl had so traumatized Becca's hen that the bird had lost a good bit of her feathers.

She'd caught Daniel watching her as she'd shooed Carl back into the stall where she was now keeping him. She tossed a handful of feed at the rooster.

"Tell me you're not laughing at me, Daniel Glick."

Instead of answering, he'd simply tipped his hat and asked her *bruder* to grab more shingles.

Yes, Daniel was avoiding her quite successfully, which was easy enough to do when he was on the roof of the barn. He wouldn't get away so easily during the Sunday meal. There was little that Becca enjoyed more than solving the unsolvable. Her *dat* had once said she was worse than a hunting dog on point. In other words, there was no distracting her once she set her mind to a thing.

Sunday arrived overcast and warm—a sure sign that the rain they'd been predicting would arrive the next day.

Her *mamm* had invited Bishop Saul and the elderly neighbors whose farm sat just to their north—Irma and Joshua Bontrager. The Bontragers had grown children over in Goshen. They were always talking about selling their farm and moving to a *Daddi Haus* on their oldest son's place, but so far, no For Sale sign had appeared on their property.

The group was rounded out with Becca's older *schweschder*, Abigail, Abigail's husband, Aaron, and their two boys—William and Thomas.

"You're bigger this time." Becca placed a hand against her *schweschder*'s stomach. "Tell him to move so I can feel it."

"Doesn't work that way. Babies tend to move in the middle of the night."

"Stubborn—like both of your other boys."

"Stop saying that. It could be a girl this time."

"Uh-huh." Becca turned back to the kitchen counter and resumed placing thick slices of ham on the platter.

"Find out anything more about your new neighbor?"

"Nein."

"But you have a theory."

"I have several, but I can't prove any of them."

Abigail sat down at the table. She was putting peanut butter spread on the bread and slicing it into triangles for the *kinder*.

"He could be undercover Amish." Becca felt foolish suggesting such a thing, but hadn't she read in the newspaper about an undercover drug agent posing as an Amish man? Or maybe she'd read it in a novel from the library. Regardless, she was glad to discuss the mystery of Daniel Glick with someone.

"Undercover? What does that mean?"

"You know…someone who is *Englisch*, a city slicker, who is merely pretending to be Amish."

"Why would someone do that?"

"I don't know. Maybe he's trying to ferret out a drug dealer."

"We don't have any drug dealers—at least none that I'm aware of. Though we did have that one boy selling his ADHD medicine at the local high school. I read about it in the paper last week. I don't know what the world is coming to."

"But back to Daniel…"

"I don't think your new neighbor is a police officer—undercover or not. For one thing, if he was, he wouldn't catch any criminals on his farm. You said yourself that he rarely leaves it, so…" Abigail let her sentence fade as she rearranged the sandwich quarters on the tray.

"I suppose you're right, but that doesn't mean he's

simply a farmer." Becca snapped her fingers. "He could be in the witness protection program."

"Witness to what? And why would he need protection?"

"I don't know." Her friend Liza had a cell phone, one with access to the internet. They sometimes watched videos together—short silly things, but some of them had been about witnesses for high-profile trials being placed in federal custody in absurd places. "You have to admit that old farm would certainly be a *gut* place to hide someone."

Abigail proceeded to add slices of apple to the tray. "You said he was replacing his barn's roof…"

"Could be part of his cover story."

"And you mentioned that he was *gut* with the horse."

"Lots of people are *gut* with horses—cowboys from Texas or Colorado or Montana."

"You read too many novels." Abigail sat back and rested her hand on her protruding stomach. "Also, he knew how to catch your rooster. I doubt a city slicker would know how to do something like that."

"Fine. Then maybe he is Amish, but he's on the run from the law."

"That's a terrible thing to think of someone."

"Maybe he got involved with the wrong people, and he didn't know how to get out of the mess, so he hightailed it out of there, flew the coop, headed for the hills."

"You certainly haven't lost your imagination."

Becca added slices of cheese to her platter, then

covered it with a dish towel and sat down beside her *schweschder.* "You have to admit it's curious."

"What's curious?"

"Buying the worst place in town."

"I don't know if it's all that bad."

"Name one place in worse shape than Daniel Glick's farm."

Abigail stared up at the ceiling a minute, then shook her head. "Okay. You might be right about that part."

"He moved in with nothing more than a backpack."

"Men don't consider furniture a necessity."

"Which is a stereotype that doesn't always prove true. Your husband was the one who insisted on a new couch."

"New to us, but remember we bought it at a garage sale."

"And if Daniel really is poor…"

"*Mamm* would say that money isn't a necessary ingredient for happiness. She would say, *Where love is, there riches be…*"

"Okay, but the only love at Daniel Glick's place is between him and that mare. Don't you find that just a little odd? I heard from Molly, who heard from Old Tim's cousin, that he sold the mare at top price. Tell me how Daniel was able to afford that, but spends his evenings in a sleeping bag on the back porch?"

Abigail raised her hands in mock surrender. "I don't know. I'll admit it's curious, but it isn't a crime. You need to remember that men think differently than women. Most men—Amish and *Englisch*—care more about how they get from point A to point B than they do about where they sleep."

Which was an observation Becca couldn't argue with.

Her own *bruder* was saving every dime he made so that he could purchase a buggy. It would come in handy for courting, but of course, a buggy required another horse. He would rather put back what little money he had in the hopes of finding a cheap buggy and inexpensive horse than spend it on something more practical like new clothes. His old clothes had been mended several times, and the hem let down more than once.

"I still look like me in anything I wear," Clyde had said with a laugh. "But no girl likes to be picked up for a date on a bicycle."

The Sunday lunch passed in its usual way—pandemonium punctuated by her father's jokes, and of course both laughter and tears from the children. Abigail's youngest was in the midst of the terrible-two stage. Thomas had insisted on eating ham with no bread. He commenced to cry because he couldn't cut his meat, then cried because his *dat* cut it for him. Which merited another riddle from Becca's father—who thought he could make anyone laugh with a well-told joke.

"What animal can you always find at a baseball game?" He combed his fingers through his beard, then leaned forward and lowered his voice as if he were sharing a secret. "A bat!"

Becca didn't want to laugh, but she couldn't help it when her *dat* cackled at his own punch line.

"Life is *gut*, *ya*?" He reached over and mussed his grandson's hair.

Thomas glanced up at his grandfather and smiled. The cut meat was forgotten for a moment, then he glanced down, frowned at his plate, pushed a forkful of ham into his mouth and said, "I want to play baseball."

Several times throughout the meal, Becca caught Daniel sitting back and watching them. He said little, though he answered pleasantly enough when someone spoke directly to him.

His manners were good.

He'd found a way to clean up, though her *bruders* had said there was no working plumbing at his house.

He managed to answer questions about his family without giving away any real information. They lived in Lancaster. He didn't expect them to visit anytime soon. He'd picked Shipshewana because he'd heard it was a *gut* Amish community—not too strict and not too liberal. Daniel laughed with everyone else when he admitted, "And the price for the farm was right."

At different points in the meal, her *dat*, Abigail's husband, Aaron, Joshua Bontrager and Bishop Saul all mentioned stopping by to help. Each time Daniel managed to change the conversation. Becca paid attention to all of this, and she'd assembled a whole list of questions in her mind for when she managed to corner him.

She didn't have to wait long.

She'd gone to check on her hens. Cola the beagle dogged her feet, hoping she was carrying a treat in her pocket. She wasn't sure why she spoiled the dog so. Cola wasn't even purely a beagle, but rather some conglomeration of other breeds with beagle-like ears. There was something about the way those ears flopped over and her eyes glanced up in hope that caused Becca to squat, pet the dog, and pull a small biscuit out of her pocket. Cola accepted it gratefully, then rolled over onto her back to show her tummy.

"One scratch. I have chickens to check on."

She came around the corner of the barn to find Daniel staring into the chicken coop.

"Want to buy a chicken?"

"Are you selling?"

"I might be if the price was right."

"You're a real little entrepreneur, aren't you?" Daniel turned to study her. With his thumbs tucked under his suspenders and his hat tipped back on his head, he looked like he'd stepped off the cover of an Amish romance novel. Not that she read Amish romance novels—or at least she didn't read them often. Occasionally her friend Liza loaned her one and then it would have been rude not to read them.

"You say *entrepreneur* as if it's a bad thing, and why don't you want anyone helping at your house?" Becca didn't believe in creeping up on a subject— best to toss it out there and catch the person you were interrogating off guard.

"I didn't say I didn't want help."

"You didn't jump at the offer, either. I noticed that you have a way of turning the conversation away from yourself."

Daniel smiled broadly for the first time since she'd known him. "Didn't realize you were watching me so closely."

"Don't flatter yourself. I'm not in the market…"

"And why is that?"

"None of your business."

"True enough, and it's none of your business why I'd rather rebuild my house by myself."

His voice was joking, but his eyes had taken on a decidedly serious squint.

"Fine by me." She turned to study her hens. "I suppose I should introduce you to the group. Princess is a golden comet. Buttercup and Egg-bert are both Rhode Island Reds, and the other four are Sussex."

"What? They don't have names?"

"Betty, Pearl, Henny and Doris."

Daniel stared at the ground a minute. When he finally looked up, she knew he was laughing at her… even though he wasn't making any sound. She could tell.

"Naming hens is a common practice. They need to feel cared for in order to lay the maximum number of eggs."

"How are things going with Carl?"

"You know good and well that things are going terribly with Carl. That's why he's still banished to our barn."

Did Daniel just flinch when she said the word *our*? Interesting.

"The new roof is *wunderbaar* by the way. I'll be able to spend a lot more time over there now that I don't have to worry about the rafters falling in on me."

That definitely irritated him. He'd crossed his arms and was frowning at something on the horizon.

She moved next to him, mirrored his position and asked in her sweetest voice, "Why did you buy the worst farm in town?"

"I'm not sure it's the worst."

"Oh, it is, trust me. I'm thinking maybe you bought it because you didn't want anyone bothering you."

"I'm not saying that's true, but I will say if what I wanted was to be alone, then my farm is a great place for that, or at least it was the first twenty-four hours I lived there."

Instead of being insulted, Becca laughed. She'd definitely managed to poke under his defensive, though polite, layer. She barely had time to enjoy the moment, though. He quickly turned the tables on her.

"Why are you so intent on making money?"

"There's nothing wrong with making money." She raised her chin slightly and tried not to notice that his smile had returned.

"Most girls in your situation would try to marry up instead."

"Marry up?" Becca clinched her hands at her side and hoped that her temper didn't pop the *kapp* off the top of her head. "You're saying I should marry up? You're actually suggesting to me that I should marry for money?"

"Oh, come on. Don't look surprised. Girls do it all the time."

"And you're an expert on this?"

"I'm not blind. I've seen it happen often enough, and I'm not saying anything's wrong with it as long as both parties are honest about their intentions."

"You're saying that the way to improve my lot in life is to hook my buggy onto some rich Amish guy's horse."

"I might not have said it that colorfully, but if the *kapp* fits…"

A low growl escaped Becca's lips. She could actually feel her blood pressure rise. Her neck and jaw muscles had gone suddenly stiff as if they'd been locked in place.

Daniel was like most other Amish men she'd met. Why had she for a moment imagined he might be different? Because he was as poor as they were? Obviously, that wasn't enough to give him a fresh perspective on life. He thought the same as every other single guy she'd ever known.

She was tired of it.

She wasn't going to demurely accept being put in her place any longer. She tried to count to ten, made it to three, and then gave up.

It was time to give Daniel Glick a piece of her mind.

Chapter Three

Daniel stepped back when Becca stepped closer.

The midsize mutt that had been dogging her steps apparently sensed the tension between them. Spotting a butterfly that was making its way across the field, the dog took off in pursuit. Daniel didn't blame him.

Things were about to go from bad to worse.

Daniel was well acquainted with a woman's temper. His oldest *schweschder*, in particular, had something of a short fuse, which made them all laugh after she'd *gone off* on someone. Amish women were supposed to be patient and kind, and Angela was both of those things once she calmed down. Still, he had learned at a young age to get out of the way when she was riled. He saw the same look on Becca's face now.

The problem was that he'd reached the limit of his patience with Becca Schwartz.

She was angry?

He wasn't exactly in the best of moods, either, so

bring it on—but from a distance. He took two steps away from the chicken coop.

Her voice dangerously low, she said, "We may be the poorest family in town—"

"I never said that."

"And we may not have a fancy new saddlebred horse—"

"What does my horse have to do with this?"

"But we take care of our own in the Schwartz family. We help one another. If my *bruder* needs a buggy and can't afford it, then I don't mind working a little extra harder to help him, and I don't need you telling me—"

"I think you misunderstood what I was trying to say."

Becca's face had taken on a decidedly red hue, her hands were slicing the air with each point she tried to make, and her gaze was jumping around as if she couldn't decide what she wanted to take down first—him or the chicken coop.

"I understood what you said just fine. You think every single woman is looking for a rich man. Ha! I guess the joke's on you, since you're as poor as we are."

"There's nothing wrong with being poor."

"But you know the funny thing? We're not really poor, because we have each other. You, on the other hand, are over there with your fancy horse and your decrepit house and you have no one. As far as I know, you're on the lookout for a wealthy Amish girl so *you* can marry up."

"I didn't move to Indiana to marry." Daniel felt

his own temper rise, and he fought to tap it down. Becca didn't know what she was talking about. She didn't know a single thing about his situation. In fact, it was almost laughable, because everything she thought she knew about him was wrong. "I moved here to be alone, so if you'd just keep your nose out of my affairs…"

"Oh, my nose is in your affairs?"

"You're over at my place every day."

"In our half of the barn."

"I saw you feeding carrots to Constance. Feed your own horse and leave mine alone!"

Again the growl, but this time she clenched her hands at her side and stomped away. He waited five seconds, stared at the ground and heard his *mammi*'s voice. *Tackle the problem, not the person.*

The problem, he realized, was that it wasn't as easy to be a loner as he had thought it would be. Well-intentioned people kept invading his space. Worse, he understood that he'd hurt her with his careless comment. That hadn't been his intention, but it had plainly been the result.

He prayed for wisdom even as he hurried to catch up with his pretty neighbor.

"Becca, I'm sorry."

"I don't want to hear it."

"But I need to say it." He reached out and touched her arm, causing her to halt so suddenly that he practically ran into her. "Look…"

When she pivoted toward him, he stepped back and raised his hands in surrender. "It's none of my business that you have a business streak, or entrepreneurial spirit, or whatever you want to call it. It's also none of my business what you hope to accomplish."

When she didn't respond, he added somewhat lamely, "And I do think it's admirable that you want to help your *bruder* Clyde."

Her chin came up and her eyes locked on his, but still, she didn't speak. Daniel's mind scrambled to remember what else he'd said, what he still needed to apologize for.

"It's actually very considerate of you to bring carrots to Constance. I'm sorry for what I said earlier—about you having your nose in my affairs. That was unkind. What I meant was that I'm not ready to talk about my life or my past. I'm… I'm a private person, and I don't…well, I don't share easily."

The truth slipped past his planned generic apology. It caught him off guard, and apparently, Becca hadn't been expecting it, either, because some of the stiffness went out of her posture.

"I plan to keep using our half of the old barn, whether it bothers you or not."

"Of course. That's fine."

She crossed her arms and squinted at him, some of the fire returning to her eyes.

"What I mean is that you don't need my permission. It's your half of the barn."

Which sounded so utterly ridiculous that he couldn't help grinning. Becca rolled her eyes and reached for her *kapp* strings.

She took a deep breath, stared at the ground, and then finally met his gaze. "I'm sorry that I lost my temper."

"*Nein.* I provoked you—unintentionally, but still I should be more careful." They both started walking back toward the picnic tables. "It's none of my business who you plan to marry or why you would want to do so."

"I'm a tad sensitive about that subject."

"Understatement of the year." He thought he'd said those words to himself, but she slapped his arm, so he must have said them out loud.

They were still out of earshot of the group, so he stopped and waited for her to turn to face him. "I'll make you a deal. You stay out of my business, and I'll stay out of yours."

"Of course."

"Seriously?"

"No problem. My life is plenty busy without solving the enigma of Daniel Glick."

He might have believed her, but then she smiled, raised her eyebrows and sashayed off toward the dessert table. He realized with sudden clarity that it wasn't him she was interested in, it was the mystery living adjacent to their property. Amish life could be slow at times, and Becca Schwartz was a nice-looking woman in her twenties, still living on her parents' farm. No doubt her life needed some excitement.

The issue was that he had no intention of providing her a welcome distraction. He wanted peace and quiet and solitude. He'd purchased those things as much as he'd purchased a rickety barn and broken-down house.

The challenge would be to stay out of her way

and not lose his temper again. He should be able to do both of those things.

Becca had reached the dessert table and was talking to Abigail. She looked back over her shoulder at Daniel, smiled too sweetly and then continued talking to her *schweschder*. They both laughed and then walked toward the house.

He didn't know how he knew it, but whatever was happening between him and Becca was just beginning.

Staying out of her way wasn't going to be easy.

Becca couldn't have explained why Daniel had aggravated her so. She certainly wasn't willing to examine her feelings on the subject of marriage. Doing so tended to put her in a funk for days. So instead, she'd sidled up to her *schweschder*, smiled back at Daniel and pretended she had a plan.

She needed a plan for dealing with their new neighbor.

Regardless of whatever his personal issues were—and he apparently did have issues that he was in no way going to talk about—he'd read her completely wrong. She was not searching for a husband in order to alleviate her family's financial problems. If she was supposed to find true love, she would. God would drop it on her doorstep—or rather God would drop *him* on her doorstep. Or maybe put the guy next door.

Ha! That hadn't happened.

So instead of worrying over Daniel Glick, she proceeded as normal for the next week—attempting to tame Carl-the-bad-tempered-rooster, helping her *mamm* with household chores, and keeping her eyes open for any new projects that might raise money for her family. Everyone called them her "get-less-poor" schemes, since a "get-rich" scheme seemed too far-fetched.

And while she did those things, she continued to try to learn more about their new neighbor.

On Friday, she decided she could use a few hours away from the farm, so she walked over to Liza Kauffmann's house to see if somehow she'd heard something that Becca hadn't. Liza had been her best friend for years and years. Liza understood her, though in many ways they were polar opposites. For one thing, Liza had plenty of beaus.

Liza was in the middle of making fresh bread. She punched the dough, turned it on the floured counter-top and then proceeded to divide it in half. "I can't believe I haven't met him yet."

"How could you? He rarely leaves his farm."

She slipped the two halves into two loaf pans, covered them, then nodded toward the window. "Walk with me over to the shop?"

"Sure."

The fall day was glorious—leaves crunched under their feet, and the sweater Becca was wearing provided just the right amount of warmth against the crisp autumn air. She'd be perfectly happy if only she wasn't so puzzled by Daniel Glick.

"Strange that he's not more interested in meeting some of the local girls."

"I guess."

"You would think that someone so…young…" Liza drawled.

"How do you know he's young?"

"Deborah told Mary, who mentioned it to me."

Becca somehow resisted the urge to slap her palm against her forehead. "The Shipshe grapevine is alive and well."

"Stop calling it that."

They walked into Liza's bakeshop, which was actually a small modular house that had been outfitted with shelves to hold the items she baked in their kitchen. Liza was an expert baker. Give her sugar, flour and any variety of ingredients, and she could create something that would make your mouth water.

She was two years younger than Becca, still enjoying the freedom of her *rumspringa*—which explained the cell phone and romance novels. Liza was also putting on at least ten pounds a year. None of those things mattered to the eligible men in their community. Liza could cook, and she had more interested males stopping by her place than she could shake a rolling pin at.

"I don't think you'd be interested in Daniel. He's older—older than us, and he's serious."

"How serious?"

"I've only seen him smile when he's teasing me about Carl-the-bad-tempered-rooster."

"Well, I'm not looking for a husband anyway."

"Still in no hurry to settle down?"

"Just because I love baking doesn't mean I want to stay home every Saturday night."

Becca shrugged her shoulders at that comment. She was used to Liza's rebellious ways.

"I just keep wondering why Shipshe? Why that farm? What's he doing here?"

"I don't know, Becca. Life can lead you to strange places. I never thought I'd go to a Notre Dame football game, but there I was last weekend in a college stadium that holds eighty thousand fans."

"Did you wear your *kapp*?"

"I wore a cap, but it had a Notre Dame logo on it." Liza winked, then smoothed out her apron. "Don't give me that look. I wore blue jeans and a sweatshirt—it was all quite proper."

"But not Plain."

"*Nein*. It wasn't." Liza squirreled up her nose. "Don't you ever want to experience things? Other things?"

"Like what?"

"I don't know. The Notre Dame campus has Touchdown Jesus in the end zone, the Basilica of the Sacred Heart, and the Grotto of Our Lady of Lourdes."

"I have no idea what any of those things are."

"Beautiful, that's what they are. You know, Amish don't have a corner on all things to do with Christ. You'd be surprised when you step out of our community how much of *Gotte* is still around."

"Well, you don't have to lecture me about it."

"Guess I'm a bit touchy about it all. *Mamm* keeps trying to set me up with Amish men—respectable Amish men. She always makes sure I understand that they are the good, decent sort."

"I suppose I should be grateful my *mamm* is too busy with the twins to meddle in my social life."

"Take it from me—you really should be."

As she walked home, Becca couldn't help wondering whether Daniel would find Liza attractive. The man could use a wife, especially one that knew how to cook. Though the thought of Liza living in a house where the roof was falling in was enough to make Becca laugh out loud.

It was later that afternoon, while she was tending to her newest project, that she had a chance to tease Daniel.

He'd been avoiding her since Sunday dinner. It seemed he kept changing the time that he brought in Constance. She'd had little chance to properly pepper him with questions. So on Friday afternoon, she brought along a cookbook and sat down to page through it while she waited for him to bring Constance into the barn.

When he did, she pounced.

"Still not working on the house, huh?"

He didn't ask what she was doing on his side of the barn. In truth, you couldn't actually split a barn in half. They shared the large open area. Daniel kept Constance in one of the stalls on his side. Becca kept Carl-the-bad-tempered-rooster and her other projects on her family's side.

"Still not working on it," he agreed.

"Aren't you worried about winter coming?"

"I'm more worried about the fields."

"Yes, I saw you out there working."

He didn't answer that. Daniel was good at not

commenting on things, which made Becca want to provoke him all the more. Although *provoke* might be the wrong word. She was simply curious. Was that such a sin?

"Seems the girls in the district are all talking about you."

"Is that so?"

"You'll have a chance to meet them at church on Sunday."

Daniel grunted.

"My friend Liza, she's a very *gut* cook—baker mostly, but she can cook just about anything."

He walked to the other side of Constance to brush her down. That horse received more attention than the average Amish wife, Becca was sure of that.

"Are you trying to set me up, Becca?"

"*Nein.* I just thought you should know what you're walking into."

"Is that why you hang out over here? Trying to provide the Amish grapevine with new information?"

"That's what I call it, too."

"Every community has one."

"It's not like we have Facebook."

"What's that?"

"Or Twitter?"

"Twit who?"

"Or Snapchat."

Daniel placed the horse brush on a shelf and walked over to open the stall door, forcing her to back up. It was a half door, so Constance could stick her head out whenever she wanted. She imagined that he spent his nights sitting outside the door, singing to the spoiled mare. As he walked out of the stall and carefully secured the door latch, he asked in a low voice, "Are you sure you're Amish?"

"Pretty sure. If not, I have a terrible sense of fashion."

"What's wrong with your fashion?"

"Look at me. Long dress, apron, *kapp* on my head."

"Would you rather be wearing *Englisch* clothes?"

"Of course not. Why are we even talking about my clothes? Let's talk about you."

"Still nosing around."

"It's natural to share. I'll start. I'm twenty-four, I'm the second oldest of nine siblings…"

"I already know all of that." Daniel crossed his arms and leaned against the closed stall door. "Have you ever dated?"

"That's a rude question."

"I thought it was natural to share."

"Except I don't want to share about that."

"All right. Tell me about your projects. What have you been doing on your side of the barn?"

"What?"

Daniel's smile brightened. He tucked his thumbs under his suspenders—which should have looked stupid, but actually made him look less stiff and more likable—and began to walk toward her side of the barn.

"Where are you going?"

"I should probably be aware of what's going on under the roof of my barn."

"*Our* barn. Remember? We both own it."

"Your *dat* and *mamm* own it. I'm sure they'd want me to keep an eye out."

"Hang on. That's none of your…"

But Daniel had already walked into the stall where she'd set up her latest project. It was closest to the outer door on her side and allowed in plenty of light so the plants could grow.

"What is this?"

"It's nothing."

He stooped closer to study the plants that were now six inches high. "What are you growing?"

"It's just a project. I received it through a mail-order service a couple of weeks ago, and I've been… you know…watering, making sure they have plenty of light, using these growing supplements they gave me."

When he turned toward her, she expected to see him laughing at her. Instead, his eyes had widened, and he was looking at her as if he'd just seen Carl dance a jig. He was looking at her with obvious disbelief.

"Do you know what this is?"

"Of course, it's…" Becca picked up the pamphlet that had come with the plants and peered at it. "From the family Cannabaceae."

"Cannabaceae?"

"I don't really know how to pronounce the word. Besides, it doesn't matter what it is. I take care of and grow the plants, then call this number and someone will come out to pick them up and pay me. It's a great deal. I can make five to six dollars a plant, which is a lot of money even if only two thirds of the plants survive."

"Becca, this is hemp."

"What?"

"It's hemp. Basically it's marijuana without the THC content."

"It is not. I wouldn't grow marijuana in my parents' barn."

"It's not marijuana. It's hemp. Did you apply for a license to grow this?"

Becca couldn't resist. Both hands planted firmly on her hips, she stomped her foot. "Read my lips. That's not what this is. It's just…it's just…"

She picked up the brochure again. "Some kind of medicinal herb." She'd meant to read the entire description, but then something had distracted her. Now she was having trouble focusing on the words. Various phrases popped out, like *industrial hemp, may contain a maximum THC content of 0.30%* and *how to deal with thieves.*

Her chest started to tighten, sweat trickled down the back of her neck, and she felt a sudden light-headedness. The words on the brochure seemed to swim before her eyes, and when she glanced up, Daniel looked as if he was standing at a slant.

Daniel grabbed both of her hands and pulled her outside, into the fading light of a bright October afternoon. "Sit there. Head between your knees."

"Why?"

"You looked as if you were about to faint."

"I'm not the fainting type."

"So you might not recognize the symptoms."

"I might have made a mistake," she mumbled.

"What?"

"I said…" But when she raised her head, he was smiling at her, and she knew that he'd understood her perfectly well.

"It's not a problem," he said. "Just throw the plants away."

"Throw them away?" That idea brought the blood rushing to her cheeks. She sat up straighter, then rested her head back against the barn. "I can't throw them away. What if someone finds them?"

"No one will find them."

"Maybe Hannah and Isabelle."

"Why would they be out here in the barn?"

"They could get high."

"No one's going to get high. It's not marijuana per se. Did you even read the pamphlets?"

"I could burn them, but then we might all get high. Imagine Carl-the-bad-tempered-rooster high." She covered her face with her hands.

Daniel moved to sit beside her on the bench. "It's all a mistake. It's just a mistake. You can fix this."

"But it is illegal?"

"*Ya.* I suppose it is since you need a license to grow hemp here in Indiana."

"So I'll get a license."

"They're backed up. It's a nine-month process."

"Nine months?" She stood and began pacing in front of him. "What was I thinking? Why didn't I read the fine print?"

"Actually it says right here on the cover that you should check your state laws before growing."

Becca snatched the pamphlet from his hands.

"How do you know so much about this? Is that what you came here for? To grow hemp?"

"I'm not the one growing it." Instead of looking defensive, he still seemed to be holding in a belly laugh.

"But you know a lot about the subject. Explain that to me."

Daniel sighed heavily, then admitted, "Both of my *bruders* applied to grow it in Pennsylvania. You're right. It's a *gut* crop, and people use it for all sorts of things that are natural. It fits right in with our Amish way of life."

"What kind of things?"

"Clothing, rope, medicinal herbs and lotions."

"But I need a license."

"*Ya.* You do."

Becca crossed her arms, drummed her fingers and tried to think. She didn't have a license. Her parents couldn't afford any sort of fine. She surely didn't want to give what little money she'd saved to the Shipshewana judicial court. With one last look at Daniel, she turned and hurried back into her hemp room.

"What are you doing?"

"I'm taking these in to the police station." She began pulling the plants out by their roots and stuffing them into a box. Stupid plants. She'd done the math. She would have made at least five hundred dollars.

"You're taking that box in to the police station?"

"Sure. I'll just explain it's all a big mistake, and ask them to dispose of these for me."

"How are you going to get there?"

That stopped her in her tracks. How was she going to get there? *Dat* had their only buggy and had gone to visit his *bruder*. She couldn't ride her bike carrying the box she was holding, and she wouldn't be able to put them all into the one box anyway.

She expected to look up and see Daniel laughing at her.

She wouldn't have been surprised to receive a lecture from him, as he seemed to delight in her projects that went awry—at least he'd laughed a good deal over Carl-the-bad-tempered-rooster. But instead of haughtiness, she saw sympathy in his eyes.

Or maybe it was pity.

The one thing Becca didn't want from anyone was pity.

The expression was gone as quickly as it had appeared. Daniel stepped closer, reached forward and tucked a wayward lock of hair into her *kapp*. His touch caused a cascade of goose bumps to parade down her arms.

Why was he looking at her that way?

Was he laughing at her on the inside?

Did he see her as some sort of entertainment factor for folks stuck on a farm?

If she'd doubted Daniel's motives, his next words swept away any questions she might have had. "I'll harness Constance. We'll go together."

Chapter Four

Daniel was sorely tempted to laugh, but one glance at Becca convinced him to hold that in check. She had been completely silent for the entire drive. As he directed Constance to turn into the parking area of the Shipshewana Police Department, Becca finally broke her silence.

"I've never been to the police department."

"It's *gut* to do something new every day."

"This from the man who doesn't leave his farm."

"What are you afraid might happen?"

"They could arrest me!"

"Doubtful. I imagine they save their cells for un-savory characters."

"They could issue me a citation."

Daniel ran a hand over the right side of his face. He'd had a few encounters with the police in Pennsylvania, mostly due to his two *bruders* acting out. On both of those instances, the police had been nothing but professional, but he didn't want to go into that story right now.

"I think you're going to be fine."

"How do I explain this to them?"

"I don't know. Start with the truth?"

She nodded as if that made sense, grabbed one of the boxes of hemp plants and took off toward the front door. Daniel grabbed the additional two boxes they'd needed and jogged to catch up with her.

The officer at the front desk had dark black hair pulled back in a braid, light brown skin and a name tag that read Raquel Sanchez.

Becca juggled the box from her right arm to her left, tugged at her apron and then blurted out, "I'm here to turn in these hemp plants."

The officer cocked her head to the side. "That's a new one. Take a seat over there." She nodded toward a small waiting area.

They waited fifteen minutes. Twice Daniel tried to start a conversation. Both times Becca looked at him as if he'd spoken in a foreign language. Finally, he leaned closer and said, "Stop worrying. You're not a criminal."

"But…in this instance, I sort of am."

"*Nein.* You're a person who misunderstood the rules and is attempting to make that right."

His words eased some of the worry from her face, though not all of it. Fortunately, Officer Sanchez picked that moment to appear in front of them.

"Sorry about the wait. I was covering for JoAnn

while she took a late lunch break. Come on back, and bring those boxes with you."

She led them into a back room that held four desks. Three of them were covered with stacks of paper, manuals and old coffee cups. Sanchez must have guessed what Daniel was thinking, because she shrugged her shoulders, sat down with a sigh and motioned to the chairs across from her.

"My fellow officers are a mess. They make fun of me for keeping such a clean desktop." She leaned forward and lowered her voice. "They say it's the sign of a sick mind. I say at least I can find my keys at the end of the day."

Daniel immediately recognized her as a kindred spirit, or at least he didn't think she was the type of officer to slap the cuffs on them first and ask questions later. Becca still seemed a bit tense. She was jiggling her knees so that the plants threatened to fall out of the box, and her hands were clutching the sides of the box so tightly that the phrase *white-knuckling it* came to mind.

Officer Sanchez turned her attention to Becca. "Miss…"

"Schwartz. Becca Schwartz, and this is my neighbor, Daniel Glick."

"Pleased to meet you both. I'm Officer Sanchez, as I guess you noticed from the name tag. Why don't you set that box on my desk before you spill dirt everywhere? That would make Johnson real happy, to come in and see potting soil all over my desk. He'd never let me hear the end of it."

Becca placed the box on the desk, then nudged it toward the officer. Clutching her hands in her lap, she launched into her explanation. "I didn't know what they were. I should have known. I should have read the entire pamphlet, but I was trying to make some extra money so my little *bruder* could buy a buggy, and I didn't stop to consider the nature of what I was doing."

She pulled in a deep breath as if she was about to dive deep, and plunged back into her explanation. "Daniel is the one who noticed what kind of plants they were. He explained to me that I need a permit or certification or something, which I don't have. And I didn't know what to do. Didn't know if I should burn them or toss them or what. So I thought the best thing was simply to bring them to you and confess."

Sanchez waited, her eyebrows raised as if she was preparing herself for another deluge of words, but Becca was apparently finished explaining. She rubbed the palms of her hands across her apron, glanced at Daniel, then turned back toward the officer.

"Okay." Sanchez leaned forward, picked up a pen and used it to push around some of the leaves on the plant nearest her. "These are plainly hemp, not marijuana, and it's true you do need a license to grow a hemp crop. Once you realized your mistake, you could have destroyed the plants—"

"I was afraid my rooster would get into them if I simply tossed them into the compost pile, or my little *schweschdern* might find them. I was afraid it would make them sick or even…even high."

"Nope. Hemp can't do that."

Becca had tucked the pamphlet into her box, and Sanchez reached for it, pausing to ask, "May I?"

"*Ya*. Of course."

She perused it for a minute. "Interesting. It sounds to me like instead of applying for their own permit, this company is depending on small independent growers to do their work for them. Saves them money and paperwork. Do you mind if I keep this?"

"Not at all."

Sanchez turned to Daniel. "Sir, you can place those two boxes over there, against the wall. I'll see that these are properly disposed of. Thank you for bringing them in."

"That's it?" Becca hopped to her feet as soon as Sanchez stood. "You're not going to interrogate us or cuff us or read us our rights?"

If Daniel wasn't mistaken, a smile twitched at the corner of Sanchez's mouth, but she managed to maintain a thoughtful look as if she were seriously considering doing any of those things. Finally she shook her head and said, "I don't think that will be necessary seeing as how you made us aware of the situation and brought in the plants. You did bring in all of the plants?"

"Oh, *ya*. These three boxes, they're all I purchased. Of course they were only seeds when they arrived in the mail, but I've been tending to them every day and they grow quite fast. They were supposed to fetch $6 a plant, but I guess that's money I'll never see."

"You might consider reporting your experience to the Better Business Bureau, and I'll turn this pamphlet over to my supervisor."

She walked them back to the front of the station. When they stepped out into the waning sunlight of a beautiful fall day, Becca pulled in a deep breath.

"Seems like we were in there forever."

Daniel glanced at his watch. "Less than thirty minutes."

"Longest thirty minutes of my life."

"Were you really worried?" He put his hand in the crook of her elbow and guided her toward the buggy.

"Worried? I kept thinking that my *mamm* would have to deal with my siblings all by herself, and that we couldn't afford a lawyer even if we knew one, and that I wouldn't look *gut* in a prison jumpsuit."

Daniel couldn't help laughing at her last point. "*Ya.* Prison jumpsuits definitely aren't Plain."

By the time he'd unhitched Constance from the post and hopped up into the buggy, Becca was leaning forward, arms crossed and resting on her knees, head bowed and face hidden in her arms.

"It's not that bad."

"Oh, but it is."

"You're being too hard on yourself."

"I wasted fifty dollars on those plants." She sat up and glared at him, as if he'd been the one to suggest she buy them in the first place. "Do you realize how much fifty dollars is?"

"*Ya*, I think I do."

"It's a lot of eggs, I'll tell you that. Quite a few of them, since I only charge $3.50 for a dozen. Let's see…that's…let me see how many eggs that is." She wrinkled her brow as she tried to do the math.

"Around one hundred and sixty-eight."

"How did you figure that so fast?"

"Simple math. It's a lot of eggs."

"Obviously."

"I think you need some ice cream."

"I can't afford ice cream!" She positioned herself in the corner of the buggy, studying him as if he'd lost his mind.

"My treat." Before she could say another word, he turned toward Howie's.

It wasn't until they were settled at a picnic table with cups of ice cream in front of them—strawberry for Becca and chocolate for him—that she seemed to pull herself out of her funk.

"I'll think of something. This is a setback, for sure and certain it is, but it's not the end. *Gotte* probably has something better in mind. I need to keep the faith, not give up. I need to move on and leave what's done—including those hemp plants—in the past." She was accentuating each phrase with her spoon and a good amount of strawberry ice cream had dripped across the table.

Daniel snagged one of their napkins and wiped it up before she stuck her sleeve in the mess.

"*Danki.*"

"*Gem Gschehne.*"

"You must think I'm crazy."

"Not at all. It's only that…well, never mind."

But he'd already stepped his foot in it. No way Becca was going to let him back out.

"Only what?" She stuck her spoon into her half-filled ice cream cup and crossed her arms. "Only what? You might as well say it. Whatever it is, you've got it written all over your face."

"I do?"

"*Ya.* Tell me how I'm wrong."

He actually thought she was adorable, but he wasn't about to say that. Whoever married Becca Schwartz would never suffer from boredom or monotony.

"You said that *Gotte* probably has something better in mind for you, but it seems to me that *Gotte* isn't a wishing well. I don't think faith works like that."

"What?" Now Becca dipped her chin and gave him a look that suggested trouble was coming. "Did I say that *Gotte* was a wishing well?"

"*Nein*, but the way you were talking, like if you do the right thing, pray the right prayer, have the right attitude, then the answer would pop up. I'm not sure that's what the Bible promises."

He thought she would argue, but instead, she stared at her ice cream, picked up the spoon and took another tenuous bite.

"I didn't mean to criticize."

"No, you're right. I try to be upbeat and optimistic, but most of the time I have no idea what I'm doing. I want to help my family. Surely I can. If I just hit on the right idea, I could improve our situation. And I believe that *Gotte* wants that. He wants what is best for my family—"

"He's already given your family what they need, Becca."

"And what is that?"

"Each other."

The setting sun cast a long shadow across the fields as they made their way home. The ice cream had made Becca sleepy—that and the emotional highs and lows of the last few hours.

Realizing her plants were illegal.

Agonizing over what to do with them.

Deciding to go to the police.

Daniel insisting on going with her.

The understanding police officer.

And beyond all of that, Daniel's assertion that *Gotte* had given her family what they need.

"Why are we so poor?" she asked, darting her glance his way, then back out toward the October evening.

"I'm not sure what you're asking."

"If *Gotte* has given us what we need, why are we so poor?"

"Are you?"

"You know we are. We are. You are. The neighbors around us are. We definitely don't live in the affluent part of Shipshewana."

"Who decides what it even means to be affluent?"

"Oh, come on." She again cornered herself in the

buggy and scrutinized him in the waning light. "Affluent. You're familiar with the word. It would mean that there's a *gut* layer of top soil on your farm, and that you don't have to try to fit ten people into one buggy, and that you would have a home with an adequate roof on it. That kind of affluent."

Instead of being offended, he laughed. Becca was learning that underneath his gruff exterior, Daniel Glick had a sunny disposition. Who would have guessed?

"I suppose my point is that we're not hungry and we're not alone. Your family, they have their health and they have each other."

"You're alone."

Daniel waved that away. He didn't even attempt to address it. "Your community is a *gut* one. I've only met a few people so far, but no one seems to look down on anyone else. They seem helpful. As you have pointed out on more than one occasion, plenty of people have offered to help me."

"And yet you turned them down. Care to explain that? Because I still don't understand."

"I don't think I owe you an explanation, Becca."

"Well, Daniel. I didn't say you owed me one. I was asking a simple question, a neighborly question. You were just pointing out the value of having helpful neighbors and family around, and yet you're all alone. What is that about?"

"It's not about anything." He frowned at Constance, something Becca had never seen him do before.

"Why are you living alone?"

"Again, none of your business." He pushed his hat farther down on his head, nearly covering his eyes, which had taken on a decidedly hostile glint.

"And how did you afford this horse?"

"That again?"

"Yes, that again. What are you hiding, Daniel? Or what are you hiding from?"

He glanced skyward, as if petitioning the Lord for answers. He pulled in a deep breath and finally glanced her way. "I was only saying that perhaps you don't need to feel so anxious. *Gotte* is still in control. We can rest in that knowledge."

Which had such a ring of truth to it that Becca felt a tad guilty about prodding him for information. "When you explain it that way, I suppose you're right. We do have much to be thankful for. It's only that life is so hard."

"Maybe it's supposed to be."

"Hard?"

"Uh-huh."

"That's a depressing thought."

Daniel laughed as he directed Constance off the main road. "Growing up, my *dat* used to ask me this question. *Is life a joy to be lived or a problem to be solved?*"

"I'll take joy."

"*Ya*, that was my answer, too, but the older I get, the more I understand that there are many problems to be solved or at least trials to be endured. The real question is whether we can maintain a joyful attitude during the process."

He guided Constance down her lane and pulled to a stop in front of the house.

"You could have driven on to the barn—*our* barn."

"I figured you might have done enough problem-solving for one day. You didn't need to face Carl-the-bad-tempered-rooster after the last few hours you've been through."

At that exact moment, the animal in question dashed across the yard, crowing and flapping his wings as he chased one of the barn kittens. Hot on Carl's tail was Cola, beagle ears bouncing, tail pointed high, eyes locked in on the rooster.

Becca placed a hand over her mouth, afraid that if she started laughing, she'd never stop. She hopped out of the buggy, waved goodbye and dashed up the steps. As he drove away, her mind replayed his words. *There are many problems to be solved or at least trials to be endured. The real question is whether we can maintain a joyful attitude.* She couldn't help wondering how Daniel could be so wise at such a young age.

Or at least he seemed wise to her.

He certainly wasn't dashing around starting new projects every week. No, Daniel's method was slow and steady, and she could probably stand to learn from that.

Though there was something about him, some mystery, that he was holding close, and she meant to solve it.

She walked into the kitchen as dinner was being served. Her *mamm* smiled and her *dat* nodded, and her little *schweschdern* scooted over to allow her a place on the bench.

They all bowed their heads and silently thanked the Lord for the food. And in that moment, Becca meant it. She didn't much care that once again they were having soup and sandwiches. She was thinking about what Daniel had said, that they really did have all they needed.

She couldn't hold on to it, though.

The peace and contentment slipped away like water you tried to cup in your hand. Her *bruder* Clyde was talking about a buggy he'd seen in town. "Needs some work, but I could get it real cheap."

David was explaining how he'd once again patched the tire on his old bike. The thing was more patches than original tire at this point.

Georgia was squinting at the book she was hiding in her lap. Probably she needed new glasses again.

Before dessert was done, Becca was once more flipping through ideas in her mind—there really were endless opportunities to earn money to help her family. It was all good and fine for Daniel to be happy in his poverty. He had no one to worry about except himself. She had a family, and she meant to find a way to help them.

As for Daniel Glick, he'd managed to distract her with his talk of contentment and *Gotte*'s provision, but if he were as content as he claimed, wouldn't he be more willing to share about his past?

What was he hiding?

What was he running from?

Daniel was a likable guy, and he'd certainly helped her out of a tight spot, but there was still a mystery there. Mysteries bothered Becca. They were like novels with the final chapter missing. Something deep inside her worried a thing until it came to a satisfactory conclusion—good or bad.

She simply couldn't abide leaving matters unresolved.

She'd figure out the details of Daniel's past. The question was whether she'd still think he was a *gut* neighbor, a *gut* friend, once she did.

Becca woke the next day with a renewed zeal to learn the details of Daniel's life. He was their neighbor. Shouldn't they know what their neighbor was up to? Didn't the Bible say they were to love their neighbor? You couldn't love someone that you knew nothing about.

Since it was Saturday, she spent the morning helping with the baking and cooking. It wasn't until after lunch that she had a spare moment to herself. She walked outside and caught her *bruder* Eli standing in the backyard, practicing his baseball swing. "Don't you have chores to do?"

"I finished mine."

He swung the bat again, watched the imaginary ball fly into imaginary bleachers. Eli was tall and thin and talented with a baseball. It was rare that he wasn't carrying around a baseball bat or rubbing oil into his baseball glove. He was in his last year of school, and Becca almost envied him that final year of childhood. Soon enough adults would be asking him what he meant to do with his life, and when he was going to join the church, and who he was going to marry.

"Say, I could use your help with something."

Again he swung the bat, following through and smiling that he'd no doubt hit another home run.

"Eli, are you listening?"

He slowly turned toward her and seemed to come back to Earth. "*Ya*. Sure. Of course I am."

"*Gut*. Here's my plan."

Fifteen minutes later, Becca and Eli had crossed their property, walked through the old barn and popped out the other side.

"You sure we won't get in trouble for this?"

"For what?"

"Snooping in someone else's house."

"I'm not going in his house. I'd never do that. I'm simply going to look around his back porch."

"Isn't that snooping?"

"Don't you want to know what's going on with our neighbor?"

Eli shrugged and tossed his baseball in the air, catching it as if it were a yo-yo attached to a string. "Daniel seems like a nice guy to me. The other day he told me that I have good follow-through on my swing."

Becca forced herself to pull in a calming breath. "Not the point."

They'd stopped near a small crop of fir trees.

"He's over there in that field, picking up rocks for all the good it will do him. Go over there and start a conversation."

"What am I supposed to talk about?"

"Rocks."

"I don't care about rocks."

"The weather, then."

Eli stared up at the clear blue sky, then looked at her as if she'd lost her mind.

"Why would I care about the weather?"

"Baseball, then."

He blinked twice. "Oh, *ya*. He used to live in Pennsylvania. Maybe he's been to a Phillies game." Suddenly embracing his mission, he hurried away.

Becca waited until they looked to be deep in conversation. Then she slipped around to the back of the house. Mounting the back porch steps, she glanced around, then walked up to a window, cupped her hands and stared inside.

The interior of Daniel's house was worse than she had imagined. He must have begun pulling out rotten floorboards because there were holes throughout. The kitchen sink had been removed as well, as had the gas refrigerator and the lower cabinet doors. Peering closer, she noticed sunlight piercing down through the roof. That explained a lot. How long had the house been this way, with rain and snow falling down into the rooms?

What a mess.

She couldn't imagine living here.

She couldn't imagine why Daniel would want to

live here, and that thought reminded her that she didn't have much time. She turned her attention toward the back porch. A sleeping bag had been placed near one wall. Next to it was an old crate with a battery lantern on it, and next to that was a camping cook stove. A few pots and pans were stacked neatly in a box, and his foodstuff was stored off the floor, stacked in another crate.

Wow.

Just—wow.

The nights were chilly now. Hadn't last night dipped into the thirties? And Daniel was sleeping on the back porch? Even if his sleeping bag was made for cooler weather, that couldn't be comfortable.

She stepped closer, nudged the sleeping bag with her foot and uncovered a journal.

Surely it wouldn't hurt to take a peek.

She glanced over her shoulder, confirming that no one was coming.

It wasn't snooping, not really. After all, the book had practically been sitting in plain sight.

She snatched it off the ground, ran her fingers over the plain cover, then opened it to the first page. His penmanship was surprisingly good.

Daniel Glick.

Lancaster, Pennsylvania.

Shipshewana, Indiana.

She walked to the corner of the porch and peered back in the direction of the field, but she didn't see anyone. No doubt Eli had talked Daniel into a game of catch.

She looked down at the journal, then turned the first page.

He who has no money is poor; he who has nothing but money is even poorer.

You are only poor when you want more than you have.

Penny-wise, pound-foolish.

Old proverbs, mostly related to money, filled the first few pages. There were also Scripture verses meticulously copied down.

Do not fear, for I am with you.

I know the plans I have for you.

When you pass through the waters, I will be with you.

Honor your father and mother.

Next to that last one was a question mark.

Interspersed between the proverbs and Bible verses were observations.

A beautiful sunrise can soothe the soul.

God's majesty is everywhere.

When a person's loyalty is divided, they cannot find happiness.

Hard work heals the heart.

She read the last one again.

What kind of hard work? Farming? Or rebuilding a house? And what part of his heart needed healing? Had he been hurt so terribly before? She ran her fingertips across the line and was so focused on the words, on what might be behind the words, that her mind didn't register the sound of boots on the porch steps.

Daniel snatched the journal out of her hands. "What are you doing? Why are you looking through my things?"

She'd seen Daniel irritated before. She'd seen him frustrated and put-out and impatient, but she'd never seen him angry. Becca glanced past him to Eli, who was standing on the bottom step, hands raised in a don't-ask-me gesture.

Daniel stared down at the book in his hands, then glanced up and shook it at her. "You have no right to snoop through my things. I want you off my property, and I want you off now."

Chapter Five

Daniel understood that he needed to calm down. His pulse pounded at his temples and a red aura surrounded his vision. Becca's expression shifted from stunned to alarmed to defensive. He strode away from her, needing space, needing to calm his anger. Unfortunately, that put him staring at Eli—a young kid who had probably been manipulated by his sister, a young kid whose biggest worry was the next pickup baseball game.

"Were you in on this?"

Eli glanced at Becca.

"Don't look at her. Look at me. Were you in on this?"

"Maybe. Becca just said we needed to know what was really going on with you."

"Oh, did she?"

Becca stepped forward to defend herself, but Daniel stopped her with an outstretched hand held up like a traffic cop.

"Tell me about that."

Eli nervously tossed his baseball from one hand to the other. "Uh, nothing to tell really. She said it was all right because she wasn't going to go inside, she just wanted to look around and make sure you weren't dangerous."

Daniel couldn't resist; he turned toward Becca wearing what he hoped was a wolfish grin. "Dangerous."

She'd crossed her arms, and there might as well have been a cartoon bubble hanging over her head.

"Save it, Sherlock." He turned back to her younger brother. "Eli, will you give me a few minutes alone with your *schweschder*?"

"Uh…"

"I assure you I'm not dangerous. If you're worried, though, you're welcome to send one of your parents over here—"

"That won't be necessary." Becca pushed forward, not stopping until she reached the porch railing. "You go on home, Eli. I'll be right behind you."

"Are you sure?"

"I'm positive. Obviously, Daniel isn't dangerous. I was being *narrisch*. Probably just reading too many *Englisch* suspense novels."

"You read those?"

"Go on home. If *Mamm* asks, tell her I'll be there in a few minutes."

Eli shrugged. "Okay. *Gut* talking to you, Daniel. Maybe you can play ball with us after church service tomorrow. You have a *gut* arm."

"Sure thing. I'm looking forward to it."

He waited until Eli was well out of hearing range before turning to Becca. His heart rate had settled, but his anger hadn't exactly cooled. He didn't deserve to be treated this way, and he was going to stop her prying into his life. He was going to do so this afternoon. They would settle this matter for once and for all.

"Look, Daniel, I'm sorry."

"You are?"

"I stepped over a line. I had no right to read your journal."

"It's not a journal, but you're correct. You had no right."

"But you can't blame—"

"Actually, I can. I can blame you for snooping through my things and for disrespecting my privacy. If you want to argue about that, we need to take this to our bishop right now—either him or your parents."

"You don't have to tattle to my parents. I'm not a child."

"You're not? Because from where I'm standing, you certainly are acting like one."

"That's not fair."

"It's completely fair. You send your *bruder* to distract me, and then you come into my home…"

"Porch. I walked up *on* to your porch, which is technically just an extension of your yard."

He closed his eyes and prayed for patience. "You came onto my porch, looking through my things—without my permission. You disrespected me, Becca. I've done nothing to deserve that."

"Is that right?"

"Yes. It is."

"Then why the secrecy?"

"Stop this."

"Why are you living on a porch?"

"That's none of your business."

"Why did you buy this house?" She stepped closer; the repentant girl who'd been caught snooping had disappeared and a woman with a glint in her eyes had taken her place. "What are you hiding from, Daniel? Are you running from the *Englisch* law? What happened in Pennsylvania? Why are you even here? And who and where is your family?"

It was the last question that punched the anger out of him. All he was left with was a deep exhaustion, the kind that turned your feet to lead and made walking a thing that seemed nearly impossible. So instead of walking away—which was what he desperately wanted to do—he sank onto the porch steps and looked out over his pitiful back field.

"I just wanted to be left alone."

"But why? If you're going to be living next to my family, next to my impressionable younger siblings, don't I have a right to know the answers to a few basic questions?"

He wanted to tell her then—tell her everything. Explain about the inheritance and the way it had torn his family apart. Describe the women who had wanted what was in his bank account. Confess how much he missed his home and his parents and his six siblings. Admit how lonely he was.

Instead, he stood and stared down at the journal before stuffing it under his arm. "*Nein*. You don't. And if I find you on my property again, I will turn you in to the authorities."

Without waiting for an answer, he turned and strode away from the house, because what he needed more than anything was to put distance between himself and Becca Schwartz.

Daniel would have given much to skip church the next day, but he understood what was expected of him. He was well aware that if he didn't attend, he'd be visited by the bishop, watched more closely by the deacons, and placed under increasing scrutiny. They didn't see it as intruding on his life. They saw it as their obligation to help along a *bruder* in the faith. After all, they were his church family.

Skipping church wasn't an option.

Best to clean up, show up and put on a smile.

Best to appear to be one of them, even though he realized he was the furthest thing from that. He was a man who didn't fit in anywhere.

Church was held at the bishop's, and the weather matched his mood. Dark clouds had rolled in, the temperatures had dropped, and a north wind had picked up.

He was used to cold weather.

He didn't mind rain.

He only wished he'd been able to fix the roof on his house before winter made its appearance, but the barn had been in worse shape than he'd thought.

The fencing and fields had needed tending to. The list of things needing done immediately was simply too long.

It was what he'd wanted, though—to have to work hard, to depend on his skills rather than his bank account, to make his own way. *Gotte* had granted his wishes, and yes, that realization did remind him of his conversation with Becca. He didn't believe *Gotte* was a wishing well, but in this case…well, it seemed as if his heart's desire and *Gotte*'s will for his life had coincided. His prayers had been answered. He wouldn't taint that by complaining.

He filed into the barn, hoping he could slip into the last pew. Bishop Saul had other ideas. He insisted that Daniel stand with him, introducing him to each family as they passed through the doors.

Becca's father smiled amicably, even as Becca pretended to be busy adjusting her little *schweschder*'s *kapp*. It was quite obvious that Samuel had no idea what had transpired between his daughter and Daniel. In fact, everyone except Eli seemed oblivious, and even Eli seemed to have forgotten. That was the way of fourteen-year-olds. Today's worries took precedence over any of yesterday's troubles.

"Can't play ball in the rain," Eli muttered. "Sure hope the weather clears." He then trudged away from them to join his *freinden*.

Daniel made a point to select a bench well away from Becca. In fact, he sat closer to the front, where he wouldn't have to see her. He thought he heard her voice a time or two during the singing, but of course he didn't turn to look. It was none of his business if Becca had a beautiful soprano voice.

He had figured that the sermon would be on loving your neighbor. That was the last thing he wanted to hear. He wasn't sure that particular commandment applied to snooping, eligible young women, but he'd rather not be reminded of the whole situation.

Since he was a young child, whenever he felt the least bit guilty about something, it seemed the pastor's words focused on that thing.

One summer he'd desperately longed for a bicycle like his friend's. It was all he could think of. He'd even stopped by the store in town to see how much it cost, though at that point they hadn't received their inheritance and had very little extra money.

The following Sunday the pastor had preached on *Thou shalt not covet.*

Another time he'd desperately wanted to be in the field, working at their harvest, rather than in church. The pastor had spoken on honoring the Sabbath.

It was a regular occurrence for the sermon to speak directly to him.

To his relief, the first sermon was not on the Golden Rule, but rather it focused on Lamentations—not one of Daniel's favorite books from the Old Testament. He remembered being assigned to read it as a teen and falling asleep every single time. Today the words pricked his heart. "It is of the Lord's mercies that we are not consumed, because His compassions fail not."

He deserved to be consumed. He was living a

lie, but how was he to tell the truth? Always his life seemed like a puzzle that couldn't be solved. Yet the words rang through his heart—*His compassions fail not.*

If he hoped the second sermon would bring some relief to his raw feelings, he was sorely disappointed. "Timothy reminds us that even when we have trouble believing, even when our faith fails, *Gotte* is faithful." Saul smiled out over his congregation.

"It's a *gut* thing, *ya*? It's a thing that pricks our hearts and eases the burden on our shoulders. Like when you unharness your horse, you ease his burden, so *Gotte* does for us…if we let Him. If we are willing to let Him carry that which troubles us."

Daniel stared at the floor.

Was that what he was doing? Trying to carry his own burdens? But it couldn't be as simple as Saul suggested. Could it?

Could he simply offer everything that troubled him up to *Gotte*? And what of his past? He had no idea what to do with his hurts and, if he were honest, his sins. Could *Gotte* actually wipe them away?

He longed to start over here, to start fresh. How? What was he to do about Becca Schwartz, who insisted on digging into his past?

If the day had been mild and the sun shining, he might have been able to avoid Becca. With the rain pouring outside, it made for a cozy and intimate affair in the barn. After the service had ended and the meal had been eaten, the children took off toward the back of the barn—to play with kittens and enjoy games of hide-and-seek. Even Eli was smiling, though Daniel heard him say that he was too old for such games.

The older members had pulled their chairs into a circle and were enjoying the time of fellowship. Most of the *youngies* stood apart, laughing and standing in groups of three or four. Several of the girls were looking his way, and Daniel knew he needed to escape before they found their courage to approach him.

It was too early to leave without drawing attention, so he stepped out of the barn doors, following the roof overhang around to the south side where the structure blocked the wind. He'd pulled up the collar of his coat and was nurturing his brooding thoughts, so he didn't watch clearly where he was going and nearly bowled over Becca.

His hands shot out to steady her, and she clasped his arms—blushing and laughing and saying that she was sorry.

"I'm the one that ran into you."

"True, but I should have been paying closer attention."

He was still holding her arms, as if she might topple over at any minute. Plainly she wouldn't. He dropped his hands and stepped back. "I didn't think anyone else would be out here."

"Only us introverts."

"You're an introvert?" He laughed, perhaps a bit too harshly, because her chin came up and her eyes narrowed. "What I mean is, you seem quite outgoing to me."

"Oh, *ya*. I'm a real partier." She trudged over to an

old rocking chair and sank into it, staring out at the rain. "Most of the people my age are already married up. The girls in there have little to worry about other than their next date. They seem younger than me."

"You have *freinden*."

"Oh, *ya*. I do. My closest friend is Liza Kauff-mann, but she was surrounded by boys as soon as the luncheon broke up. She's not really interested in dating right now, but she's too polite to tell them that."

"Maybe you should have rescued her." Daniel perched on the other rocking chair. He wasn't sure he was staying, but at the same time, outside with Becca seemed preferable to inside with all the eligible girls staring at him. Not that he considered himself such a great catch. It was just the way things were, especially when someone was new in a community.

"*Nein*. Liza can take care of herself. Trust me."

Becca studied him so long that Daniel began to squirm.

"What?"

"I don't know. What?"

"I mean why are you staring at me that way?"

"Only trying to figure you out. I thought you'd do everything possible to avoid me today." Before he could answer that, she pushed on. "I have to admit I didn't pay much attention to the sermons. I was too busy dealing with my own guilt."

"Your guilt?"

She fiddled with the sleeve of her dress, which was a pretty autumn orange. Daniel waited, not sure he should interrupt.

Clearing her throat, she finally looked up. "What

I did yesterday was wrong. I suppose I knew that as I was doing it, but I justified my actions by saying that I needed to know what type of person you are. Already my *bruders* are looking up to you—"

"They are?"

"And I worry about people who might be a bad influence on them."

"I'm a bad influence?"

"None of that justifies my actions. Snooping is wrong. I'm sorry." Now she met his gaze directly. "Really I am. I'm not that kind of person, and I promise that I will keep a proper distance in the future."

He was a bit stunned.

He hadn't expected a direct apology at all.

If anything, he'd regretted how harsh his words had been—when he wasn't still angry at what she'd done.

Perhaps it was time that he be honest with Becca. He didn't have to tell her everything, of course. He didn't need anyone in Shipshe knowing that he was an Amish millionaire. The term still struck him as something out of a novel.

But he could tell her a little, enough to ease her worries about her *bruders*. Perhaps he could stop guarding his past so closely. Maybe he could trust that burden to the Lord.

Watching Daniel, Becca almost started laughing. His range of expressions reminded her of looking through the twins' kaleidoscope. Just like those colors and shapes shifted and blended and altered, it seemed that Daniel's emotions changed and merged and finally settled.

She decided it was best not to say anything.

Instead, she waited.

Finally, he tapped the arm of his rocking chair and sent her a tiny smile. "I apologize if I've come off as secretive."

They both knew that he had been just that, so she again opted for saying nothing. It wasn't natural for her. A whole backlog of words was building up in her throat.

"It's just that when you move to a new place you're not sure who you can trust—who might be a gossip or who might ridicule you. I don't care too much what others think, but I don't want to spend time correcting rumors that are false." He crossed his arms. "Living with other people is a mess."

"Oh, and living in the woods alone is easy?"

"How would I know? I haven't tried it."

He wiggled his eyebrows, and Becca laughed. This was a Daniel she could like. Gone was the brooding, angry man from yesterday. Not that she blamed him one bit for his brooding or his anger. She'd deserved every ounce of it.

Daniel's mood shifted again. She sensed it immediately, like a change in the wind. She didn't know him so very well. How was it that she was able to read him so easily?

"I don't want to go into my past, Becca. Not now. Maybe not ever. I honestly can't say if or when I'll feel able to do that."

"All right."

"But I can assure you that it's nothing nefarious. Whatever crazy ideas you've concocted in your brain about me, they're not true."

"You're sure?"

"Yes." He looked at her and sat back, relaxing for the first time since he'd nearly ran her over. "Try me. Give me your craziest idea about me—the most far-fetched thing that has crossed your mind."

"Okay. You're part of the federal witness protection program."

"Definitely not. I heard they put those people up in pretty nice places, and my farm doesn't really fit that scenario."

"All right. Running from the law?"

"I've never broken a law. So, no."

"Left a girl at the altar—heartbroken and confused?"

He only hesitated a millisecond, but it was enough that Becca knew she'd hit a nerve. She cocked her head to the left and waited.

"There was a girl, back home in Pennsylvania. I broke it off well before our wedding day. Furthermore, she was not confused or brokenhearted. She knew very well why I ended our relationship."

"Hmm. Well, I'm sorry, then…for whatever heartache you've been through."

"Danki."

Becca stood and paced to the edge of the roof overhang. The rain continued to fall, but more softly now. The land looked to her as if it was drinking the water, storing the resource for spring, when all of nature would need it for new growth and rebirth. She'd always loved fall and winter—it seemed to her the time of year when everything rested and prepared for what was to come.

She turned toward Daniel. "What about your family? I don't mean to pry. Honestly, I don't, but you and I both know that Amish are all about their family. It just seems so odd for you to show up here—alone."

"All right. That's a *gut* point."

"You don't owe me an answer, Daniel. I understand that now. You don't have to speak of this."

"*Nein.* I said I would answer your questions if I can, and that one I can." He joined her at the edge of the roof overhang. Together they looked out at the day, and it seemed as if they could watch fall change to winter before their eyes.

She thought of Daniel's back porch—the sleeping bag and little cook stove.

She wondered how he would make it through the winter if he didn't accept anyone's help.

But she didn't say either of those things. Instead, she waited, and though Becca had been somewhat cold earlier, she suddenly felt flushed. Perhaps she was coming down with something. She wouldn't be surprised to discover she had a fever. Even her heart was beating faster than it normally did.

"I have two *bruders*, both younger. Benjamin is twenty and still at home. Joseph is twenty-four, and he has left the faith."

"I'm so sorry. Did he become Mennonite?"

"Actually, I don't think he's become anything yet. He's a bit lost. I tried speaking with him, tried writing him, but he isn't ready to hear anything I have to say. Not that I'm the best person to offer advice. I haven't figured this life out, either."

"What about your parents? Do they have any influence with him?"

"*Mamm* and *Dat* try, but they argue quite a bit." He sighed, stretched his neck to the left and right. "They seem to be having trouble finding their own way. I don't think they'll be much help to Joseph."

"That must be hard on you. My *dat* is always telling silly jokes, and he doesn't seem to care at all how poor we are, but he's been a solid example for us."

"You're fortunate to have a father like that."

"And my *mamm* loves him. They're…well, they're a sweet couple. I always wanted someone to look at me the way my *dat* looks at my *mamm*." She ran both hands around the back of her neck. Of all the scenarios she'd imagined Daniel to be in, a broken family wasn't one of them. "Do you have any *schweschdern*?"

"I do. I have four."

"Have they remained Amish?"

"They have, but…" He crossed his arms and leaned against a wooden column, turning toward her as if he needed to gauge her reaction. "Sometimes it seems as if you can remain a part of something, but not genuinely be fully committed to it anymore. Does that make sense?"

"When a person's loyalty is divided, they cannot find happiness."

To her surprise, Daniel laughed. "Yes, you have a *gut* memory."

"I shouldn't have read your journal."

"It's not a journal."

"Whatever it was—I shouldn't have snooped."

"The book you found—I just call it my notebook—it's very personal to me. It's a place where I jot down things that I think might be true."

"That's the very definition of a journal."

He nudged his shoulder against hers. "Journals are for girls where they write about their feelings and practice penning their new last name."

"Maybe in fifth grade!"

"Did you have a journal like that in fifth grade?"

Becca rolled her eyes. "Did you forget what a big family I have? A journal in my house would not be wise. Pages would be borrowed for tic-tac-toe games, or a homework assignment, or a letter to our kin in Ohio."

"I didn't know you have family in Ohio."

"Oh, *ya*. My *dat* has a lot of *bruders* there. Cousins everywhere."

Hannah and Isabelle picked that moment to dash around the corner of the building, chasing one another and shouting at the top of their voices. It felt like being bombarded by a whirlwind. They were there and then gone.

Becca didn't want the conversation with Daniel to

end, but she was probably needed inside. "I should go and see to the snack for the young ones."

"I'll help."

"You will?"

"Nothing else to do, and I'm avoiding all of those girls who are staring at me like I'm a new bonnet they'd like to try on."

Becca smirked and said, "Well, you're not humble."

"It's not that I think I'm *Gotte*'s gift to Amish women. It's only that I'm new in town."

"No worries." She patted him clumsily on the arm. "Someone newer than you will come along, and their attention will be diverted."

"One can hope."

They turned and began walking back toward the main room of the barn. Halfway there, Daniel tugged on her arm. She stopped, pivoted and looked up at him. Daniel Glick had a strong jawline and very attractive eyes.

Which didn't matter to her one bit.

Staring into someone's eyes was what a person did on a date, and she and Daniel were certainly not dating. In fact, dating was the furthest thing from her mind.

"So we have a truce?"

"Oh, *ya*. Now that I know you're not running from the law or anyone else."

"Excellent."

"Still don't know why you won't accept help on that ramshackle house."

"Still none of your business."

"You can't plan to sleep on the porch all winter."

"There's always the barn, which is in pretty *gut* shape."

"You and Constance can keep each other company."

"And Carl-the-bad-tempered-rooster."

"Never trust that bird. I wouldn't put it past him to peck you while you sleep."

"I'll make sure he's safely penned up before sleeping in the barn."

"Uh-huh. You don't know how clever he can be. I've yet to find a way to keep him in a pen."

And with that banter, their friendship—if that was what they wanted to call it—seemed to shift to solid ground. She could definitely do worse than having Daniel for a neighbor. It was better than a doting old couple. He'd come out of his funk eventually, meet some girl who caught his fancy, marry and have a passel of kids. She could watch it all happen from her side of the barn.

For some reason, that thought didn't please her nearly as much as it should have.

Chapter Six

Two weeks passed; October gave way to November, and the truce between Daniel and Becca held. She had stopped snooping, as far as he could tell. She seemed satisfied with the less-than-complete answers he'd given her.

The only answers he could give her.

Daniel understood that Becca was worried about protecting her family. Somewhere along the way, she'd designated herself as the mother hen, in spite of the fact that her mother, Sarah, seemed perfectly capable of handling anything that came along. It was a large family, though, and Daniel was slowly feeling closer to all of them. It was hard not to. Sort of like having a litter of Labrador puppies next door that constantly frolicked in front of you, asking to be noticed.

Not that he was comparing Becca's family to a litter of pups. Okay, he'd just done that very thing, but the comparison fit.

"Are you sure you want to do this today?" Becca's *bruder*, David, was staring at him quizzically.

"Finish this field and all the winter crops are in."

"*Ya*, but...you don't look like you feel so good."

Daniel used his sleeve to swipe beads of sweat from his forehead. "I'm fine."

"You're sweating."

"I always sweat while I'm working."

"It's forty-five degrees out here—tops. There's a north wind, and it's cloudy." David pulled up the collar on his coat. "I think you're coming down with something."

"And I think you're avoiding my south field." Daniel attempted a grin though it hurt his head to do so. "Or maybe you can't keep up with me."

"Dream on, old man."

They spent the next four hours planting a cereal rye cover crop. When they paused for a break, David peppered him with questions.

"You're not going to harvest this?"

"*Nein*. We till it under in the spring."

"Why plant it if you're only going to till it under?"

"Provides biomass, crowds out weeds, and deer will graze on it."

"You plan on hunting?" Now David was grinning. "We only have the one deer rifle, but we try to harvest a few deer each year."

"Most Amish do—it's free meat, and most families can use that."

"My family certainly can." David was unerringly good-natured. His family's financial situation didn't seem to bother him a bit. "*Dat*'s never planted a cover crop."

"When we're done here, we'll take the extra seed over to your *dat*. See if he'd like us to plant it."

"He's working at the RV plant this week. He doesn't like the hours, but we needed the money."

"All the more reason to share the extra seed. You and I can take care of the planting as long as he thinks it's a good idea. You can ask him tonight."

"Sounds like a plan."

But by that evening, Daniel knew that he wouldn't be planting in the Schwartz field the next day. His body hurt all over, and he couldn't eat the meager dinner he'd put together. Shivers racked his body, but sweat dripped from his face. He had definitely caught some sort of bug. Hopefully it was the twenty-four-hour variety.

His living arrangements probably didn't help. He'd taken to sleeping in the house as the temperatures had dropped, but there was no way to heat even one of the smaller rooms because the roof still needed so much work. Not to mention there were gaps around the window frames that he'd stuffed with newspapers.

"Next week," he croaked as he hunkered down in his sleeping bag. He should have started working the roof sooner, but the crops had taken precedence. The roof could wait. If he didn't plant the cover crops, next year's harvest would be half what it could be.

He fell into a troubled sleep, peppered with images of Constance looking through his house window, David sitting in the middle of his field pulling up plants by the roots, and Becca standing at the fence, jotting notes on a pad of paper that she stuck in her pocket. He tried to call out to each of them, but no one seemed to be able to hear him.

And then he was back in Pennsylvania, at his parents' home.

They were arguing about Joseph moving to town. His *bruder* was standing on the front porch, his arms crossed and his back to his family, and Daniel? Daniel was where he'd always been, standing in between them, trying to forge some type of peace.

He woke to a cool hand on his forehead and sunlight streaming through the window. Blinking to clear his vision, he took a moment to realize that Becca was popping in and out of his line of sight, and even longer to realize that she was speaking to him or at least about him.

"I don't know what you were thinking."

He attempted to sit up, but the room tilted. He fell back against the sleeping bag.

"Stubborn. That's what this is about, and maybe a lack of common sense. I'm really not sure which is the most dangerous."

He tried to reach out his hand, to stop her as she moved away. The last thing he heard was her calling to someone.

"David, go and get *Mamm*. Bring *Dat*, too, if he's home. We're going to need help moving him, and bring the buggy."

He wanted to argue that he wasn't going anywhere, that there was work to do, that he needed to look in on Constance. The words wouldn't form. He tried to swallow and felt intense pain stab through his throat, and then he was falling into the darkness that threatened to consume him.

Daniel opened his eyes, blinked and realized it was once again dark and that he was no longer sleeping on the floor.

Then where was he?

He rolled onto his side. The room seemed to tilt, and someone was groaning. He was groaning. The weight on his chest felt impossibly heavy, and he couldn't stop shivering.

Becca turned on a lamp, placed another blanket around him and murmured, "Try to rest."

He glanced up to see her face in the lamplight—concern, worry and maybe fear colored her features.

What was he doing in their home?

Why was she sitting next to him?

How late was it?

What day was it?

None of those questions made it to his lips. He slipped back into a deeper darkness.

"You found him yesterday?" The person speaking placed a hand on Daniel's shoulder and shook him gently. "Can you open your eyes, son?"

He did and flinched away from the bright light.

"One more time."

He didn't want to, but he did want this man to go away. He needed to sleep, needed to burrow down in the blankets and find some warmth.

"Now your throat."

Squeezing his eyes shut, he complied.

A tongue depressor was stuck in his mouth, and then someone swabbed his nose. He jerked his head away.

"I'm sure it is influenza. We have a particularly nasty strain going around this year. Everyone else in the house had their flu shots this year?"

"Ya." The voice was Becca's *mamm*'s, but it seemed to be coming to Daniel from across the pasture. "Bishop Saul is adamant about everyone having their vaccinations."

"Not all Plain people do. Tell Saul I appreciate his help." The man sighed and moved away from Daniel. "Here's a bottle of Tamiflu."

"We can't—"

"Pay for it? This one's on me. I'd suggest putting him in the hospital, but I suspect I know what your answer to that will be. Just follow the directions on the label, try to get fluids down him, and be sure to wash your hands after touching him or anything he's used."

"But the vaccinations…"

"They help, Sarah. An exposed person who has been vaccinated can still contract the flu, but they will have a lighter case. I'd rather there be no more cases coming from this household, so keep the kids at a distance and you and Becca wash your hands often."

Daniel wanted to open his eyes and see Becca.

He wanted to ask her to look after Constance.

He wanted to thank her for finding him, but he couldn't do any of those things. Maybe after he rested...

"He's coming around." Becca rinsed the washcloth in the basin of water and wrung it dry. When she placed it back on Daniel's head, his eyes popped open. "Welcome back, sleepyhead."

He attempted to struggle off the couch, but Becca put a hand to his chest and gently pushed him back. When had she become so strong?

"Not so fast."

At that point, Sarah bustled into the room, followed by Hannah and Isabelle.

"Is he awake?"

"Can he play with us now?"

"Why does his hair look like that?"

Both girls flung themselves into a chair on the far side of the room, staring at their guest.

"We can't sit closer," Hannah explained.

"Cause you're sick."

"Bad sick."

"And we could catch it."

Daniel offered a small wave. Hannah and Isabelle giggled and waved back. Before Daniel could say anything, Sarah stuck a thermometer in his mouth.

"Hold your questions," she said, sitting down on

the coffee table in front of the couch. "Dr. Neal said that if your temperature didn't break today, you had to go into the clinic, so we need to check this."

He raised his arm as if he intended to remove the thermometer, but Becca popped into his field of vision, shook her head and nodded toward her *mamm*. "You want to do what she says. *Mamm* isn't to be messed with when it comes to the flu."

Sarah smiled at him and tapped her foot against the floor. The girls' voices had dropped to a whisper, though Daniel was able to make out the words "horse" and "house" and "workers."

Finally Sarah took the thermometer from his mouth and held it up to the light from the window. "Only one hundred. Much better."

"Doesn't feel better." His voice came out resembling a bullfrog's, and he winced against the rawness in his throat.

"Hannah and Isabelle—I want you two cleaning up your rooms like I told you before. Becca, could you see that Daniel gets down at least a full cup of water? I'll go and heat up some chicken broth. I do believe you've turned the corner, Daniel." And then she patted his shoulder as if he'd done something praiseworthy.

The girls dashed from the room in a flurry of giggles and shouts.

Sarah picked up a tray and glided into the kitchen.

Becca took her place in front of him, perching on the coffee table. She held up a cup of water. "Want to give it a try?"

He nodded, though he couldn't take his eyes off her. Somehow the afternoon light had formed a halo around her head. Her lips were more pink than he remembered, and her freckles seemed to pop with the smile she wore. It was her eyes, though, that gave him pause—the look of concern caused a lump to form in his throat that had nothing to do with the flu.

He took a sip of the water, both their hands steadying the cup. He winced at the pain of swallowing and then drained the rest.

"I don't remember..." He tried to clear his throat, but Becca shook her head.

"You're only going to make it hurt more. Here, try one of these cough drops."

She unwrapped it and dropped it into his hand. He sucked on it for a few minutes while she watched him.

"I don't remember coming here, or...anything."

"What's the last thing you do remember?"

"Planting the cover crop with David."

"That was three days ago."

Becca almost laughed at the look of shock on his face, except it wasn't really funny. Nothing about the past three days had been funny. She'd been terrified when she'd found him burning with fever and unresponsive. She'd spent the last four days hovering and praying and trying not to worry.

"What happened?"

"You were supposed to bring the extra seed over

on Tuesday morning. When you didn't show, David went looking for you."

"And?"

"He could see you through the window, lying on the floor in your sleeping bag. He tried tapping on the window to wake you, shouting at you, but nothing worked. He didn't know what to do, so he came and got me."

"You told him to fetch your *mamm* and *dat*, and to bring the buggy."

"I did."

"You came into my house."

She dared him with a look. "I did not snoop this time. Obviously something was wrong. I wasn't going to let you just die there."

"Danki."

"Gem Gschehne."

Becca's *mamm* returned carrying the tray, which now held a steaming bowl of chicken broth and another cup of water.

"Becca, please help Daniel eat this—all of it. Also, it's time for another dose of his flu medicine." Sarah sat the tray on the coffee table next to Becca, smiled at them both and went back into the kitchen.

Becca wasn't sure if there was work in there, or if she was giving them time alone. Her *mamm* seemed to think there was something going on between them. Becca had tried to disabuse her of the idea, but it only made her *mamm* more convinced that she and Daniel were hiding their feelings for one another.

"I remember an old guy—" Daniel scrubbed a hand across his face. "He shone a light in my eyes and said for you all to stay away from me."

"Doc Neal. *Mamm* says he worries too much, but she did insist the girls keep their distance."

Becca picked up the soup bowl and the spoon. "Think you can handle this?"

"*Ya*. I can feed myself."

She didn't argue. Instead, she handed him the spoon and bowl, but his hand shook so badly that the soup sloshed right back into the bowl.

"Um. Maybe you could help me."

"I'd be happy to."

As he obediently swallowed each spoonful, she caught him up on what he'd missed the past four days. "*Dat* and David planted the extra seed in our back field. That was after they moved you here. Your temperature topped out at a hundred and five. Clyde and David went back to your place and fetched a few things—a couple changes of clothes, your hat and coat, and your journal."

"Notebook."

"Right, and in case you're wondering, I didn't so much as take a peek."

"I wasn't wondering." His eyes met hers and a shiver slipped down her spine. "That argument seems rather childish after…after this."

"Indeed." She cocked her head, so relieved to find that he was eating and talking that she felt a strong urge to give him a hard time for it all. "Quite impressive. I've never seen anyone with a temperature that high."

"I'm an overachiever."

"Apparently." She spooned more of the soup into his mouth, then offered him a napkin. He wiped his mouth, then sank back onto the pillow.

"Who turned this couch into a bed?"

"Oh, I did that—Francine and Georgia helped."

"How did your family get by with no sitting room?"

"That wasn't a problem. We just stayed in the kitchen, though honestly, if it weren't for you being contagious we could have danced a polka in here and you wouldn't have known."

"You know how to dance a polka?"

"Beside the point. You were out." She scooted the tray away, crossed her legs, propped her elbows on her knees and her chin in her hands. "Did you know that people talk a lot when they have a high temperature?"

"Uh-oh."

"Oh, *ya*. There was one name you called out over and over…"

David's eyes widened. "Who…"

"We tried to tell you she was fine, but you wouldn't be comforted." Becca would have liked to keep teasing him, but her *mamm* walked through carrying a stack of clean towels and popped into the middle of their conversation.

"Never heard a man go on so about a horse," Sarah said, smiling.

"Indeed." Becca wriggled her eyebrows. "She must be the love of your life, Daniel."

"She's okay?"

"She's fine," Sarah assured him. "David's gone over twice a day to see to her. You don't need to worry about Constance."

Her *mamm* walked back to the bathrooms, so Becca dared to lean forward and lower her voice. "You'd have been better off in the barn with that horse, than in that drafty old house. What were you thinking?"

He looked as if he was about to answer, but then another sound caught his attention.

"What was that?"

"What was what?"

"It sounded like…hammering."

"Oh, that. *Ya.* The community is rebuilding your house." Becca stood and began tidying the things on the coffee table, dropping the thermometer, cup of water and wet cloth onto the tray.

"Wait. What did you say? They're…"

"Rebuilding your house, Daniel. They've had prep crews here the last two days. The actual workdays are tomorrow and Saturday. It's a real shame that you won't be there. I guess you'll have to trust that they do the work the way you would have wanted it done."

"Wait. I didn't want…" He tried to sit up, but he ended up grasping the back of the couch and taking deep breaths.

She almost felt sorry for him, but really, wasn't this his fault? If he hadn't been so secretive, if he'd accepted help when they'd first offered, he might not be in this mess.

Which wasn't quite true. He'd still have the flu. She knew it wasn't caused by sleeping in a drafty house. It was a virus that was caught from other people. They'd had half a dozen members at church come down with it. Daniel's case seemed to be the worst. That could've been because of his living conditions or the terrible state of his pantry.

He'd finally caught his breath, and reached for her arm. "They can't do that."

"They are."

"But I'll take care of it."

"You'll rebuild your house? Before the first snowfall? Did you forget that we're already in November?"

He flopped back onto his pillow and closed his eyes, then threw his arm across his forehead. The expression on his face was pure agony. He was definitely being more dramatic than the situation called for. The Amish helped one another.

What was his problem?

Why was he embarrassed?

Was he actually too proud to accept help?

Or maybe he was feeling guilty that he hadn't taken care of his home before his fields.

She couldn't begin to imagine what was going on in Daniel Glick's mind, but she paused when he reached out and laid a hand on her arm. "I need to talk to the bishop."

"Okay. I'm sure he'll check on you tomorrow."

"*Nein*. I need to talk to him before tomorrow, before the real work begins. Can you…can you call him?"

"No need for that. I saw his buggy go by on the way to your place. I suppose he's there helping. If it's so important, I'll send Francine or Georgia over to fetch him."

Daniel closed his eyes and nodded.

He looked more than worried. He looked distraught, but the flu didn't seem to care about his new worries. The flu was still having its way with his body. By the time Becca had carried the tray to the kitchen door, she heard his soft snores behind her.

Her mind slipped easily back into its old track.

What was Daniel hiding?

Why the urgent need to talk to Saul?

And on top of those questions, a more pressing one: Why did she care so much about the concerns of Daniel Glick?

The sky was nearly dark by the time Bishop Saul walked into the Schwartz sitting room. Fortunately, the entire family seemed to be gathered in the kitchen. Daniel could hear their conversation and laughter and the general chaos that usually accompanied such a large household.

"Daniel, it's *gut* to see you awake."

Daniel pushed himself into a sitting position. He was suddenly aware that it had been several days since he showered, but that was trivial compared to what he was about to do.

"I need to speak with you…" He glanced toward the kitchen, knowing they couldn't hear what he was about to say, but worried that they might. "If now is a *gut* time."

"Now is an excellent time. There is no time better than the present to unburden your soul." Saul sank into the chair closest to the couch.

Daniel guessed his age to be near eighty. The man's face was a myriad of wrinkles that fanned out into gentle folds, and his neatly trimmed, white beard reached his chest. It was his eyes, though, that belied his calling in life—they were gentle, patient, kind.

"I haven't been honest about my past, and the work over at my house…well, I think it should stop."

Saul didn't argue, simply made a go-on gesture with his hand.

"I have perhaps misrepresented myself. That is to say, though I purchased a less than pristine property…"

"A bit of an understatement."

"I actually have quite a bit of resources."

Saul didn't answer, didn't react in any way.

A nauseous stomach now added to Daniel's other aches. He pushed the thought away. Nausea was the last of his troubles.

"What I'm trying to say is… I'm rich."

"I see."

"*Nein.* I don't think you understand. I'm a millionaire."

And then the story poured out of him. He explained about inheriting the money, how it had torn his family apart, how it had ruined his relationship with the woman he'd expected to marry. The sounds in the kitchen turned to cleaning dishes and home-work questions and a game of chess, but that was all background to Daniel as he gave up the burdens of his heart to this man that he barely knew.

"I decided to move away, to live as if my life had never changed, to live as if I had nothing." He crossed then uncrossed his arms as he finally ran out of words.

Saul ran his fingers through his beard, tapped the arm of the chair and then sat forward—elbows on his knees, hands clasped together.

"It is not a sin to be wealthy, Daniel."

"It's not?"

"*Nein.* Remember the parable of the talents."

"I never understood that one."

Now Saul smiled. "*Gotte*'s word can be difficult. *Ya?* And at various times in our lives, it can speak to us differently. Go back and read the twenty-fifth chapter of Matthew, as you're recuperating. I think that you'll find comfort as well as instruction there."

"That's it? That's all you have to say? Read Mat-thew?"

"Paul is *gut*, too. In the first book of Timothy, he commands those who are rich to not be arrogant." Saul waited, a smile tugging at the corner of his lips. "Search your heart, Daniel. Have you been ar-rogant?"

"*Nein.* Stubborn, perhaps."

"Which we can deal with at a different time. Paul

also says that the rich are to put their hope in *Gotte*, not in their wealth."

"My wealth has been nothing but trouble for me. *Gotte* has been—up until now at least—the only constant in my life."

"*Gut*. That's *gut*." Saul sat up straighter. "Paul goes on to say that the rich are to be generous. I suspect you have been generous with your resources, since you're certainly not spending them on yourself."

"But don't you see? People are going to show up tomorrow to work on my house. They're going to give of their time and use resources from the benevolence fund. That's not right. It's not fair. I could easily hire a contracting firm to come and do that. I wanted to live simply, to live without the money, but then this happened, and now I don't know how to fix it."

"It would seem to me that you've started down that path already, by talking to me. I will pray that you have wisdom in this matter, Daniel. We'll both pray that you know with certainty who you should share this with and when you should share it—if at all."

"But what about tomorrow?"

"What about it?"

"They're going to all show up to help, thinking that I'm poor."

"I'm not sure that's true. Our community would show up to help, regardless of your financial situation."

"Okay. Maybe you have a point." Daniel scratched at the stubble on his cheeks. He needed to shave. He needed to bathe, and his stomach was starting to grumble. But more than those things, he needed to settle this now. "But what about the cost? The materials will be paid for out of the benevolence fund."

"That's not a problem. We often have anonymous donations. Search your heart, then donate what you can. If you'd rather not give it directly to Deacon Miller, I'll be happy to pass it along."

Saul stood, stepped closer and placed his hand gently on the top of Daniel's head. He prayed that Daniel would have wisdom and clarity in all things. What pierced Daniel's heart was when this man, who really knew very little about him, thanked *Gotte* for bringing Daniel to their community, for adding him to their numbers, and for turning him into a strong man of *Gotte*.

He wasn't sure those words described him.

But one thing he was certain of—he wished that they did.

Chapter Seven

Becca hadn't given up on the idea of earning extra money for her family. Clyde was still saving for his new buggy, but he also gave a portion of what he earned each week to his parents. He needed help. And Christmas was coming. Becca wanted Hannah and Isabelle to have something new. Georgia would love a new book, and she probably needed new glasses. Francine…she really had no idea what Francine would like. Apparently Francine had decided she was in her *rumspringa*, though she wasn't even done with school yet. If asked what she wanted for Christmas, she'd probably say she'd like a new pair of blue jeans or to have her ears pierced.

Of course, gift giving wasn't the focus on the holiday, but still Becca dreamed of being able to surprise her family with a few nice things. She had a couple of new leads on earning a little extra money. Hopefully, during the next week, she'd have time to pursue them more.

Carl-the-bad-tempered-rooster wasn't exactly working out the way she had hoped. At least her hens had become used to his moody behavior. They no longer ran from him, but instead moved to the end of the chicken coop and watched him carefully. Sort of reminded Becca of the group of young women at church watching Daniel.

Oops.

How had that image popped into her mind? It wasn't exactly a kind one.

Which was beside the point. As she walked back from Daniel's house Sunday afternoon, a westerly wind pulled at her coat and nearly tugged the bonnet off her head. She only wore the black bonnet over her *kapp* in the worst of weather because it was old and not particularly flattering. She felt rather like a crow with it covering her head, but it did protect her from the wind, which was apt to change and come from the north any moment. November in northern Indiana was a tumultuous time.

Speaking of tumultuous, Daniel was standing on the front porch when she reached the house, and the look on his face reminded her of the stormy sky at her back—brooding.

"How do things look?"

"Aren't you supposed to be inside?"

"Is there anything left for me to do?"

"You mean besides running a farm? *Nein.* That's it."

"Good grief." He limped over to the porch swing and collapsed on it. "My entire farm is being renovated, and I can't even see it."

"You're getting stronger every day. Before you know it, you'll be healthy enough to escape."

"Now you're mocking me."

"A little."

"I suppose I deserve it."

"You do."

"I'm not ungrateful."

"Uh-huh."

"Seriously, I'm not. And your family..."

She sat down beside him on the swing because he once again had that faraway look in his eyes. She peered at him more closely. He looked rather lost. He'd always seemed to be a bit of an introvert, but since his illness, he seemed to drift off into his own thoughts even more often. Several times she'd walked into the living room to find him with his journal in his lap, a forgotten pen in his hand, and his gaze locked on something outside the window.

He had the ability to disappear right before her eyes.

She raised her hand and snapped her fingers to get his attention, then smiled when he looked at her as if he was surprised she was there.

"Where did you go?"

"I was thinking about your family."

"They're a lot. My family can be overwhelming, even to me, and I grew up with them."

"*Nein.* That's not what I meant."

He hesitated, and she thought he'd change the subject. That was usually what he did when she prodded. There was still something mysterious about Daniel

Glick, and a small part of her remained determined to figure out what it was. She no longer thought he was nefarious, but there were other reasons that one went into hiding.

He shook his head and laughed, though there wasn't much happiness in it. "My family was big, but it wasn't like yours. We didn't play games together at night..."

"Is Eli bugging you about chess again? None of us know how to play, so I suppose he sees you as fresh competition."

"No one wanted to read aloud a passage from the book they were reading..."

"Georgia will read to anyone who is sitting in one place for more than thirty seconds."

"And none of my *schweschdern* would have asked me what type of color she should dye her hair."

"She won't do it. I know Francine better than she knows herself. She was only teasing. At least I *hope* she was only teasing."

"The point is that my family wasn't close in that way. There were a lot of us, and sure, we sat around the dinner table together, but it wasn't the same."

"Oh." Suddenly she did understand what he meant, and she felt an almost overwhelming love for her big, loud, crazy family. Instead of sharing that, she wrapped her arms around her middle. "You seem anxious to go home."

"I can't believe they remodeled the entire house without me."

"Oh, *ya*. You won't recognize the place. There's a roof and everything."

"I'm strong enough to go home. Your *mamm* worries, but I think I'd be fine."

"And she would have agreed except that your temperature spiked again last night. Dr. Neal said forty-eight hours without a fever, and she's going to hold you to that."

"Maybe tomorrow."

"Maybe so." She cast a sideways look at him. "Off-Sundays are laid-back around here."

"I enjoyed the devotional."

"*Ya*, *Dat* has a real flair for making a passage in the Bible quite entertaining. He has a dramatic voice for reading." Her *dat* had read them the verses about Abram and his nephew Lot—how they'd disagreed and Abram had given Lot his choice of land. Lot had taken the best for himself, although it didn't end well for him. This was all before Abram had accepted *Gotte*'s calling on his life and become Abraham.

Becca wasn't sure how the story related to her and her siblings, although they did occasionally bicker over minor matters. Was that why her *dat* had picked it? Of course, after the Bible study and prayer, he'd snuck in a joke.

Who was the smartest man in the Bible?

Abraham. He knew a Lot.

"It was nice to see your *Onkel* Jeremiah."

"He'll be gone most of December, visiting family in Ohio."

"And Abigail…she gets bigger every time she comes by."

Becca swatted his arm. "Better not tell her that. You'll have to hear her what-it's-like-to-be-pregnant stories."

"How about you sneak me out to the barn to see Constance?"

"I suppose I might be able to pretend that I need your help." They'd moved Constance to the closer barn, which made for easier feeding.

"Great." Daniel practically jumped off the swing. Just as she thought he probably was well enough to return home, he started a fit of coughing that lasted a good minute and a half. She wasn't glad that he was still ill. That was most certainly not the emotion she was feeling. But she also didn't want him to go home just to have a relapse. He'd scared a year off her life the first time. He owed it to her to be completely well before moving back into his own place.

"After we check the horses, *Mamm* should have dinner ready. It's usually just cold sandwiches on Sundays."

"Sounds *gut*."

"And I'm pretty sure there'll be a game of Pictionary after that."

"Never played it."

"You've never played Pictionary?"

"Nope."

"*Gut*. You should be easy to beat."

She bumped her shoulder against his as they walked back into the house. Twenty minutes later they were in the barn, brushing down Old Boy and Constance. Becca couldn't imagine who Daniel would ever let close enough to even have a relationship, let alone marry. Whoever the gal was, she'd need a lot of patience, because he absolutely adored that horse.

A girl who cared about him could get jealous over such a thing. Not that she would know anything about that.

It was actually Thursday before Daniel was able to go home. He did have a relapse—this time only running a low fever, but it was the cough that complicated things. It felt as if his ribs were bruised. He couldn't imagine trying to cook for himself or do his own laundry or even take care of his own horse.

That last one really rankled him.

He knew that Clyde and David and even Eli were caring for the mare, but she was his responsibility.

As the week progressed, he slowly regained his strength.

Thursday morning, he'd showered, shaved and agreed to stay until lunch. Then he was going home—for good. He hadn't even seen the place since the workday. He was quite eager to look over what had been done. It couldn't all be finished, as Becca had suggested. Surely there would be work for him to do?

As he attempted to restore the sitting room to its pre-infirmary condition, he marveled that he'd been staying with the Schwartz family for ten days. Had he ever stayed in anyone's home that long? Come to think of it, he'd never stayed with anyone at all—except for his parents, of course.

The last ten days had offered his first insight into how other families lived, and as he'd confessed to Becca, it had helped him to realize that his own family was dysfunctional in more than one way—in more ways than just the wealth they'd inherited. He'd had two more visits with Saul, and the older man had been a great sounding board—only offering his opinion when Daniel flat out asked for it.

His most recent suggestion had been that Daniel write to his parents. Daniel wasn't sure he was ready to do that, but he was at least considering it. Saul's words reverberated in his mind at the strangest times.

Anger is a heavy burden for the one who carries it. Best to let it go.

Could it possibly be that easy? Could he just let it go? It wasn't as if he could tie his feelings to a balloon and watch them float away. Could he forgive his family for all the hurtful things they'd said to one another? He hadn't been completely innocent, either. There were things he needed to apologize for. He was already composing the letter in his mind, though he wasn't ready to commit it to paper.

Becca walked in the room and looked around in surprise.

"You're ready."

"Nearly."

"Lunch will be in a few minutes."

"*Gut.* I'm starved."

"Your appetite has definitely returned." She

walked over to the bookcase and picked up his journal. She turned toward him, holding the journal in one hand and a duster in the other. She was a beautiful woman—golden blond hair peeked out from her *kapp*, freckles dotted her cheeks and nose, and her blue eyes were something a guy could get lost in.

At the moment she was pretending to be quite serious, but her eyes gave her away. Becca's eyes nearly always held laughter, in spite of her obsession to work her family out of their state of poverty.

"You don't want to forget this."

"Danki."

"I know you've explained that it's just your thoughts and that it's not a journal." She shook her head and laughter brightened her eyes. "But where do you find this stuff?"

The last few evenings he'd had trouble sleeping, so he'd sat at the kitchen table and written in it. The first time Becca had joined him, he'd immediately shut the book, but as he grew more comfortable around her he'd begun sharing snippets. When she hadn't mocked him, he'd shared more, so now he knew her question was in earnest.

"Some of it you just learn the hard way."

"Is that so?"

"Ya, you being so young, you probably can't imagine that."

"I keep forgetting you're an old man of thirty while I'm a young chick of twenty-four. Okay, learn it the hard way. What else?"

"Read. Some things you can learn from reading."

"The Bible."

"Sure, but other books, too. Men and women have been sharing what they learned through writing for a very long time."

"Now you sound like Georgia." She ticked off his answers on her fingers. "Learn the hard way. Read about it. Are those my only options for finding wisdom?"

He stepped closer and breathed in the scent of her. For reasons he couldn't have explained, his ex-fiancée, Sheila, popped into his mind. He could remember how it felt to be hurt by her, but looking back now, it was as if those things had happened to someone else. He supposed he still bore the scars of her betrayal, but it no longer bothered him like it once had. "Heartbreak. I think you can learn from that."

She cocked her head and looked up at him. "Has your heart been broken, Daniel?"

"Yes. Once. I seem to have healed."

"Uh-huh. I think I'll pass on that one. Any other avenues of wisdom open to me?"

"Age, which we sort of already covered."

"You're telling me to get older?"

"Sure." He reached forward, tucked a wayward lock into her *kapp* and allowed his hand to linger there. Her eyes widened, practically daring him to… to what?

Fortunately, her *mamm* called them to lunch then. Instead of turning and walking away, Becca tucked her hand into the crook of his arm. "Come on, old man. Maybe you can share your wisdom during our meal—entertain my *mamm* and *dat*."

Daniel barely heard what she was saying. He was focused on the feel of her hand on his arm, the closeness of her, the way that life seemed simple to Becca—family or not family, helpful or hurtful, wise or naive. It wasn't so much that she saw things in black-and-white as it was that for her, life had been uncomplicated to this point. He could only pray that it would remain so for her. She needed to find a guy who had a family like hers. Then they'd have a dual support system, as most Amish newlyweds did.

He didn't know why his thoughts were focused on Becca's future marriage, when to his knowledge she wasn't even stepping out, but he could see her in a house of her own. He could see her surrounded by children and wayward chickens and hound dogs. What he couldn't see was her with another man.

Which was ridiculous.

It wasn't as if she would be interested in the likes of him, even if he was in a place to look for a *fraa*.

Which he wasn't. He wasn't even close.

The last thing she needed was in-laws with a history of problems, especially ones that had become an integral part of their lives.

No. Becca Schwartz would be better off stepping out with a normal guy—one who could provide her with a normal house and farm and family.

One of the things he'd written in his book, one

that he hadn't shared with her, pretty much summed up his life and how it would not be a good life for her.

Money, especially excess money, brought with it a world of trouble.

Becca tried not to laugh as Daniel climbed the steps of his front porch. Of course, he'd insisted on moving Constance and stabling her first. The mare looked quite content, if a horse could look satisfied, pleased and happy to be home.

Now he stood staring in disbelief at his house.

"How did they manage to do all of this?"

"Surely you've been to a barn raising before."

"This wasn't a barn, though."

"We do the same for houses all the time." Becca thought the place looked fantastic. There was no longer any danger of falling through the porch's floor. The railing was solid. The new paint gleamed in the bright November sunshine.

Daniel opened the screen door—then closed and opened it again. "Works better."

"Because it's a new door. I thought the workers would be better off tearing down your old place and building a new one, but Silas King—he's usually the foreman of our work crews—said your place has good bones."

"He told me the same when he stopped by, and he described the work, but…"

"But what?"

"I didn't envision this, couldn't imagine it at all."

They walked into the house and Daniel stopped in

the middle of the sitting room. He turned in a circle, looked up at the ceiling, went over and tapped the window frame, then dropped his bag on the floor and put his hands on his hips. "Where did the furniture come from?"

"That old couch?"

"Doesn't look that old."

"It was somebody's who didn't need it anymore. You know how it is with Plain people. We rarely throw things away."

He clomped into the kitchen, turned and looked at her with his mouth slightly ajar, then strode to the pantry and jerked the door open. Becca knew what he was going to see. She'd helped to stock the shelves. Rows and rows of canned goods that people had donated from their own harvest, plus paper goods and staples they'd purchased with money from the benevolence fund.

"This is terrible."

"What? That you can eat something besides oatmeal?"

Daniel sank into a chair at the table he hadn't owned before he was sick. "I knew they were going to rebuild the place, and I didn't see a way to stop them."

"Why would you?"

"But they've furnished it, given me enough food to see me through the winter..."

"You'll still need meat, fresh eggs and dairy." Becca opened the refrigerator and scanned it, then removed a small pitcher of milk. She set the kettle on the used stove that had been placed in the corner of the kitchen. "There's only enough for a couple of weeks."

Daniel's reply was a groan. When she glanced over at him, he was sitting at the table with his head in his hands.

"This tea will fix you right up. You're probably just tired."

"You don't get it. You don't understand."

She sat across from him. "Then explain it to me. Why is all of this bad?"

"Because they're giving out of what they don't have."

"Many in our community have more than enough."

"And many don't." Daniel scrubbed his hands over his face, then finally looked at her. "Many don't, and they've given part of what little they have to me. That's not right because I—"

He stopped midsentence, a pained expression on his face.

"What? You had nothing here, Daniel—except your horse and your sleeping bag and your journal. People wanted to help from day one, but you wouldn't let them. It took your coming down with the flu before you'd accept help. Now don't ruin it by letting your pride become involved."

"It's not pride."

"What is it then?"

"I can't... I can't explain why this is such a terrible thing, Becca. Just trust me. I should not have accepted this much help."

She stared at him a moment, waited until he raised those beautiful brown eyes to hers. When he did, she smiled, ducked her head and gave him a pointed look. "You can't take any of it back, so I suggest you get used to the new Daniel Glick homestead and learn to say thank you. That's all people expect."

"That's it? That's your advice? Say thank you?"

"Uh-huh. Oh, and be ready to jump in when they need help, because that's what neighbors do."

The kettle whistled, and she hopped up to fix his tea. In truth, Daniel's house only held minimal furniture now. Yes, he had a bed, a couch, an old patched recliner and a table with seating for four. He had a new roof, new siding, tight window frames and a porch where he wouldn't break his legs. He had a used propane stove and refrigerator, and when he finally made it to the mudroom, he'd see a nearly archaic wringer washing machine.

He had the minimum, but you'd think by the look on his face that people had furnished his place for an *Englisch* magazine photo op. She didn't understand that. She didn't understand his need to live so sparsely.

He seemed to be stuck on the fact that he was poor.

Her family was poor, too, but they didn't mind having food and clothing and a furnished home.

Men were a mystery to her, and Daniel Glick? Daniel was a paradox. For a guy who carried around a book and filled it with words of wisdom, she thought he had a lot of learning to do.

Chapter Eight

The next week and a half passed in a blur. Daniel went to town as soon as he felt strong enough, withdrew more money and gave it to Bishop Saul.

The good bishop simply patted him on the shoulder and assured him that he would "see it went into the benevolence fund—another anonymous donation."

On the Sunday after he moved back home, he stood up at the church meeting and thanked everyone. It was both harder and easier than he'd expected. Harder because it had been a long time since he had felt anything resembling kinship to other people. Easier because the response was laughter, cries of "We'll call you when our harvest is ready," and murmurs that at least now he could begin courting without fear of scaring off the woman.

But he had no intentions of courting.

He set himself to the work of a farmer in winter— mending fences, buying and transporting hay for

Constance, and ordering seed for the spring. The first snowfall brought over a foot of white powder, and he found an old, tattered horse blanket in the loft of the barn for his mare. She tossed her head when he put it on her, but when he released her into the field it appeared she had forgiven him.

The Schwartz brood came by with sleds and insisted he accompany them to the top of a small hill at the back of the property. There was only a foot of snow on the ground, and the hill wasn't that large, but you'd have thought they were at a famous ski resort the way they carried on. He didn't think Becca could look prettier. Wrapped in what must have been her *bruder*'s coat, well-worn mittens, a bonnet and a scarf, she looked like a snow princess to him.

It was while they were having hot chocolate at his place, all seven of her younger siblings spread out on the living room couch and floor, that he realized she was up to something.

He tugged her arm and pulled her into the kitchen.

"What are you doing?"

"What do you mean what am I doing?"

"You were texting someone on Francine's phone. How does Francine even have a phone?"

"Not that it's any of your business, but it's not her phone. It's her friend's phone. You know she thinks she's on her *rumspringa*."

"She's only twelve."

"I know that. Go speak to her about it if you dare. As to who or why I was texting on it, I don't want to talk about that with you."

He scowled at her, but it did nothing to intimidate her into confessing.

Before they left, he tried talking to Clyde and David.

"Don't know," Clyde admitted. "Another one of her get-less-poor plans."

David wrapped his scarf tightly around his neck. "She's still a bit put out that Carl-the-bad-tempered-rooster hasn't brought any new baby chicks. Seems the hens are hiding from him."

"He's a nice-looking Brahma, though." Clyde ran a hand up and down his jawline, attempting to look serious and thoughtful. "Maybe we can roast him for Thanksgiving."

The two *bruders* high-fived, then turned to trudge off after their *schweschdern*. Daniel couldn't have explained what he did next—it was pure instinct. He jogged after the group and motioned Clyde toward his barn.

"Has she asked you to let her use the buggy? What I mean is, has she asked you not to take it to work?"

Clyde had been working for a big Amish farm across town—the owners were actually in another church district, but they paid well, and he was still saving for his own buggy.

"Actually, *ya*. She said she could take me to work tomorrow, use the buggy and then pick me back up in the afternoon."

"Is that unusual?"

"Can't remember her doing it before."

"So it has to do with this new plan?"

"It could. Why? Is that a problem?"

Becca had never told her family about the CBD plants. Something told him that this might be like that. Getting in over her head again. Not that Becca Schwartz needed him to follow her around and protect her. But they were friends, right? What was it she had said standing in his kitchen? *Be ready to jump in when they need help, because that's what neighbors do.*

That was exactly what he was going to do then— jump in and help.

"Go ahead and take your buggy. I'll give her a ride to town."

"You're sure?"

"Absolutely. I need to run some errands anyway."

"Sounds *gut* to me. I'll let her know."

Daniel was glad he wouldn't be there when Clyde shared the change in plans. He was pretty sure that whatever Becca was doing in town, she did not want her family to know about it.

That thought was confirmed an hour later when she came barging into the barn.

"What is your problem?" Her bonnet was askew, she was only wearing one mitten, and she'd forgotten to button her coat.

Daniel had been in the middle of giving Constance her daily brush-down. He turned back toward the horse and resumed his work. "Wasn't aware I had one."

"Why did you tell Clyde you'd take me to town?"

"Because neighbors help each other. Remember?"

She tried pinning him with an aggravated look. When he didn't jump to the bait, she picked up the horse comb, walked over and commenced combing out Constance's mane.

"Why are you doing that?"

"I'm helping. That's what neighbors do."

"*Ya*, but Constance and I were doing just fine without your help." He was hoping to aggravate her, to provoke her into stepping away—or even better, leaving his barn altogether. *Their* barn. It was their barn. He had to keep reminding himself of that. Regardless, Becca looked too adorable to be standing so close to him. He moved to the other side of the mare.

"I understand." She leaned forward and smelled the mare's neck, then glanced over at him. "I was doing fine without your help. So why did you stick your nose into my affairs?"

"Because you're up to something."

"I have no idea know what you mean."

"It's another get-rich scheme. Isn't it?"

"I don't want to be rich. I just want to be less poor."

"Haven't you outgrown this absurd idea? Didn't the hemp plants teach you anything?"

"They taught me to be more careful." She raised her chin a fraction of an inch. "This is completely aboveboard."

"Oh, is it?"

"Uh-huh. I have the man's business card and everything. I even checked out his website."

"Business card? Website? Are you listening to yourself? You sound like a *youngie*."

"Look, Daniel. I know you can't understand this because you're living over here all by yourself, but I have a family—a very large family. Plus, Christmas is coming, and I want to be able to give them nice things. Is that so wrong?"

"It is if you're going to get yourself in trouble."

"I *won't* get in trouble."

They were glaring at each other over Constance's back, and the mare nodded her head as if to say, *go on…*

"Tell me what you're doing, and if it doesn't sound dangerous, I'll let you borrow Constance and my buggy and go by yourself."

"I do not need your permission to go to town alone."

"Of course not."

"But it would be convenient to use your horse and buggy."

"Exactly."

"Fine." She put the comb back on the shelf, then walked over to stand next to him. Pulling a piece of paper from her pocket, she unfolded it and pushed it into his hands.

"What is this?" Daniel's thoughts scrambled as he stared down at the sheet of paper. It showed a picture of an Amish woman with two small children walking away from the camera. There was the slightest indication that the woman was about to look back over her shoulder and smile at the person taking the photograph.

As he read the words below the picture, he thought his head might pop right off his shoulders.

Plain & Simple Glamour Shots
Tastefully Done
Earn extra money for your farm, family or community

"Tell me you are not going to do this."

"Why wouldn't I?"

"Because we don't pose for pictures."

"Look. It says right here, Tastefully Done. When I checked the web page, there were quite a few testimonials from women saying they'd worked for two to three hours and earned plenty of extra money."

"Becca, look at me."

She reluctantly raised her eyes to his.

"Don't do this. You can't believe this piece of paper or that website. Anyone could make up those things."

"But why would they? See, I've thought of that, but why would they make it up? There's no reason to. They simply want photographs for their magazines, and since it never shows our face, and we're even allowed to wear Plain clothing… Well, what's the harm?"

Daniel handed the sheet of paper back to her, but instead of resuming the work with Constance, he walked out of the stall into the main room of the barn. He was very aware that if he said the wrong thing, Becca would go off and do what she wanted to do. She wanted to believe this was legitimate. Maybe it was. Who could say?

But a warning alarm in his heart told him it could be dangerous.

Finally, he turned toward her. "Let me go with you."

"What?"

"Let me go with you. When are you supposed to meet him?"

"Tomorrow, but I don't need you with me."

"What time?"

"None of your business."

"Let me go with you, and if everything seems legit, then I'll go wait for you in the buggy."

"In the cold? You're going to wait in the buggy in the cold for hours?"

"Sure."

"Ridiculous. You'd probably end up sick again. Plus, there's no reason for you to do such a thing. You could simply wait on the other side of the coffee shop."

"That's where you're meeting? Which coffee shop?"

"The Kitchen Cupboard, in Davis Mercantile, but I don't need someone watching over me, Daniel. I'm a grown woman."

"Oh, *ya*." He rubbed his chin, then shot a hopefully serious look her way. "But I need some supplies in town, and I do love a *gut* cup of coffee."

He thought she'd be offended.

He expected her to storm away after forbidding him to come.

Instead, she walked over to where he was, standing close enough that he took a step back and bumped into the wall.

"You're worried about me."

"Well, you know. Neighbors…"

"Helping neighbors. I heard you before, but this is different. Are you getting sweet on me, Daniel?"

He crossed his arms and scowled at her. "Stop it."

"What? A girl has a right to be flattered."

So that was her plan. She'd embarrass him, and then he'd call it off. Only he wasn't falling for that. He was going to stay focused on the objective, which was to see Becca safely through another crazy scheme.

"What if I am, Becca? Are you interested?" Now he stepped toward her, only she didn't back away as he'd expected. Instead, she looked up at him, laughter in her eyes.

"We'll continue this conversation tomorrow after my meeting."

"Sure. Okay."

"After you see that I am a capable, independent woman who doesn't need to be looked after."

There was that spunk he was expecting to hear from her.

"But I have to say, I'm flattered that you care so much."

More bait. He wasn't going to respond. She was almost to the door, when he thought to call out to her. "What time should I pick you up?"

"Nine o'clock sharp."

With a backward wave of her hand, she was gone, leaving Daniel to wonder what he'd just gotten himself into.

The next morning, Becca stood staring at her four dresses. She wanted to wear her best dress to town, but she knew that would make her *mamm* suspicious. She only wore that dress on church Sundays. Best to wear her second-best and avoid the scrutiny. She did take a little extra time with her hair and *kapp*, not that the man would be photographing her today, and besides, it would only be from the back when he did start taking pictures.

Still, she'd like to look her best. So she made sure that her hair was braided nicely and tucked into her *kapp* except for a soft fringe around her face. She didn't have any makeup, had never had much of a *rumspringa* herself. She momentarily thought about checking with Francine to see if she had any blush or powder or lip gloss, but that would only be encouraging her *schweschder*'s rebellious ways.

"It is what it is," she murmured to the small mirror, then hurried downstairs.

Her *mamm* was too busy with Thanksgiving preparations to notice that Becca was up to something.

"You're sure you don't mind getting all these supplies for me while you're in town?"

Becca stared down at the long list in surprise. Her *mamm* wanted all these things? Were they feeding their family or the entire neighborhood? And where had the money come from? As if reading her mind, her *mamm* pressed a wad of bills into her hand. "Clyde's been helping out and your *dat* was paid for his work over at the factory. *Gotte* provides, Becca."

"Yes, he does," she said, but what she was thinking was that *Gotte* provided for those who worked. Didn't it say that somewhere in the Bible? She'd have to ask the bishop next time she saw him. Regardless, she planned to contribute some to the holiday meal herself, or if she didn't have any money that soon, she could at least help purchase Christmas gifts for her siblings.

Her thoughts were focused on that as she helped with breakfast, scooting everyone off to school and cleaning up the kitchen. She was surprised when she heard the clatter of buggy wheels and realized Daniel was there.

"I'm so happy that you two are doing things together, dear." Her *mamm* didn't even try to hide her enormous smile.

"It's not like that."

"Often it's not...until it is."

Becca thought of arguing, but she had a feeling that the more she protested, the more she sounded like a teenage girl with a crush on the new boy in town. So instead, she kissed her *mamm* on the cheek, snagged her coat and hurried outside.

Daniel was speaking to her *dat*, who was grinning as if Christmas had already come. She arrived in time to hear him ask, "What did the farmer say when he lost one of his cows?"

"Hmm. I can't imagine." Daniel looked at her and wriggled his eyebrows.

"He said, *What a miss-steak!*"

Her *dat* would have launched right into another joke, if Becca hadn't intervened. "I guess we better hurry so we make it to town before the stores get too busy."

Daniel looked skyward, as if he expected help from that direction. At least he didn't argue with her in front of her *dat*.

"So they don't know?" he asked in a low voice.

"Of course they don't know."

"Don't you feel guilty about that?"

"Did you tell your parents everything when you were twenty-four?"

Daniel scrubbed his hand across his face. "*Nein*. I didn't, but this isn't about me."

It was a beautiful day, but Becca could hardly appreciate it with butterflies fluttering around in her stomach. She told herself that it was about the interview, but it was also about the man sitting next to her. When had she begun to think of Daniel in *that* way? She shook off the thoughts and suggested he drop her off at the mercantile's front door.

"I thought we'd walk in together."

"And I thought it would be better if it didn't look like we were a couple."

"Fine."

"Fine."

The scowl on his face was almost comical, but he didn't argue with her. She didn't bother looking back as she slammed the buggy door shut. She could do this. She could be an independent woman, and she could show Daniel Glick that she knew how to take advantage of a good business opportunity when she saw one.

She hurried into the mercantile, past JoJo's Pretzels and into the coffee shop. The place smelled like baked goods and freshly ground coffee, and the shelves were covered with packaged teas, coffee and mugs. A mere eight tables were scattered throughout the space, so it was pretty easy to spot the man who had given her the flyer when she was last in town.

"Hi, I'm Becca."

"And I'm Sean Wilson. Would you like a coffee?"

"Ya. Danki." She told him how she liked her coffee and tried not to crinkle her nose at the smell of his too-strong cologne. Sean Wilson used a little too much hair gel, too. In fact, without his baseball cap on, he seemed older than she'd first thought. Why would anyone comb their hair over and plaster it down? The look was somewhat ridiculous, but then she supposed *Englisch* had different styles than Amish. She knew the women did, so perhaps the men did, as well.

She settled into the table he'd been waiting for her at, while he went to purchase her drink. There was a stack of flyers on the table, or perhaps they were simply full-size photographs. The first was the one she had seen, where the Amish woman and two children were walking away.

Becca glanced up, confirmed that Sean Wilson's

attention was with the barista, and scanned through the pictures. Only the top three were similar in nature. As she quickly glanced through the others, she was alarmed to see that they were women looking directly at the camera, some in Amish clothes, some not in Amish clothes, and some in poses that struck her as quite flirtatious.

Her mouth went suddenly dry, and she could feel her heartbeat pulsing in her temples.

It was really none of her business what types of photographs Sean's company used in their advertisements. Didn't she see the same thing on every *Englisch* magazine at the store? She would never pose in such a way, and she would make that quite clear.

As Sean walked back toward the table with her coffee, he passed Daniel. Daniel turned, gave her a thumbs-up, then ordered his own coffee. By the time Becca was able to direct the conversation to any possible work, Daniel was seated two tables behind them facing her. Close enough in case she needed him, but far enough away to give them some semblance of privacy.

"I'm glad you responded to our ad." Sean restacked the photographs. If he noticed she'd looked through them, he didn't remark on it. "How long have you wanted to be a model?"

Becca nearly spilled her coffee. "Oh, I have no desire to be a model."

"No?"

"*Nein*. I mean, no. I'm willing to have a tasteful photograph taken, like this one on top." She tapped the stack of photographs. Best to get this out in the open now. "But I'd never pose like some of those beneath—where the woman is looking right at the camera or where she has her shirt off her shoulder."

"You're shy."

"I'm not shy in the least, but I wouldn't go against our *Ordnung.*"

"I see." He sipped his coffee and studied her. "You have beautiful features."

Becca didn't know how to answer that, so she didn't. Then she remembered something her *dat* had said recently. *Straight ahead is shorter than round about.* Best to plunge in and get this over with.

"Mr. Wilson—"

"Sean."

She nodded, but she didn't use his first name. It seemed too personal—as if they were friends, and she wasn't at all sure about that.

"The question isn't about my features, not really, since any pictures I would do for you would be facing away from the camera. The question is simply where, when and how much you're paying."

"I like a gal who gets straight to the point."

Gal? Did he just call her a gal? Something about this meeting wasn't going as planned. The butterflies in her stomach had switched to the feeling of a lump—something in between having eaten too much and having a stomach bug.

"I rather like straight answers."

"All right." He again straightened the stack of photographs, then met her gaze head-on. "The truth is that I have plenty of women who are willing to put on a bonnet—"

"It's a *kapp*."

"Plenty of gals who will wear a badly designed dress and walk away from the camera. I can get that any day of the week. Would we pay you for it? Probably not, but you'd at least be gaining some experience and photo shoots that you could add to your portfolio."

"I don't need experience, and I don't have a portfolio."

Sean continued, as if she hadn't interrupted him. "What pays better—you'd be surprised how much— is for you to let us give you some fashionable clothes, let your hair down, literally, and then allow some private viewings of your photography shoot."

Becca stood up so quickly that she jostled the coffee out of both of their cups, right onto the stack of photographs. She didn't care. In fact, she had the irrational thought that she'd like to pick up his stupid stack of pictures and toss them on the floor.

Some part of her mind recognized that Daniel had stood and was moving toward them. She didn't pause. She wasn't waiting for her knight in shining armor to arrive and save her from the bad man. She was ready to give the bad man a piece of her mind.

"This is not what you advertised, and it is not what I agreed to."

Oh, if only she could wipe the smirk off his face.

"You should be ashamed of yourself, Mr. Wilson. If that's even your real name. You can be sure that my bishop will be hearing about this—"

"And the police." Daniel's steady presence beside her calmed her quaking nerves.

"Yes, and the police."

Sean Wilson laughed. "Don't you think you're overreacting?"

"*Nein*. I don't. What I do think is that some of the girls in these pictures were underage, and I'm wondering if you had their parents' permission to photograph them."

A cold and hostile expression passed over Sean's face. "Don't even think about messing with me, lady. Just because you think you're too good…"

"She is too good." Daniel was now standing shoulder to shoulder with Becca. "And we both think it would be best if you leave now. Or would you like me to call the owner over? We'd be happy to tell her that you're running a business—very likely an illegal business—in her coffee shop."

Sean Wilson was already gathering up his things. Without another word, he stormed out the door. Becca walked to the window while Daniel went to speak with the shop owner. When he returned, he asked, "Are you okay?"

"*Ya.*"

"What's that?" He nodded toward the folded sheet of paper in her hands. It was the flyer that Sean had given her when she'd first met him, and on the back, she'd written the type of car he was driving, as well as his license plate number.

"I think we need to go to the police again."

Chapter Nine

Daniel directed Constance toward the police station. Once there, they told the receptionist that they'd like to speak to an officer, and then sat down in the waiting area. Just like before.

Becca had been completely silent on the way over. Now she looked at him, misery etched on her face, and admitted, "I feel like a fool."

"Don't do that."

"Don't do what?"

"Don't take someone else's poor actions and blame yourself for them."

The worry lines between her eyes eased. She didn't quite smile, but neither was she staring blankly at her hands. It was an improvement.

"Is that something written in your book?"

"Nein."

"Maybe it should be."

Before she could tease him more about his notebook, Officer Raquel Sanchez appeared in the doorway. "You two again."

Becca and Daniel stood.

"More CBD plants?"

"Nein." Becca stepped forward, and Daniel was relieved to see that some of the color had returned to her face. "But I think we need to report a crime."

Sanchez tilted her head, then said, "Better come on back."

Daniel noticed the other desks in the large room were still a mess, and Sanchez's was still a beacon of cleanliness and order.

There was one chair sitting next to Sanchez's desk, and she moved over another. She pulled out a pad of paper and a pen, then said, "Okay. Tell it to me from the beginning."

Becca did, and Daniel didn't interrupt. Sanchez wrote down a few notes, then asked, "Did you feel threatened in any way?"

"He seemed threatening to me." Daniel glanced at Becca who nodded once. "Especially after Becca told him he had misrepresented himself on the advertising sheet."

"And are you sure the photographs were of underage girls?"

"They seemed awfully young to me, but here's the thing…" Becca glanced nervously to her right and left, then lowered her voice, though they were the only ones in the room. "I think I recognized a couple of the girls. I think they're Amish girls, from our community. At least I'm pretty sure one is, and

I know she's only twelve—same age as my *schwe-schder*."

"Okay." Officer Sanchez sat back in her chair, causing it to creak. "It's not illegal for teenage girls to have modeling gigs. On the other hand, it is illegal to misrepresent yourself, to coerce girls into modeling that they're not comfortable with, and you definitely need parental permission if the girl is a minor." She sat forward, elbows on her desk, fingers steepled. "Are you willing to give me the name of the girl you saw?"

"I wouldn't want to get her in trouble with her parents."

"I understand." Sanchez waited a moment, then picked up a pen and tapped the sheet where she'd written the information regarding Wilson's car. "On the other hand, you might be protecting her."

"Protecting her in what way?"

"Are you familiar with human trafficking?"

"I've read a few articles about it."

Daniel shifted in his seat. "Our community in Pennsylvania was briefed on it by local law enforcement. They were afraid Plain girls might be an easy target."

Sanchez sat back, causing her chair to squeak. "We've had chatter lately about a human trafficking ring that has set up along the I-90 corridor. Those girls sometimes get lured in thinking that they've signed up for a modeling job, only to find that much more is expected of them."

"That's terrible."

"If we could talk to this girl, see what she has to say…then possibly we'd have enough to put an All Points Bulletin out for Sean Wilson."

Becca glanced at Daniel.

"Think if it was Francine," he said, which he knew would push her toward doing the right thing.

Becca gave Sanchez the girl's name and directions to her house.

"Can you give me some idea how her parents will react to this?"

"Her *dat*'s pretty strict, and her *mamm* is… I guess you could say she's a bit timid."

"Okay. This is in your church district?"

"Ya."

"And Saul Lapp is your bishop?"

"He is."

"Then I'll swing by and speak with Bishop Saul first, see if he'd like to go with me. In these instances, it can help to keep everyone calm and reasonable if we have a clergyman along."

"Is there anything else we can do?" Becca stood, pulled her purse strap tight over her shoulder and stepped closer to Daniel. He liked that—that she would find some comfort from his presence.

"Nothing I can think of at the moment, but I appreciate your coming in. A lot of people wouldn't. They'd just think they misread the situation or that they were overeager to make a buck. The fact that you were willing to come forward and talk to us— it shows a real level of maturity. It shows how much you care for your community." Sanchez walked them out of the office and thanked them again. She promised to let them know if there were any developments in the case.

When they stepped outside, Becca stood there on the steps, her face turned up to the November sunshine.

"Are you okay?"

She closed her eyes and breathed in deeply before answering. "Feels like this day has already lasted forever."

"Nope. Only—" he checked his watch "—ninety minutes."

"Unbelievable."

"We still have time to go shopping for the things on your *mamm*'s list. Only two days until Thanksgiving. I imagine she's going to be pretty busy cooking the next few days."

"Thanksgiving." Becca hooked her arm through his and they walked toward the buggy together. "I have a lot to be thankful for this year."

"Even though the job didn't work out?"

"Even though." She turned to him as he opened the buggy's door. "*Danki*, Daniel. It was *gut* having you there with me. I like to think of myself as an independent woman—"

"You *are* an independent woman."

"But even so, having a friend along is a *gut* thing. *Danki* for being there for me today."

He felt his face flush, thought of kissing her, then wondered if he'd gone a little crazy to consider doing such a thing in public in broad daylight. "Just being a *gut* neighbor."

She hopped up into the buggy. He untethered Constance, then climbed into the driver's seat. They were nearly to the store when Becca said, "I owe you."

"You do not."

"And I mean to pay you back. You've helped me out of a tight spot twice now."

"Nothing to pay back." He could tell that her mood had shifted, though, and that the spunky, playful Becca was nearly back. "But if you did, um, pay me back...what did you have in mind?"

She rubbed her hands up and down her cheeks, patting them slightly. "Oh, I don't know. Maybe some turkey, dressing, cranberry sauce..."

"Homemade?"

"Of course it's homemade. Then there will be the vegetable casseroles, fresh bread, cakes and pies."

"Stop," he groaned. "I haven't had your *mamm*'s cooking for almost two weeks."

"Still having canned soup at your place?"

"Guilty as charged."

"So you wouldn't be averse to accepting a dinner invitation?"

"I wouldn't."

Becca laughed. "We were going to ask you anyway. *Mamm* reminded me before you showed up this morning."

"Is that so?"

"*Ya.* You're like an honorary family member, Daniel."

For reasons he didn't want to examine, a lump

formed in his throat. He swallowed past it and tried to focus on the road. Becca was headstrong and somewhat naive in certain situations, especially those outside a Plain community. She was also kind, free-spirited, and passionate about life.

He couldn't think of anywhere he'd rather be on Thanksgiving, anywhere better than with the young woman sitting beside him and her family.

Becca pulled out the shopping list her *mamm* had given her. They might live on one of the worst farms in Shipshe, but on Thursday they would thank the Lord for the things they had. They'd pray and eat and laugh and be together. And that wasn't a bad way to spend Thanksgiving. In fact, looking at Daniel, who was suddenly grinning like a child on his birthday, she realized that she was actually looking forward to the holiday.

The next hour passed pleasantly enough as she and Daniel filled the cart with items for the Thanksgiving meal.

"I'd like to help pay for this."

"Oh, no, you won't."

"But…"

"Uh-uh. Not going to happen. We don't ask guests to dinner and then have them pay their way." She pulled out the bills her *mamm* had given her and paid the cashier.

Fortunately, the buggy Daniel had purchased had a storage compartment mounted on the back. Between that space and the back seat, they were able to store all of the supplies. Once they were back in the buggy, Becca realized she would need to tell her parents about today. She didn't have to, but she'd feel better if she did. Keeping things from them only made her feel childish and on edge. Better to have the hard conversation.

She chuckled lightly.

"What's funny over there?"

"I was thinking of something you could put in your book of wisdom."

"Oh yeah?"

"Have the hard conversation."

"I don't get it."

She turned in the buggy, her back against the space where the seat met the door so that she could better watch him. Daniel was a handsome man, and he was older than she was. It seemed that in some areas he was pretty inexperienced—especially when it came to relationships.

"Explain it to me," he prodded. "If I'm going to put it in my notebook, I need to understand it."

"Okay. Say that you hire my *bruder* to come over and help you plant your field."

"I did hire your *bruders* to help me plant my field."

"Uh-huh, but say they did a terrible job."

"They did a great job."

"Work with me here."

"All right. I'm pretending they did a terrible job."

"Now, would you tell them so? Or would you thank them, pay them and send them on their way."

"Hmm. I'd be tempted to do the latter, and then just not ask them to help again."

"Exactly!" Becca reached over and patted his arm. "I knew you would get it."

"But I don't get it."

"Look. If you did what you just said—thanked them, paid them, sent them on their way, then how would they learn? They'd go on being terrible farm workers, and word would get around, and then they wouldn't be able to find a job."

"But if I had the hard conversation…"

"Which is difficult to do because you don't want to hurt anyone's feelings, and it's awkward, and you could be wrong."

"I'm pretty sure I know a bad farm worker when I see one."

"Right, and doesn't the Bible say to speak the truth in love?"

"I believe it does."

"Only you have to search your heart first—to see if it is love that's motivating you or if it's something else."

Daniel directed Constance down their road, and then into Becca's lane.

"I could have walked from your place."

"With all these groceries?"

"Oh, right."

He pulled Constance to a stop, set the brake, then turned to study Becca.

"So this hard conversation that you're about to

have... I assume it's about what happened at the coffee shop."

"It is." Becca watched Daniel closely. She didn't see any condemnation there. He hadn't said a word about how silly she'd been. No I-told-you-so. Just compassion.

"Would you like me to stay, provide emotional backup?"

She leaned forward, kissed him on the cheek, then patted his arm again when he blushed bright red. "*Danki*, but this is something I need to do on my own."

The next two days passed in a flurry of preparation. In addition to Daniel, they'd have *Onkel* Jeremiah, plus Abigail and her family. Becca kept rechecking her tally, and each time she ended up with sixteen. Or was it seventeen?

"Stop with the list." Her *mamm* reached across and tugged on the sheet of paper, then set it out of her reach. "We've prepared plenty of food, and we'll make room for whoever shows up. It's going to be fine, Becca."

"I guess." Her mind was spinning with all the things to do before the luncheon, which was traditionally held around one thirty.

"What do you think it means to be Plain?"

That pulled Becca out of her planning mode as if she'd been splashed with cold water.

"Huh?"

Her *mamm* stood, refilled their coffee cups, then

sat back down. Her *dat* and Clyde and David were in the barn caring for the animals, and the rest of the family was still asleep. It was the precious part of the day before the pandemonium started. In a family as big as theirs, every day held its share of chaos, but Thanksgiving more than others.

"Tell me what you think it means to be Plain."

"I've already joined the church, *Mamm*. I know what Plain means."

"Right. I know you've been through the bishop's classes, and I'm pleased that you did commit yourself to the Lord, our church and our way of life."

"But?"

"But what do you think it means to be Plain?" Her *mamm* smiled over the rim of her coffee mug. "Humor me."

"Okay. Well, it means our life is simpler, that we strive to be *in* the world but not *of* it, and that we choose to do things the old way. We do sometimes embrace change, like the solar panels that are going up on everyone's houses, but we do so carefully and slowly."

"*Gut* answer."

"*Danki.*" Why did she feel like she'd received an A on a school paper? She sipped her coffee and tried to guess what her *mamm* was up to, because she was definitely up to something. Her expression was smiling, but her eyes were quite serious.

"We strive for simplicity." Her *mamm*'s voice was soft, almost as if she were speaking to herself. "But with our large families, sometimes life is anything but simple."

"You can say that again."

Her *mamm* leaned forward, as if she was about to share a secret. "The simple part is in your attitude, Becca. Our lives are as complicated as anyone's, but if we keep our focus on what matters and don't allow ourselves to be caught up in the whirlwind of modern living, then we can have the peace that many strive for."

"You're telling me to forget about the seating chart."

"It'll never work, and it doesn't matter."

"I suppose." For some reason, she was especially concerned about the holiday meal going well this year. "I guess I want today to be perfect."

"Things will never be perfect. Perfect is overrated."

"I'll take your word for it."

Her *mamm* stood, walked to the sink and then came back and stood behind Becca's chair. She put her hands gently on Becca's shoulders, leaned forward and kissed the top of her head. It felt like a blessing of sorts, and for reasons Becca couldn't have explained, it brought tears to her eyes. "Enjoy today. We're only able to experience each day once, and it'll pass in the blink of an eye."

Then her *dat* came in, and her siblings stumbled to the table, and they were soon praying over the light breakfast and the day to come.

But suddenly Becca's mind stopped racing.

She forgot to worry about the next minute.

She allowed herself to enjoy the present one.

Enjoy today. It'll pass in the blink of an eye.

Definitely something that Daniel needed to write in his journal.

Maybe it was because Daniel had lived in their house for ten days when he was sick.

Or maybe it was because he'd grown accustomed to having all of Becca's *schweschdern* and *bruders* around. It could have even been that he missed her *dat*'s jokes.

Whatever the reason, Daniel relaxed the minute that he arrived at the Schwartz home. Becca wouldn't let him pay for the groceries, but she couldn't stop him from bringing food to the meal. Everyone did that. Daniel had gone back to town on Wednesday and purchased everything he could think of that might go with the meal Becca and her *mamm* were cooking.

Now, as David and Eli helped him carry the sacks into the house, both Becca and her *mamm* stopped to stare at him.

"What is all of that?"

"Oh, just some…you know. Food. And stuff."

Becca gave him a glare that seemed to say, "Didn't we talk about this?"

But her *mamm* only walked over, kissed him on the cheek and said, "*Danki*, Daniel. That was very thoughtful."

Hannah and Isabelle had started to paw through the groceries, and both squealed when they found the gallons of ice cream.

"Six? You bought six gallons of ice cream?" Becca walked over to him, stood close enough that Daniel could smell the scent of the shampoo she'd used, and peered up into his face. "Did you get a little carried away?"

"Well, there was a special, and I didn't know what flavor everyone liked."

"Lucky for us, looks like you bought every flavor they had."

"Is there room in the…"

"Freezer? *Ya*. The girls will show you where it is."

The freezer was gas-powered and old, but it kept the food cold. Hannah and Isabelle led him out to the mudroom, he stuck the ice cream way down in the bottom, and they returned to the kitchen in time to find that Georgia and Francine had found the games he'd purchased.

"A new board game, and look—it's a Plain version." Georgia pushed up her glasses as she stared at the box. "I can be the horse."

"Then I get to be the lamb." Francine was actually laughing, something she hadn't done much of lately. For the day, at least, perhaps she could forget her focus on her *rumspringa*.

There were also three types of card games—Uno, Skipbo and Dutch Blitz.

"There must have been a sale in the game aisle, too." Becca tossed him a knowing look.

But Daniel understood that she didn't really know his secret. She thought he'd simply been caught up in the holiday spirit and thrown caution to the wind.

The truth was that he'd been looking for a way to pay the Schwartz family back for taking care of him, and today seemed like a natural way to do that.

Eli lined the liters of soda on the counter. "We never have soda, and hardly ever have ice cream."

"*Ya*, but you have your *mamm*'s cooking."

"True." Eli tapped one of the bottles. "Maybe tonight we can make root beer floats, after I beat you at chess."

"Dream on, kid."

Daniel thought it was funny that the boy liked chess nearly as much as he liked baseball. Perhaps it was just the playing that he liked, anticipating the next move, trying to outthink someone. He was athletic, but he also had a good mind. There was no telling what the lad would grow up to be.

Eli was already heading toward the chessboard, but Samuel walked into the room and claimed he needed help outside. As Daniel followed him, Becca's dad admitted, "Need to use up some of their energy. Plus, it helps Sarah to have them out from underfoot for an hour or so."

Daniel didn't know if his *dat* had ever done that for his *mamm*. He didn't think so. At least he didn't remember it. His parents' marriage had been strained for so many years—by the inheritance and the choices their children were making, maybe even by the way the community treated them differently— that he really couldn't remember a holiday like the one Becca's family was enjoying.

In Becca's family, everyone seemed to actually like each other.

If he ever married, he'd give up every dollar in his bank account to have this sort of home and this sort of relationship. He hadn't thought it was possible. He hadn't believed that people genuinely cared for each other so much. But as they walked to the south pasture and everyone scattered looking for items to place in the Thanksgiving bowl, he started to believe that he'd been wrong.

An hour later they were back in the house. *Onkel* Jeremiah had arrived while they were gone, and he'd stoked up the fire in the big stove that heated the sitting room. The place felt warm and cozy, and if his stomach wasn't growling Daniel might have been tempted to sit on the couch and nap a bit. But then Abigail and Aaron arrived with their two sons. Abigail was now eight months pregnant, and though she was obviously uncomfortable, it seemed that there was an aura of happiness around her.

And why wouldn't there be?

Aaron obviously doted on her, and they were expecting their third child. He wasn't too surprised to see her slip a small knitted bootie into the Thanksgiving bowl.

Becca and her *mamm* hurried from the kitchen and took their place in the haphazard circle. Becca had explained this tradition to him, but seeing it firsthand was an entirely different experience. The sitting room wasn't especially large, but they were all seated together. Everyone was hungry because of their light breakfast, but no one complained. The feast to come would more than make up for any current hunger pains.

Onkel Jeremiah sat in a rocker, with his Bible open in his lap. "The Lord be with you," he said.

"And also with you." Hannah and Isabelle practically bounced as they recited the age-old words with the rest of their family.

"This year I thought we'd read Psalm 107."

The murmurs around Daniel varied from "That's a *gut* one" to "Have we read that before?" to "I hope it's short." That last was from Clyde, and instead of being in trouble, he elicited laughs from everyone.

Then Jeremiah began to read, his voice rich and deep and filled with more wisdom than Daniel could write into his book if he lived another fifty years.

"O give thanks unto the Lord, for He is good; for His mercy endureth forever."

They all quieted, settled, focused.

"Let the redeemed of the Lord say so, whom He hath redeemed from the hand of the enemy..."

Daniel felt suddenly redeemed. He was nearly overpowered by a feeling of humility.

"And gathered them out of the lands, from the east, and from the west, from the north, and from the south. They wandered in the wilderness in a solitary way..."

Daniel had done exactly that. His wilderness had been of his own making, though. His solitary way had been a choice. He understood that now, and the understanding lifted a weight off his shoulders that he hadn't realized he'd been carrying.

He must have spaced out, because Jeremiah closed his Bible and quoted the last verse—a verse that seemed written especially for Daniel. "Whoso is wise, and will observe these things, even they shall understand the loving kindness of the Lord."

Amens circled the room, and Samuel offered a short prayer, and then it was time for the Thanksgiving bowl.

Becca loved the old ceramic bowl that sat in the middle of the table. Her *mamm* had explained that it belonged to Becca's great-grandmother, and that it was used before there was running water—when they would place a pitcher of water and a bowl on the nightstand so that in the morning you could splash cold, clean water on your face.

They didn't have many things in their home. The furniture was tattered after years of use. There were no fancy lanterns or store-bought lap blankets or machine-woven rugs. Most of what they had was homemade or used. Somehow none of that mattered when she looked at the Thanksgiving bowl brimming with items.

"Everyone has placed an item in the bowl, *ya*?"

Each person in the room nodded. Samuel passed the bowl to his wife, who put her hand in, pulled an item out without looking, and smiled. "This seems to be a baby bootie, and I believe that it's from Abigail, who is grateful for the child soon to be born."

"That was too easy," Eli insisted, but he took the

bowl from his *mamm,* shut his eyes and pulled out a book. "Ha. This must be from Georgia, and I think I remember her saying that her teacher gave it to her for helping all semester at school."

And so the bowl was passed around the room, each person pulling out an item and guessing who was grateful for the thing and what it represented.

Daniel pulled out a wooden car that one of Abigail's boys had put into the bowl.

Georgia pulled out the newspaper clipping of a buggy. Everyone knew that was Clyde's item.

"Once he owns his own horse and buggy, he'll be able to go out every night with Melinda," David teased.

When it was Becca's turn, she pulled out a bright red rooster feather. "This could only belong to Carl-the-bad-tempered-rooster, and I can't imagine who would…"

But then she noticed Daniel staring at the floor, trying not to laugh.

"Daniel? And why would you be thankful for my unruly rooster?"

"Don't you remember the day I met you? You were trying to fend him off with a rake." Which started everyone laughing and telling stories of Carl. It wasn't until they'd dispersed to the kitchen that Becca realized Daniel hadn't explained exactly what he was grateful for. "A rooster?"

"Not exactly." He pulled her back into the living room, making sure they were alone, and then kissed her softly on the lips. "I'm thankful for you, Becca. Every single day."

Chapter Ten

The time between Thanksgiving and Christmas passed like a blur in front of Becca's eyes. Every trite expression she'd read about being in love felt like a reality.

Her feet barely touched the ground.

Her stomach was filled with butterflies.

She'd find herself putting the milk in the cabinet and the fresh baked bread in the refrigerator.

If her family noticed, they didn't tease her about it, but everyone was busy with Christmas preparations, as well as the upcoming school program. She was grateful that no one's attention was on her.

No one's except Daniel's.

They enjoyed walks through his fields.

He told her his plans for spring crops.

They took buggy rides for no other reason than that the days were fine, the winter sunshine was beautiful and they wanted to be together.

Twice more he kissed her—once in the barn and another time in the buggy.

She found herself wishing she kept a journal, so she could write down each precious memory. But she knew she'd never forget.

Was she falling in love with Daniel Glick?

Was he falling in love with her?

Beneath those questions lay a more difficult one. If they were, and if he asked her to marry, was she willing to accept a life of poverty? It was the only thing to mar her happiness—knowing that if she agreed to a life with Daniel, she'd be turning her back on any chance to help her family financially.

Not that he would dissuade her from her get-less-poor schemes, but Becca was old enough to understand how these things went. They'd marry, and before five years were passed, they'd have three children. She'd continue having children for the next ten to fifteen years, as many as the Lord saw fit to give them.

And part of her wanted that. Each time she looked at her *schweschder* Abigail, she thought, *That could be me this time next year.* Her heart would flutter and she'd have to step outside to gather her thoughts.

But what of their living conditions?

Was she ready to give up on the dream that they might one day have more?

Someone else might chastise her for focusing on material things—someone who hadn't lived her life, someone who had those material things she wasn't supposed to hope for.

But she'd been poor a long time.

She understood what it was like to sit with a feverish sibling, hoping her temperature would drop so they wouldn't need the doctor—wouldn't have to dip into the benevolence fund yet again.

She'd eaten soup not just for days on end, but once for an entire month as they waited for the harvest from their own garden, and money from the crops, and the chance to hunt for deer so they'd have meat.

In some ways, she thought Daniel's situation might be worse than theirs. He was undoubtedly as poor as they were, but at times he'd spend money as if he had baskets full of it. The items weren't for himself, but did it make any difference? It seemed to Becca that he was purchasing things for others while he still had no money to buy furniture for his own house. He'd recently added two lawn chairs to his living room furniture. That was it. No coffee table. No bookcase. No rocking chair.

Was she ready to go into even deeper poverty?

Then he'd show up on her front porch with a basket of pine cones or a jar of red berries, or simply wanting to read to her from his journal, and she'd think, "Yes. I could live that way. If two people really care for one another, they can endure any hardship."

It was her first thought each morning and her last thought as she drifted off to sleep. Then nineteen days after Thanksgiving and one week before Christmas, she fell asleep in her room at the back of the house and dreamed of walking through a mist.

She seemed to hear her family as if from a great

distance, along with urgent barking from Cola the beagle. There was something she needed to find in the fog. There was someone she needed to see and talk to. She walked on and on, with occasional dark shadows looming close to her. Once she caught a glimpse of Carl-the-bad-tempered-rooster. A bird had set to beeping somewhere close to her. At other times, sounds that she couldn't distinguish reached her.

Her pulse began to accelerate and her skin went clammy.

She began to run, with no real destination in mind—only the certain knowledge that she needed to get away and she needed to call for help.

But her voice made no sound.

She couldn't outrun the ever-thickening fog.

She was still alone and afraid and unsure what to do next.

A loud bang caused her to sit up in bed. The fog that had plagued her throughout the dream surrounded her, and she could hear Cola's desperate barking in the distance. She pulled in a deep breath, which only caused her to cough and gasp for air as she dropped to the floor.

It wasn't fog.

And it wasn't a dream.

It was a fire.

The beeping came from the fire alarms they'd placed in key places throughout the house.

She shared a room with Francine and Georgia. They must still be here. They wouldn't have left without her. She put out a hand, bumped into the door of their room and held her palm against it. It wasn't hot. Good.

Everything she'd been taught in school about fires came back to her in a rush.

Check the door—not the doorknob—with your fingertips.

Smoke is toxic, so stay low.

If you can't safely leave a room, keep smoke out by covering cracks.

Signal for help with a flashlight.

But they were at the back of the house. Who would see them? Did anyone else even know that there was a fire? Surely someone could hear the dog barking.

She tried yelling, but it only made her cough louder and longer and deeper. The sound woke Francine and Georgia, who also began coughing.

Becca grabbed three garments from the cubbies that held their clothes. She made her way to their beds, pulled them onto the floor and spoke in their ears.

"Stay low. Hold this to your mouth. Francine, keep your other hand on my back. Georgia, you do the same to Francine. We're going to the window."

Twice they ran into beds and realized they were going the wrong way, but finally, they made it to the window. She fumbled with the latch, and then as she pushed the window open, air rushed into the room— good air, though still tinged with the smell of fire.

Becca gulped it as if it were water, filled her

lungs and then turned to help her *schweschdern* climb outside.

"Go to the front of the house. Wait by the old tree. Stay there until someone comes."

"But where are you…?"

"Just go." But instead of pushing, she pulled both girls to her, kissed them each on the cheeks, and then helped them climb through the open window.

She couldn't go. Not yet. Because she was thinking of Clyde, whose room was around the corner from hers, a room that had no window.

Daniel was in a sound sleep when he woke to the smell of smoke.

His first thought was the barn. He pulled on his shoes, pants and a shirt, grabbed the blanket off his bed in case he needed to beat out flames, and hurried outside, praying that Constance wasn't trapped.

His barn was fine, silhouetted against the December sky by the half moon—a moon that provided enough light for him to see smoke coming from the Schwartz place.

He didn't bother going back inside for his coat. Instead, he dashed through their shared barn and across the adjoining field. What he saw when he topped the hill caused him to put his hands on his knees, both of which were trembling.

The Schwartz family was huddled near a tree in the middle of their front yard.

A fire truck with its sirens blaring and lights flashing was barreling down the lane.

Fire was rapidly devouring the house, but at least everyone was out.

Homes could be rebuilt. That thought circled round and round his brain as he ran toward Becca's family. He was nearly on top of them before he realized they were all staring toward the house. Francine and Georgia were crying. Hannah and Isabelle stood close together holding hands. Sarah was pleading with her boys not to rush back into the house.

"Your *dat* went. He'll find her."

He didn't have to ask who. Instead, he turned and ran toward the burning building. He was nearly to the porch when Samuel tumbled out of the house, a blanket wrapped around Becca, both of them gasping for breath.

Instead of asking questions, he supported Becca on the other side and helped walk her to her family. He wanted to pick her up and carry her. He wanted to pull her into his arms and never let her go.

He thought Becca might collapse into her mother's embrace, but instead, she dropped the blanket around her shoulders and ran to her *bruder* Clyde.

"I thought you were in there. Thought you would be trapped because your room has no windows."

"I was with Melinda. We were out late. When I came home, I saw… I saw…" And then he turned and walked away from the group, his head bowed and his shoulders shaking.

"He's okay. He'll be okay." Samuel hurried after Clyde, put his arms around the young man, gave him all of his attention even as the firefighters were climbing out of their truck and the house was collapsing behind him.

"You're okay?" Daniel reached for Becca. He needed to touch her, needed to look in her eyes. "Tell me you're okay. You're not hurt?"

"I'm fine…"

"I was so terrified, Becca. So afraid…" And then he pulled her to him and held her until her shaking lessened.

The firefighters began to spray water from the pump truck onto the perimeter of the fire. There was nothing to be done for the structure, but they made sure that it wouldn't spread to the fields or barn beyond.

Before they'd even finished, neighbors began arriving with blankets and coats and thermoses of hot coffee.

Bishop Saul was one of the first on the scene, speaking with Sarah and Samuel first, then taking a moment with each of the children.

Paramedics arrived and checked out everyone's breathing, put some salve on Samuel's hands, which had been burned slightly when he went back into the house looking for Becca.

Each of their neighbors—Amish and *Englisch*— came over and shared their condolences, and then they offered clothes, showers, a place to stay. Several times Daniel heard someone proclaim, "A week before Christmas. What a tragedy."

Sarah looked overwhelmed, and her children

were traumatized, confused and exhausted. It was the bishop who finally stepped in.

"The firefighters will stay and make sure there are no flare-ups."

He was interrupted by an older gentleman wearing a firefighter's uniform. "We won't know the cause for certain until the blaze is completely out and we can sift through the wreckage. Did you have a wood-burning stove in the middle of the house?"

"Ya." Samuel's voice was shaky. "In the sitting room."

"The fire appeared to be hottest there. My guess is it started in the stove pipe." He pulled off his helmet and wiped a beefy hand over his face. "Can't tell you how glad I am you had those fire alarms installed. I'm aware some Amish don't, but tonight, they saved your lives."

"*Gotte* saved our lives," Samuel said.

"Perhaps *Gotte* provided the smoke alarms." Bishop Saul thanked the fireman, then turned back to the family. "Where were we?"

"You were telling us what's been done."

"Oh, yes. The Bontragers have taken your gelding to their place for now. I suggest that you all come to my house. We'll feed the children, have some coffee and figure out what to do next."

"We'll never all fit in your buggy," Samuel pointed out.

Which was the opening that Daniel had been waiting for. "I'll run and fetch mine."

"That would be very kind, Daniel. Thank you,

and thank you for staying with my family through this night."

Had the night ended?

Was that the pale light of dawn at the edge of the eastern horizon?

He had no idea, and it didn't matter. What mattered was that Becca was okay and none of her family had been injured. Daniel wasn't ready to let any of them out of his sight.

He jogged back to his house, paused to grab his hat and coat, then harnessed Constance, who looked rather surprised to be going somewhere so close to dawn.

Within the hour they'd loaded the entire family up and traveled the short distance to the bishop's home. They walked inside to find three of the women from their district there. They'd already made coffee and set out milk and juice for the children. The kitchen cabinets were covered with breakfast casseroles, breads and fruit salads.

The room was full to overflowing, but when Saul raised his hands, everyone quieted. Though he didn't bow his head, Daniel understood that he was offering a prayer on their behalf.

"We are grateful, this day, for the well-being of this family—our *bruders* and *schweschdern*. We are grateful to you, *Gotte*, that you have provided, even as our hearts grieve for what is lost. We are grateful for one another."

Amens filled the room, then everyone was filling their plate and talking about the events of the night.

Becca took her plate to a corner of the living room, and Daniel thought maybe she wanted to be alone. Then she looked up, right at him, and it was as if he could hear her thoughts.

He crossed the room in four long strides and sat on the floor beside her.

"Are you okay?"

"You already asked me that."

"But are you?"

"*Ya.* I am." She stared at her plate, then set it on the floor and covered her face with her hands.

"Talk to me, Becca."

"I had a…a dream, and then when I woke and realized what was happening, I was so afraid."

"Anyone would have been."

"Even as it was happening, I thought, *This will be okay. We know what to do. We're okay.*"

"I'm so grateful you were."

"But then I remembered Clyde. Clyde, who snores so loud that I can sometimes hear him through the walls. He sleeps so hard that he once slept through an entire train ride to Ohio to see our cousins—whistle stops and conductors and passengers jostling back and forth." She crossed her arms around her middle, no longer trying to hide the tears streaming down her face. "I was terrified that he hadn't heard the alarms, that he'd sleep through the fire. That he'd die because he wouldn't wake up. I've never been that afraid."

Daniel understood that there was nothing he could say to that, nothing he needed to say. So instead, he pulled her into his arms and let her weep.

Someone was sent to tell Abigail that they were fine. Since she was in her final month of pregnancy, they didn't want her to hear of the fire and worry for even one second.

The next hour passed with everyone eating their fill. Eventually the neighbors who had prepared the breakfast left, and the bishop finally called a meeting in the kitchen.

Becca and her *mamm* and *dat* filed back into the kitchen. Saul and Sarah and Samuel sat, but Becca remained standing, so Daniel did, as well.

Daniel glanced from Samuel to Becca, then back again. "If you'd like me to go…"

"*Nein*. It's *gut* for you to be here." Samuel placed his hand over his wife's.

Saul cleared his throat. "We will rebuild your home, of course. There's plenty of money in the benevolence fund, so there won't need to be an auction." Saul glanced at Daniel, held his gaze for a moment.

Daniel had the slightest fear that Saul would spill his secret, but instead, the bishop nodded and continued.

"Unfortunately it looks like we're in for some wintry weather the next few weeks, so it will be past the first of the year before we can get started."

"However long it takes," Samuel said. "We appreciate it. We really do."

"You have done the same for others, Samuel. Your appreciation is noted, but don't start thinking that you owe anyone. You do not. You are an important part of our community, and as such, we support one another. Am I clear?"

"Ya."

"Gut. Now the more immediate problem is where you're to live until the house is rebuilt. *Gotte* has blessed you with a big family. We've had several come forward already and offer a spare room."

"We'll have to be split up…" Understanding dawned on Sarah's face. She looked up at her husband, and Samuel shrugged.

"If it's the only way."

"It'll only be a few weeks." Saul tapped the table. "We'll begin rebuilding as soon as the weather allows."

Daniel didn't think about what he said next. If he had, he would have realized that it was a selfish thing—wanting the entire Schwartz family near him, wanting Becca near him. They'd become such an integral part of his life. He couldn't stand to see them farmed out, not even for a few weeks.

But all of that occurred to him later.

At the moment, he didn't bother analyzing what he was about to do. Instead, he stepped forward and said what was on his heart. *"Nein,* you don't have to break up the family. You can all stay with me."

Chapter Eleven

Becca, her parents and the bishop all turned to stare at Daniel. It was Saul who found his voice first. "You're saying that you'd take the *entire* family into your home?"

Mamm had closed her eyes, clasped her hands together and was uttering a prayer of relief. *Dat*, for once, seemed speechless, and Becca couldn't believe that she'd heard Daniel correctly. It was one thing to offer sympathy for a neighbor, another thing entirely to change your life for them.

"Why's everyone looking at me as if I suggested something outrageous?"

"Because our family can be a lot." Becca glanced into the bishop's sitting room. All seven of her younger siblings were piled on the couch—Hannah on Clyde's lap, Isabelle on David's. Eli, Francine and Georgia were squished in next to them—as if they needed to be close, needed to be certain that the entire family was intact. "They're quiet now because they're still in shock, but you're talking about allowing ten people to move in with you."

"I can count. I certainly don't want to argue, but I also don't see what the big deal is. You are my neighbors. You're my closest friends in Shipshe. Why should your family be separated if they don't have to be?" He stared up at the ceiling for a moment, then added somewhat defiantly, "There's plenty of room."

Saul looked to Samuel, waiting for him to decide. But Samuel had already made his decision, Becca could tell that as plain as day. From the tears in his eyes to the way he clasped her *mamm*'s hand, it was obvious that he would accept. He stood, stepped toward Daniel, placed a hand on his shoulder and tried to speak. He cleared his throat twice, as if he could dislodge the sorrow there, and then swiped a hand across his eyes.

Seeing that—seeing her *dat*, who always had a handy joke to tell and a smile on his face, break down—undid her more than even the sight of their family home in flames. She felt the tears slip down her cheeks and was afraid she might break into giant sobs. The exhaustion of all that had happened felt like a heavy blanket that threatened to weigh her down.

"A friend is never truly known until a man has a need. This day my family had a need, and you have stepped forward to fill it. *Danki*, Daniel. We accept, and we thank you with all our hearts."

Samuel pulled Daniel into a hug. Becca looked up in time to catch the expression on Daniel's face, the way his eyes closed and the sigh escaped his lips, as if he were the one setting down a giant burden—and perhaps he was. Maybe *Gotte* was using this tragedy to heal Daniel in ways that Becca couldn't completely understand.

Samuel turned to Sarah and slipped his hand in hers. "Let's go tell the *kinder*."

Before she followed her husband into the other room, Sarah walked over to Daniel, stood on tiptoe and kissed him on the cheek.

Saul smiled and said, "It's settled, then." With a wink, he turned and followed Becca's parents into the sitting room.

Daniel looked as if he was afraid Becca might burst into tears again. She didn't. She squared her shoulders, wiped her cheeks dry and sank into a kitchen chair. "I hope you know what you're doing."

"It's not that big a deal, Becca."

"You moved here to be alone."

"It's not as if your family is going to live with me forever."

"Might seem that way, though." She tried to smile to soften the words, but it felt as if she were stretching her lips in an awkward angle.

"Your family isn't that bad."

"Oh, don't misunderstand me. I love them. And I appreciate what you're doing." She stared at the table, tracing the swirls in the wood with her fingertips. "Living with Hannah and Isabelle is like living with twin tornadoes. Clyde rarely remembers to wipe his feet. David eats more than a single person should be able to, and Eli has an old harmonica that he has taken to playing at odd hours in the barn."

Daniel sat down next to her, reached forward and thumbed a smudge of soot off her face.

"David is hardly around at all—just long enough to eat and leave dirty laundry tossed about."

"What about Francine and Georgia? Aren't you going to warn me about them?"

"Georgia's all right—though you'll trip over her because she's plopped down somewhere to read a book. Francine is still insisting she's begun her *rumspringa*, though we all keep telling her she's not old enough."

"And your parents?"

"*Mamm* will be cooking all the time. You'll probably put on ten pounds."

"Are you saying I'll get fat?"

"As for *Dat*, you know how it is with his jokes, he seems to have an endless supply."

"Anything else?"

"Only all my projects..." The horror of what they'd been through hit her then. She pressed her fingers to her lips, closed her eyes and tried to calm her emotions. Her heart had other ideas. It tripped and rattled and seemed to push against her rib cage.

She felt as if her heart was going to collapse and explode all at the same time.

She felt as if the world was simply too much.

Daniel stood and pulled her into his arms, and Becca allowed herself to stop being the strong one. For the first time since smelling smoke, she allowed the fear and sorrow to have its way. She wept for all that they'd lost, for the terror she'd felt when she thought Clyde was trapped inside, for the anguish of seeing the home she'd grown up in disappear in flames.

Daniel didn't try to reason with her.

He didn't point out that everything would be okay or that they had much to be thankful for. He held her and let her weep. It was during that moment of intense grief both felt and shared that Becca accepted what she'd probably known for a long time—that she'd fallen in love with Daniel Glick.

The rest of the day passed in a blur of activity. By the time they reached Daniel's house, Bishop Saul had already put out the word. Hour after hour, people from their church as well as *Englischers* from the community showed up with clothes, bedding, mattresses, even extra food.

"Early Christmas," Daniel muttered as he stuffed yet another casserole into his refrigerator.

Christmas was ten days away. Becca didn't want to think about it. The few gifts she and her *mamm* had made had been destroyed in the fire. Instead of dwelling on that, she said, "I warned you about the ten pounds, and *Mamm* hasn't even started cooking yet."

Dinner was a somber affair, owing to the fact that nearly everyone was falling asleep in the chicken soup that Abigail had brought over. It was hard to believe that her baby was due before the end of the month.

At least the impending birth gave everyone something to look forward to.

If Becca thought about it too hard, the winter stretched in front of them like an endless parade of cold days, days she would be forced to stay inside, days in close proximity to Daniel, whom she had such strong feelings for. She didn't completely understand those feelings yet. She couldn't even flee to the barn for private time, since it was his barn as well as theirs.

She'd just have to put a lid on her feelings. Daniel couldn't have been more clear about where he stood. How many times had he said that he wasn't looking for a *fraa*? Every time one of the unmarried women at church threw a look his way, he practically ran for a rabbit hole.

She believed he did care for her, but she also understood that he had no intention to marry anytime soon. When she thought about it in that light, she convinced herself that his feelings for her were not serious. There had been a few kisses, but now it seemed as if those lighthearted moments had happened a hundred years ago. As for his comforting her earlier in Bishop Saul's home, no doubt he'd been doing just that—comforting a friend who had just lost their home.

No, she would not be confessing her feelings to Daniel.

Her heart had endured quite enough for one day.

Throughout the meal, she'd steal a glimpse at him, prepared to see a look of regret on his face. Surely he was beginning to understand the enormity of what he'd done by inviting the entire family into his home. If he was regretting it, then he was hiding it well.

He even laughed at her *dat*'s joke.

"What do you call a horse that lives next door?" Samuel barely waited before delivering his punch line: "A neigh-bor."

Hannah and Daniel were the only ones to laugh aloud.

Isabelle, attempting to butter her piece of corn bread, said, "Our horse will live here now. Right? Since the Bontragers brought him back? I wonder if Old Boy is scared, being in a different place and all."

Becca guessed that everyone at the table understood Isabelle wasn't speaking only of the horse. It was Daniel who suggested checking on the animals. "We can go out together, maybe take both Old Boy and Constance a carrot."

"I wanna go, too." Hannah moved her spoon around in her soup. "Maybe I can take them my peas. *Mamm*, do I have to eat these peas?"

Which turned the conversation to all the food that had been donated, how generous their neighbors had been—both *Englisch* and Amish. Daniel met Becca's gaze and winked. Oh, but he was a charmer when he wanted to be.

By nine that evening, everyone was in bed. They'd found a place for each person to sleep, barely. The five girls managed to fit into one room with a bit of creative rearranging. Clyde, David and Eli spread across the living room, and it wasn't lost on Becca that Eli was using Daniel's sleeping bag—the same sleeping bag he'd once slept in on the back porch.

Well, at least no one was in the barn. Her parents took the smallest guest bedroom, claiming there were only two of them, so they didn't need as much space. Daniel tried to give up his room, but everyone put up such a fuss that he raised his hands in surrender.

Becca lay on the mattress she was sharing with Hannah and Isabelle and listened as her *schwe-schdern*'s breathing slowed. Why couldn't she fall asleep? Shouldn't she be exhausted? But there were too many images flipping through her brain—rushing through the smoke, flames shooting out of the top of her house, Daniel standing in the cold with her siblings, her family huddled together as the fire-fighters worked to contain the blaze.

She tried deep breathing, praying, even counting sheep. Finally she stood, reached for her robe and tiptoed out of the room. If she'd been afraid of waking her *bruders*, that thought evaporated when she slipped through the living room. They were all snoring loudly.

Once in the kitchen, she pulled the pocket door closed, turned the switch on the battery lantern Daniel kept on the counter and set about making herself a cup of tea. Filling the kettle with water, setting it on the stove, putting the tea bag into a mug—all of those things were such normal, ordinary things to do that they calmed her nerves and quieted her thoughts.

Her stomach growled, reminding her that she'd eaten very little at dinner. She foraged through the pantry and came away with a container full of oatmeal bites. She inhaled deeply of her best friend's baking—no one made oatmeal cookies like Liza, and the miniature ones were the absolute best. Just last week, Becca had joked that they were tiny bites of goodness, sprinkled with sugar.

She stood there in the pantry, holding the container, smelling their goodness and letting the trauma of the past twenty-four hours slip off her shoulders. Of course, it was at that moment that Daniel appeared.

"They taste even better than they smell."

"Oh! You scared a year off my life."

Instead of answering that, he reached around her, plucked a cookie from the container and popped it in his mouth.

"Water's still hot if you'd like some tea."

Which was how they found themselves huddled on the far side of the table, the lantern turned to low, eating cookies late at night.

Daniel kept thinking about how he felt when he'd put his arms around Becca. He'd experienced an overwhelming sense of having finally come home, as if after a long and tedious journey he'd found where he belonged. Could holding a person represent so much?

It had been so hard to watch her struggle all day, harder even than watching the fire devour her family's home. As far as opening his house to her family, how could he not?

They'd welcomed him when they knew nothing about him.

They'd taken care of him when he was sick.

And the entire community had helped to rebuild his home.

He liked to think he would have made the same offer to anyone in need, but he was honest enough with himself to realize that Becca had claimed a special place in his heart. He thought maybe she felt the same way about him.

But would she if she knew the truth?

If she knew who he really was, would she still care for him? He wasn't willing to risk it. Not yet, anyway. Maybe in a year or two, when she had a chance to know him better.

"You're awfully quiet." She studied him over the top of her mug.

"Can't gather my thoughts with the sounds of three trains in my living room."

"*Ya*, my *bruders* snore quite loud. Are you having regrets about inviting us here?"

"Not at all." He reached for another cookie, allowed his hand to brush against hers, and looked up to see her blushing in the glow of the lamplight.

"How are you holding up…really?"

"My mind won't stop spinning."

"I can imagine."

"I keep seeing the smoke, and then it's as if I re-experience the fear that my family might be inside the burning house. My heart starts racing and my palms start sweating…" She shook her head. "I sound crazy."

"Not at all. You've been through quite a trauma, Becca. Give yourself some time to process all that has happened."

"I was so scared."

"Scared is what praying's for."

She'd been staring at the table, but at his words, her head popped up. "I thought praying only when you're in need was…you know…bad."

"Is that the only time you pray?"

"Nein."

He studied the cookie he'd retrieved, then pushed it across the table to her. She picked it up and nibbled around the edges.

"I don't think *Gotte* minds that we cry out to him when we're afraid. Didn't Job do the same thing? And Jonas? And Abraham? You're in *gut* company if you pray when you're scared."

"When did you get so wise?"

"Didn't say I was."

"It's because of all those things you jot down in your journal."

"Notebook."

"Whatever."

Daniel sat back, feeling on more solid ground when they were teasing one another. "I know I probably don't know what I think I do…"

"You lost me."

"Well, all that stuff I write…it makes sense to

me when I jot it down, but it doesn't mean that I'm wise or anything. Only that..." He shook his head, unwilling or unable to go on. He wasn't sure which.

"Only that what, Daniel?" She leaned closer, stared up into his eyes, and Daniel fell a little bit further in love.

"Um, only that..." What had they been talking about? His notebook and truth and life. "Only that it seems some of it you can learn that way, by paying attention, I mean."

"Hmm." Becca sat back and sipped her nearly cold tea. "I guess. Life is hard."

"That it is."

"I thought it was hard before, when we were poor. Now we're homeless and poor, so you know... I realize life wasn't so hard yesterday."

"The bishop is already scheduling a workday to rebuild."

"I know he is, and I know I'm lucky to be Amish. If I was *Englisch*, I'd have to wait for an insurance check, then a contractor..." She gave a mock shudder.

"How do you know so much about *Englisch* ways?"

"Look around you. Half our neighbors are *Englisch*. Half the boxes of stuff people brought today are from the *Englisch*. They're *gut* people, only different in the way they choose to live their lives."

"I guess." He turned his mug left, then right, thinking of his *bruder*. Finally he raised his eyes to hers. "Have you ever thought of leaving..."

"Shipshe?"

"*Nein*. Our faith. Have you ever thought of not being Amish?"

"Maybe once, when I was a *youngie*. Younger than Georgia is now. When I was nine years old I'd read this book about a girl who was an Olympic gymnast, and I thought that would be an awesome thing to become."

"A gymnast?"

"Don't look at me that way. I could do a mean cartwheel." She stared across the room, no doubt seeing another place and another time. "I asked *Mamm* about it, and she explained that Amish don't seek recognition on a world stage. She reminded me that we strive to be humble and set apart."

"And how did the nine-year-old Becca respond to that?"

"I took my school bag, stuffed my extra dress, *kapp* and pillow in it, and trudged off down the road."

"You didn't." Yet somehow he could picture this. Apparently, she'd been full of spunk even then.

"I did. Made it to the mailbox, took a left, then another right, and then suddenly I was lost."

"You hadn't gone far?"

"*Nein*. Only over to where Abigail is now, but it seemed farther. I was so afraid and I sat down on this rock. I sat down and hoped someone I knew would walk by."

"And did they?"

"*Ya*. My *onkel* Jeremiah. He asked me what I was doing, I told him that I was running away to be an Olympic gymnast, and he said maybe I should go home for dinner, then start out early the next day."

"Smart guy."

"Exactly. By the time he'd walked me home, I was

so happy to see our house that I ran into my *mamm*'s arms and told her I'd missed her." Becca closed her right hand into a fist, rubbed it against her heart. "*Mamm* told me years later that I'd only been gone an hour, that she thought I was out playing in the barn."

"That's a *gut* story."

"I think that's when I understood what home meant—that it was a safe place with people who love me." She laughed, a soft delicate sound. "It was the only time I thought I might like to not be Amish. This life is what I know, and it's who I am. Does that make sense?"

"It does to me."

She'd leaned forward, and Daniel could no more have stopped himself than he could have stopped water flowing from the sea. He pushed their cups out of the way, framed her face in his hands and brought his lips gently to hers.

He kissed her once, and then again.

With her eyes closed, she put her hands on top of his, and Daniel almost groaned. Wait a year to tell her how he felt? How was he going to be able to do that? He wanted to ask Becca to marry him now. He wanted to bare his soul, explain his past, beg her forgiveness for all the half-truths he'd told.

Becca squeezed his hands, stood and whispered good-night.

Leaving Daniel sitting in his own kitchen, wondering how his world had managed to turn into something that he didn't even recognize.

Chapter Twelve

Daniel could barely understand what had happened to his barn or buggy or home.

All that he owned had been taken over by Christmas elves—mainly in the persons of Hannah and Isabelle, though he suspected they had help. Holly sprigs decorated every windowsill, as did small battery-operated candles. Red berries that the boys had found along the Pumpkinvine Trail adorned the fireplace hearth and the center of the kitchen table.

Though the Schwartz family had escaped their fire with only the clothes on their backs, still there were secret meetings, newspapers disappearing to reappear later wrapped around mysterious boxes, bright red ribbons on packages that were hidden behind couches, in the pantry, even under his bed.

How did a box large enough to hold a man-size coat appear under his bed?

He left it there, shaking his head and telling himself that in only two more days the craziness would stop.

He had a strong feeling that his life would never return to what it had been before, and he found that thought didn't bother him as much as it might have a year or even a month ago. Becca and her family had only been in his home a week, but already their routines were precious to him.

Samuel's jokes as they ate each meal around the table.

Clyde's muddy boots leaving trails from the mudroom to the kitchen and back again.

David's appetite, which was indeed quite amazing.

Georgia's stack of books—where did she get them all? Some were stamped Shipshewana Public Library; others were quite worn around the edges.

Francine's *Englisch* blue jeans and hoodie that she thought no one knew about.

He'd even grown used to the plaintive sound of Eli's harmonica as he did a final walk-through of the horses—always with Hannah and Isabelle trailing next to him.

His life was fuller, richer than it had ever been, and Daniel realized with a start that he was happy. He hadn't been this unburdened since…since his family had inherited the money.

What a curse that blessing had turned out to be.

Only it wasn't the money that had been the problem. He understood that now. His family had been waiting to fall apart at the seams. The money had just caused that disintegration to happen a little faster than it might have otherwise.

He walked from his bedroom through the kitchen.

A new drawing sat on the table—the girls left him one nearly every day. This one had two stick horses with extraordinarily large heads. One was labeled *Ol Boy* and the other *Constant*. He smiled at the misspellings, but what tugged at his heart was the stick-figure man standing in between them. He had arms twice as long as his legs, a pear-shaped head wearing an Amish hat, and on his shirt was a big heart, instead of a pocket. In case he didn't recognize himself, someone had penciled the word *Daneel* underneath.

Becca's *mamm* walked into the room and caught him staring at the picture. "The girls left that for you."

"*Ya*. Their penmanship is improving."

"Can't say the same for their spelling, but in this case, I suppose it's the thought that counts."

"Indeed."

She patted him on the shoulder as she passed him by, but must have seen something in his eyes, because instead of continuing to the stove she backed up. "Is everything okay?"

"*Ya*. It's fine."

That was another thing. Though Sarah never seemed to stop working, nothing slipped past her. She was the first to bandage a scratched knee, find a misplaced *kapp* or counsel a bruised heart.

"You looked a bit sad, there, for a minute."

"Thinking of my family, I guess." The admission surprised him, but Sarah only nodded her head in understanding.

"I don't know the details, and I don't need to, but I pray for you and for them every night."

She left it there, not expecting or needing an explanation. Daniel wondered at the simple way she cared for her family, even as he hurried outside to be sure both horses were hitched up and ready to go. By the time he walked back into the kitchen, everyone had gathered at the table and a steaming bowl of chicken soup was at each place.

He scooted into his normal seat at the end of the bench, and each member of the family bowed their head to pray.

It occurred to Daniel then that Christmas was about so much more than gifts hidden under the bed. This family had no money to speak of, yet they were filled with joy—for each other, for the gifts they'd made, for the Christ child. As he helped Isabelle take a pat of butter for her bread and then pass the dish on, he realized that he was actually looking forward to the school play they were about to attend and the festivities of the next few days.

How long had it been since he'd felt anything but sadness and remorse on the holidays?

But this year was different.

This year he was surrounded by *freinden*, and he was sitting across from the girl he hoped to marry.

Becca glanced up, caught him staring and immediately reached for her napkin, which only made him smile wider.

It wasn't food on her face that made him stare, it was what she'd come to mean to him—and he meant to find a private moment to tell her before the Christmas holiday had passed.

They fitted into two buggies, though it was a bit snug. He still didn't understand how the Schwartz family had ever managed with only one. He couldn't help reaching for Becca's hand and squeezing it, which was immediately noticed by Hannah.

"Are you going to kiss her?"

"Hannah, that's rude."

Daniel turned to smile at Georgia, who was pushing up her glasses and tugging Hannah back onto the rear seat bench.

"Why was it rude? I'm just asking a question."

"And we saw them kissing yesterday in the barn." Isabelle piped in. "So it's natural to wonder."

"Still, it's private. How about we play a game of I Spy?"

Daniel started to laugh. Becca shook her head, but she didn't pull her hand away. "Those two are a handful."

"So you've mentioned."

The schoolhouse was decorated in snowflakes cut from local newspapers, construction paper formed into chains of garland, and pine cones decorated with glitter. Apparently, whoever had been in charge of the glitter had been a bit overzealous, as the stuff seemed to be everywhere—on the floor, in the seats, and even a bit on the ceiling, Daniel looked up and saw. How did glitter land on the ceiling?

With five of the Schwartz children still in school, there was at least one member of the family in every skit, song and recitation. The punch and cookies afterward were especially good, but Daniel's mind was on something else. When was he going to ask Becca to marry him? Where could he possibly do it? Finding a single private moment wasn't easy. Finding several private moments was almost impossible.

Becca stepped closer and put a hand on his arm. "We can go if you want."

"Oh, okay. Sure. Where…?"

"They've all gone."

"Who has all gone?"

"My family."

"I don't understand."

She raised her eyes to his as a light blush splashed across her cheeks. "They already went home, is what I'm saying—home to your house."

"All in your *dat*'s buggy?"

"*Ya.* I mean, I think Clyde and David and Francine left with *freinden*, but *Mamm* took the younger ones home."

"Oh."

"They thought we might like to be alone."

A moment alone was exactly what Daniel had been wishing for, so perhaps this was a little push for him to do what he'd been wanting to do for nearly a week now. He wasn't one to dawdle once he'd made up his mind, and he had definitely made up his mind that he was in love with Becca Schwartz.

Once they were in the buggy—alone—he couldn't think of where to go.

"Would you like to drive to town and get a piece of pie or something?"

"*Nein.* I'm full. Unless you're hungry…"

"I'm full, too." He called out to Constance, but when he reached the road, he didn't know which direction to go. His brain felt a little addled, like when he woke up after a particularly deep sleep.

"Perhaps we could drive around and look at Christmas lights for a little while."

"*Ya*. That's a *gut* idea."

"Constance seems to like the snow."

"She likes to go—doesn't matter if it's sunny, raining or snowing. She's sort of like Hannah and Isabelle."

There was a light dusting of snow on the fields, not enough to affect the roads, but enough to give the landscape a nice Christmastime feel. *Englisch* houses sported inflatable yard decorations and large light displays. Amish homes were easily recognizable by candles in the window. He drove slowly through the streets of Shipshe. Becca chatted about the school festivities, the Christmas displays, and how much she was looking forward to Christmas Day. But Daniel barely heard what she was saying. He was growing more and more nervous by the minute.

His hands had begun to sweat, and twice he'd dropped the horse's reins.

"Are you cold?"

"*Nein*. This blanket is warm, and your heater works well." She sighed. "*Dat* would love to have a heater in our buggy. *Mamm* would, too, though she'd never ask for one."

"Your *mamm* isn't one to complain."

"No, she's not."

A familiar look came over Becca's face then, and he knew that she was planning another scheme, another way to pull her family out of poverty. Only she didn't need another scheme. She had him. She just didn't know it yet.

So he drove to the city park, where the trees had been decorated with tiny white lights. Fortunately they had the place almost to themselves—a church van full of youth was loading up to leave on the far side of the parking lot, and an older couple had parked their truck and were walking hand in hand down the path.

Now was the time.

Now was when he needed to tell Becca how he felt.

He directed Constance beneath the boughs of a fir tree and set the brake. He then turned to the woman he'd grown to love and covered her hands with his.

"There's something I want to talk to you about."

"There is?" Her eyes widened, not in surprise so much as anticipation. She couldn't be surprised, could she? Surely she understood how he felt.

He swallowed around the lump in his throat. "I care about you, Becca."

"You do?"

"Ya." He nodded his head, feeling like an idiot. Why couldn't he just spit it out? "In fact, I love you, and I want to marry you."

She stared at him a moment, then leaned forward and kissed him gently on the lips. "I care about you, too, Daniel. I do. You're a kind man with a generous heart, but…"

"But?" He hadn't expected a *but*.

"But I don't really know anything about you."

"Oh." Daniel couldn't form a cohesive thought. He'd been so keyed up about asking that he hadn't considered what he'd say next. Yet here Becca was, waiting for his answer.

"Um. You don't know anything about me?"

"Not about your past, not really, and I understand that. I do. After our talk. You remember, the talk that you gave me when you caught me snooping?"

He nodded, trying to focus on what she was saying and not the sweetness of her smile or the pinkness of her lips.

"You told me a little then, like about your *bruder* leaving the faith. But you said…what was it? That you didn't want to go into your past—*not now, maybe not ever.*"

He winced at the words.

"Which is fine for *freinden*, Daniel. But if I agree to marry you, to be your *fraa*, then I need to know your past every bit as much as you need to know mine."

She sat back, hands folded in her lap, watching him.

When had Becca become the wise one?

And why was he hesitating to tell her everything?

He cleared his throat. "You're right. There should be no secrets between us."

"Exactly."

"And I know I can trust you with the details of my past."

"Of course."

"Only it's hard." He stared out at Constance. The horse didn't seem bothered by the cold evening or the light snow. For all he knew, she was enjoying looking at the lights. He understood as much about the thoughts of horses as he did about the thoughts of women—make that one woman.

"It's hard to talk about a thing after you've stayed silent for so long." He turned his complete attention toward Becca. He knew he needed to look her straight in the eyes when he told her about his past. "I'm a millionaire."

"Excuse me?"

"I inherited a large sum of money when I turned twenty-five, we all did. That is, everyone in my family did."

Becca had sat up straighter and was looking at him as if he'd sprouted ears out of the top of his head. "Is this a joke?"

"*Nein*. Listen to me. Becca…" He reached for her hand, pulled it toward him and stared at it as he traced his thumb over her palm. "My *mamm*'s *bruder* was Mennonite. I barely remember the man. Only met him a few times. He was *gut* at writing code for computers—"

"Code?"

"And he developed some app, something *Englischers* use on their phones. He sold it and made a lot of money, and then some big corporation used his code for their apps. The entire thing snowballed. Apparently, it surprised even him, and I don't pretend to understand it all."

"You're a millionaire?"

She wasn't smiling. She didn't look thrilled about this revelation. In fact, she looked as if she'd been chiseled from ice.

"Each member of my family inherited a portion of the money. We receive it when we turn twenty-five, and even then we only receive so much a year, or I might give it all away. I suppose my *onkel* knew we might do that. He understood the Amish life. I guess that's why he set it up the way he did, where we receive a certain percentage each year."

"A million dollars?"

"A little more than that." From the look on her face, he was pretty sure he shouldn't tell her just how much more, not right now. Perhaps the entire revelation had been too much. Maybe he should have broken the news more gently. But how?

"It's why my parents fight all the time, why my *bruder* left the faith, and why even my *schweschdern* seem so…changed."

"Is this why you broke off your relationship with the girl you were to marry?"

"I found out she didn't care for me at all…only for my money." He was once again surprised that the memory of Sheila no longer felt like a knife in his heart.

"So you moved here and pretended to be poor?"

"Well, yes, but no. It wasn't like that."

"Were you laughing at us this entire time?"

"*Nein.* Of course not."

"Our simple meals and our plain clothes and… No wonder you made such a big deal about our single buggy. You and your fancy horse."

"I can explain about the horse." She was staring at him with such disbelief that he found himself stumbling over his words. "I didn't want the money. Didn't want to live that way anymore, but then, when I got here, I knew that it would be a waste of money to purchase an older horse."

"Like ours?"

"I reasoned that a horse was something I'd be using for the next twenty years. I could live in a dilapidated house on a run-down farm, but when I saw Constance I knew that I—"

"Take me home."

"What?"

"You heard me. I want to go home right now."

"Becca, you're taking this all wrong."

"You have been lying to me since the day you arrived—me, my family, our community. You've been pretending to be just like us when in fact you were sitting back and laughing."

"I never laughed at you." He felt his temper rise, knew that he needed to shut his mouth or he was going to say something that he'd regret.

"Take me home, please."

"I thought you cared about me."

"And I thought I knew you." If she'd shouted the words at him, they wouldn't have hurt nearly as much. But the look on her face, the expression of disappointment, tore at his heart.

They rode home in silence.

Daniel tried to figure out where he'd gone wrong. How had this evening turned so horribly bad? How should he have handled it? But he knew the answer to that. He should have been honest from the beginning.

Still, he had to try one more time. As he directed Constance into his lane, he glanced Becca's way, but she wouldn't look at him.

"Becca, this doesn't have to be a bad thing. You care for me. I know you do, and I care for you. The money, well, it could be a good thing. It could help your family."

"I don't need you to rescue me, Daniel." Her chin rose a fraction of an inch. "I don't need your money. My family doesn't need your money. What we needed was your friendship—and friends don't lie to one another. They don't pretend to be something that they're not."

He'd barely stopped the buggy when she jumped out and fled up the porch steps.

The next twenty-four hours felt like an eternity to Becca. She avoided Daniel whenever possible, which wasn't easy given the amount of snow falling outside and the amount of people inside.

Their family tradition was to spend Christmas Eve with only the immediate family, but this year that included Daniel. It would have been strange to leave him out, given they were living in his house.

Though her heart felt bruised, she couldn't help seeing what was happening around her.

Daniel helping her *mamm* slice the chocolate cake.

Daniel playing chess with Eli.

Daniel sitting with Hannah and Isabelle and reading to them.

When her father told a Christmas joke—*What do sheep say to each other at Christmas? Merry Christmas to ewe*—Daniel laughed.

When Georgia misplaced her book, Daniel helped her find it.

And when Clyde fell despondent because he couldn't walk to his girlfriend's in the snowstorm, it was Daniel who told him to take his buggy.

The truth was that he cared about her family.

That wasn't fake.

That wasn't a lie.

It was an uncomfortable truth—uncomfortable because it made her question whether he cared for her. It seemed as if he did, but then, why had he lied to her for so long?

It was after she helped to clean the dinner dishes, finished the last preparations for the next day's celebration, and tucked Isabelle and Hannah into bed that her *mamm* tugged on her arm and suggested they walk to the barn together.

Becca walked straight to the stall that now held all of her chickens. Carl-the-bad-tempered-rooster was sitting on top of the chicken house they'd built. The hens peeked out from their nests. She didn't believe for a minute that her wayward rooster had changed his stripes, but she was grateful that for this one evening he'd chosen to behave.

Becca made her way to Old Boy's stall, intent on giving him all the carrots in her pockets. Then Constance stuck her head over the door, nudging her arm, and she couldn't help laughing. It was ridiculous to be angry with the horse. It wasn't the mare's fault that her owner was dishonest.

Her *mamm* stepped in front of Old Boy's stall, cooing to him and scratching him between the ears.

That image—of her mother so completely satisfied with life—caused Becca's tears to flow freely. She tried to swipe at them casually, but little passed her mother's notice.

"Want to talk about it?"

"I don't know."

"Okay. So start, and if you change your mind, you can stop."

"You make it sound so easy."

"There's nothing easy about being hurt, Becca. Now tell me what happened."

So, she did. She confessed her feelings for Daniel, his feelings for her, his proposal the evening before and what seemed to her to be this insurmountable thing between them.

"Let me see if I have this straight. You're angry because he's rich and he didn't tell you that from day one."

"Not day one. I'm not naive. I know you don't share those sorts of details with just anyone. But *Mamm*, he knew our family's situation…"

Becca stopped talking when her *mamm* began shaking her head. "Let's keep those two things separate for now. It's certainly not Daniel's fault that we have limited resources."

"We're poor. Just call it what it is."

"Do you really think so?" Her *mamm*'s smile was gentle, but her voice held a tinge of impatience. "Becca, I wish that you didn't struggle with this. I wish I had *gut* advice to give you for every possible problem you will encounter. But I have never wished for a different life. Your *dat* has been a *gut* husband, and I love my family."

"But—"

"There is no *but* on this point. What you insist on seeing as a huge obstacle is no more than an insignificant detail—like the bow on a gift. What counts is the intention behind the gift. What counts in this family is that we care for each other, not whether we can afford a new buggy."

Becca felt appropriately chastised but still confused. "So you don't think he was wrong?"

"Wrong about what?"

"About keeping the truth of his finances a secret. About pretending to be poor. What if…what if he was laughing at us the whole time?"

"Do you think he was?"

"I don't know."

"You do." Her *mamm* stepped closer, waited for her to look up and then repeated her question. "Do you think Daniel was laughing at this family?"

"Nein." She felt miserable admitting it, but also

as if a giant burden had been lifted. "I guess I'm a bit sensitive on the subject."

"A bit?" Her *mamm* reached forward and thumbed away her tears, then straightened her *kapp*. "What's really bothering you?"

"I know how to be poor. I've done it all my life, but I have no idea how to be rich." The confession startled her. Was that really what was bothering her? Fear of the unknown? An unknown that she had been chasing for years?

"Then we will pray that *Gotte* grants you wisdom and clarity in this area. One thing I know is that if you agree to marry Daniel, you have to accept all of him, including his past. It's time for you two to grow up and understand that there are some things in life we don't get to choose. Instead, we trust *Gotte*'s design for our life and then do the best we can."

She hooked her arm through Becca's, they said good-night to the horses and rushed back across the snow-filled night to the house.

Becca was relieved that Daniel wasn't waiting for her.

She needed time to think and pray.

Christmas morning dawned with a clear blue sky and sunshine that would probably melt the snow before evening. Hannah and Isabelle were already at the table by the time Becca made it downstairs.

"We're fasting," Hannah declared.

"That means only milk for breakfast." Isabelle

sipped hers carefully, then whispered, "Because the baby Jesus didn't have much when He was born."

"*Ya*, and we want to remember that."

"But later we get cake."

"And ham."

"And presents."

Becca ruffled the hair of both girls, remembering Christmases past—the first time she'd understood what it meant to fast, the time her grandparents from Ohio had come to stay with them, the year when the twins were only babes.

Her *mamm* pushed a mug of coffee into her hands, and before she'd drank even half of it all the men came in through the mudroom, stomping their feet and declaring it a perfect Christmas morning.

It was during the reading of the Christmas story that she finally met Daniel's gaze. The entire family was there—even Abigail, Aaron, William and Thomas. Abigail would have her baby in the next few days. She'd have to. There was simply no way she could get any bigger.

It wasn't uncomfortable with all of them crowded into Daniel's living room. It was cozy. It felt good and right that they should be together like this.

Would she want a bigger house?

It wouldn't make a bit of difference. She could see that now. What mattered was that they were together.

"Why did Baby Jesus have to sleep in the barn?" Hannah asked.

Isabelle perked up. She always perked up when she knew an answer. "Because the motel was full."

"Inn," Francine said. "The inn was full."

"What's an inn?"

"It was a place where people stayed when they were away from home—a long time ago." Georgia pushed up her glasses. "The barn must have been cold and a little smelly."

"It's probably true that it wasn't where Mary and Joseph wanted to have their baby." Her *dat* stared down at the open Bible in his lap. "But it wasn't a surprise to God the Father. Listen to what the angels told the shepherds. *Ye shall find the babe wrapped in swaddling clothes, lying in a manger.* It was a divine appointment they had, and the birth of the Christ Child in a manger? That was *Gotte*'s plan all along."

Hannah squirreled her nose. "I'd rather have a divine appointment in a house than in a stinky barn."

"But barns are nice, too." Isabelle clasped her hands in her lap. "When the hay is fresh, and there's that horsey smell. I kinda like barns."

"I think there's more to this story than whether the babe was born in a smelly stall or a clean room." Clyde shifted in his seat.

Watching him, Becca realized that he'd become a man. When had that happened? While she'd been chasing schemes to improve their lot in life, her *bruder* had grown up. She'd missed it. Glancing around the group, she realized she didn't want to miss anything else. She didn't want finances to be her focus. Maybe she could trust her parents to care for them. Maybe they didn't need her help. Maybe *Gotte* had a plan.

"Explain what you mean by that, son."

"It's that there was no pretense. Can't go much lower than a barn. I think the point might be that we can all approach the Christ child, we can all approach the Lord, without worrying about our status in life."

"Oh, come let us adore Him," Daniel said.

Which started the twins singing, and soon they all joined in. It was a precious moment, one that didn't last nearly long enough. Becca thought that perhaps when she was very old—if she lived to be very old—she would remember them all crowded into Daniel's sitting room as they sang that age-old hymn.

Daniel searched his memory, trying to recall a Christmas like the one he was experiencing, but he couldn't. His family had never had the kind of peace he saw in the faces around him. He was sure that on one level his family did love each other, but there had always been friction between them. The money they'd inherited had only intensified those feelings.

After their Scripture reading, everyone drifted off to various spots. The next few hours passed in a sweet atmosphere of quiet and contemplation. He read his Bible, wrote in his notebook, prayed for himself and this family surrounding him, and he prayed for Becca. He asked that *Gotte* would guide them, even as he realized that he'd lost his heart to her long ago. There was no going back. Regardless of what she decided, he loved and would always love Becca.

He gradually became aware of folks moving around, dishes being heated in the kitchen, laughter and teasing. When he finally walked out of his room, he gasped at the spread on the kitchen table.

"Did you think we were going to eat sandwiches?" Sarah handed him a platter filled with a giant turkey that she must have cooked the day before. It was stuffed with dressing full of carrots and celery. His stomach growled so loudly that Abigail laughed and nudged him with her elbow. "I'm supposed to have the stomach that draws all the attention."

"I suppose you're ready to have that *boppli*."

"We both are," Aaron admitted. "The rascal wakes us both up in the middle of the night."

Soon they were all gathered around the table, a veritable feast laid out before them. After the blessing, Daniel glanced up and caught Becca watching him. She didn't look away. Didn't blush or smile but simply waited, and Daniel knew what she was waiting for.

He knew what he needed to do.

What he should have done long ago.

So, as the turkey was passed, and the vegetable dishes were shuffled back and forth, he cleared his throat and dove in.

"There's something I'd like to share with each of you—something I should have shared many weeks ago, but I didn't know how. I suppose I was a little embarrassed. To be truthful, in the past when people learned the truth about me, the result wasn't always *gut*."

He had everyone's attention now, and he didn't

want the wonderful meal that Sarah had prepared to go cold, so he got right to the point.

"I'm rich. I inherited a large sum of money a few years ago—my entire family did. It caused quite a bit of strife between everyone. My *bruder* even left the faith, though I hope and pray every day that he will find *Gotte* on whatever path he chooses. That's all beside the point. I'm sorry that I wasn't honest, and I appreciate the way you've made me feel at home here in Shipshewana."

David leaned toward Eli and said in a mock whisper, "That's how he paid for Constance."

Which started everyone laughing, then the meal proceeded as if he hadn't revealed this long-held secret.

"Why shouldn't you tell a secret on a farm?" Samuel asked. He glanced at Daniel—eyes sparkling and a smile pulling at the corners of his mouth. "Because the potatoes have eyes and the corn has ears."

Groans and laughter echoed around the table.

Even Becca smiled and rolled her eyes. The conversation turned to the meal and gifts and the return to school the following week.

His big revelation hadn't made much of an impression on this group, and that, more than anything else, convinced him that he'd done the right thing.

Now he only had to wait to see if Becca would forgive him.

Chapter Thirteen

After the leftovers had been put away and the dishes washed, they all gathered in the sitting room again. This was one of Becca's favorite moments of Christmas—not because she cared about what gifts she received. She loved watching the expressions of her *bruders* and *schweschdern* as they opened their presents.

Each person pretending to be surprised.

Each person exclaiming over a small thing that was either handmade or cost very little.

Because of the fire, this year they had even less than usual. In fact, they had practically nothing, but somehow everyone had scrambled and managed to come up with gifts.

Hannah and Isabelle received new dolls and new frocks. Both had been donated by members of their church, but they didn't know that. They threw their arms around their *mamm* and thanked her over and over.

Georgia received not one but three new-to-her books.

Francine had taken up knitting, and she received a set of circular needles and a bag of yarn. Becca had stopped by the yarn shop in town hoping to find something on clearance, and the owner had insisted on donating the items. "Fires are terrible things. My parents lost everything in one years ago, and I'll never forget the tragedy of it. The community pulled together, though. That's what they did then, and I think it's what we should still do now."

She wouldn't even consider letting Becca set up a payment plan for the items.

David and Eli received new work tools that they claimed they'd been eyeing for months.

Clyde received buggy blankets for the buggy he hadn't purchased yet. "Glad the money I've managed to save wasn't lost in the fire."

"Where was it?" Daniel asked.

"In the bank—definitely not under my mattress."

Abigail's little boys received puzzles, a new ball, and two used bicycles that had been hidden in the barn when the fire occurred. They were used, but her *dat* had cleaned them up with a coat of paint and new seats.

Abigail and Aaron were given the only thing that actually cost money, and the entire family had pitched in. "A gift card? But…"

"We all contributed, dear." Sarah wrapped an arm around her daughter's shoulder. "It's so you both can pick out what you need for the baby—once you know whether it's another boy or a girl."

"Danki," Aaron said. "We didn't expect that."

There was a surprise for Becca's parents, as well. They all had to troop over to the barn to see it.

"Oh, my." Sarah's fingertips covered her mouth. Sitting in the middle of the room were two rocking chairs.

"For the new front porch, once the house is rebuilt." Abigail put a hand on her stomach.

When it seemed her *mamm* and *dat* still didn't know what to say, Clyde stepped forward. "We didn't waste money on them. Don't worry about that. We found them in town, at a garage sale. The guy had heard about our fire and insisted on giving them to us. We all spent a little time out here the last few days refinishing them."

"Danki," her father said. "This was very thoughtful, and it helps us…"

He swiped at his eyes, then smiled at his family. "It helps us to focus on what's to come rather than what we've lost."

He stared at the ground a moment, then looked up at his family. "I hope you all know that we thank *Gotte* every day for your safety. That house on the hill that's simply a charred ruin now…it doesn't matter. What matters is each person in this room."

Becca felt as if her heart were being wrung like a dish towel. Why was it that her heart felt so tender? Watching her parents, her siblings, even Daniel, reminded her that she'd been focused on the wrong things for too long.

She realized with a start that she didn't feel poor. Their circumstances hadn't changed, not really, but she felt very wealthy.

Her somber thoughts were interrupted by Hannah and Isabelle shouting, "Now for Daniel's present."

"But I didn't get you all anything."

"Because we told you not to, Daniel. Because you're giving us a place to stay." Becca's *mamm* reached over and squeezed his arm. "That gift means more than any other ever could."

Clyde, Hannah and Isabelle had run to one of the back stalls. Now they walked out with a long box holding Daniel's gift.

"I believe I saw that box under my bed."

"*Ya*, it was there, but we had to move it. Didn't want you finding it." Francine ran her fingers up and down her *kapp* strings. "I hope you like it."

"I'm sure I will." Daniel glanced at Becca, his eyes questioning, but she only shrugged. She wasn't going to spoil the surprise now.

He opened the box to reveal a brand-new dark gray horse blanket with the word *Constance* embroidered across the bottom.

"In case we have a cold front, and she needs it."

"Everyone knows how much you care for the horse."

"It was at Lydia Kline's, being embroidered the night of the fire."

Becca heard all the comments from her family,

but her attention was on Daniel. Were those tears in his eyes? Over a horse blanket?

But of course, it was more than that. It was that they had, out of their poverty, found a way to give to him. Which was what neighbors and friends were supposed to do. The only question was whether Daniel Glick was merely a friend and neighbor, or did she want him to be more?

Later that evening, when once again she couldn't sleep, Becca made her way to the kitchen. When she saw Daniel sitting there at the table, she almost backed away.

"Please. Don't leave on my account."

"I didn't mean to interrupt you. I didn't think anyone else would be here."

"I was sort of hoping you wouldn't be able to sleep."

"Is that so?"

"Came out wrong." He tapped his journal, then looked up at her and smiled. "What I mean is, I was hoping to have a chance to be alone with you for a few minutes."

"My family is *wunderbaar*, but there are a lot of them."

Daniel was sitting at the end of the table. He nudged the chair closest to him out with his foot, then nodded toward the platter on the table. "There's still a few pieces of chocolate cake left. You know you want one."

"Only if there's cold milk to go with it."

"There is."

"You talked me into it, then."

It felt good to banter back and forth, but Becca knew that she needed to apologize for her earlier behavior. It was too hard living in the same house, dancing around one another, and feeling guilty for her rudeness. Best to clear the air.

She sat across from him and accepted the piece of cake he'd cut for her. Suddenly, she couldn't imagine eating a bite. Her stomach was doing somersaults. Why did she turn into a silly *youngie* when she was around Daniel? What was it about the way he looked at her that sent her feelings soaring and her pulse thumping?

Was that love?

If it was, how did people live with it over an extended period of time? She felt as if she could run a race, and as if she might be sick, all at the same time.

"Don't you want it?"

"Maybe later." She cleared her throat, stared at the glass of milk, then dared to look up into Daniel's eyes. She'd expected a wide range of responses from him—pity, anger, acceptance, even a brotherly friendship. Yes, he'd said he loved her and wanted to marry her, but after the way she'd acted, she rather suspected that offer had been withdrawn.

Now, as she looked at the man sitting across from her, she saw only love in his eyes, and it humbled her more than anything else that had happened to date.

He set aside his journal. Under it was a plainly

wrapped gift with a bright blue ribbon. "This is for you."

"But you weren't supposed to buy us gifts. You're giving enough just letting us live here."

"I bought this before the fire." He pushed it across the table, leaving his fingertips on the edge of the package.

As she reached for it, she was taken aback by the image before her—his hand, her hand, both holding a Christmas gift.

They were so different, and it was evident even in their hands. Daniel's was calloused from hard work, tanned even in the winter, with small scratches here and there.

Hers was smaller, her skin softer and younger.

And the gift? It was probably some simple thing— she hoped it was. Yet she understood that gifts had a way of binding people together.

"Aren't you going to open it?"

"*Ya*. Sure." She'd received a book on raising backyard chickens from her siblings. She hadn't expected anything else. Any other year, she might have felt depressed that their gifts were so few. This year, it hardly mattered.

She untied the ribbon and set it aside. It was long enough to braid in Hannah or Isabelle's hair. She pulled the wrapping paper away and stared at the clothbound book.

"It's a project book."

"Oh."

"For your projects." Daniel scooted closer. "See?

Each section is for a different project. There's room for fifty. It includes a place to project costs and materials, then make notations about what works and what doesn't, and finally a cost analysis section."

Becca bit her bottom lip as tears sprang to her eyes. Did he know what this meant to her? He understood her need to help her family. He didn't expect her to wait for a man to swoop in and make everything right. He was no longer suggesting that his money could solve her problems.

"This is very kind. *Danki*, and I'm embarrassed that I don't have a gift for you."

"I didn't expect a gift."

"Daniel, I want to apologize."

"You don't have to do that."

"*Ya*. I do. It was wrong of me to be so angry with you. I was… I guess I was embarrassed. It's been a fear of mine since I was a young child."

"What has been?"

"That people were laughing at me." She shook her head, ran a finger down the binding of the book. "It might have started when I first went to school. Before that, I don't think I realized I was poor. At home, we were all the same. When I went to school, even an Amish school, I realized that my clothes were different—more patched, older, a little too large or a little too small."

"And did they laugh at you, Becca?"

"Maybe. I'm not even sure. I don't remember that part. I only remember how it made me feel, and so

I've spent the last few years trying to make sure Hannah and Isabelle don't have to endure the same."

"It's plain how much you and your family care for each other."

"*Mamm* said something to me earlier that caught me by surprise." She thought about admitting that she'd confessed all to her mother, but decided it was best to stay on track. "She told me that she'd never wished for another life. Isn't that amazing?"

"That she has found contentment? It doesn't surprise me. Your *mamm* is a wise woman, Becca. I believe she would be content whether she was rich or poor."

"I thought she was simply putting on a brave front for the rest of us. As for my *dat*, I thought he was simply clueless."

"But he's not."

"*Nein*. It's very clear to me now that he understands what the most important things are—that we have each other, that we're a family, that we put each other and our faith before other things."

Something akin to pain crossed Daniel's features. "If my family understood all of that, I believe they could be happy even with their wealth."

"Which is what I need to apologize for."

"I don't think you do. You were right. I should have been honest with you—maybe not from the first day, but as we became *freinden*."

"Possibly. We can't go back." Becca tugged on her braid, pulled it over her shoulder. "I judged you for being rich, in the same way I was afraid other people had judged me for being poor. I understand now that prejudice goes both ways, and it's wrong. We should see the person, not the bank account behind the person, or what does it mean to be Christian? What does it mean to be Plain? I'm sorry, Daniel. Truly, I am."

"Apology accepted."

Becca worried her bottom lip. She was still nervous but also hungry, so she set the journal aside, loaded a piece of cake on her fork and popped it into her mouth.

Daniel's smile grew, and she knew he was trying to hold back his laughter.

She tried to ask *what?* but it came out as "Wha?" owing to the large piece of cake in her mouth. She managed to swallow, then washed it down with the cold milk. Daniel was still clearly amused.

"Chocolate," he explained, then leaned forward and thumbed the frosting from the corner of her mouth. His hand lingered there, cupping her face.

Becca found herself leaning forward and closing her eyes, and then Daniel's lips were on hers—sweeter than the cake, more tender than a child's fingertips, more precious than any gift she could have received.

Pulling in a deep breath, he rested his forehead against hers.

"I love you. I hope you know that."

"I do."

"Can I ask you again?"

"Yes," she whispered.

"Becca Schwartz, will you marry me?"

"I will."

"You're certain?"

Now she opened her eyes, pulled back and studied him. "I love you, Daniel Glick."

"Ya?"

"Ya. Don't look so surprised."

"Happy. I'm happy and maybe a little surprised."

"I'm happy, too."

"And you think that you can…accept my life? It's not as easy as you might think, having money."

Her laughter was light and bright and from a place that she'd forgotten existed—a carefree place that trusted things would be okay.

"I know how to be poor."

"You're very good at it."

"I suppose I can learn to be wealthy."

He stood and pulled her into his arms. "We'll love each other all of our days."

"For better or worse."

"For richer or poorer."

Which really was all they needed to say. The details could be worked out another time. They stood in the middle of the kitchen, their arms wrapped around one another, and enjoyed the last few minutes of a very special Christmas, one Becca knew she'd never forget.

Epilogue

Seven months later

Becca stood on the front porch of her house—her and Daniel's house—and shaded her eyes to better see across the yard.

"Looking for Carl-the-bad-tempered-rooster?" Daniel walked up behind her and slipped his arms around her waist.

"How did you know?"

"Because you're frowning."

"That rooster is going to take five years off my life."

"He's out by the road."

"The road?"

"Chasing the mailman."

"He chased the mailman?"

"Don't worry. The mailman was in an *Englisch* car. He made a clean getaway."

She wrapped her arms around his. In the distance,

she could make out her *bruder* working in the field alongside her *dat*. By the street was a simple sign that read G&S Organic Farm—Produce and Eggs. The two properties had become one, as had the two families.

From the corner of their porch, she could just see her parents' new home that had been built in the spring—plain, sturdy and paid for by the *freinden* in their community. Daniel had made a large, anonymous donation to the benevolence fund—more than enough to cover the cost of materials. As for the labor, there was no way to repay that except by being willing to help when someone else needed assistance.

Before they were married, she and Daniel had met with the bishop and discussed how to handle their finances. His advice had been remarkably clear and wise.

Live simply.

Help others when you can.

Be grateful.

Becca was surprised that very little in their lives had actually changed. She no longer felt the desperate need to help her parents financially. In fact, her parents were doing quite well. Turned out that her *dat* was a natural at organic farming.

"I passed your *schweschder* on my way down the lane."

"Abigail?"

"Ya."

"Did she bring Baby Tabitha?"

"She did."

Becca spun in Daniel's arms, reached up and touched his face. "Now would be a *gut* time to tell them that we're expecting."

"I was thinking the same thing."

He slipped his hand into hers, and they walked across the property that was bathed in the afternoon's summer sunshine. Becca couldn't help feeling that they were walking into their future.

Together.

* * * * *

THE AMISH WIDOW'S
CHRISTMAS HOPE

Carrie Lighte

For my mother, who reads my books first and fastest

And, lo, the angel of the Lord came upon them,
and the glory of the Lord shone round about them:
and they were sore afraid. And the angel said
unto them, Fear not: for, behold, I bring you
good tidings of great joy, which shall be
to all people. For unto you is born this day in the
city of David a Saviour, which is Christ the Lord.
—*Luke* 2:9–11

And the Word was made flesh,
and dwelt among us, (and we beheld his glory,
the glory as of the only begotten of the Father,)
full of grace and truth.
—*John* 1:14

Chapter One

Fern Glick crouched down so her face was level with her children's faces. "I should be home by lunchtime. Remember to use your best manners and do whatever Jaala asks you to do," she instructed them.

Patience, five, nodded obediently, but Phillip was distracted by the chatter of Jaala's grandchildren as they put on their coats and boots in the mudroom at the opposite end of the kitchen.

"Can we go outside, too, *Mamm*?" the six-year-old asked.

"*Jah*, of course you may. Be sure to button your coats to the top buttons—it's chilly out there," Fern answered. Rising, she kissed the tops of their heads before the pair raced to the mudroom. Fern smiled when she heard the other children welcome them enthusiastically.

"The *kinner* sound like they're already having *schpass* and they haven't gotten out the door yet," Jaala said as she entered the kitchen and took the broom from its hook. "Didn't I tell you the more the merrier?"

"That's true for *kinner*, but not necessarily for *eldre*. Especially when it means there aren't enough beds to go around. I feel *baremlich* about imposing on you like this when you already have company here for *Grischtdaag*."

"They're not company—they're *familye*," Jaala said with a wave of her hand. "You and the *kinner* don't have to leave on the twenty-third—you're *wilkom* to stay here and celebrate *Grischtdaag* with us."

Despite Jaala's warm hospitality, Fern couldn't wait to leave Serenity Ridge, Maine. The only reason she was staying until the following Saturday was because that's when she could secure the most affordable transportation home. If it was up to her, she wouldn't have returned to Maine in the first place.

Earlier in the month, she'd been contacted by an attorney regarding her recently deceased uncle Roman's estate. The attorney said Fern was to receive an inheritance, but he couldn't provide additional details until she met with him in person. Which meant Fern and her children had to journey nearly one thousand miles from their home in Geauga County, Ohio.

Fern had arranged to stay with Jaala and her husband, Abram, the district's deacon, but Jaala hadn't known her two sons and their families would be visiting at the same time—they weren't supposed to arrive for another week. The Amish had a knack for making room for everyone, but Jaala and Abram's modest house was stretched to the limit.

Jaala was the only person Fern had kept in touch with since she left Serenity Ridge eight years ago, so it didn't seem right to call on anyone else for lodging. Getting a room at a local inn was also out of the question: Fern spent every cent of the meager savings she'd managed to scrape together on transportation to Maine.

"Roman must have bequeathed you something substantial," Jaala speculated as she bent to sweep crumbs into the dust bin. "Otherwise, whatever he left you could have been shipped to Ohio."

Fern couldn't imagine her uncle leaving her anything of significant value. While it was true she'd helped her cousin Gloria care for him for over a year while he was recovering from a stroke and then she'd lived with them for two more years after that, Fern had rarely communicated with Roman since she left Maine. She never visited, either. In fact, she'd even missed Gloria's funeral five years ago because she'd just given birth to Patience and couldn't travel with a newborn. And Fern hadn't been able to leave Ohio to attend Roman's funeral this past November, either, since she was tending to her cousin's wife, who was on bed rest during the last month of her pregnancy.

"I assume he gave the *haus* and any savings he had to Gloria's daughter because she's Roman's closest living relative," Fern suggested. She supposed it was greedy, but once or twice she caught herself hoping whatever Roman left her, it was something that could be sold quickly so she could use the money to compensate for the expense of their trip.

"But Jane's only seven," Jaala commented. "If Roman left the *haus* to her, Walker will either have to manage the property or sell it and put the money in a trust fund for her until she's of age."

Fern turned her back and rinsed a couple stray coffee cups in the sink so Jaala couldn't read her expression. Walker Huyard, Jane's father, had been the love of Fern's life. Or so she believed during the two and a half years they'd secretly courted when Fern lived in Serenity Ridge. The couple had planned to get married the autumn they turned twenty-one, but that September, Fern was called back to Ohio to care for her ailing aunt.

Initially, Fern thought she'd return to Maine in time for wedding season, but when it was clear she'd be delayed indefinitely, they both pledged to wait however long they had to in order to become husband and wife. Yet Fern had barely been away for two months when she learned Walker had wed Gloria instead. Jane was born the following summer.

Fern wasn't merely hurt, angry and disappointed; she was in shock. Barely able to eat, sleep, pray or speak for weeks on end, it was as if she were in mourning for someone who'd died a sudden and unexpected death. She was just beginning to recover physically and emotionally when the aunt she'd been caring for passed away and her aunt's house was repossessed by the bank, leaving Fern homeless. It was desperation, not love, that had caused Fern to marry Marshall, a widower twelve years her senior. More accurately, it was *resignation*; Fern had given up believing there *was* such a thing as true love.

But in Marshall she'd found a man who, although not outwardly affectionate or expressive, was kind and considerate and until he fell ill, he'd given her a house and stability. In turn, she did her best to offer him companionship and care. The unspoken truth between them was that he'd married her out of loneliness and she'd married him out of poverty. Over time, their fondness for each other deepened and although Fern never felt toward Marshall the way she once felt toward Walker, she didn't regret marrying him. How could she, when he'd fathered their two beloved children? *Besides, Marshall never hurt me the way Walker did...*

"Ouch!" Fern yelped as the water scalded her fingers, snapping her back to the present.

"Are you all right, dear?" Jaala asked.

"I'm fine. I'd better get going—it's almost nine o'clock."

Fern bundled into her coat and covered her prayer *kapp* with her best winter church bonnet, then stepped outside. It was only the fifteenth of December, but Jaala mentioned that two days before, a heavy rain had frozen over, coating everything with ice. It had since melted, but this morning the air smelled of impending snow. Fern glanced across the dirt driveway toward the barn, where the children were straddling the fence, pretending they were riding horses.

As Phillip bounced up and down, Fern visually

assessed the railing and determined it wouldn't give way beneath his weight. He was such a sturdy child, built like his father. He had his father's dark hair and eyes, too. But Marshall's demeanor was so understated he seemed detached, whereas Phillip couldn't contain his exuberance for life and his affection for people.

Patience, on the other hand, was a diminutive replica of her mother—fair-haired, fair-skinned, freckled and petite—but Fern hoped that's where the similarities ended. *Waifish* was the word someone once used to describe Fern as a girl and she didn't want her daughter to grow up feeling like a ragamuffin, too.

Gott willing, maybe I can get a full-time job at Weaver's Fabric Shop and I'll be allowed to bring the kinner *to work until they're old enough to start* schul. *Then I might be able to afford to rent a place of our own*, Fern schemed.

Shortly after Fern's husband died two years earlier, she'd had to sell their house—at a loss—because she couldn't keep up with the mortgage payments. Fern and the children moved in with Fern's cousin on her mother's side, Adam, and his wife, Linda, and their children. Fern contributed what she could to the family's expenses and she helped mind their brood, too. She'd even given up her part-time job so she could manage the household while Linda was on bed rest during her fifth pregnancy. However, in spite of Fern's helpfulness, the couple had been strongly hinting it was time for her and the children to find another place to live.

Having lost both of her parents when she was still a baby, Fern was accustomed to being shifted from one relative's home to another. Whenever someone in her extended family needed an extra person to work on a farm, mind children or tend to an infirmed elder, Fern would pack up her suitcase and go stay with them until her help was needed elsewhere. It wasn't that she didn't want to be of service to her extended family members, nor was it that anyone was unkind to her. But Fern had grown up longing for a permanent place to call home.

I'm twenty-nine and not much has changed, she reflected. *I* still *want a permanent place to call home...but now I want it more for my* kinner *than for myself.*

Patience's waving from across the driveway snapped Fern out of her daze. She giggled; the child had misbuttoned her coat, but at least it was fastened to the top. Fern lifted her gloved hand to wave back and then started down the lane.

Walker climbed into his buggy, hoping the meeting with the attorney wouldn't take long; this was a busy week at work. During the warmer months, he was employed full-time by an *Englisch* tree service, but in winter, he took odd jobs here and there. From Thanksgiving until Christmas, Walker helped out at Levi Swarey's Christmas tree farm in the mornings, cutting and baling trees and loading them onto

Englischers' vehicles. The nearer Christmas drew, the more frantic the customers became, and Walker especially regretted leaving Levi short staffed on a Friday, their second busiest day of the week.

I imagine Roman bequeathed the haus *to Jane*, he thought as he guided his horse toward Main Street. He figured he ought to feel grateful, but instead the prospect overwhelmed him. Walker wasn't adept at negotiating legal matters and completing paperwork. Besides, the Lord had already provided him with a good living, and the house he shared with his daughter and mother had room to spare. *Either I'll have to sell the* haus *and put the money in a trust fund or rent it out until Jane becomes an adult and can decide for herself what to do with it.*

Walker didn't like picturing his daughter as an adult; she was growing too fast already. He smiled as he thought of her practicing for the annual Christmas program at school; she was so excited it was all she could talk about. Jane had been assigned three Bible verses to recite and although she'd memorized them thoroughly, she kept practicing, worried she might stutter or forget a word. *She probably developed that anxiety from being around her* groossdaadi. *Gloria's* daed *was so particular; everything had to be just right and even then, he was rarely satisfied.*

Walker immediately felt guilty for thinking ill of Roman. There was no doubt in his mind the man had loved Jane dearly and wanted the best for her. The problem was, Roman's sense of what was *best* often bordered on perfectionism. His standards were al-

most impossibly high and he had virtually no toler-
ance for mistakes, big or small. *If only he'd exhibited
more mercy...* Walker shook the thought from his
head, remembering one of his mother's oft-quoted
sayings, "*If only* is a complaint dressed up as a wish."

As he journeyed through town, Walker spied a
tree toppled in an *Englischer*'s front yard. It wasn't
a large tree, but its weight was enough to splinter the
nearby fence when it landed on it. *At least it's only
wood that was fractured. A fence can be replaced.*

Just like that, the memory of the tree-trimming
accident came rushing back, as instantaneously as
the accident itself. One moment Walker had been
strolling across a customer's lawn toward his employer's bucket truck. The next moment it felt as if
he'd been knocked between the shoulder blades with
an anvil. Then there was a black, blank void.

When he came to, Walker was in the hospital.
His foreman explained one of the ropes the crew
used to bring limbs down had snapped, causing a
twelve-foot branch to swing in the wrong direction.
Walker assumed the limb had knocked him flat, but
he was told the force he'd felt against his back was
his *Englisch* friend and coworker, Jordan, shoving
him out of harm's way. Although his helmet was
cracked, Walker survived the accident with nothing more than a minor concussion. Jordan, unfortunately, suffered a broken neck and skull fracture
and perished at the scene.

It had been eight years, but Walker still shuddered
at the memory. Or maybe that was partly from the

weather; it was definitely cold enough to snow. He pushed his hat down over his ears and worked the horse into a quicker trot.

Once he reached Main Street, he stopped to get out and hitch the horse to a post behind the library and then he jogged across the street to the attorney's office. The receptionist was on the phone, so he hung up his coat and hat and waited until she was free to usher him to the attorney's office.

"I'm Anthony Marino," the attorney said, extending his hand. "Have a seat. The other party should be here soon. Would you like something to drink? Coffee? Water?"

"No, thank you," Walker replied in *Englisch*. He sat down before repeating, "The other party?"

"Your father-in-law named two heirs for the majority of his estate," Anthony explained just as the receptionist tapped on the door. He crossed the room to open it, saying, "Looks like she's here now."

Because the woman was wearing a bonnet, Walker couldn't immediately see her face from where he was sitting. But after Anthony introduced himself, she replied, "And I'm Fern Glick. It's nice to meet you."

Walker gasped audibly and both Fern and Anthony swiveled their heads in his direction. Anthony chuckled, saying, "Obviously, there's no need for me to introduce the two of you."

Fern's eyes, which were as gray as the snow clouds outside the window, opened wide with apparent disorientation as she looked at Walker. He hardly had a chance to register that she still had a faint smattering of freckles across her nose and cheeks before she glanced away. *"Neh,"* she answered the attorney. "We're already acquainted."

Acquainted? The word was like a snowball right between Walker's eyes. *Acquainted?* They'd once pledged their undying love for each other! Of course, that was over eight years ago and they'd both married other people since then, but did Fern have to reduce their past relationship to nothing more than acquaintances? Walker tugged at his shirt collar, as if that would help him breathe better.

"Please, make yourself comfortable, Fern," the attorney said, gesturing to the chair next to Walker's.

As Anthony turned and emptied a decanter of ice water into two glasses, Fern perched on the far edge of her seat, her elbows pressed to her sides and her hands folded on her lap. She'd always had a way of drawing into herself, as if to take up as little space as possible, but today her posture seemed like a rebuff of Walker's presence. He tried to think of a greeting that wouldn't sound trite, but his tongue felt thick and his mind was woolly. He hadn't felt this unnerved since the first time he'd ever sat so close to Fern.

Anthony handed them each a glass and Walker gratefully took a gulp of water. The attorney sat down behind his desk and explained Roman had required both Walker and Fern to be present for the reading of his will. "I can go through the document with you word-by-word, but the long and short of it is that Roman named you two as beneficiaries of his estate."

"You mean he named Fern and my *dochder*, Jane, as beneficiaries, right?" Walker clarified.

"No, he actually bequeathed his possessions and estate to Fern and you, not to your daughter. Roman indicated he trusted you implicitly to do right by Jane."

That's surprising—he never said a complimentary word about my relationship with my dochder *when he was alive.*

Anthony added, "He also understood it would simplify things if he named you as a beneficiary because there are very precise stipulations to the inheritance."

Now that *sounds more like Roman.* "What are those stipulations?"

"First, Roman bequeathed the house solely to Fern for as long as she chooses to reside in it."

The brim of Fern's bonnet obscured her profile but Walker heard her inhale sharply. She leaned forward and placed her water glass on a coaster on Anthony's desk. "What if I don't choose to reside in it?"

"Then you may sell it. But in that case you and Walker will split the profit, fifty-fifty."

Fern's response was immediate and decisive. "That's what I'd like to do, then. Can you help me arrange the sale?"

Anthony balked. "I'd be glad to, but wouldn't you like to give it more thought? The last time I spoke with Roman, he led me to believe you didn't have your own—"

"I don't need to think it over," Fern interrupted.

"I have absolutely no intention of living in Maine ever again."

What she means is she has no intention of living around me *ever again*, Walker thought.

"I care less about getting market value than I do about selling the house as soon as possible," Fern asserted. "I understand there are real estate investing franchises that can expedite a cash sale. I'd like to contact one of them."

Anthony picked up a pen and rolled it between his fingers. "That's fine, as long as Walker agrees. According to the conditions of the will, he has the first option of buying you out—"

"I'm not interested in acquiring another house," Walker objected. Eventually he'd just resell it, so it wasn't worth the added hassle of buying out Fern's share first.

"Okay, in that case the house becomes joint property for you to sell. You'll have to agree on how you want to go about that."

Walker cleared his throat. "I'm not sure we should rush into working with an investing franchise instead of a local realtor. For one thing, it's a very big decision to make on the spot. For anoth—"

"You've made big decisions on the spot before," Fern broke in, staring directly at him. Her face, always thin, had become more angular with age. Or maybe it was her cutting remark—an obvious reference to his decision to marry Gloria—that made Fern's features appear sharper.

Clenching the water glass, he averted his eyes

and addressed Anthony instead. "The other reason I think we should wait is that the recent ice storm brought down two trees in Roman's yard. One blocks the lane and the other clipped the edge of the *haus* and damaged the roof. We'll get a much better price for the property if we at least make that repair and clear the yard before we show it to prospective buyers, whoever they are. I could fix everything up myself within a couple of weeks."

The attorney leaned forward and spoke to Fern. "Walker's right. Even a real estate investing franchise is going to appraise the house before making an offer. A little yard work and a minor repair might make the difference between thousands of dollars." When Fern was silent, Anthony pressed, "May I ask why you're in such a hurry to sell?"

"I—I—I'm only going to be in Serenity Ridge until the twenty-third," Fern stammered. "I want to get the process started in person now and I can't always get to the phone shanty."

"That's no problem. I can mail you the necessary documents for signing when the time comes, and I'll give you my personal cell phone number so if you have questions, you can call me whenever it's convenient for you." Anthony smiled convincingly.

"Denki," Fern said. Walker noticed they both kept slipping in and out of *Deitsch*.

"Just a couple more things concerning Roman's estate," Anthony said, shuffling through his papers. "It looks like he left his livestock and buggy to the Fry family."

Sarah Fry had been widowed two years ago and she was struggling to feed her seven children, all under the age of twelve. After Roman's death in early November, the deacon tasked the two eldest Fry boys with caring for Roman's horse, milk cow and chickens at their home until the will was read. Walker was touched to learn Roman wanted them to have the animals and buggy permanently, as he knew how much it would benefit them. *I guess there was a side to him I didn't always see*, he admitted to himself.

"As for Roman's possessions in the house, stable and workshop, similar rules apply—Fern would have inherited them in full if she'd taken up residence. Since she's chosen not to, the two of you need to decide together what you'll do with the furnishings and tools, et cetera."

"I don't want anything from the *haus*, but if Walker does, he can take whatever he'd like. Otherwise, I think we should give the material goods to someone in need or include them in the sale of the house," Fern said.

Anthony rubbed his temples, clearly bewildered by her snap decision to forfeit any material goods. "You're already in town, so I'd urge you to take a look through the house and workshop first."

After a brief silence, Fern unexpectedly agreed. Walker was further taken aback when she questioned, "Since the *haus* is unoccupied, may my *kinner* and I stay in it for the week? The woman I'm visiting, Jaala, received unexpected company, so the extra room would be *wilkom*."

"That's fine, as long as Walker has no objections."

"No, no objections." Although the roof was damaged superficially, from what Walker could see in passing, the house was structurally sound. "However, I'm starting a full-time contractor position after the first of the year, so if I'm going to work on Roman's *haus* and yard, I'll have to get started on it next week."

Wrinkling his forehead, Anthony shrugged. "I can't see that presenting a problem, will it, Fern?"

Fern's discernible pause indicated she thought otherwise, but she answered, "*Neh.* I'm sure we won't disturb one another."

Too late for that, Walker thought ruefully.

After Anthony handed her the house key and a folder of paperwork, Fern said goodbye and hurried into the restroom. She ran warm water over her hands, trying to gather her composure.

The attorney never mentioned anyone else would be attending the meeting, so Fern assumed Walker had already been informed of the terms of the will during a separate appointment. And while she expected she might have seen him from afar at church on Sunday, she'd planned to avoid coming within speaking distance of him. Or at least, she'd planned to stay far enough away so that she wouldn't have been able to smell the lemongrass soap he still used or to hear the rustle of his pant legs when he shifted in his chair the way she could in Anthony's office.

So any elation or gratitude she felt over what the

inheritance would mean for her future was temporarily eclipsed by how unsettling it was to have to sit in such close proximity to Walker for the past fifteen minutes.

You're being lecherich, she told the mirror. It didn't matter; a tear trickled down her cheek anyway. Fern thought she'd forgiven Walker and moved on but the hurt, anger and confusion felt as raw and real today as they had felt eight years ago. Of all things, it had been his mustache that set it off again...

The Amish communities in Maine were among a handful in the country that permitted the men to wear mustaches, as well as beards, when they married. When Fern glimpsed Walker's dark, coppery-brown facial hair, which appeared as thick and soft-looking as the hair on his head, she remembered the secret signal he used to give her. When he was across the room at church or a singing, he'd stroke the skin beneath his nose with his index finger and thumb, as if smoothing an imaginary mustache. The gesture was his way of saying, "I can't wait to be married."

Oh, he couldn't wait to be married all right—just not to me*!* she fumed. Fern pulled a paper towel from the dispenser and dried her hands, then adjusted her bonnet. Stalling until she could be sure Walker had left the building, she idly thumbed through the folder of paperwork. She didn't even like seeing Walker's name and hers together on the same page. How was she going to endure being on the same property with him for the next seven days?

"Please, *Gott*, give me strength and grace," she whispered before exiting the restroom.

Fern could barely glance my way, much less greet me or say my name, Walker silently brooded as he drove toward the Christmas tree farm to begin his shift. *I understand why she'd resent me for marrying her* gschwischderkind, *but she doesn't know the full story.*

That was just it: *no one* knew the full story, except Walker. And he and Gloria had solemnly promised, for Jane's sake, they'd never tell another soul about what led to their sudden marriage shortly after the tree accident claimed his coworker's life.

As aggrieved as Walker had been by Jordan's death, he soon discovered Gloria was even more despondent. Walker knew Gloria and Jordan had socialized together—nearly eighteen, Gloria was still on her *rumspringa* and frequently hung out with *Englischers*—but he wasn't aware of the extent of their relationship until after the funeral. Walker was giving Gloria a ride home in his buggy when she broke down, confiding she was pregnant with Jordan's baby.

"We planned to get married next week on my birthday," she'd sobbed. "Now what will I do? My *daed* will never forgive me. He'll turn me out of the *haus* if I tell him about the *bobbel*."

Racked with guilt, Walker felt he couldn't allow Jordan's child to grow up homeless, as well as fatherless—not after the *Englischer* had given up his life to save Walker's. So, after intense agonizing, he sacrificed his own future for the baby's and wed Gloria instead of Fern. Although he believed he'd made an honorable decision, Walker was heartsick about ending his courtship with Fern, anticipating it would hurt her as much as it hurt him.

However, it appeared Fern's pain was short-lived; she hadn't even waited until the following autumn wedding season to marry Marshall. According to Jaala, they'd wed in the spring, a mere seven months after Fern told Walker she'd rather remain single forever than to pledge her life to any man other than him.

Granted, Walker had said the same thing to her. The difference was, despite all outward appearances, *he* had meant it. *I didn't* want *to marry Gloria, but at the time I didn't seem to have any other choice*, he rationalized. *If the shoe were on the other foot and Fern had been forced to marry someone else, I would have stayed single for the rest of* my *life...*

Which was exactly what he planned to do from now on, but it was no longer because he clung to any enduring love for Fern. On the contrary, his breakup with Fern had taught him what a mistake it was to give his heart to her. To *any* woman.

Likewise, although Walker cherished Jane as much as any father cherished his daughter, in retrospect he realized he shouldn't have married Gloria. If he hadn't been so traumatized by the accident, Walker likely would have come up another way to help her and the baby that didn't involve keeping such a burdensome secret. That didn't involve living a lie.

I can't change the past, but with Gott's *help, I can make better decisions in the present,* he reminded himself as he turned down the lane to the Christmas tree farm. *And for the next week that includes keeping as much distance between Fern and me as she seems to want.*

Chapter Two

Filtered through a cloudy sky, the sunlight cast a white glare, and Fern squinted as she peered down Main Street toward the small *Englisch* market located on the other side of the bank. Shopping there was more expensive than at the superstore on the opposite side of town, but since she didn't want to walk that far in the cold from Roman's house with the children, Fern decided she'd better pick up some groceries now.

A jangling bell announced her arrival as she opened the door, but a quick scan of the aisles fortunately revealed the only other people in the shop were *Englischers*. Given her weepiness, it was better if Fern didn't have to face someone else from her past today. She selected beans, rice and a few other staples from the shelves, but she decided against buying flour or vegetables until she saw what Roman had left over in his pantry and cellar. Since he'd given away his livestock, Fern reluctantly added a half gallon of milk and a dozen eggs to her basket, too. Store-bought eggs were never quite as tasty as those she collected from the henhouse herself and these were labeled Organic, which meant they'd be twice as pricey as the kind sold at the superstore. *I'll just have to cut back somewhere else in our food budget,* she decided.

By the time she got to Jaala's house, it was flurrying. The children had their mouths open to the sky as they attempted to catch snowflakes on their tongues.

"Don't eat too many or you'll spoil your appetites for lunch," Fern called, teasing. Phillip and Patience immediately dashed over to give her a hug. She never tired of their fervent greetings, which more than made up for all the times she'd ever second-guessed how her relatives felt about having her live with them when she was a youth.

Jaala said her daughters-in-law were in the basement feeding the laundry through the wringing machine and her sons were in the workshop, so Fern took advantage of the opportunity to speak with Jaala in private, telling her about the meeting with the attorney and her plan to stay in Roman's house for the rest of her time in Serenity Ridge.

Jaala frowned. "Are you sure, dear? You don't have to leave on our account. The *kinner* are getting along so well. They're going to be terribly disappointed to be separated."

"They're *wilkom* to visit anytime. Roman has that big hill in the backyard—if the snow keeps up, the *kinner* can go sledding." Fern had no idea how she'd feed everyone if they came during lunchtime, but she'd think of something. For now, it felt good to be the one in the position of offering hospitality to someone else, even if staying in Roman's house was undoubtedly going to dredge up unpleasant memories.

After lunch, Fern fetched the suitcase she shared with Phillip and Patience. Jaala was right; all of the children were disappointed they were leaving, but they brightened when Fern invited Jaala's grandchildren to visit as soon as the snow was deep enough for sledding.

Since Abram had come home for his lunch break, he gave Fern, Phillip and Patience a ride to Roman's house on his way back to the lumberyard. Fern's stomach fluttered in nervous anticipation as they wound along the familiar roads toward her uncle's property on the outskirts of town. For most of her life, she had lived with relatives in large Amish settlements in Ohio or Pennsylvania, where she could look in any direction and see vast stretches of farmland punctuated by barns and silos. Not so in Serenity Ridge, where large stands of tall pine trees separated one family's property from another's. The hills in this part of Maine were steep and rocky, and because Serenity Ridge's Amish settlement was only about twenty-five years old, it was still a relatively small community—although Fern did notice several new Amish houses that hadn't been built when she lived there.

"You can see the ice storm did quite a bit of damage," Abram pointed out. "Tomorrow there's a frolic to repair the Blanks' *haus*, weather permitting. A tree crashed straight through two of their upstairs bedrooms and came to rest in the gathering room. Thank the Lord, no one was hurt."

"I'm told there are a couple of trees down in my *onkel* Roman's yard, too, but they didn't damage his *haus* much," Fern said.

Abram responded that there was a second work frolic the following weekend to repair the Schwartzes' barn, but he said he could arrange for the men to clean up Roman's yard on Saturday, December 30.

"*Denki*, but Walker is going to make the repairs in the afternoons during the upcoming week. He said it shouldn't take him long so the trees must have been fairly small."

But when they rounded the bend and Roman's yard came into view, Fern was surprised to see the size of the downed trees. One of them, a cedar, had completely uprooted and was blocking the driveway. The other, which was actually a large section of an oak tree, not the tree in its entirety, had split in such a way that the base of the branch was still partially attached to the trunk, although the rest of it had toppled over and was wedged against the ground, forming an upside-down V with the tree. Smaller limbs littered the yard. *Roman would have hated how messy his lawn looks*, Fern thought.

Abram brought the suitcase to the porch before hurrying off to work. Fern was glad he didn't want to come inside; her stomach was still upset and she needed time to adjust to being back in her uncle's house again. Instead of taking the key out of her purse, she set her bag of groceries down, turned and motioned to the lawn. "You may play anywhere in the yard except under the tree by the side of the *haus*, okay?"

"Jah," the children agreed in unison.

"There's a big hill in the backyard and you're allowed to climb to the very top of it and run or sled all the way to the bottom, but you mustn't go into the woods without me," she instructed them. "Would you like me to show you around? We can look in the barn and in the workshop, too."

"I'm cold. Can we go inside?" The tip of Patience's nose was pink.

"Jah, I want to see what the *haus* looks like first," Phillip said, and Fern knew she couldn't put off entering it any longer.

"Sure, but we have to take our boots off at the door. There's no mudroom." She found herself automatically repeating the rule her uncle had frequently cited when she lived there, despite the fact she and Gloria were long past the age of needing a reminder not to dirty the floors. The children were so eager to get inside they pulled off their boots before she could steady her hands enough to turn the key in the lock.

The tiny square-shaped house opened to a small living room on the left and a staircase on the right. Still able to find her way through the house in the dark, Fern edged along the wall and pulled the shades up to let in more light. A small maroon sofa and matching armchair, as well as a rocker, were angled toward the woodstove. There was a round braided rug in the center of the floor and a smaller, rectangular braided rug near the door. Nothing hung on the walls except a single shelf just large enough to hold a clock. The clock's battery must have died because its hands read nine thirty-five. There was a gas-powered lamp built into a rolling table at one end of the sofa, and a Bible rested atop the flat surface. The wood bin was located at the opposite end, closest to the stove; it was still full.

There was a tradition among Serenity Ridge's Amish women to clean the house for the family of someone who had just died. Largely, this charitable act was done because after the funeral, the family was expected to host a gathering at their home. In Roman's case, Jaala and Abram had hosted a gathering at the church instead because the Serenity Ridge district, like the Amish community in nearby Unity, was unique in that its members met in a building for worship instead of in each other's homes. But Fern could tell by the faint scent of vinegar in the air the women had cleaned Roman's house anyway. Not that there would have been much to do—he insisted on keeping everything extraordinarily tidy, even by Amish standards.

Phillip sat down on the sofa and bounced twice, testing the springs, whereas Patience stood in the middle of the room and turned a slow circle, tentatively taking in her surroundings.

"Kumme," Fern said to them after she got a fire going. "I'll show you the kitchen."

They followed her through the living room to the equally tiny kitchen. It housed a gas stove, a gas-powered refrigerator and a table with four chairs. Two additional chairs were in the corners of the room. Fern resisted the urge to peek in the cupboards to see what staples Roman still had on hand; she'd do that later, when the children weren't around. Patience was so perceptive she'd recognize her mother was taking inventory, and then the young girl would worry there wasn't enough for them to eat.

Next Fern showed the children where the bathroom was, and then the three of them stuck their heads into Roman's bedroom across the hall. Fern's eyes stung as she recalled that immediately after Roman's stroke, she and Gloria had to wrap his arms around their necks to lift him from bed until he was capable of walking by himself again. *Those were such difficult days for him, yet they were some of the happiest for me because of how much I enjoyed living with Gloria. And because I'd just met Walker...*

"Let's go upstairs," she said quickly, brushing a tear from her cheek. The children hadn't uttered a word and she was concerned they were still upset about having to leave Jaala's to come to such a cold, empty shoebox of a house. *Maybe this was a mistake...*

There were two rooms at the top of the stairs; Fern pointed to the one on the right. "This used to be my room when I lived here," she told them, and

Phillip pushed the door open farther and bounded inside. "My *gschwischderkind*, Gloria, slept in the other one."

Patience hung back, her eyes as big as saucers. "You had a room just for yourself?"

"Jah."

"Look at this, Patience. *Mamm* had her own double bed and a dresser and a chair! Her own closet, too," Phillip announced from inside the bedroom.

The children's astonishment troubled Fern. While she valued that they had learned at a young age how to share joyfully with others and to be satisfied with whatever God had given them, she wished they'd known what it was like to have a *little* more personal space—or at least a bed for themselves. *But that will change as soon as this* haus *sells and we can move out of Adam and Linda's home*, she thought. It was really starting to sink in that for the first time in her life she wouldn't have to be dependent on anyone else—and especially not on a man—for a place to live.

"Weren't you lonely sleeping by yourself?" Patience asked.

"Sometimes," Fern admitted. She understood her daughter's fear about sleeping alone, but she didn't want it to keep her from getting a good night's rest while they were there that week—or once she permanently had a bed to herself. "But I'd read or pray or else Gloria would tiptoe into my room and we'd talk until we were tired enough to fall asleep. And once you're sleeping, you're not lonely, are you?"

As she spoke, Fern had to fight back tears again, recalling her late-night chats with her cousin, which were sometimes serious, sometimes silly, and almost always involved secrets they didn't want Roman to hear. Three years younger than Fern, Gloria had also been an only child and she'd lost her mother as a girl, so in those ways the two young women had a lot in common. Even though they'd never met until Fern came to Maine, they bonded with each other immediately and grew even closer over time.

She was like my little schweschder, Fern recalled. But there wasn't an ounce of sibling rivalry between them. That was partly why it was so baffling and hurtful when Gloria married Walker. Fern hadn't ever told her cousin she was in love with Walker and planned to wed him that autumn—she and Walker had kept that a closely guarded secret. But Gloria was aware Walker had been Fern's suitor for over two and a half years, so she knew better than to enter into a courtship with him the moment Fern left for Ohio.

At least, that's when Fern initially *assumed* Walker and Gloria's relationship began. But after a while as she reflected on her cousin's behavior, she realized Gloria hadn't quite seemed herself that summer; she'd grown jumpy and secretive, as if she was hiding something.

As Fern stood in the hallway, she remembered the last late-night conversation she'd shared with her cousin. Much to Roman's consternation, Gloria was still on *rumspringa* and her father had told her either she had to put her running around period behind her and join the Amish church in the spring following her eighteenth birthday or she'd have to find somewhere else to live. That evening, Gloria was uncharacteristically doleful as she confided how conflicted she'd felt about making that decision.

"I don't know if I can be *gut* all the time the way we're required to be once we become members of the *kurrich*," she'd said.

"No one but *Gott* is *gut* all the time. The rest of us need the Holy Spirit to empower us not to sin and Christ's grace and forgiveness when we fail," Fern had replied. "If sin disqualified someone from joining the *kurrich*, there's not a person on earth who could join."

"*Jah*, but you don't know some of the *baremlich* things I've done. The things I'm *tempted* to do…"

"Scripture says nothing can separate us from the love of God in Christ and that if we confess our sins, God is faithful to forgive us. It also says He'll provide a way of escape from temptation."

"That's just it. I don't know if I want to escape the things I'm tempted by…or if I'd rather escape the *Ordnung*," Gloria had mumbled before bursting into tears.

Back then, Fern had interpreted Gloria's hesitance to join the church as a reflection of how much pressure she felt to live up to her father's standards, not the Lord's. But in hindsight, Fern suspected getting involved with Walker romantically was one of the "terrible things" Gloria had alluded to doing or being tempted to do long before Fern went back to Geauga County that fall.

But Fern had never once noticed a change in Walker's behavior toward her. If anything, they'd become closer than ever that summer. Maybe he was better at covering it up than Gloria was, but if he had developed romantic feelings for her cousin that summer, why would he have suggested they get married in the fall? So Fern had concluded years ago that Walker and Gloria's relationship *had* to have started after she left for Ohio. *Out of sight, out of mind,* she thought sourly.

"Let's look in the other room," Phillip urged, tugging Patience's hand and pulling her back into the hall—and Fern's thoughts back into the present. He gallantly offered, "You can choose which one you want to sleep in."

But Patience didn't need to look at the other room to know she wanted to sleep in Fern's old room. "I can pretend I'm *Mamm* when she was a little *maedel.*"

"I wasn't a little *maedel,* Patience. I lived here from the time I was eighteen until I was twenty-one."

"Then I can pretend I'm you when you lived here and you were all growed up. I want to be just like you, *Mamm.*"

Oh, sweetheart, I want more for your life than that. "Let's go get our things from the porch," she suggested. But before Phillip and Patience scampered down the stairs, her son threw his arms around Fern's waist.

"This is a great *haus*, *Mamm*!" he said. "It's got so much space and there aren't a lot of things we have to be careful not to bump into or break!"

"*Denki* for bringing us here," Patience added. "I wish we could stay till *Grischtdaag*."

With those few words, Fern's children utterly changed her perspective, as they'd frequently done throughout their young lives, just by being themselves. Fern may not have found the kind of love she'd once hoped for in a man, but she'd been blessed with two children she couldn't have imagined in her fondest dreams. A few tears rolled down her cheeks and when Patience noticed, she asked what was wrong.

"Nothing. I'm crying because I'm so grateful *Gott* gave you to me," she replied. *You're all the* familye *I'll ever need or want.*

Walker spied Jane standing on the steps of the one-room schoolhouse, licking her mitten. It had stopped flurrying but a dusting of snow—the first of the season—had collected on the railing and she must have wiped her hand over it so she could have a taste. Her lips and chin always got so chapped in winter from eating snow off her hands like an ice cream cone, but Walker had given up trying to dissuade her; she'd outgrow her childish antics too soon anyway. When she spotted him she clapped, ran across the yard and boarded the buggy.

"Guess how many days until our *Grischtdaag* program?" she asked as he tucked a blanket around her legs to keep her warm; the temperature seemed to have dropped a good seven degrees since that morning.

The annual school Christmas program was one of the Amish community's favorite traditions. The presentation included a Biblical recitation of the nativity story by the children, carols, a gift exchange and a wide array of seasonal refreshments. Usually it was held on the last weekday before December 25, but the teacher, Amity Speicher, had requested to go out of town for Christmas, so the school board decided to hold the program on Wednesday, December 20. Unlike *Englisch* children, Amish children usually didn't get a long Christmas break, but this year they'd have December 21 and 22 off, in addition to Monday, December 25.

Walker scratched his head, pretending not to know when the event would occur. "One hundred and eighteen?"

"*Daed!* How could there be one hundred and eighteen days left when there were only six days yesterday?" she asked incredulously.

"Aha! If there were only six days left yesterday, that means there are only five days left today," he deducted.

"You tricked me!" Jane accused him, but she laughed and he laughed, too. His dark-haired, pudgy-cheeked daughter's smile had that effect on him; even more so now because she was missing two teeth. Usually Walker thought she was the spitting image of Gloria, but every once in a while when she was overly tired and her eyelids were half-mast, she reminded him of Jordan. Although the similarity brought Walker comfort because it was like catching a glimpse of his *Englisch* friend's face, he was relieved no one in their community had known Jordan well enough to notice the resemblance.

"Want to hear me say my Bible verses?" Jane asked.

She had rehearsed saying them so many times, Walker knew them by heart himself, but he answered yes, so she recited Luke 2:9–11, which went:

> And, lo, the angel of the Lord came upon them, and the glory of the Lord shone round about them: and they were sore afraid. And the angel said unto them, Fear not: for, behold, I bring you good tidings of great joy, which shall be to all people. For unto you is born this day in the city of David a Saviour, which is Christ the Lord.

When she finished, she asked, "Now do you want to practice 'Hark! The Herald Angels Sing' with me, *Daed*?"

The pair sang the rest of the way to their home, which was located on the west side of town close to an *Englisch* neighborhood. Walker had built the house the spring after he married Gloria; until then, he'd been living with his mother, Louisa, and sister, Willa, in his childhood home. Walker's father had died when Walker was sixteen, and his two older brothers had long since married. One moved to Fort Fairfield, a small settlement in the northern part of the state, and the other relocated to Canada.

After Gloria and Walker's wedding, the couple rented a *daadi haus* until Walker could build his current home. Then his sister got married the following year and she moved to the district in Unity, a neighboring town, so his mother sold the family house and went to live with Willa and her husband. When Gloria died, Louisa moved back to Serenity Ridge so she could help Walker raise Jane. She was the closest person to a mother Jane could remember, and Walker didn't know what he would have done without her help. Although he sometimes felt guilty about allowing her to believe he was Jane's biological father, Walker knew telling Louisa the truth wouldn't change one thing about his mother's relationship with Jane or decrease her love for the child.

Mamm has been more of a groossmammi *to Jane than Jordan's* mamm *ever was*, he thought. Gloria had visited Jordan's parents shortly after the funeral to tell them about her pregnancy, but they'd accused her of lying and said they wanted nothing to do with her or the baby. Their rejection of their son's child was another reason Walker felt compelled to marry Gloria.

As he and his daughter lifted their voices in song, he couldn't help but think, *Poor Jane. She might not have any of my genes, but she's as tone-deaf as I am!* It delighted him that they both belted out the carols anyway.

"*Groossmammi*, do you want to hear me recite my verses?" Jane asked the moment she got in the door. Another round of caroling followed and then a third round after supper.

Once Jane went to bed, Louisa invited Walker to have a cup of chamomile tea in the gathering room. Since the tree farm had been so busy that day and Walker had missed half his morning shift, he'd stayed there until it was time to pick Jane up, so he hadn't had a chance to tell his mother about the meeting.

"What did the attorney have to say?" she questioned. "Did Roman bequeath the *haus* to Jane?"

"*Neh.* He actually bequeathed it to me on her behalf."

"Ah, that makes sense."

"But he named a co-heir. His niece, Fern Troyer— I mean, Fern Glick." Walker lowered his eyes to blow on his tea so he wouldn't have to look at his mother. Because the Amish were customarily discreet about who they were courting, he'd never told his mother he was Fern's suitor. But he'd frequently sensed his mother suspected they were courting, and he didn't want his expression to give it away now.

His mother nodded. "That's as it should be. Fern is his relative, too, and she was such a blessing to him after he had the stroke. Gloria wouldn't have been able to manage his care on her own."

Walker remembered how often Gloria used to tell him the same thing. "Fern coming to live with us was the best thing that could have happened to me," she'd say. "Not only did she help enormously during *Daed*'s illness, but she was like a *schweschder* and a *mamm* and a best *freind* all rolled into one. I was so glad she stayed with us in Serenity Ridge even after *Daed* recovered."

I was so glad, too...

"Walker?" His mother interrupted his thoughts. "What's wrong?"

"Nothing." Walker hadn't realized he'd been glowering. His mother probably thought she'd made him lonely by mentioning Gloria, but really it was the memory of his and Gloria's broken relationships with Fern that saddened him. He had disciplined himself not to dwell on it over the years, but seeing her again had brought the regret to the forefront of his mind. "Anyway, neither Fern nor I want the *haus* for ourselves, so we're going to—"

"When did you speak to Fern?"

"This morning. She was there, at the attorney's office."

"Oh, that's *wunderbaar*! How are she and her *kinner* doing?"

Walker shrugged. "Fine, I guess. I don't really know."

"You didn't inquire about her *kinner* or her life in Ohio?"

She probably wouldn't have answered me if I did. "It wasn't the right time or place, *Mamm*. We were there to discuss the will. Afterward she darted off to the restroom and I had to hurry back to work."

"I'm surprised at you, *suh*. There's always enough

time to catch up with a *freind*," his mother admonished him. "Especially when it's someone like Fern. She was such a tenderhearted *maedel* and the two of you got on well, if I recall. I even used to think you were courting her... I remember one time after *kurrich*, Roman told me he'd caught you sneaking down his lane in your buggy. I was sure you'd been there dropping off Fern, not Gloria."

Walker furrowed his brows. He and Fern had been even more discreet about their courtship than most Amish couples, mostly because they didn't know how Roman would react if he found out. There was nothing wrong with Walker being Fern's suitor, since they started courting when they were both eighteen and their behavior was completely respectable. But Fern always insisted Walker drop her off at the end of her street, even in the rain. It used to drive him crazy. "I won't melt," she'd coyly tease after they'd kissed good-night. "I'm already melted."

"I—I don't remember that," he said honestly, referring to Roman seeing him near the house. "I'm fortunate he didn't chase me off the property with a garden hoe."

"Oh, Roman wasn't that strict. He was just looking out for his *dochder*'s best interests," his mother said, causing Walker to swallow his tea wrong. He coughed into his sleeve as his mother asked, "Where is Fern staying while she's here?"

"She was at Jaala's *haus*, but now she and the *kinner* are going to spend the week at Roman's place."

"Didn't you tell me a tree hit his *haus*?"

"Grazed it, *jah*. It's only superficially damaged. A couple shingles missing from the roof, that's all. I'll patch it up this week and chop up the tree for firewood, too. Fern wants to put the *haus* on the market as soon as possible so I've got to get it ready for an appraisal and inspection."

"You ought to get started tomorrow, then. Jane will be thrilled to meet her *gschwischderkinner*. I'll bring a pie and we can all have lunch together."

Walker wiggled his leg. "*Neh*, we can't do that. There's a frolic at the Blanks' *haus*, remember?"

His mother's shoulders drooped. "*Ach*. I forgot. I don't know where my mind is. We'll have to visit her for supper on *Sunndaag* instead."

"I—I don't think that's a *gut* idea. You know how tiny Roman's *haus* is." When his mother squinted at him, Walker realized how unconvincing his excuse sounded. He embellished it, reasoning, "Besides, Fern is only here for a week. Roman left the *gaul* and buggy to the Fry *familye* so she doesn't have transportation to the grocery store. She probably won't have enough leftovers to feed us supper on the *Sabbat*. I don't want to embarrass her."

"Oh dear, you're right. Better we should invite her and the *kinner* here, instead."

"*Neh!*" Walker uttered.

His mother set her teacup in its saucer and cocked her head at him. "What in the world is wrong with you, *suh*? Fern was a member of our *kurrich* and she and her *kinner* are the only relatives Jane has left from Gloria's side of the *familye*. Why wouldn't you want them to meet each other?"

"I—I—I—" Walker's cheeks were blazing. For lack of any other plausible excuse, he said, "If I'm helping you host Fern and her *kinner*, I can't go for a walk with Eleanor Sutter on *Sunndaag*."

His mother pulled her chin back as if she couldn't believe her ears. Walker didn't blame her; he couldn't believe his *mouth*. But that's what happened when he was desperate—he panicked and made a rash decision.

Louisa replied, "You go ahead and have *schpass*. I'll host Fern and the *kinner* myself, but you'll have to give us all a ride home before you pick up Eleanor."

Why didn't I think of that before I opened my big mouth? My entire purpose in going for a walk with Eleanor after kurrich *was so I could avoid any close contact with Fern.* Walker wished he could take it back, but it was too late to change his plans now. "Okay."

As he rose to leave the room, his mother beamed at him. "It's *wunderbaar* you're going to try courting again, *suh*."

"Going for a walk with a woman isn't the same thing as *walking out* with her, *Mamm*," he emphasized.

Despite his mother's pronounced hinting over the past several years, Walker had adamantly refused to even consider courting anyone again. What was the point, since he had no intention of remarrying?

But if he ever *had* been open to the possibility of a courtship, it most definitely wouldn't have been with Eleanor Sutter, whom he found to be immature, gossipy and prone to complaining.

Oh well. Spending an afternoon with her wouldn't be nearly as uncomfortable as spending an afternoon with Fern. At least, he hoped it wouldn't.

Chapter Three

Fern woke on Saturday to the sound of her own stomach growling. The evening before she'd been disappointed to find Roman's pantry and cellar were completely bare. No canned fruit or vegetables, no salt or sugar, not even any flour for making bread. Uncertain if or when anyone would be visiting the house again, the women in the district had probably cleared the house of all foodstuff so it wouldn't spoil or so mice wouldn't get into it. *But that means there's less variety of food for me to feed my two little mice until we go to town on Muundaag,* Fern fretted as she gazed at Phillip and Patience asleep on either side of her.

Patience had gotten out of bed almost immediately after Fern tucked her in on Friday, claiming she'd heard something knocking against the rooftop and she was afraid another tree was about to fall. So Fern had given her permission to sleep downstairs for the night, planning to show her in the morning how sturdy the trees were. When Phillip learned he'd be the only one sleeping upstairs, he came into Fern's bed, too. Fern didn't want to make it a habit, but oddly, despite being elbowed in the ribs by Phillip and crowded by Patience, she had one of the best night's sleep she'd had in years.

She tried to ease out of bed but as soon as she sat up, Phillip popped upright, too. "*Guder mariye, Mamm.* Are we going to explore the yard today?"

She tousled his hair and replied in a hushed tone, "After breakfast and chores."

"What chores, *Mamm*?" Patience opened her eyes slowly. "There aren't any *hinkel* and this *haus* is so clean we can eat on the floor."

Fern suppressed a giggle at Patience's phrasing of the idiom. "There are a lot of fallen branches we need to pick up in the yard."

"If we find pine branches, can we decorate the *haus* for *Grischtdaag*? They don't cost any money. Please, *Mamm*?"

Fern winced; Phillip was too young to be so conscientious about their financial circumstances. "We won't be staying here until *Grischtdaag*. We're going back to Ohio next Saturday, which is December 23. But I suppose we can decorate anyway, as long as we take everything down before we leave."

After eating plain scrambled eggs for breakfast, the trio tromped outside. Patience and Phillip retrieved branches and twigs that had come down in the ice storm and brought them to Fern, who snapped them into smaller pieces and then stacked them in a heap beside the woodpile. Once they cleared the front section on the right side of the house, Fern suggested they trek up the hill in the backyard.

As they walked, Fern told the children about how she and Gloria would hike to the edge of the woods after they'd finished their morning shifts as house-keepers at the *Englisch* inn down the road. There was a large domed boulder there and they'd climb atop it with a picnic lunch. Afterward they'd take a shortcut through the woods to buy double-scoop cones of chocolate fudge brownie and cotton candy ice cream from a little Amish ice cream stand off of the main highway.

"Can *we* hike through the woods to get ice cream after lunch?" Phillip asked.

"*Neh, lappich,* it's too cold—the ice cream stand is closed for the winter," Fern said lightly, but the thought of it made her mouth water, too, especially since they were going to be eating eggs, beans and rice all weekend.

Fern realized Jaala had probably thought it would have been unfair to suggest the three of them attend the work frolic since they were only visiting, but Fern wished they'd been included. She knew what a de-lectable assortment of food the women would put out for everyone who came to help. Maybe there would be leftovers and they'd bring them to *kurrich* tomor-row. But even if there weren't leftovers, Fern was looking forward to the traditional after-church lunch, which consisted of cold cuts, cheese, church peanut butter, bread, pickles and pickled beets, homemade pretzels and dessert.

"Jaala usually brings spice *kuche* with cream cheese frosting to *kurrich*," she said, partly to herself and partly to the children. "We'll enjoy an *appenditlich* dessert tomorrow."

"Okay," Phillip agreed so good-naturedly it made Fern wish she could buy him an entire gallon of ice cream. "I want to roll down the hill anyway!"

"Be careful," Fern warned. "The ground's frozen."

Phillip had already dropped to his side. Bending his arms tightly against his chest, he spiraled down the hill like a log. Patience remained upright, traipsing behind him while clasping Fern's hand. At the bottom, they waited until Phillip regained his balance before they scoured the perimeter of the yard for fallen pine boughs and cones to decorate the windowsills, as well as to make a wreath.

They also collected wire, glue and fishing line from Roman's workshop. The Amish generally didn't embellish their Christmas greenery with elaborate bows or tinsel, but Fern decided their wreath needed a touch of color. So after lunch, she took the children across the road and down a hill toward a swampy area to search for wild winterberries.

"Sometimes moose like to roam in this area," she informed them. "They don't like to be frightened, so we should sing *Grischtdaag* carols, and that way they'll hear us coming."

They spotted the stunning red berries before

they'd even finished singing the second stanza of "Joy to the World," and in no time they'd collected enough to brighten the wreath and tuck into the boughs they'd arrayed across the windowsills. To their delight, Fern found candles—admittedly, in mismatched heights and shapes—in one of Roman's kitchen drawers. After carefully securing them among the arrangements on the sills, she lit their wicks and then hung the wreath on the door.

As the trio stood on the porch and admired their handiwork, Patience breathlessly exclaimed, "It's too bad *Onkel* Adam and *Ant* Linda and Emma and Thomas and Benjamin and Miriam and the *bobbel* can't see how pretty our *haus* looks."

Fern fought the impulse to remind her daughter they were only staying there temporarily. Instead, she suggested, "Maybe you and Phillip could draw pictures of the *haus* to show to your *gschwischderkinner* when we get back to Ohio. But first we need to eat supper."

After their meal—this time Fern served fried eggs with their rice and beans—she did the dishes as the children drew on the back of the junk mail envelopes Fern had pulled from the box earlier that afternoon, since that was the only paper she could find. Then she gave each child a bath and put them to bed in their own rooms. All the outdoor activity must have worn them out because they fell asleep without any fuss.

After bathing and washing her own hair, Fern retreated to the living room to read from her uncle's Bible. It was so quiet that each time she turned a page, she was keenly aware of the sound of the paper rustling. For as often as she wished she and the children had a space of their own, Fern found herself longing for another adult to talk to, and by the end of the evening she could hardly wait to go to church—even if it did mean she might cross paths with Walker again.

Sunday dawned warmer than usual, which made walking to church especially pleasant. Fern, Phillip and Patience had just arrived and were hanging up their coats in the foyer when a voice from behind them asked, "Fern, is that you?"

She turned to find Walker's mother standing behind her with outstretched arms. "Hello, Louisa," she replied, giving her a swift embrace.

Fern had always liked Walker's mother, but she was concerned that if Louisa had just arrived, it meant Walker couldn't be far behind. Usually the men and women entered the church and sat separately during worship services in her district in Ohio, but here in Maine, the families sat together. Figuring Walker had dropped Louisa off near the door, Fern inched backward, hoping to take a seat before he entered the building, but Louisa had her cornered.

"I was so surprised to hear you were in town. I'm sorry it was a sad situation that brought you here, but I'm glad to see you again."

Fern couldn't honestly say she was glad to be there, so instead she replied, "*Denki*. It's *gut* to see you, too." Then she introduced Phillip and Patience to Louisa.

"Your *gschwischderkind*, Jane, can't wait to meet you," the older woman told them and gestured toward the door off to their left. "Here she comes with her *daed*."

Fern mechanically turned toward the door. When she saw the little girl holding Walker's hand, her breath snagged and her knees went soft. Despite the age difference, Fern felt as if she could have been looking at her cousin, instead of at her cousin's daughter; Jane's dark hair, round face and pert brown eyes were identical to Gloria's.

"Jane, this is Fern, your *mamm*'s *gschwischderkind* I was telling you about."

"*Guder mariye,*" Jane replied cheerfully, revealing two missing teeth when she grinned. Walker added his greeting to his daughter's, but Fern could scarcely reply to either of them. Seeing Jane had simultaneously sparked loneliness for her cousin and anger at both Gloria and Walker. As irrational as the notion was, especially in light of how she felt toward Walker now, Fern couldn't help thinking, *This was supposed to be* my kind *with Walker, not Gloria's.*

"*Guder mariye,*" Fern finally repeated. She pulled Patience and Phillip in front of her body, like a shield. "This is my *dochder*, Patience. And this is my *suh*, Phillip. *Kinner*, meet Jane, your *gschwischderkind*."

The children said hello to each other and then Phillip gazed up at Walker. "Are you our *onkel*?"

"*Neh*. Walker is Jane's *daed* but he's no relation

to us." Fern spat out the words as if they burned her tongue. "Not like your *onkel* Adam is anyway. You should just call him Walker."

Walker could hear the indignation in Fern's voice when Phillip mistook him for being the children's uncle, but he tried to shrug it off. "Hello, Patience. Hi, Phillip," he said to the two small children, and their warm replies compensated for Fern's frostiness.

With her pale complexion, wispy stature and gentle smile, Patience was definitely Fern's daughter. But Phillip looked nothing like her. *He must take after his* daed, Walker assumed. Judging from the boy's dark, curly hair and healthy physique, Walker could only guess Fern's husband had been handsome and strong. Hadn't Jaala once mentioned he worked in construction? A stab of envy caught Walker off guard and his jaw went tight.

"I'm pleased we caught up with you before anyone else did," Walker's mother said. "We'd like you to *kumme* to our *haus* after *kurrich* so the *kinner* can get to know each other better."

Fern visibly blanched. "I—we—we—" she stammered.

Louisa seemed oblivious to her discomfort. "I'd love to hear about your life in Ohio. It will just be us women, though, since Walker is going—"

"Hiking," Walker cut in, mortified at the possibility his mother may have been on the brink of telling Fern he was going for a walk with Eleanor.

When Fern still didn't accept the invitation, Louisa added, "I made a peanut butter cream pie just for the occasion."

"Peanut butter cream pie?" Phillip marveled. "That's my favorite pie in the world."

Fern placed her hand on his head. "You mustn't interrupt adult conversation, *suh*," she said.

"I'm sorry, *Mamm*. My mouth made me interrupt because it loves the taste of peanut butter cream pie so much."

Fern's cheeks pinkened but Walker's mother let out a hearty chuckle. "Then that settles it, doesn't it, Fern?" she pushed.

Walker was incredulous. *Can't* Mamm *see how reluctant Fern is to* kumme *to our* haus?

"*Denki*, we'd enjoy that," Fern politely conceded. "Excuse me, but I need to use the restroom before worship service begins. *Kumme*, Phillip and Patience."

Just like yesterday, Fern couldn't seem to get away from Walker quickly enough. *It's not as if I want to keep company with her, either*, he thought.

"I'll take your *kinner* inside with me so you can have your privacy," his mother offered. "We usually sit in the fourth or fifth row from the back on the right side of the aisle."

Walker recognized the look of alarm in Fern's eyes, but she deferred to his mother's authoritative tone. *"Denki,"* she said and bustled toward the stairwell.

"I'll show you the bench I like best because it's near the window." Without a moment's hesitation

Jane took Patience's hand as if they'd been friends all their lives. Phillip followed the two girls and Louisa followed him, which put Walker at the end of the line.

He assumed that was the same order they'd sit on the bench, but instead his mother commented over her shoulder, "I'll sit on the far side so we can sandwich the *kinner* between us and keep an eye on them."

Once Fern sees me at this end, she'll go sit on the other side of Mamm, Walker assured himself. But right before Fern returned, an elderly couple, the Knepps, took a seat next to Louisa, so there was nowhere else Fern could sit except next to Walker. The group already occupied almost the entire bench as it was, so he shifted closer to Phillip in order to give Fern more room. She folded into herself as usual, taking up no more space on the bench than her son, but she was still close enough for Walker to smell the lavender scent of her shampoo. He quickly redirected his focus to the worship service.

A few minutes after the singing ended and the sermon had begun, Phillip put his hands flat on either side of his legs and pushed his arms straight, lifting his feet from the floor and his bottom from the bench. He balanced this way for an impressive amount of time before his arms gave out and he dropped onto his backside again, jostling his sister beside him. The commotion caught Fern's attention and she leaned forward to peer down the aisle, waving a finger at her son. Phillip sat straight up again and so did Fern.

Walker gave her a sidelong look. Now that she was only wearing a *kapp* instead of a bonnet, he could take in her profile, which, save for a line or two cupping her pale pink lips, hadn't changed since he'd last seen her. From her flaxen-blond hair to her equally light eyebrows and eyelashes to the sprinkle of freckles across her straight nose, almost everything about Fern's face was understated. Everything except for her big gray eyes. Depending on her mood, they sometimes appeared flinty and cold, but more often than not, Fern's eyes glimmered like polished silver. "Like precious coins," he used to describe them. Walker jiggled his knee; he usually hung on every word of the sermon but today he was impatient for it to end. Being so close to Fern was unnerving him.

"Your *mamm* is going to scold you if you keep fidgeting like that," Phillip whispered loud enough for everyone around them to hear. Fern immediately bent forward to see past Walker again, a finger pressed to her lips. In response, Phillip slapped his hands over his mouth, bunched his shoulders to his ears and nodded affirmatively.

Walker stopped shaking his leg but laughter gripped him from the belly upward and he had to bite the inside of his cheek to keep it from escaping his lips. The more he tried to control his amusement at Phillip's mischievousness—or maybe it was just nervous laughter—the harder his body quaked. Fern, meanwhile, was posed as rigidly as a statue. *She must think I'm setting a* baremlich *example.*

Walker could sense Phillip's eyes on him, so he

looked down and winked. Phillip grinned. Then, when Walker set his mouth in a serious line, crossed his arms over his chest and lifted his face toward the deacon, the boy copied him. *No matter how I feel about his* eldre, *I really like this* bu, Walker thought.

After the service, the three children took off to play outside with Jaala's grandchildren, and Fern and Louisa went downstairs to the kitchen to help prepare lunch. Walker helped the other men stack the benches atop each other so they could be used as tables the *leit* would stand around as they ate. Then he headed outside to see if the two men in charge of watering and feeding the horses that week needed any help, but he happened to spot Eleanor on the top landing of the stairs. Not surprisingly, she was loitering with her eyes closed and her head tipped toward the sun instead of assisting the other women with the food preparation.

Walker regretted that he was going to have to ask to pick her up later instead of offering to give her a ride home from church and stopping on the way to take a hike. Somehow, calling on her at home made it seem more deliberate. More like a date.

"It's a pretty day," he remarked awkwardly. "Warm."

She opened her eyes and blinked at him. Or was she batting her lashes? "*Jah*, it is. I've had a cold so I'm soaking in some vitamin D."

"I thought it was vitamin C you were supposed to take when you had a cold." Walker hadn't asked a woman to spend the afternoon with him since...

since he'd courted *Fern*, but it wasn't nerves that was making him procrastinate like this. It was dread.

Eleanor, who was nearly as tall as he was, nudged his shoulder. "Sunshine doesn't have vitamin C in it, *schnickelfritz*."

"I know. That's what I meant—" Walker didn't bother to explain further. Taking a deep breath, he forged ahead, saying, "Since today might be the last of the nice weather, would you like to go for a ride to Serenity Lake? We could take a walk on the trail through the woods."

Eleanor lifted her eyebrows. "*Jah*. Walking with Walker—what a way to while away the day!" she said, giggling at herself.

Walker was already getting a headache. "I'll pick you up at two. Would you mind meeting me at the end of your lane, near Pinewood Street?"

Eleanor bobbed her chin up and down. "Ah, I get it, you don't want anyone to know we're courting."

Courting? I never said anything about courting.
"*Neh!*" he protested. "I mean, *jah*, you're right, I don't want anyone to know that I'm picking you up, but—"

Eleanor's brother, Henry, hopped through the door at that moment. "Hey, Walker. Do you want to go hunting with Otto and me? It's the last weekend of expanded archery season and Otto said he'd show us how to use his compound bow."

Walker wasn't especially interested in learning to use the bow, since he couldn't imagine himself ever buying one, but tagging along in the woods with Henry and Otto would have been preferable to spending the afternoon with Eleanor. Or with Fern. Once again, he realized in his haste to avoid an unpleasant situation, he'd missed out on a better opportunity that would have accomplished the same purpose. *When will I learn?*

"He can't," Eleanor piped up. "He's going for a hike with me."

For crying out loud! Walker should have known there was no need to worry about other people seeing him alone with Eleanor and spreading gossip—she'd beat them to the punch.

"Voll schpass," Henry said, implying his sister was joking. He knuckled Eleanor's arm as if they were Jane's age instead of in their twenties. "So, how about it, Walker?"

"I—uh—I really am going on a hike with Eleanor," Walker admitted.

Henry's mouth dropped open. "Oh. Okay…"

"You're *wilkom* to join us."

"He is not!" Eleanor objected.

"I already told Otto I'd go with him," Henry said. Then lifted his nose in the air. "Smells like they're bringing the food upstairs. I'm going inside to grab a spot at the table."

"I'll *kumme*, too." Although the *leit* sat together with their families during church, the men and women ate lunch separately afterward, and Walker was glad for the excuse to get away from Eleanor.

"See you at two o'clock," she said with an exaggerated wink. "I can't wait."

"See you," Walker muttered.

* * *

After Fern helped serve lunch to the men and children, she took a place at a table with Jaala and Jaala's daughters-in-law. She'd briefly caught up with some of the other women she used to know as they were preparing the meal together, and she supposed she ought to get to know the newer members of the district, too, but she felt emotionally spent and she still had a long afternoon ahead of her. As the women around her chatted vivaciously, Fern wondered, *How did I get roped into going to Walker's haus?*

She knew the answer. It wasn't politeness that had kept her from turning down Louisa's invitation; it was peanut butter cream pie. Fern didn't want to deny her son the pleasure of eating something he loved so much, something he never got to indulge in at Adam's because Emma was allergic to peanut butter. Besides, Fern understood why the children wanted to play with their cousin, and she didn't mind spending the afternoon with Louisa, either. But what vexed her was *where* they'd be spending it.

Before Walker broke up with Fern, they'd take long walks through the woods or sit on the shoreline of Serenity Lake, daydreaming about the house he'd build for her once they were married. He'd even sketch its design in the sand with a stick. And then he'd draw a garden in the front yard that contained flowers nearly as tall as the house itself because Fern once told him that when she was young she rarely lived anywhere long enough to see the gardens she'd helped plant come up the following year.

It was upsetting enough to meet the dochder *Walker had with Gloria*, she lamented. *Now I have to spend time in the* haus *he built for Gloria? It's like rubbing my nose in the fact he married her, not me.*

Fern instantly felt terrible for having such thoughts. *What kind of petty person begrudges her deceased* gschwischderkind *a* haus? *Besides, Walker didn't invite us over—Louisa did. And she never knew anything about my courtship with him, so it's not really that anyone is trying to make me feel bad.*

"Are those beets too vinegary?" Jaala asked, causing Fern to realize she had puckered her mouth into a knot.

"*Neh*, they're *gut*," she answered. But after eagerly anticipating lunch since the day before, Fern had suddenly lost her appetite and she struggled to finish her meal.

A few minutes later as she and Walker's mother herded the children across the lawn toward his buggy, Louisa directed, "You sit up front with Walker. I'll join the *kinner*."

Fern would have preferred to run alongside the horse rather than to sit next to Walker again today, but out of respect for Louisa's age, she acquiesced. *If I made it through a three-hour* kurrich *service sitting next to him, I can survive a short ride to his* haus.

As they began rolling down the steep hill, Fern strained to hear what was happening in the back seat; Jane's voice was barely audible as she recited the verses she'd learned for her school's Christmas program to Louisa, Phillip and Patience.

"I wonder if Serenity Ridge will have a white *Grischtdaag* this year," she heard herself saying absently.

"We might. It flurried on *Freidaag* and I'm told there could be a nor'easter headed our way toward the end of the week, but I'd never guess it judging from how warm it is today," Walker replied, briefly twisting in her direction.

Fern had always thought he looked especially handsome in his dark winter wool hat, but now his neatly trimmed sideburns, mustache and beard gave his rectangular-shaped face a maturity he hadn't had before, and their burnished color made his green eyes appear more vivid than ever. She shivered, despite the warmth of the sunshine streaming in through the buggy's storm front.

Flustered, she babbled, "I'm glad it's so nice out— it means the *kinner* will be able to run around outside and burn off some of their energy. I'm sorry if Phillip distracted you in *kurrich* today. He has a hard time sitting still."

Walker chuckled. "That's to be expected for a *bu* his age, especially one who is so athletic. He's strong, too—he must take after his *daed.*"

"*Jah*, he does. I—I mean he *did*… I mean *jah*, he's husky and tall like Marshall was." Fern didn't know why, but she felt uncomfortable talking about her former husband with Walker. She'd feel even more uncomfortable talking about *Gloria* with Walker, but she recognized she somehow ought to acknowledge her cousin's passing. It would have been odd to offer condolences, especially after so much time, so instead Fern touched on the subject indirectly by remarking, "Jane is very sweet. She looks exactly like Gloria did."

"I think so, too," Walker agreed. "And Patience looks exactly like you. She has your eyes."

It was undoubtedly intended to be an innocuous comment, but it made Fern recall how Walker used to compliment her on the color of her eyes. "They're so silvery they shimmer," he'd say. "It's as if they're lit from inside."

"If that's true, it's only because they reflect how *hallich* I feel whenever I'm with you," she'd banter back, unabashedly saccharine.

But that was ages ago. Fern was a different person now, and if her eyes reflected anything it was how overwhelmed she was. She had expected that coming back to Serenity Ridge and facing the past would be difficult, but she didn't think it would be *this* difficult. And she certainly didn't think she'd have to make small talk with Walker about their children or the weather, as if nothing had ever happened between them. As if Walker hadn't shattered her heart to bits.

Just then, Patience's melodic giggle rose from the back of the buggy, followed by Phillip's boisterous laughter, and then Jane said something Fern couldn't quite hear but it caused everyone to laugh harder.

It's only one afternoon, Fern reminded herself. *And I'm doing it for the* kinner. She could do just about anything for her children.

* * *

Walker noticed Fern recoiling from his remark. He sensed he shouldn't have expressed his observation about Patience's eyes being like her mother's, but he wasn't sure why not. It was meant to be a compliment, but clearly Fern didn't take it that way; she shifted in her seat to stare out the other side of the buggy and journeyed the rest of the way in silence.

Once they reached the house, Walker let everyone off in front before continuing down the long driveway toward the barn. There was no sense unhitching Daisy because Walker was only going to run into the house and change out of his church clothes before leaving again. When he was courting Fern and they'd go for a walk after church, Walker always stayed in his best Sunday attire, but today he didn't want anyone—least of all, *Eleanor*—to get the impression he was behaving the way a potential suitor would behave toward a woman he wanted to court.

He replenished the wood bin and stoked the fire before bidding goodbye to his mother and Fern, who were already sipping tea in the living room. Outside, he carefully navigated the buggy past Jane, who was letting Patience and Phillip take turns riding her yellow scooter up and down their paved driveway. While he loved how welcoming and generous his daughter was, Walker hoped she wouldn't get too attached to Fern's children; after today, he didn't want them playing together. Mostly because he didn't want to have to spend another afternoon with Fern.

Nor did he want to have to spend another afternoon *avoiding* Fern.

Especially not if it meant hanging out with Eleanor, who seemed determined to extend her time with Walker for as long as possible. Once they got to the lake, she tiptoed along the path through the woods at a snail's pace, regaling him with a story about helping her nephew memorize his verses for the Christmas program. Even after they'd reached the water and scaled a large, flat boulder that provided the perfect vantage point for viewing Serenity Lake, she blathered on and on.

Walker alternately murmured "hmm" or chuckled when it seemed she was waiting for his response. But his mind was light-years away as he recalled stargazing from this very rock with Fern shortly before she left for Ohio. They'd had a rare argument because Walker didn't want her to go but Fern maintained her aunt had no one else to care for her. Which wasn't exactly true—she had her son, Adam, but at the time he was still on his *rumspringa* and was living out his rebellion among the *Englisch* somewhere in Dayton.

"You know what *Gott*'s word says about caring for people in need, especially in our *familye*," Fern had wept. "Please understand why I have to do this, Walker."

Walker *had* understood. Fern's sacrificial care for those who were sick and help for those who needed help was one of the qualities he'd loved most in her. "Just promise you won't stop loving me while you're gone."

"I'll *never* stop loving you," she'd claimed and Walker had believed her. But that was before his world literally came crashing down around him...

"Yoo-hoo," Eleanor sang, snapping her fingers in front of his nose. "Penny for your thoughts."

"They're not worth that much," he said wryly, shaking his head. "*Kumme*, it's getting late. We'd better head back to the buggy now."

He scooted down the rock on his behind, and then reached for Eleanor's hand so she wouldn't slip on the boulder's icy sheen. *The last thing I need is to be responsible for anyone else getting hurt*, he thought ruefully.

Eleanor prattled all the way home and by the time Walker stopped on Pinewood Street to drop her off, his head was buzzing.

"*Denki* for a pleasant afternoon," she said as she stepped down. "I'm looking forward to Wednesday evening."

Wednesday? Walker had been distracted through most of Eleanor's twaddle so he couldn't fathom what she was referring to until he was halfway down the street. *Ach! She must be going to the* Grischtdaag *program at the* schul, *too*, he realized with an ache in his stomach that rivaled the one in his head. *Oh well, at least talking isn't allowed from the audience during the presentation. Afterward, I'll just have to grab something to eat and make myself scarce.* Which was the same strategy he intended to employ when he got home in a few minutes, too.

Chapter Four

As uncomfortable as Fern was initially about spending the afternoon at the house Walker built for her cousin, once she got there her qualms diminished. Whether it was because it was located in a residential area and was much smaller than Fern expected it to be or because it seemed more like Louisa's home than Gloria's, whatever envy or bitterness Fern might have felt fell to the wayside. The house was just a house, and she grew increasingly relaxed being in it after Walker left.

It helped that the children were getting along so well, too. They spent nearly every minute of their visit with Jane outdoors running around or learning how to use her scooter. Patience took a spill and although her mittens and winter coat cushioned her hands and elbows, she scraped one of her knees and tore a hole in her long stockings. Fern was amazed Patience hadn't cried at all and she figured her daughter was doing her best to prove she could hold her own among the older kids. At home she usually pulled back when the other children were doing something physically challenging, so Fern was happy to notice this small change in her behavior.

Phillip, on the other hand, was his usual risk-taking self. With his hat abandoned and his coat unbuttoned, he sailed up and down the driveway on the scooter long after the girls decided to take a rest on the porch. He zipped back and forth so quickly Fern would have gone outside to warn him to slow down but he was as adroit as he was fast, maneuvering the scooter as easily as if it were an extension of his own body.

Meanwhile Fern enjoyed hearing updates about Serenity Ridge from Louisa, as well as news of Louisa's children, especially since Fern had gotten to know Walker's sister fairly well when she lived in Maine. In fact, Fern had first met Walker after Willa invited her to a quilting sister day at their house. Fern remembered how Walker had gotten in trouble with Louisa for helping himself to the peanut brittle Fern had brought before any of the women at the gathering had a chance to taste it.

Later, although he'd had plans to go bowling with some of the other single men in the district, his mother urged him to give Fern a ride home since it was raining and no one else was headed in her direction. Once they were courting, Walker confessed how disappointed he was because Fern had cut their conversation short that afternoon, asking to be dropped off several blocks from Roman's house.

She recalled feeling as if she could have talked to him all afternoon, too—a stark contrast with how she felt during today's buggy ride.

"It must be close quarters with seven *kinner* and three adults living together in a small *haus*, isn't it?" Louisa asked at one point.

"*Jah*, but we're used to it," Fern replied, forcing a bland smile.

She shied away from questions like these about her living situation. It wasn't that Walker's mother asked her anything especially private, but Fern assumed anything she said could be repeated and she didn't want Walker to know how much she'd struggled over the past couple of years. It was a matter of pride and pride was sinful but there were still certain topics—such as her financial challenges—Fern didn't wish to disclose.

She had hoped Louisa would serve the peanut butter cream pie in the late afternoon so she, Phillip and Patience could begin their long trek home before the daylight waned, but the children remained outside for so long the older woman said she'd serve the pie after their meal.

Fern hadn't planned on staying at Walker's home through supper, but Louisa's leftover roast beef, mashed potatoes and gravy were a welcome change from rice and beans. And now that Walker wasn't around, Fern's appetite was really kicking in, so she eagerly set the table while Louisa heated the food.

"Walker told me not to wait for him if he wasn't

home by five, but let's add a plate just in case he shows up," she suggested.

Sure enough, just as everyone was settling into their chairs, they heard footsteps on the porch.

"Perfect timing, *suh*. Hurry and go wash your hands—we'll wait to say grace," Louisa instructed, causing Fern to wonder if she'd still be reminding Phillip to clean up for supper when he was Walker's age.

When he returned to the room, Walker took the open seat at the foot of the table to Fern's left. "I'll pray," he volunteered.

Before everyone could bow their heads, Jane piped up, "Let's hold hands."

Fern and Phillip automatically joined hands but she hesitated before sliding her fingers onto Walker's open palm. As he gently curled his fingers around hers, she remembered all the times they'd sat knee to knee, hand in hand, praying about their relationship. It was through prayer that they'd come to believe they were God's intended for one another. *How could I have been so mistaken?* Fern wondered.

As everyone began passing serving bowls around the table, she once again felt too queasy to eat. Phillip, however, was clearly ravenous.

"*Suh*, there are five other people at the table," Fern said under her breath as the boy scooped himself a huge serving of mashed potatoes.

"There's plenty more where that came from," Louisa said with a wink at Phillip. "As long as you eat what's on your plate, you can take as much as you like."

"Where did you go on your hike, *Daed*?" Jane questioned.

"Through the woods by Serenity Lake." Walker answered tersely, as if he didn't want to talk about it.

That's probably because he only left so he wouldn't have to be around me, Fern thought. Noticing he hadn't cracked a smile since he'd arrived, she figured he was disappointed to discover she, Phillip and Patience were still there. She hoped Louisa intended to bring them back to Roman's house so Walker wouldn't feel further inconvenienced about having to give them a ride.

"You went hiking alone? That doesn't sound like *schpass*," Jane commented.

Walker avoided a direct answer, replying, "I'm sure you three *kinner* had a lot more *schpass* being together, right?"

"*Jah.* We went horseback riding."

Walker's eyebrows jumped up. "On whose horse?"

"Not a real one—we were pretending the scooter was a horse. Phillip even let go of the reins with one hand."

"While your horse was trotting?" Walker asked Phillip, sounding impressed. Fern was surprised he was playing along; maybe she had misjudged his mood.

"*Neh*, it was running full speed," Phillip blustered, causing Fern to cover her smile with her napkin. "My *hut* flew right off but that's okay because my head usually gets too sweaty anyway."

"My head gets sweaty, too, especially when I have to wear a helmet for work," Walker commiserated. Then he asked Patience if she let go of the horse's reins with one hand, too.

"*Jah*, but I fell off," Patience admitted softly as she struggled to cut her meat with her fork. Walker reached over and sliced the roast beef for her.

"Did you get hurt?" he asked so compassionately, Fern's heart bloomed with unexpected fondness.

"My knee bleeded a little and I ripped my stockings," Patience answered. "*Mamm* will have to sew them because I'm not big enough to wear Emma's hand-me-down stockings yet."

Fern cringed at her daughter's revelation of just how poor they were, but Jane piped up, "You can have my hand-me-downs, can't she, *Groossmammi*?"

"I don't think Patience wants your old stockings, Jane," Walker interjected. "They *schtinke*."

"*Daed!*" Jane exclaimed. Then she addressed Patience, saying, "My stockings don't really *schtinke*. Not after *Groossmammi* washes them anyway."

Patience giggled and Louisa spoke up. "I actually think you have a few dresses you've outgrown. We can take a look in the trunk after supper. I may have stowed them away for quilting but it would be a much better use of the material if Patience could wear the dresses."

"I never get to hand down anything because all my littler *gschwischderkinner* are *buwe*," Jane explained sadly, as if she'd been cheated of an important privilege.

"That's too bad," Patience sympathized before turning to Fern. "Did you get to hand down your clothes to Jane's *mamm* when you lived together?"

"*Neh*. Gloria was taller than I was, even though she was younger. But one time she gave me a pretty lilac dress of hers. She took up the hem first."

"*Groossmammi* said my *mamm* didn't like to sew and she'd do anything to get out of it."

"That's true. But she took the hem up anyway as a surprise because she really wanted me to have the dress." Fern remembered this with affection. Gloria was as nearly as poor as Fern was, but she was always generous with whatever she had. Fern saw that same personality trait in her daughter, even if her mother had perished before Jane was old enough to copy her behaviors. *Maybe that characteristic is to Louisa's credit. Or to Walker's.* "Your *mamm* was very generous," she told Jane.

"What else was she like?"

Fern hesitated only briefly before singing Gloria's praises. In light of how kind Walker was being to her children, she knew she couldn't be stingy-hearted about Gloria in front of Jane, who understandably wanted to hear more about her mother from someone who'd known her well. "Your *mamm* was a very hard worker. And she looked just like you—she had the same deep brown eyes. She loved to sing and she had a very pretty voice."

"*I* love to sing. For the *Grischtdaag* program we

learned lots of carols. I can sing one for—" Jane began to say but Walker cut her off.

"There's no singing at the table, remember?"

"We can sing it on the way to your *haus*," Jane promised Patience.

"I don't think you should ride with them," Walker contradicted. "You need a bath before bedtime."

"Please?" Jane implored her grandmother, not her father. Fern noticed Louisa often had the final say in family matters and she wondered if it ever bothered Walker.

"It won't take very long to go to Roman's *haus* and back," Louisa reasoned, addressing her son. "If you leave right after dessert, there will be plenty of time for Jane to take a bath when you return."

If Walker was taken aback to be told he was giving Fern and the children a ride home, it didn't show on his face. He grinned at Phillip, suggesting he accompany him to hitch the horse, and the boy happily traipsed after him into the mudroom.

Meanwhile, Louisa went off in search of Jane's hand-me-downs and Fern and the girls cleared the table and rinsed the dishes. Just as they were finishing, Louisa returned with three dresses that she said she'd include in a bag full of ingredients for Fern's pantry since she knew the women in the district had completely emptied Roman's cupboards.

"You don't need to do that. We're walking to the store on Main Street tomorrow," Fern politely declined.

"It's supposed to rain tomorrow. Just take a few

things so in case you don't go, you'll still be able to make fresh bread."

Fern was tickled to receive flour and fresh eggs, and she noticed the woman wrapped up the last piece of pie for Phillip, too. The children helped her carry the bags to the buggy, where Walker loaded the items into the back of the carriage. After tucking a blanket around the children, he unfolded one for Fern, too.

"Warm enough?" he asked after she'd spread it over her lap.

"Not yet," she used to answer when they were courting. He'd hand her a second blanket, inch closer to her on the seat and ask again. "*Neh*, not yet," she'd always reply. Then he'd slide close enough to wrap his arm around her from the side. "There," she'd say, snuggling against him. "*Now* I'm warm enough."

The memory brought heat to her cheeks and she couldn't help but wonder if Walker remembered it the minute the words were out of his mouth, too. She quickly answered, "*Jah*, I'm fine. *Denki.*"

Then she began jabbering on about how her *Ordnung* in Ohio had recently begun allowing propane heaters in buggies but Adam didn't consider them safe, much to Linda's consternation, and the couple would have the same argument almost every Sunday they traveled to church, which was a terrible way to begin the Sabbath. Fern had no idea where she was headed with her story but fortunately, the children broke into a Christmas carol, which interrupted Fern's nonsensical ramblings and spared

Walker from having to reply. The five of them sang all the way to Roman's house.

"*Denki* for bringing us back," she told him when he dropped them off. "You can feel free to use whatever tools you need from the barn tomorrow, of course. We'll probably be gone when you *kumme*."

At least, that's what Fern had planned, although it no longer seemed imperative to avoid the very sight of him. *I might not want to spend time alone with him, but with the* kinner *present, being in Walker's company is rather pleasant*, she thought.

In the morning, she woke to a hard rain hitting the windowpanes. Or was it sleet? In either case, Louisa had been right; the precipitation meant they wouldn't be walking into town that morning.

"Can Jane *kumme* to our *haus* to play?" Patience asked as she dug into her French toast at breakfast. They didn't have any syrup, but Fern had brought a small jar of strawberry jam in her purse to make sandwiches on the way from Ohio, so they spread that on the top of their French toast. It felt like such a treat.

Fern wished her daughter would stop referring to Roman's house as *their* house. "*Neh*. She has to go to *schul*, remember?"

"After she gets out she could *kumme* for supper," Phillip chimed in.

Fern appreciated how much her children wanted to spend more time with their cousin, but it would mean Walker would have to accompany Jane. Even if Fern was finding it easier to be around him, she was on such a strict grocery budget she doubted she'd be able to afford to buy meat from the store in town, and she couldn't imagine serving Walker the kind of meal she *could* afford, especially not after he'd worked up an appetite sawing and chopping wood all afternoon.

"*Neh.* If the rain stops, Jane's *daed* is going to be here chopping up the trees in the afternoons. So he'd have to go all the way to the *schul* and then *kumme* all the way back here with Jane. Then after supper he'd have to go all the way to their *haus.* I don't think he'd want to do that."

"I can ask him when he gets here," Phillip offered.

"*Neh!* You're not to talk to him about it," Fern snapped. She immediately felt bad and added, "But when he arrives, I'd appreciate it if you'd tell him he can use the stable so his *gaul* doesn't have to stand in the cold."

"Maybe I should ask him if he needs help with the tree, too," Phillip suggested.

"I don't know about that. He might be using dangerous equipment." Fern tousled her son's hair. "But once the sky clears, we'll all go outside and pick up branches from the other side of the *haus.* That will be very helpful."

But the rain kept up all morning, and by lunchtime Fern wondered if Walker would be coming at all. However, he showed up around one-thirty even though it was still drizzling. Since Phillip had to tell Walker about stabling the horse anyway, Fern allowed both him and Patience to go play outside for a while.

"Just stay away from Walker while he's working. If he's using a chain saw, he won't be able to hear you coming."

She watched through the window as Phillip ran to Walker's buggy wagon, the vehicle Amish men used to transport their larger equipment and supplies. Phillip was gesturing animatedly as he spoke, and watching him, Fern felt a pang of wistfulness. Phillip could hardly remember his own father, and he'd been asking a lot of questions about him lately. Fern wished he had a stronger male influence in his life. There was Adam, of course, but he had five children of his own and he worked such long hours he was rarely home as it was.

Fern sighed and ambled into the kitchen to make more bread—she intended to make eggs on toast for supper. She was glad they'd each had a good helping of broccoli the night before at Louisa's house, but Fern really needed to get to the store so they'd have more variety in their diet.

The revving of the chain saw disrupted her thoughts, and Fern set aside the bowl and wooden spoon to peek out the window and make sure the children weren't getting too close to Walker. But they were on the opposite side of the house, gathering branches and stacking them by the woodpile.

Marshall would have been pleased to see they're becoming so helpful, she mused. Once, when he realized it was only a matter of weeks before he succumbed to cancer, Marshall expressed concern about Phillip's future without him. "Patience has you to help her grow into womanhood, but who will Phillip have to teach him how to be a man?" he'd asked. "I hope you'll consider remarrying after I'm gone. Don't wait too long—a *bu* needs a *daed* to shape his character most when he's young."

He'd said it so matter-of-factly that Fern would have been appalled, but she knew that was how Marshall expressed himself. He was just being practical and he made a fair point, but Fern had no intention of marrying again. She'd married out of necessity once, but she wouldn't do it a second time, not even for her son's sake. *Maybe when I get back I could pair Phillip up with one of the men from* kurrich *and he could help with yard work or a carpentry project...*

Fern's mind wandered as she kneaded the bread dough. Then she molded it into a big round lump, plopped it in a bowl and draped a dishcloth over the top before setting it by the woodstove so it would rise nice and high. Wiping her hands on her apron, she discreetly peered out the window again—she didn't want Walker to think she was spying on him.

Fern noticed Patience was standing to the side of the house, her neck craned upward, but Phillip was nowhere in sight. She looked out the other window, but she still didn't see him, so she opened the door and walked to the end of the porch.

"Patience, where's your *bruder*?" she called.

Patience pointed to the large section of tree that had toppled and was wedged upside down between the ground and the trunk, forming a sharp incline. Fern gasped when she spotted Phillip, who had climbed halfway up the branch like a bear cub.

Flying across the yard in her stocking feet, Fern screamed, "Phillip, you stay right where you are!"

She needn't have worried; bent at the waist, the boy was frozen in a half-standing, half-crawling position. He gripped a small side limb with one hand and supported his torso with the other. His feet were planted against the trunk in such a way that his legs were extended straight up and his bottom stuck out.

"I'm stuck, *Mamm*," he said when she got closer. "The bark is too slippery for my boots. I can't move."

"Hold on, I'll *kumme* get you!" she shouted as she pulled her socks from her feet so she'd have traction. As soon as she began scaling the broken tree, her skirt twisted around her legs. Trying to kick free, she lost her footing and would have fallen to the ground were it not for Walker's arms encircling her.

"Absatz!" he barked into her ear and set her upright on the frozen earth.

"Let me go!" She pushed his hands from her waist. "Can't you see my *suh* is in danger?"

"I do see," Walker said in a low voice despite the panic rising in his chest. "I also see this branch is in a very precarious position. Any more weight on it and it could split from the trunk. Phillip could get hurt and so could you."

They both eyed the young boy. His legs were beginning to shake from being fixed in the same position for so long. Sweat collected on the nape of Walker's neck. He shifted so he was standing beneath Phillip, who he estimated was about twelve feet from the ground.

"Roman must have a ladder in the barn. Go get it," Walker commanded Fern. He wasn't sure she could carry it herself, but he was positive if Phillip fell, she wouldn't be able to catch him, so Walker had to stay right where he was, posed to catch the boy himself if Phillip's endurance gave out.

"My legs are tired. I'm going to fall," Phillip whimpered.

"*Neh*, you aren't. You're a very strong *bu*. I noticed that about you right away," Walker told him, just as the tree creaked. The ladder was a bad idea— they couldn't put any more weight against the branch. Besides, with his body situated as it was, Phillip wouldn't be able to shift onto the ladder by himself.

"I've got it!" Fern yelled as she and Patience dragged the ladder across the frozen ground.

Phillip turned to look over his shoulder toward his mother.

"Don't look at your *mamm*—look down here at me!" Walker barked. "Listen to me and do just what I say. When I tell you, I want you to hold on tight with your hands and lower yourself onto your belly. You're going to walk your feet backward like this."

Walker crouched onto the ground below the branch and imitated the movements he wanted Phillip to copy. Then he said, "Once your belly touches the trunk, then you're going to wrap your legs around it. Okay, now."

Planting himself below the branch with his arms upstretched, Walker prayed, *Please, Lord, keep him from falling. Please, please, please don't let the branch break.*

"That's right," he encouraged the child as Phillip eased his feet backward until his stomach was almost resting on the trunk of the branch. His foot slipped and he instinctively wrapped his legs around the branch, which bounced from the force of the sudden shift of his weight. Walker continued to coax him. "That's *gut*. Now, you just hug that tree for a moment until you catch your breath." *And until I catch mine.*

"He's too heavy. It's going to break." Fern was at Walker's side trying to upright the ladder. "We have to get him down from there."

Walker wrestled the ladder from Fern's arms and nearly knocked over Patience in the process. He didn't have time to explain. Through gritted teeth he commanded her and Patience to clear the area before turning his attention to the boy again.

"Okay, Phillip, now I want you to swing your body around so you're hugging the tree from beneath the branch. I know you've probably let yourself down from a tree the same way before, right?"

"*Jah*, one time I did. But this tree's a lot higher."

"That's okay. I'm going to be standing right under you so if you fall, I'll catch you."

Once the boy had maneuvered so he was twisted

to the underside of the branch, Walker instructed him to dangle his legs. He had to work quickly, knowing the boy could lose his grip at any second. "You're being very brave. As soon as you dangle your legs, I'm going to count to three and then you're going to let go with your hands so I can catch you. Ready?"

Phillip followed his instructions perfectly and Walker managed to grab him right beneath his armpits, breaking his fall. The tree limb bounced upward and Walker yanked Phillip out of the way, just as the huge branch crashed down a couple yards to their left. Pieces of branches and bark flew up around them. Patience screamed and ran toward the house.

"Phillip!" Fern sobbed as she rushed to embrace her son.

"I'm okay, *Mamm*," he said, patting her back. "I'm okay."

In just that amount of time, all of Walker's concern and fear turned into irrepressible fury. "*Jah*, you are okay this time, but you could have been beneath that branch instead of standing here with your *mamm*!" Walker roared, pointing at the tree branch, his arm shaking. "Don't you ever, ever play by a cracked tree again, do you hear me?"

Phillip's lower lip trembled and his eyes welled, but Walker figured he'd rather the boy cry now than risk his life again in the future.

Fern released her son and pounced toward Walker like a lioness. "And don't *you* ever, ever yell at my *kind* like that again!" she warned, glaring up at him.

"Somebody has to—you obviously haven't taught

him how dangerous it is to fool around on fallen trees!"

"Well, that somebody sure isn't *you*. You're not his *daed*!" Fern retorted. She shot him a final withering look, spun around and plucked her stockings from the ground where she'd shed them. She pulled Phillip with her as she made her way to the porch, where Patience was crouched on the steps with her head buried in her arms.

That's the thanks I get for rescuing her son? Fine! Leaving the ladder lying on its side, Walker wasn't going to stand around and be treated like that. He retrieved his chain saw and stormed toward the stable, where he piled his tools into the back of his buggy wagon, hitched the horse and then headed for home. His chest was so tight he felt as if it would burst open if he so much as inhaled, and there was a terrible racket in his ears, as if the chain saw were still abuzz. Halfway home he had to pull off to the side of the road because he got sick to his stomach.

He's okay, he told himself, wiping his mouth with the back of his hand. *Phillip's okay. He's not Jordan. He's okay.*

When he came through the door, his mother immediately questioned, "Why are you home so early? I thought you were going to work on the trees in Roman's yard."

"It's raining," he said, even though it was barely drizzling. "And I don't feel great. I'm going to take a shower." But afterward, Walker felt like he couldn't get warm again. He was still shivering as he set out to pick up Jane from school.

"Guess how many days until the *Grischtdaag* program?" she asked. "I'll give you a hint. It's less than three but more than one."

"Two," he said absently, pushing up his hat to rub his temple. Whatever Jane chattered on about for the rest of the ride, he didn't know. His mind was somewhere else; his mind was in the past. Despite all the times he'd prayed for the Lord to help him let it go, Walker feared the past would never be completely behind him.

He spent the rest of the afternoon in a daze, but he snapped to attention at supper time when Jane asked, "Can I invite Phillip and Patience and Fern to *kumme* to the *Grischtdaag* program?"

"That's a lovely idea," Louisa agreed.

"Neh," Walker said at the same time.

"Why not?" Jane asked.

"You know better than to question an adult's decision. Now eat your green beans," Walker said firmly, pointing at Jane's plate.

His mother started to object but Walker scowled at her and she went silent. He appreciated how much help his mother had given him raising Jane, but sometimes he resented it that Louisa seemed to think her decision was the only one that counted. It was as if Walker were still as much of a child as Jane was.

After Jane was in bed, Louisa told him, "I need to go shopping tomorrow when you're done at the tree farm. If you pick me up on the way to Roman's *haus*, I'll ask Fern and the *kinner* if they'd like to go with me, since she likely didn't walk into town in the rain today."

"Fine." Walker preferred Fern and the kids weren't anywhere near him when he was working anyway.

However, avoiding them physically and avoiding thinking about them were two different matters, as Walker later discovered when he closed his eyes to sleep and images from the afternoon filled his mind. He'd put himself in harm's way to deliver Phillip from danger—and to keep Fern from experiencing the kind of sorrow Jordan's parents had suffered—and all she could do was berate him for scolding Phillip?

Amish parents frequently corrected each other's children as if they were their own, especially when they were jeopardizing themselves or someone else. Walker couldn't help but think if any other man had reprimanded Phillip after rescuing him, Fern wouldn't have flown off the handle the way she'd done today. Her words, "you're not his *daed*," echoed in Walker's mind. Her tone was so bitter it was almost as if she were blaming him for the fact her son's father died. Or maybe what she was really blaming him for—what she was really pointing out, once again—was that he'd married Gloria, not her.

Even though she doesn't know I never wanted to marry Gloria, isn't it time Fern got over her anger at me and moved on? Walker brooded. But considering how long he seethed into the night, he could have been asking himself the same question.

Chapter Five

Fern was so upset she hardly slept a wink. First, she was distressed because of the fright Phillip had given her. Second, she was livid because Walker had yelled at him and criticized her for being a bad mother. *Does he really think I'd allow my* kinner *to take unnecessary chances?*

That was a laugh—half the time, Fern fretted she was being *overly* protective of the children, especially of Phillip. And Walker was wrong if he thought she didn't admonish her children when they did something they shouldn't have done. But Fern hardly thought screaming at her son the instant after the branch practically came crashing down on his head was an appropriate way to handle the situation. So she waited until the following morning to discuss the incident with Phillip.

After breakfast she sat him down in the little front room and asked, "Do you remember what I told you about playing by the fallen tree?"

"*Jah*. You said not to play under it," Phillip somberly recited her instruction. "So I didn't. I only climbed on top of it."

Seeing his earnest expression, Fern realized he wasn't being cheeky—he had taken her directions to heart, word for word, and he guilelessly thought he'd obeyed them. It wasn't the first time. In Ohio, Fern recently had permitted the children to go outside after a rainstorm, but since she'd just scrubbed the kitchen floor she said they'd better not track even a speck of dirt into the house when they returned. Long after the rest of his cousins had come inside, Fern found her son on the porch, using his shirt hem to wipe the grooves of his boots. He was very literal-minded at this stage and he honestly tried his best to do what was asked of him. Fern couldn't fault him for that. She could only help him develop his comprehension.

"Why didn't I want you to play under the tree?" she asked, hoping to teach him to come to logical conclusions.

"Because the wind could blow it down on my head."

"*Jah*. Or it could have shifted on its own. If that happened and you were under it, you could have gotten crushed. But if you were on top of it, you could have fallen and broken your bones." Fern paused, giving him a chance to take in what she was telling him. "Next time I forbid you to play *under* something, I also mean don't play *on* it or anywhere *near* it. Otherwise, you could get hurt, and that would break my heart because you and your *schweschder* are the most precious things in my life."

Phillip nodded. "I'm sorry."

"It's okay. I know you won't do it again. But why did you climb it in the first place?" Fern was curious because Phillip rarely climbed trees at home, even though his cousins frequently did. He seemed to prefer speed over height and was more likely to spend his time outdoors hurdling fences and racing the goats.

Phillip studied his hands on his knees as he admitted, "Jane said the *Englischers* pay her *daed* to climb trees and cut their branches down. He doesn't just chop up the fallen parts."

His reply took Fern's breath away. *Phillip climbed the tree to impress Walker—to show Walker he could be like him!* In light of that realization, Fern grew even more incensed over how harshly Walker had reprimanded the child. It was one thing for Walker to crush *her* feelings the way he'd done, but for him to hurt her son's feelings was unconscionable. *What's wrong with him, losing his temper like that? Can't he see how much the* bu *looks up to him?*

Fern kissed Phillip's forehead and told him to scoot upstairs to make his bed, but she couldn't dismiss her acrimony toward Walker so easily, even though she prayed about it as often as the feelings of ill popped into her mind. *If there's any consolation in all of this it's that I recognize now more than ever what a mistake it would have been to marry him,* she thought. *Marshall wasn't perfect, but at least we saw eye to eye about how to raise the* kinner.

She planned to wait until right before Walker arrived to go to the store so she and the children wouldn't be at home while he was working in the yard. But after lunch Patience was so droopy she asked if she could lie down for a little while. To Fern's surprise, Phillip said he was tired, too, so both children crawled into their beds for a nap.

A few minutes later, Fern heard Walker's carriage pull into the yard. Rather than glancing out the window, she continued reading from her uncle's Bible until Walker knocked on the door. *He's probably here to offer an apology*, she thought. But since she didn't feel prepared to accept it, she dallied before opening the door.

She found Louisa, not Walker, standing on the doorstep. "Hello, Fern. I have to get groceries and I'm going to the superstore. Would you like to *kumme*?"

Fern bit her lip, hesitating. Although she'd prefer to limit her time with Walker's family, the superstore was so much cheaper than the market in town. "I'd appreciate that. The *kinner* are taking naps, but please *kumme* in and I'll get them up."

"*Neh*, don't wake them. I have time for a cup of tea first," Louisa said, even though she hadn't been offered one. Fortunately, Fern had four tea bags left over in her travel bag, which she surreptitiously retrieved while Louisa was using the bathroom.

After the water came to a boil, Fern poured the

older woman and herself each a cup. "I'm sorry I don't have any honey. Do you take sugar?"

"*Jah.*" Louisa dumped a heaping teaspoon into her cup and stirred the steaming liquid. "They say we're going to get a snowstorm this weekend. I hope it doesn't start up on *Samschdaag* before we leave for Willa's *haus* in Unity. She's expecting us for *Grischtdaag.*"

"I hope it doesn't start on *Samschdaag,* either," Fern said. "We're scheduled to leave in the morning, too." *And I don't want anything to prevent us from going.*

"It's such a shame you can't stay longer. Jane loves being with her *gschwischderkinner* on Walker's side of the *familye,* but lately she's been curious about her *mamm,* especially since Roman died. Walker doesn't talk to her enough about Gloria, if you ask me. So it's been *wunderbaar* for her to meet you and to spend time with Phillip and Patience."

"They've enjoyed it, too," Fern murmured. What was Louisa expecting her to say? That she hoped they could get together again? Fern didn't plan on the children spending any more time together; she wanted to keep them as far away from Walker as possible.

But Louisa didn't broach the topic again. Instead, she rocked silently in the chair, frowning at the cup in her hands for so long Fern finally asked, "Is something wrong with the tea?"

"Oh, *neh,* dear. I'm sorry. I'm just so sleepy.

Walker kept me awake last night. He was shouting in his sleep."

He did a lot of shouting during the day, too. "Did he have a nightmare?"

"I imagine so, but he clammed up when I broached the topic. Funny, but he hasn't had one that bad since..."

Despite how angry she was at Walker, Fern wanted Louisa to finish her sentence. It sounded as if Walker suffered nightmares repeatedly. *Probably the sign of a guilty conscience.* "Since when?"

"Since right after the accident, when he was living at home still. I thought the terrors, as I call them, were from the concussion, but the doctors told me sometimes they can be a reaction to trauma," Louisa explained. "Which was understandable, considering his friend died right next to him. He was in such a dark mood for a long time afterward."

"Hmm," Fern murmured sympathetically, but she was thinking, *He wasn't so grieved that he postponed his wedding to Gloria.*

As if Louisa had read Fern's thoughts, she said, "I probably shouldn't be telling you this, but I pleaded with him not to marry Gloria—I didn't think he was in his right mind. But he was so insistent I began to think maybe marrying Gloria would help him. Instead, he seemed worse after that. She told me he had the terrors almost every night—they had to sleep in separate rooms for fear his thrashing would injure her or the *bobbel*. It wasn't until Jane was born that the nightmares subsided and Walker began to seem more like his old self again. Or at least not as depressed. I think becoming a *daed* helped him heal."

Fern swallowed. It wasn't easy hearing about how impatient Walker had been to marry Gloria, and there was no way Fern could chalk up that decision to his head injury because that would have been letting him off too lightly. She didn't relish hearing how happy it made Walker to have a baby with Gloria, either. But she understood why fatherhood would have changed his perspective, since having children had increased her joy, too.

"I haven't heard him yell out like that in his sleep during the entire time I've lived with him here, though." Louisa clucked her tongue against her teeth. "He's been so sullen these past couple of days, too. I don't know what's triggered it again after all this time."

Fern's hand trembled, causing her cup to rattle against its saucer. *She* knew what triggered Walker's terror: the incident with Phillip climbing the tree and the branch breaking. *That's* why Walker reacted as he did. He must have been reliving Jordan's accident. Fern should have known because being in the house where she'd tended to Roman had caused her to relive many upsetting memories, and they were minor compared to Walker's trauma.

"I think I know what's triggered it," she said softly. Then she described what had happened the previous afternoon, stopping short of telling her about how Walker had reacted afterward.

"Oh, that might explain it," Louisa acknowledged.

"Walker works for the tree trimming company nine months out of the year, and being around falling limbs never seems to faze him. I guess the difference is that yesterday someone's safety was at stake. Maybe the situation with Phillip brought back memories of Jordan."

A shudder racked Fern's body as the full weight of Louisa's words sank in. *Walker wasn't* angry *at Phillip—he was* frightened *for him.* She glanced out the window. "He must be freezing out there. I think I'll take him a cup of tea before I wake the *kinner.*"

"*Gut.* That will give me a chance to take a little snooze," Louisa said, leaning her head back against the rocking chair.

Fern filled a mug and donned her coat, eager to apologize to Walker and to thank him for saving her son's life.

When Walker saw Fern coming toward him out of the corner of his eye, he reluctantly turned off the chain saw he'd borrowed from his employer. He expected her to chew him out again, but instead she smiled and extended a mug.

"It's warm."

"*Denki.*" He took a swallow.

"Sweet enough for your liking?" she asked, and for a moment he thought she was facetiously referring to her change in attitude. "Two sugars, right?"

Had she remembered that's how he took his tea or had his mother prepared it for him? Knowing Louisa, she'd probably *ordered* Fern to bring it to him, too. *"Jah."*

"Gut. Because after my behavior yesterday, I figured you probably need something warm and sweet," she said, dipping her head and tapping at the frozen ground with the toe of her boot.

What brought this on all of a sudden? Now Walker *really* suspected his mother's interference.

"Listen, I'm sorry for getting so angry at you for yelling at Phillip," she apologized. "I realize now how frightening it must have been to see him in a potentially perilous situation like that considering… you know, your accident."

So *that* was it. His mother heard him shouting in his sleep the night before and she told Fern about his nightmares. But Walker didn't need Fern's sympathy—he needed her to appreciate what a foolish thing her son had done by climbing the broken section of the tree.

"Yelling at Phillip had nothing to do with Jor— with the accident. I wasn't frightened—I was angry," he firmly informed her. "He shouldn't have been climbing the tree and quite frankly, I blame you for that. You should have warned the *kinner* to keep away from it the minute you came to stay here."

"I *did* warn them to keep away from it!" Fern protested, her eyes flashing.

"So he was deliberately being disobedient? Then he probably needs a man to teach him how to make better choices instead of just having his *mamm* coddling him after he's misbehaved."

"That's true. He does need a man to teach him. Not to intimidate or holler at him, but to *teach* him," Fern retorted. "Unfortunately, his *daed* is dead, so he's left with me. I'm doing my best…" Her eyes were brimming and Walker felt terrible, knowing his words had brought her to the brink of tears. She took a deep breath before continuing, "Phillip climbed the tree because he wanted to impress you, Walker. Don't ask me why, but for some reason, he admires you."

She spun on her heel to leave but Walker swiftly reached for her arm. "*Neh*, wait. Don't go." She wouldn't turn to face him but she stopped walking. "You're right. I overreacted. Wh-what happened with Phillip did remind me of—of the accident. I lost my temper at him because I'd never want another *elder* to suffer the way Jordan's *eldre* suffered after they lost their *suh*."

Now Fern twisted around, her slate-gray eyes still watery as she searched his face. "You've suffered deeply, too, haven't you, Walker?"

Jah, but not only because Jordan lost his life—but because I lost the life I dreamed of having, too. His voice was barely audible when he replied, "Not nearly as much as his *familye*."

"You've still suffered."

"The Lord has healed much of my sorrow."

"But it still grips you sometimes, when you least expect it, doesn't it?"

What else had his mother been telling her? Walker took a step backward. "How do you know that?"

"From being with people I care about who were

ill. Who were dying." Fern shivered. She paused before changing the subject. "I'm sorry for not thanking you for rescuing Phillip yesterday. I don't want to think about what would have happened if I had climbed the tree or used the ladder to try to get him down myself."

I don't want to think about that, either. Walker's voice trembled as he expressed contrition, too. "I'm sorry for criticizing you as a parent. From the little bit I've witnessed, I can see what an excellent *mamm* you are, although I appreciate how difficult it must be raising the *kinner* on your own."

"I'm not really raising them on my own—Adam and Linda help."

Remembering all Fern had done for her relatives, Walker doubted Adam and his wife were as much of a help to Fern as she was to them. "My *mamm* helps me, too, but sometimes, I could use a little *less* help, if you know what I mean," he joked about his mother's bossiness.

Fern giggled impishly. It was the first time since she'd been back that Walker had heard her laugh, and he hoped it wouldn't be the last. "Speaking of your *mamm*, I should get inside now. The *kinner* are probably up from their naps, and Louisa is taking us shopping."

"Okay," he said, although he regretted their conversation drawing to a close. He handed her back the mug, wryly thinking, *Jah, that was* definitely *warm and sweet enough for my liking.* And by that, he didn't mean the tea.

* * *

Inside the house, Fern found Louisa helping Patience button her coat as Phillip was pulling on his boots.

"Did you have a *gut* rest?" she asked.

"Jah," Louisa answered. Fern smiled; she'd actually been asking the children, but she was glad to hear Walker's mother had had a refreshing cat-nap, too.

When they got outside, Walker approached. "Hi, *kinner,*" he said cordially, as if nothing ever happened the day before. While Phillip returned Walker's greeting, Fern noticed the boy averted his eyes until Walker asked, "Hey, Phillip, instead of going shopping with the women, can you give me a hand here? I can't cut wood and stack it, too."

Phillip puffed up his chest. "I can stay here, can't I, *Mamm*? Walker needs me."

"Jah. Just steer clear of the saw and do whatever Walker tells you to do." Filled with gratitude for Walker's kindness, Fern caught his eye and mouthed the word *denki*. When he winked in return, she felt her cheeks burning all the way to the superstore.

Once there, she and Patience separated from Louisa, agreeing to meet back at the buggy when they were done shopping. Fern placed a small ham in her cart, as well as milk, oatmeal and frozen vegetables. She would have preferred to buy fresh produce, but frozen was cheaper and she wanted to have enough money to bake a dessert to have on hand in case Jaala and her grandchildren came by. Or to offer Walker.

In case he needs sustenance while he's doing all that work outside, she told herself.

Snickerdoodles were easy and inexpensive, but since there was a sale on peanuts, she decided to make peanut brittle instead, since the children had never tasted it. After collecting the necessary ingredients, as well as a few more staples, Fern estimated her total bill. Thanks to the meals and pantry items Louisa had shared, Fern figured she had enough money left over to purchase a warm pair of stockings for Patience, so they swung by the clothing department before checking out.

Louisa took longer to shop than Fern did, so by the time the older woman circled back to the buggy, it was so late they had to go directly to the school to get Jane. Patience, who was usually such a wallflower in new surroundings, surprised Fern by asking if she could wait on the stairs for her cousin to come outside. She balanced on the bottom step, hugging the newel post until the doors opened and the children flooded out. Then she moved off to the side until Jane came trudging down the stairs. Although Fern couldn't hear their conversation, she could tell by the big hug Jane gave Patience that she was tickled to see her there.

"Hi, *Groossmammi*, hi, Fern," she greeted them when the girls climbed into the buggy. "I thought *Daed* was going to pick me up."

"Isn't it nice that we've *kumme* instead?" Louisa prompted.

"*Jah.* It's *schpass* to be with just *meed* for a change," Jane chirped from the back seat.

"Your *daed* and Phillip are probably at home saying how much *schpass* it is *not* to be with just *meed* for a change," Fern joked.

"They might think so, but they don't get to eat *kuchen* like we do," Louisa said. Then she instructed her granddaughter to open the package of shortbread cookies and pass them around. "Don't tell. It's our little secret."

"What is?" Fern teased. "That we're eating *kuchen* before supper or that you bought the *kuchen* instead of made them yourself?"

"Both," Louisa said with a hearty laugh, and Fern was pleased her fretful mood had lifted.

When they got back to the house, Louisa went inside to warm up, and Jane and Patience carried Fern's groceries to the porch so Fern could check in on Walker and Phillip.

"Wow, you've made some *gut* progress here," Fern complimented them. Phillip's cheeks were ruddy but he didn't stop piling small logs into the wheelbarrow.

"That's because many hands make light work," Walker said. "Or even an extra pair of hands makes light work when the hands are as capable as Phillip's."

The girls ran up at that moment, calling, "Hi, Phillip!"

"Hi," he said over his shoulder as he tossed another log into the wheelbarrow.

"Do you want to go race down the hill with us?" Jane asked.

"*Neh*, I'm working."

"Actually, Phillip, I think we're done for the day. You can go play with the *meed*," Walker suggested.

Phillip lifted his hat to wipe his brow. "You sure you can manage wheeling this load over to the wood-pile by yourself?"

Walker bit his lip and Fern stifled a chuckle, too. "I think I can handle it. *Denki* for all your help today."

"You're welcome. I'll meet you here the same time tomorrow," Phillip said as if he were Walker's hired hand. Then he was a young boy again, darting off and challenging the girls to beat him to the top of the hill.

"*Denki* for letting him stay with you. He really hates shopping," Fern said.

"No thanks needed—he was a huge help," Walker said, tossing a wood chip onto the tarp he'd spread nearby. "But I understand why he hates shopping. Especially at this time of *yaahr*. I can't stand it, either."

"Really? You never let on when I'd ask you to take me shopping. Remember that year I couldn't decide whether to get Gloria a stationery set or a glass pie plate for her birthday? You must have taken me to five different *Englisch* stores. You were so patient."

Walker's smooth mustache broadened with his grin. "How could I forget? After going back and forth and back and forth, you bought her teacups instead. Didn't they have flowers on them?"

"Tulips, *jah*."

The china was as beautiful as it was impractical, and Fern could only afford to purchase two cups and saucers. Gloria kept them hidden away in her bedroom because she said she didn't want her father to accidentally break them, although Fern suspected what she really feared was that Roman would consider the decorative pattern too "worldly." On special occasions after he went to bed, Gloria would take them out, and the girls would sneak upstairs so they could chat and drink tea in the elegant cups in private.

Thinking about it, Fern felt a hollow achiness deep inside. Despite what Gloria had done, Fern had loved her cousin. And she realized if she missed Gloria, Walker must have missed her three times as much. Feeling ashamed she'd withheld her condolences for this long, Fern uttered, "I loved Gloria deeply and I know you must have loved her even more. I'm sorry she's gone."

Walker's green eyes dimmed and his mouth settled into a straight line in such a way he almost looked angry instead of sad. In a low tone he said, "*Denki*. And I'm sorry you lost your spouse—sorry that Marshall died, I mean."

"*Denki*," Fern replied simply.

There was something about directly acknowledging Gloria's death that made Fern feel as if she'd taken a step closer to...well, not to reconciling the past, necessarily, but to being a little more at peace with it. And maybe even with Walker.

* * *

Fern headed inside and Walker delivered the final load of logs to the woodpile, reflecting on the exchange they'd just shared, as well as on their conversation from earlier that afternoon. As he considered Fern's comments, he realized he'd been underestimating her capacity for empathy, not only toward her cousin, but also in regard to how the accident had affected Walker.

If she can be that understanding of me, I can definitely be more charitable about Jane inviting her gschwischderkinner *to the* Grischtdaag *program,* he thought. *Especially now that Fern and I are getting along better.*

So, after he'd stowed the chain saw and wheelbarrow in the barn, Walker called loudly in the direction of the backyard, "Jane! *Kumme* here!" All three children came scampering from around the house.

"Do we have to go already?" Jane whined. "I just got here."

"*Jah*, but you can see Phillip and Patience again tomorrow night."

"*Neh*, I can't. Did you forget about the *Grischtdaag* program, *Daed*? It's tomorrow after supper."

"Ah, so it is." Walker scratched the hair on his chin. "Then I suppose you'll just have to invite them to the program."

The whites of Jane's eyes went as large as eggs. "But you said—"

Walker put a finger to his lips to shush her before saying, "Provided their *mamm* says *jah*, they can *kumme*."

"Let's go ask her. I'll race you!" Phillip was off like a shot with Jane close behind him, but Patience hung back, clearly tuckered out.

"I don't want to race, either," Walker said, slowing his pace so she could keep up with him.

After a few yards, she remarked, "*Mamm* says you know a whole bunch about trees."

Really? That was complimentary of her. "Maybe not a whole bunch, but I know a few things. Why— is there something you want to ask me about them?"

Instead of posing her question directly, Patience told him, "*Mamm* says if there was another tree in the yard that was going to fall, you would have seen it and chopped it down before we got here. She says it's only a little branch hitting my ceiling at night but that doesn't mean the whole tree is going to tip over."

Ah, now Walker understood. He stopped and pivoted in the direction of the tree nearest the house. After studying it thoughtfully, he said, "Your *mamm* is right. That's a very sturdy, healthy tree. It's just sort of waving its limbs around in the wind, kind of like you do when you're really happy to see someone or you want to get their attention. And it's so close to the roof, it taps against it, that's all. But if it keeps you awake at night, I can cut the branch down tomorrow." He began moving toward the house again.

"How?" Patience asked, slipping her hand into his and trotting alongside him just like Jane would have done.

"I'll use a tool called a pole saw."

"Will you have to climb the tree?"

"I'll go up on a ladder, *jah*."

Patience fiercely shook her head. "*Neh*, that's okay. I don't care anymore if it taps my ceiling."

It occurred to him that Patience didn't want him to go up in the tree because she was traumatized by Phillip's near accident the previous day, too. *If I'm going to climb any ladders or trees, I'd better not do it in her presence*, Walker decided as he and Patience caught up to Jane and Phillip on the porch.

"Look, *Daed*—they lit candles in the windows!" Jane exclaimed.

"The *haus* has never looked so pretty, has it?" Walker remarked. Roman didn't permit Christmas decorations; he thought they were too showy. It always disappointed Jane, just as it had disappointed Gloria before her.

Before he could rap on the door to let his mother know he was ready to leave when she was, Louisa and Fern stepped outside.

"Can we go to the *Grischtdaag* program tomorrow night, *Mamm*?" Phillip asked, hopping from foot to foot. "Jane invited us."

Fern hedged, "We don't have a way to get there and it will be dark—"

Louisa interrupted, "When he's done working here, Walker could bring you with him to pick up Jane from *schul* and then circle around to our house. We'd all eat supper and then we'd go to the *schul* together. Walker will bring you home, too."

Walker got the sense his mother had hatched this scheme even after he'd told Jane she couldn't invite Patience, Phillip and Fern to the program. But instead of feeling chagrined that she must have suspected he'd change his mind, Walker was glad she'd come up with the idea.

"*Denki*, that would be *wunderbaar*," Fern said. "Wouldn't it, *kinner*?"

"*Jah!*" they chorused, jumping up and down.

Walker's heart leaped, too, much like it had the very first time Fern accepted an invitation to spend an evening out with him.

Chapter Six

Fern was glad she'd purchased ingredients to make peanut brittle because now she'd have a treat to bring to the Christmas program to share with the other families. She also told Louisa she'd make scalloped potatoes with ham for supper. Louisa tried to object but Fern insisted, so the older woman said she'd prepare stewed tomatoes and green beans to go with the potatoes and ham. Which meant the meal would help compensate for the vegetables the children had been missing in their diet.

As Fern took a mixing bowl from the cupboard on Wednesday after they'd eaten an early lunch, Patience asked, "Can I help you bake, *Mamm*?"

"I'd appreciate that," she answered. "Do you want to help, too, Phillip? There are lots of potatoes to peel."

"*Neh*. I want to move the logs we didn't get to yesterday," he said as pushed one arm through his coat sleeve.

"Aren't you going to wait for Walker to get here?"

"*Neh.* The more I do now, the less Walker will have to do on his own once I leave," Phillip replied seriously.

As he headed out the door, Fern noticed he wasn't wearing his hat again, but she didn't remind him. He was right when he said it made his head sweat, and Fern was more concerned about him running around with wet hair than with cold ears.

"I wish I could be in a *Grischtdaag* program," Patience said a few minutes later as she spread butter around on a cookie sheet to keep the peanut brittle from sticking to it.

Patience was usually so bashful she wouldn't speak in front of a group of her peers, much less in front of an audience of strangers. There was something about her being with Jane that emboldened her in a way being around Emma didn't. Fern sensed it was that Jane was more tolerant, more encouraging, whereas Emma understandably tired of Patience shadowing her.

"Well, you'll get to be in one when you go to *schul.*"

"I wish we could stay here and I could go to *schul* with Jane."

"What about your *gschwischderkinner* in Ohio? Don't you want to go to *schul* with them?" Going to school with her cousins was something Patience had been anticipating ever since Emma started school.

"*Jah,*" Patience answered. "But they have lots of *kinner* in their *familye.* Jane doesn't have a *schwester.* Or a *bruder.* So she'd probably like it if Phillip and I went to *schul* with her."

Fern was touched that Patience was concerned Jane might have been lonely. At the same time, she had to keep her daughter's hopes about remaining in Serenity Ridge in check. "That's true. If we lived here, Jane would love going to *schul* with you and your *bruder*. We have to leave on *Samschdaag*, but I know Jane is very *hallich* you get to visit her *schul* tonight."

Patience held up the cookie sheet so Fern could make sure she hadn't missed buttering any spots. Fern pointed to a corner and Patience traced it with the stick of butter, asking, "*Mamm*, why don't you want to live here?"

"It's not that I don't want to…" Actually, it was. Fern started again. "We already have a home in Ohio."

"That's *Onkel* Adam and *Ant* Linda's home, not ours. Emma said so."

Fern tried not to let her annoyance come through in her tone. "Everything anyone has comes from the Lord. He's the One who gives us a *haus* to live in and a *kuh* for *millich* to drink and a *gaarde* of food to eat. All those things are His, but He shares them with us because He's so generous. So you see, the *haus* in Ohio belongs to *Gott* even more than it belongs to your *onkel* or *ant*. Or to Emma. *Gott* is just letting them use it for now. And they're sharing it with us."

Patience was quiet. After she finished buttering the corner of the cookie sheet, she set it flat on the table and asked, "Does this *haus* belong to *Gott*, too?"

"*Jah*." Fern smiled brightly, pleased her daughter understood her point. "It does."

"Then I'm going to pray and ask *Gott* if He'll let us live in it."

Inwardly, Fern groaned. She hadn't told her children anything about the inheritance or her plan to sell Roman's house and get a place of their own in Ohio. For one thing, it wasn't appropriate to include them in adult matters; for another, she didn't want them to get too excited too early in case her plans went awry. However, she was beginning to think it might be a good idea to tell them sooner rather than later. *Maybe I'll tell them at* Grischtdaag, *sort of as a gift.*

For the moment, she said, "Patience, all of our relatives are back in Ohio."

"Not all of them. Jane isn't." Patience was being unusually assertive. "Walker isn't."

"Walker isn't your relative." Technically, he *was* related, but only by marriage, and for some reason, the distinction was important to Fern.

"But if we lived here, maybe he'd ask you to marry him and then he'd be my *daed.*"

"Patience!" Fern yapped, slapping her mixing bowl down on the table. "I don't want to hear you talking nonsense like that again, do you hear me?"

Patience's nose went pink, like it did when she was cold, and her eyes simultaneously filled with tears. *"Jah, Mamm,"* she rasped. Then she fled the room, and the pattering of her footsteps as she scurried up the stairs tattered Fern's heart. Nothing hurt a mother more than causing her own children pain.

Why did I react so strongly? she reproached herself. *Am I really so worried she'll tell Jane about her absurd wish that Walker will marry me?* Even if she did and Jane repeated it to her father, Walker undoubtedly would have recognized it as being a child's fantasy, not an idea that originated with Fern.

Disgusted at herself for being overly sensitive, Fern washed her hands and dried them on her apron before climbing the stairs. She expected to find Patience curled up on the bed, but instead she was standing at the window, her back to the door. Although Fern couldn't hear her, she could tell by the way her daughter's shoulders were moving up and down that Patience was sobbing.

Fern sat on the bed. "Patience, *kumme* here. Please *kumme* sit with your *mamm.*"

Hanging her head, Patience edged toward her, stopping a couple of feet shy of her mother. Fern reached out to pull the girl onto her lap and cuddled her to her chest, the way she did when she was an infant. Whereas Phillip was always on the move—his restlessness even kept Fern awake during her pregnancy with him—Patience always liked being rocked. *How much longer will she let me hold her like this?*

"I'm sorry for snapping at you," she murmured into her daughter's fine hair. "I didn't mean to be so crabby."

Fern hummed, rocking a few minutes more before Patience pulled her head back to ask, "Don't you like Walker, *Mamm*?"

"*Jah*, he's our friend and he's been very helpful to

us," Fern answered diplomatically. "But two people need to *love* each other in a special way in order to get married."

Patience seemed to think this over before questioning, "Can I still ask *Gott* if we can live in this *haus*?"

"You can ask, but *Gott* might have another *haus* for us to live in. One that's in Ohio, close to *Onkel* Adam and his *familye*," Fern cautioned, planting the possibility in Patience's mind. "Now, we'd better get downstairs and finish making that peanut brittle or we won't have anything to share at the *Grischtdaag* program."

"Can I wear the dress Jane gave me tonight?"

Fern tapped her daughter's nose. "If we finish baking lickety-split so I can take in the seams."

By the time Phillip came in, the peanut brittle was beginning to cool and Fern had peeled and sliced all the potatoes. After guzzling down a glass of water, he remarked, "Walker will be *hallich* to see how many more logs I piled into the wheelbarrow."

It occurred to Fern that Phillip was becoming as fond of Walker as Patience was of Jane. *I'm glad they're forming a connection but I hope they don't get too close to their gschwischderkind or to Walker,* she worried. *Because if they do, no one knows as well as I do how difficult it will be for them to leave Serenity Ridge.*

Walker had reason to whistle on his way to Roman's house. For one thing, he'd slept through the night without stirring even once. For another, the customers he interacted with at Swarey's Christmas Tree Farm had been in such cheery moods it was contagious. Most importantly, his daughter's greatly anticipated Christmas program that evening was going to be all the more meaningful to her because Phillip, Patience and Fern would be in attendance—and there were few things in life that made Walker as joyful as witnessing Jane's delight.

When he arrived at Roman's house, Phillip was waving from the porch. Walker noticed the rest of the wood they hadn't collected yesterday was now stacked high in the wheelbarrow.

"Did you stack all those logs yourself or did you have a team of men helping you?" Walker asked once he'd unhitched and stabled the horse.

"*Neh.* I did it alone," Phillip answered, as if Walker sincerely suspected otherwise. "But I couldn't move the wheelbarrow myself. It's too heavy."

"Looks like it's pretty full. It might be too heavy for me, too."

"I could lift one handle and you could take the other side," Phillip suggested, but Walker figured they'd end up tipping the barrow, so he said he'd give it a try first.

After wheeling the logs to the woodpile, he told Phillip he had a very important job for him—holding the ladder while Walker ascended it. Before Walker began cutting up the smaller of the two trees that had been damaged, he wanted to trim the branch that was knocking against the roof above Patience's bedroom.

Since she was indoors, this was an opportune time for him to do it without her seeing him.

They retrieved the ladder from the barn and Walker's pole saw and two helmets from his buggy. "I doubt any branches will drop on our heads, but it's better to be safe than sorry," he told Phillip as he tightened the helmet strap beneath the boy's chin.

It only took a couple of minutes for him to saw through the small branch, and after Walker descended the ladder, he said, "*Gut* job. You've got a firm grip."

"I'm going to work construction like my *daed*," Phillip told him. "Or maybe I'll be a tree cutter, like you."

Over the years, Walker had occasionally imagined what it would be like to have a son to follow in his footsteps, but because he wasn't ever going to marry again, he'd trained himself to disregard the daydream as soon as it sprang to mind. However, working with Phillip gave Walker a glimpse of what he might have been missing, so he relished the opportunity to mentor the boy, if only for a few days.

The pair worked for nearly an hour and a half before Fern appeared on the front porch. She cupped her hands to her mouth and called, "Would either of you like a snack?"

Phillip answered for both of them. "*Jah*, we would!"

Walker trailed him into the house. They both took their shoes off at the door before following the mouth-watering aroma into the kitchen.

"We sure worked up an appetite," Phillip announced, and from the twinkle in Fern's eye, Walker could tell she found the child's adult mannerisms as amusing as Walker did.

"The potatoes and ham you smell are for later, but sit down and have some peanut brittle and *millich* to tide you over until supper."

"Peanut brittle?" Walker repeated. He pulled out a chair and seated himself next to Phillip as Patience tiptoed toward him, carefully balancing a small plate heaped with candy. He told her, "It looks and smells *appenditlich.* Your *mamm* always made the best peanut brittle in Serenity Ridge."

"Denki," Fern mumbled. "But I didn't make this myself. Patience helped."

"The piece on top is for you," Patience told him, holding the plate beneath his nose. "You get the biggest one because you cut down the branch above my window."

He smiled at the little girl as he selected the treat she'd indicated was his. "You saw me doing that?"

"Only for a little bit, and then I went into the kitchen with *Mamm.* She couldn't watch because it made her nerves afraid, too," Patience explained as she offered the plate of peanut brittle to Phillip.

Fern's nerves were frayed? Walker realized plenty of people were afraid of heights and he shouldn't take it personally that watching him had made Fern nervous, yet he was still touched by her concern for his safety. "I was fine. Phillip was holding the ladder nice and steady for me."

"That's because I'm getting practice for when I go to work," Phillip said, accepting a glass of milk from Fern. She set a glass in front of Jane and Walker, too, and then took a seat at the table across from him.

"Mind your teeth," she warned the children. "Peanut brittle is crunchy."

The four of them bit into their candy at the same time and Walker gave a contented moan when he tasted the buttery richness of the dessert. He took another bite and when he finished chewing, he told Patience in a magnified whisper, "Don't tell your *mamm* I said so, but this peanut brittle is even better than when she used to make it by herself."

Patience gave a self-conscious smile and leaned over to confide, "That's because we did something secret when we were making it."

"Did you add a pinch of love?" Walker guessed. He quoted a cliché Fern used to say: "Everything tastes better when it's made with love."

Phillip snorted. "That's *lappich*."

But Patience scrunched her eyebrows together in thoughtful consideration. *"Neh,"* she replied slowly. "If you put love in something you bake, it would melt."

It took every ounce of Walker's willpower not to crack up and Fern was covering her mouth, too.

Patience, fortunately, was oblivious. She took a swallow of milk before revealing, "The secret is you have to warm the cookie sheets first because that gives you extra time to spread the mixture on them."

"Aha!" Phillip pointed at her. "You just said what

the secret was. It's not a secret anymore." Patience's shoulders drooped as her brother laughed; it was the only time Walker had seen any hint of discord between them.

"That's okay," Fern comforted Patience instead of scolding Phillip for taunting her. "Most people are *schmaert* enough to know if they tell a woman's cooking secrets or criticize her baking, she'll probably serve them the smallest piece of dessert the next time she makes it."

"That's right," Walker confirmed, patting Patience's head. Then he ribbed Fern, "You *did* hear me say how *appenditlich* your peanut brittle is, didn't you?"

She rolled her eyes, but her riposte was playful. "Most people also know that flattery will get them nowhere. But if you want more, please help yourself, Walker."

"Denki," he said with a smug grin, reaching for the candy.

"What's flattery?" Phillip asked.

"It's when someone says something nice to you that they don't really mean."

"But I *did* mean what I said about your peanut brittle being the best in Serenity Ridge," Walker insisted. *I meant every word of everything I ever said to you.* With more seriousness than the conversation warranted, he looked directly at Fern and reiterated, "It wasn't flattery. It was the truth. I wouldn't tell you something unless I meant it."

In this light, Fern's eyes were pearly gray and as

she returned Walker's unblinking stare with an intense gaze of her own, it seemed she understood he was no longer discussing candy. "I believe you," she said, her voice barely audible.

She believes what? *That I wasn't lying about the peanut brittle or that I wasn't lying about how much I loved her?*

"*Kumme.*" Phillip tugged on Walker's sleeve. "We still have work to do outside, right, Walker?"

"Right," he answered, rising quickly. He wasn't sure what had just transpired between Fern and him, but whatever it was had taken his breath away. He needed fresh air and he needed it fast.

Because Patience volunteered to pick up stray wood chips and other debris near the fallen tree, Fern was left alone to finish hemming the dress from Jane. She was glad for the solitude, which allowed her to ponder Walker's reaction to her teasing. *He sure got awfully serious all of a sudden*, she thought. *It was as if I'd personally maligned his character just because I suggested he was flattering me about the peanut brittle.*

But deep down, Fern wondered if Walker's vehement response had less to do with food than with his feelings. When he said, "I wouldn't tell you something unless I meant it," could he have been referring to his past declarations of love for her?

As Fern deftly worked the needle in and out of the fabric, her thoughts continued to drift. What if Louisa was right, and Walker only married Gloria as a result of the trauma? It was possible his near-death experience had given him a sense of urgency about moving forward with his life. Maybe Walker had decided he couldn't wait for Fern to come back—that he wanted to be married and have a child as soon as possible, lest something else happen before he had the opportunity.

Suppose that's the case. What does it really change anyway? she asked herself. Even without understanding the reasons behind Walker's decision to marry Gloria, Fern had already come to a truce with him. What more did she need to know? The past was over and by this time next week, she'd be back in Ohio, hopefully researching new places to live. *How exciting that will be!* she mused, setting her mending aside.

Before calling the children inside to get ready for their outing, she took advantage of her time alone to wash her face, comb her hair and put on her good church dress without any interruptions. Then, as the children cleaned up and changed their clothes, she transferred the potatoes and peanut brittle into portable containers. Walker pulled up in front of the house just as Fern and the children opened the door.

"For me? You shouldn't have," he joked, taking the containers so she could climb into the buggy unencumbered.

Fern giggled, glad to put the strangeness of their earlier interaction behind them. Once everyone was seated and the buggy was rolling down the street, she began pointing out landmarks to her children, who leaned forward to look out the front window.

"That road leads past the ice cream shop I told you about," she said over her shoulder.

"You mean Brubaker's?" Walker asked.

"Jah."

"It's not there anymore. They moved back to Ontario the summer after you left."

"Really? That's a shame."

"It's okay, *Mamm*. Jane will show us a different ice cream shop this summer," Patience consoled her.

"This summer?" Walker sounded perplexed.

Fern surreptitiously tapped his arm and put a finger to her mouth, shaking her head. She didn't want to ruin the festive mood by reminding Patience they wouldn't be in Maine in the summer. In a voice loud enough for the children to hear, she asked him, "Where do people go to get ice cream cones in Serenity Ridge now?"

"We go to Foster's. They still have a shop on Lincoln Avenue."

Fern was familiar with the *Englisch* creamery, but she'd never been there herself. "Do they have cotton candy ice cream?"

"I don't think so."

"That's too bad. Cotton candy was Gloria's favorite flavor." Fern was surprised by how natural it felt to mention Gloria now. A little farther down the road, she told the children, "There's the street that leads to the library. Walker used to pick me up there when—"

Fern cut her sentence short, mortified she'd almost disclosed that Walker used to pick her up at the library when they were courting. They'd chosen that location because Roman never visited the library, so there was virtually no chance of him traveling down the small side road during the day. Fern's uncle was usually asleep by the time Walker brought Fern home, but Walker would drop her off at the end of the street by her house, just to be on the safe side.

Ever attentive to the smallest nuance, Patience asked, "When *what*, *Mamm*?"

"When it was raining and I needed a ride to visit our friends," Fern said. She quickly added, "He'd give Gloria a ride, too." Fern silently prayed Walker wouldn't elaborate on her response, which was technically true but shamefully misleading. Walker *had* picked Fern up in the rain. Occasionally Gloria accompanied them, too, and they continued on to attend singings with the rest of the youth in Serenity Ridge. However, more often than not when Walker picked Fern up, it wasn't raining and they were headed off to go hiking or out to supper alone, not with Gloria or anyone else. But Fern had never told the children that Walker had courted her before marrying Gloria, and she didn't want them to ever find out.

Patience was still puzzled. "Why didn't he pick you and Gloria up at *Onkel* Roman's *haus*?"

Fern's mouth went dry. To her relief, Walker replied, "Because the library was halfway between our *heiser* and both Gloria and your *mamm* loved to read. So they'd take the shortcut through the woods and read while they were waiting for me to *kumme* get them."

His answer relieved Fern and satisfied Patience, who sighed and said, "*I* love to read, too."

"*I* love to explore the woods," Phillip piped up. "Will you show us the shortcut tomorrow, *Mamm*?"

"Maybe. It depends on the weather."

"You'd better be careful," Walker warned. "There was a moose sighting in the woods before the ice storm. A bull, too, in broad daylight. Unusual for this time of year."

Overhearing him, Patience whined, "There's a moose in our woods?"

Even though Fern had told the children there might have been a moose wandering in the swampy area across the street from their house, she'd tried to present the possibility in a way that indicated the moose would be scared of *them*, not that they should be scared of the moose.

Walker must have heard the fear in Patience's voice because he punned, "Well, if there is, he's probably a *Chrismoose*, so you'd better leave some *Grischtdaag kuche* out for him!"

Phillip cracked up and Patience giggled, too, but Fern anticipated the damage had been done; before Patience's bedtime, Fern was going to have to field a lot of questions about moose. *At least it will be better than answering any more questions about Walker picking me up in his buggy*, she thought.

When they arrived at the school, it was still in

session, so Phillip and Patience hopped out of the carriage and ran to wait on the staircase for Jane.

"Sorry about that," Walker said to Fern, giving her a sheepish look. "I shouldn't have mentioned the moose in front of Patience."

"It's okay." Fern wanted to apologize for what she'd said about him picking her up at the library, but she would have felt awkward alluding to their courtship again.

Setting his gaze on the schoolhouse door, Walker nonchalantly asked, "What did Patience mean about going to the ice cream shop in the summer? Have you reconsidered selling the *haus*?"

"What? *Neh!*" Fern exclaimed.

Walker leaned back in the seat and Fern couldn't read his expression by his profile. Was he relieved? Disappointed? "Are you sure? Because if you did change your mind, that's fine with me."

"Fine with you?" she repeated dumbly.

"*Jah.* I mean, even though we told Anthony we were going to sell it, it's not too late to make other arrangements. The Lord has, ah, blessed me monetarily, so it's not as if I'm counting on the sale…"

Oh, so that was it. Walker was only letting her know if she changed her mind, it wouldn't put him under any financial duress. While she appreciated his assurance, Fern felt her heart settle an inch lower in her chest. *What was I expecting him to say? That he wants me to stay in Serenity Ridge?* She wouldn't, of course, even if he'd asked her to, so it was ridiculous to feel disappointed he hadn't. *It must be that seeing so many old sights has made me nostalgic,* she realized. *But I'm nostalgic about being young, not about being with Walker.*

"*Denki,* but staying here is Patience's prayer, not mine. I let her talk about the possibility because I don't want to discourage her from taking her requests to the Lord, but I absolutely intend to go through with the sale as soon as possible."

"I see," Walker replied noncommittally, just as someone flung open the school door so forcefully the wreath nearly flew off its hook. It was Jane.

She clamored down the stairs and exuberantly embraced each of her cousins. Then Phillip charged back to the buggy, but Patience unbuttoned her coat and Fern recognized she was showing Jane that she was wearing her old dress. Whatever Jane said in response caused Patience to hug her cousin a second time. As the girls joined hands and galloped across the schoolyard together, they reminded Fern so much of how close she'd once been to Gloria she didn't know whether to laugh or cry.

For the rest of their trip, Walker and Fern quietly listened to the children chattering about the evening's upcoming event. As Phillip's, Patience's and Jane's laughter filled the carriage, Walker found himself wishing Fern weren't so adamant about leaving Maine right away. Jane would have loved to have her cousins living so close by for a while longer, and they obviously would have enjoyed more time with her, too. *I wouldn't mind having Fern nearby, either.*

Now that we've broken the ice, I wonder why she's still in such a rush to leave.

Ordinarily, Walker would have speculated Fern wanted to get back to Ohio because she had a suitor waiting for her there, but his mother informed him she'd found out on Sunday that Fern wasn't being courted. *I suppose it's none of my business why she's in a hurry to go,* he thought. *They're leaving soon and that's that. For tonight, it's a blessing for the* kinner *to be together.*

When they arrived at Walker's house, the children ran off to retrieve Jane's scooter from the barn. Fern and Walker went inside, where they found Walker's mother in a tizzy. She told them that afternoon Jaala had taken her to the phone shanty to call Willa, as was their Wednesday afternoon practice. But it was Willa's husband, Mark, who answered the phone at the agreed upon time. Apparently Willa and her children were suffering from high fevers and body aches. Willa could scarcely take care of herself, much less tend to her four little ones.

"Mark's beside himself. I regret missing Jane's program, but I ought to leave as soon as possible to help him. Since today was Jane's last day of school this week, I could take her with me, but I don't want her to come down with whatever Willa's *familye* has."

"Don't worry about Jane. She can *kumme* to the tree farm with me in the mornings and then I'll take her to Roman's *haus* in the afternoons."

"Or you could drop her off at our *haus* before you

go to work on Thursday and Friday," Fern immediately offered. "The *kinner* would be thrilled they get to spend two entire days together."

Walker didn't hesitate to accept. Although Jane could have played with the Swarey children at the farm, he knew she'd prefer to be with her cousins while she could. "I'll go call a driver," he said. There were two dependable *Englisch* drivers in Serenity Ridge and three more in Unity, so he was confident he'd be able to arrange transportation to the neighboring town.

"Louisa, you go pack. I'll put supper on the table," Fern suggested, and Walker's mother readily complied. They'd all finished their meal just as the driver pulled up shortly before six o'clock.

"It's too bad you're going to miss the *Grischtdaag* program, *Groossmammi*," Jane expressed sincerely.

"I would have loved to see it, but I'm glad you recited your verses and sang the songs so often with me. I'll be able to picture it in my mind," Louisa replied. She bent to whisper something in her granddaughter's ear and Jane nodded in agreement.

Then Louisa gave everyone else a hug and wished Fern and her children a merry Christmas. As Walker escorted her to the van, she instructed him to call her at eleven a.m. on Saturday to make sure everyone had recovered enough for him and Jane to visit for Christmas.

"I will, *Mamm*—unless there's a blizzard and I can't make it to the phone shanty," Walker teased, but his mother was too worried for jokes.

"*Gott* willing, that won't happen, too," she murmured, wringing her hands. "But if it does, don't even think about venturing out into the snow. It's more important you and Jane stay safe than you arrive at Willa's for *Grischtdaag*."

After helping her into the van, Walker stood on the side porch, waving until the vehicle rolled out of sight. As he turned to open the door to the mudroom, he glanced through the kitchen window. Inside, Fern was washing the dishes and the children were drying and putting them away. Listening closely, he recognized they were singing, "All is calm, all is bright," which was exactly how he would have described the feeling in his heart at that moment.

Chapter Seven

Once they arrived at the schoolyard, the children rushed off so Jane could introduce Patience and Phillip to her friends before the program started, but Fern waited for Walker to hitch the horse. Standing just beyond the foot of the buggy, she balanced her container of peanut brittle atop two containers of sugar cookies Louisa had prepared. There was just enough moonlight to see the faces of other parents and children, and whether she recognized them from when she lived there or not, Fern exchanged warm greetings as they passed on their way into the building.

One man said hello and then stopped short and swung around. "Fern Troyer?" he asked incredulously.

"Jah," she said, answering to her maiden name.

He pulled his scarf away from his chin. "It's me, Stephen Hertig."

"Hello, Stephen, how are you?" Fern stalled. He obviously knew her when she lived in Serenity Ridge, but she hadn't seen him in church on Sunday and she couldn't immediately place him in her memory. Stephen must have noticed her hesitance because he chuckled.

"You've forgotten the first man to court you when you moved to Serenity Ridge?"

Fern instantly remembered—Stephen had only taken Fern out twice but that was enough for her to know he was charming, but he came on too strong for her taste. Judging from how openly he'd referred to their courtship just now, he was still as audacious as ever.

"My apologies. I didn't recognize you with a beard. Is your wife inside? I'd like to meet her," she said emphatically, hoping to embarrass him into demonstrating more discretion.

"Neh." Stephen tugged the brim of his hat lower. "She died last year from cancer."

"Oh, I'm so sorry!" Fern felt horrible. She softened her voice to confide, "My husband died from cancer, too."

She shifted the goodies to one arm so she could reach out and give his hand a sympathetic squeeze, but the containers slid across one another. Stephen grabbed the top two before they fell and Fern managed to keep her grasp on the bottom one.

"I can carry these in for you," he offered. "So, are you visiting or have you moved back to Serenity Ridge for *gut*?"

"Neh. I'm only here until *Samschdaag*. I, um, had some family business to take care of after my *onkel* Roman passed away."

"I was sorry to hear about that, although sometimes *Gott* works in mysterious ways. You never know what else He might have in mind by bringing you back to Serenity Ridge." It was too dark to be certain, but Fern thought he winked at her.

Unsettled, she simply thanked Stephen for his condolences. *What's taking Walker so long?* she wondered, just as she saw movement in her peripheral vision. Walker took a step forward and Fern noticed his hands were clenched.

"Hello, Stephen," he said curtly.

"Hi, Walker," Stephen replied with a grin. "Don't tell me you're the man responsible for keeping Fern waiting out here in the cold with her arms full?"

Walker's voice was so low it sounded like a growl. "Fern came with me because her *kinner* are Jane's *gschwischderkinner* and Jane invited them to see the *Grischtdaag* program. We ought to get inside now."

As Walker brusquely squeezed past Stephen and Fern and strode toward the school, Fern thought, *He sure made a point of letting Stephen know I'm only here with him because Jane wants Phillip and Patience to see the program.* Fern supposed his caution was understandable, considering how quickly rumors caught fire in their community. Still, she was flustered by Walker's gruffness.

Trying to make up for it, she conversationally asked Stephen, "How many *kinner* do you have?"

"None. Anke and I were only married for a year when she got sick, but *Gott* willing, I'll be blessed with lots of *seh* and *dochdere* when I remarry."

"Oh, you're remarrying?" Fern felt foolish for worrying Stephen had been flirting with her. "Is she someone from Serenity Ridge?"

"*Neh*, I was speaking hypothetically," Stephen said. "Right now, I'm on my own. I actually live in Unity—that's where Anke was from so we built a *haus* there. But I visit my *bruder*'s *familye* as often as I can. In fact, I came early for *Grischtdaag* to surprise my nieces and nephews. They have no idea I'll be here at the program tonight."

As they climbed the stairs to the schoolhouse, Walker said over his shoulder, "It's almost time for the program to start. I've got to go talk to Abram for a minute. Fern, you'd better round up Phillip and Patience."

"I will, as soon as I deliver the goodies to the dessert table," Fern replied indignantly. *It would be nice if you gave me a hand instead of giving me instructions.*

"I'll help," Stephen offered, holding the door for her.

After Fern and Stephen eased their way through the crowd to add Fern's and Louisa's treats to the refreshment tables set up in the corner of the room, Stephen left to stand by his brother along the back wall with the rest of the men. The scholars, as the students were called, and the teacher had arranged two rows of chairs for the women; the teenagers and visiting children were expected to sit on the floor in front of them.

Fern spotted Phillip and Patience seated midway

down the aisle with Jaala's grandchildren, but all the chairs behind them were filled. Fern waved and placed a finger to her lips to indicate they were to be quiet during the presentation, even though she had no doubt they'd be on their best behavior. Then she took a seat at the end of the row next to Eleanor Sutter, a young woman Fern knew when she lived in Maine. They had chatted briefly in church the previous Sunday, but this evening they barely had time to exchange greetings before the teacher walked to the front of the room and welcomed everyone to the event.

The first part of the program included a Biblical skit about the nativity story, Scriptural recitation, and songs by the scholars. Although there were no costumes or props, Fern noticed Phillip and Patience hung on every word, and she caught herself moving her own lips when Jane recited her verses. The young girl spoke distinctly and solemnly, without missing a word, and after she finished, Fern wicked away a tear. *Gloria would have been so delighted.* She scanned the back wall to see if Walker was standing nearby so she could give him a smile in acknowledgment of Jane's accomplishment, but he wasn't in her range of vision.

After the presentation, the school board awarded the teacher a financial gift, and then the audience was invited to sing Christmas hymns with the scholars. After the last song, the teacher announced the children would give the parents the gifts they'd made for them—a pencil case for their fathers and travel sewing kits for their mothers—and invited everyone to indulge in the refreshments.

As the women rose to their feet, Eleanor turned to Fern and remarked, "That was a *wunderbaar* program, wasn't it?"

"*Jah*. It was delightful. The children and their teacher must have worked very hard on it." Fern craned her neck; she'd lost sight of Phillip and Patience.

"I couldn't help but notice you came in with Stephen Hertig," Eleanor hinted.

"*Jah*. He spotted me in the schoolyard and my arms were full so he helped me carry my desserts inside," Fern replied flatly. Eleanor had always been something of a gossip and Fern didn't want her to start any rumors. For that same reason, she didn't add that she'd actually come in with Walker, not Stephen.

Eleanor tittered. "There's no need to be coy with me, Fern. I understand if you want to keep it quiet that the two of you are striking up a long-distance courtship. I won't tell anyone."

Flabbergasted, Fern repeated, "Stephen was merely helping me car—"

But Eleanor spoke over her, saying, "Walker Huyard, my suitor, is very secretive about our relationship, too. He was so afraid of anyone finding out about it that on *Sunndaag* after we went out, he dropped me off at the end of my road instead of bringing me all the way home. Can you imagine?"

The din in the room was nothing compared to the racket inside Fern's head. *Walker is courting*

Eleanor? Louisa had never mentioned Walker was courting anyone—and there was precious little the older woman hadn't told Fern about her children and grandchildren in the past few days. Fern couldn't exactly account for why she felt so let down to learn Walker was Eleanor's suitor, other than she couldn't imagine him choosing a woman like Eleanor. Then again, Fern never foresaw Walker marrying Gloria, either.

"Some people are more discreet than others," she replied pointedly.

"I suppose. But I hope when he gives me a ride home tonight, he doesn't expect me to walk down the lane in the cold and dark."

"Walker's giving you a ride home tonight?" Fern echoed. *He must have forgotten all about it.* Between the tumult of Phillip's tree-climbing escapade and Louisa's sudden departure, she could understand why it slipped his mind.

"*Jah.* Why do you sound so surprised?"

"Be-because I would have thought he'd have to get home early to put Jane to bed." She deliberately didn't tell Eleanor that Louisa had gone out of town. Nor did Fern say Walker was supposed to give her and the children a ride home, too; it was up to him, not her, to deliver that news to Eleanor.

"He's probably arranged for Jane and his *mamm* to ride home with someone else," Eleanor said, waving her hand. "It wouldn't be much *schpass* to have them tagging along."

It's not going to be any schpass *for me, either,*

Fern silently lamented. *Especially if you're peeved at Walker for forgetting he'd made plans with you.*

Just then, Jane squeezed through the cluster of people standing to Fern's left and announced, "This is for you!" She extended a box wrapped in gold paper and tied with a red bow.

Knowing the traveling sewing kits were intended for the scholars' mothers, Fern cooed, "Oh, Jane, that's so sweet! I would love to accept this, but don't you think your *groossmammi* might feel bad if you give it to me instead of her?"

"*Neh*. She told me I could," Jane insisted. "When you visit again you can bring it with you to hem the next dresses I hand down to Patience."

Moved by Jane's earnestness, as well as by her wish to have them visit again, Fern couldn't refuse. She thanked the girl, hugging her tightly and adding, "You did *wunderbaar* tonight. I could hear every word of your Bible verses, and I liked it that you smiled when you sang. I think the Lord must be very pleased with you."

"You do? Menno Ausberger said my singing sounded like I have a cold, but I don't."

"Hmm. Maybe *he* has a cold and his ears are stuffed up," Fern suggested. "Anyway, you were singing for the Lord's ears, not Menno's."

"Hi, Jane!" Phillip had burst through the crowd with Patience in tow, and both of them immediately told Jane how much they liked the program. Since Eleanor was engaged in a conversation with someone else, Fern and the children slipped away to the dessert table, where they helped themselves to cookies and other treats. Patience wanted to see where Jane's desk was, so Fern settled the children around it to eat their snacks. But then Phillip spilled his cider and Fern went to fetch a napkin.

On the way back, she crossed paths with Stephen again. "I should have mentioned this earlier, but if you need anything while you're in town, I'll be right down the road at my *bruder*'s *haus*," he said.

Fern bit her bottom lip, wavering about whether to ask him for a lift home. After the kind of remarks Stephen made earlier, she didn't want him to get any ideas about her being interested in him romantically, but it would be awkward for all three adults if Fern "tagged along" with Eleanor and Walker. Reluctantly, she answered, "If, um, if you wouldn't mind giving the *kinner* and me a ride home tonight, I'd appreciate it."

Stephen's eyes lit up. "Of course I don't mind! I was on my way to hitch my horse now."

Circling back to tell Phillip and Patience it was time to go, Fern discovered the cider had been mopped up and Walker was leaning against the wall by the window near where they were eating. "Oh, there you are!" she exclaimed. "Listen, the *kinner* and I are going to leave now. I've arranged for someone else to take us home—"

"Why would you do that?" Walker interrupted.

Fern hadn't planned to tell him about her conversation with Eleanor. Considering how hard he'd worked to keep his courtship a secret, Fern figured it would embarrass Walker that she knew about it. Instead, she'd intended to say it would be less strain on Walker's horse if Stephen gave her a ride, since he lived much closer to Roman's house. But she was so ruffled by Walker's accusatory tone, she snitched, "Because *you* apparently forgot you were giving Eleanor a ride home. It's one thing if you have your *dochder* with you, but I don't think she'll appreciate three more people in the buggy."

"What are you talking about?" Walker cupped Fern's elbow and steered her farther away from the children. "I'm not giving Eleanor a ride home. Why would you think I was?"

"Because she told me you were."

He shook his head. "*Neh.* That's not the truth."

Fern bristled. "Are you saying *I'm* not telling the truth about Eleanor telling *me* that or *Eleanor's* not telling the truth about *you* telling *her* that?"

"I'm saying I never had any plans to give Eleanor a ride home, so someone is mistaken." Walker crossed his arms. "And it isn't me."

"Well, my ears work fine, so I'm not the one who's mistaken, either," Fern retorted. "I guess that means Eleanor must have dreamed it all up! Just like she must have imagined you're her suitor and you went out with her on *Sunndaag.*"

The complacence melted from Walker's face. He faltered backward, dropping his arms to his sides. "I—I—I *did* go for a walk with her, but I never said I'd take her home. And I'm certainly not courting her—or anyone else, for that matter. She must have gotten the wrong impression."

Just like I *must have gotten the wrong impression about how you felt about* me? Fern took a deep breath and let it out before responding. "Apparently, there's been a misunderstanding, and I wish you two the best in working it out, but I have to go. Stephen is waiting—"

"*Stephen* is bringing you home?" Walker sneered. "Then by all means, you ought to hurry off to be with him. Don't give us a second thought!"

Fern had had enough. "What is your problem?"

"We had an agreement! It isn't right for you to change your mind after making plans with me."

It's only a buggy ride—you *changed* your *mind about committing to spend the rest of your life with me!* Fern's cheeks prickled with heat. Digging her fingernails into her hand, she stared Walker down and replied as evenly as she could, "For one thing, I thought I was doing you a favor, so you wouldn't get into hot water with Eleanor. For another, I don't see what the big deal is about Stephen bringing me home."

"The big deal," Walker articulated deliberately, "is that Jane was looking forward to taking Patience and Phillip past a specially decorated *haus* in an *Englisch* neighborhood. It was supposed to be a surprise."

Fern blinked, but she kept her chin in the air. "Well, I'm sorry about that, but as I said, I was trying to help you out of a sticky situation. Good night, Walker."

She swished over to the children, who were now flipping through a book, and crouched down next to Jane. Walker couldn't hear what Fern said, but he could tell by their expressions that all three children were crushed their evening together was ending prematurely. As Walker moved closer, Fern consoled them, "You'll get to see each other tomorrow."

After Fern and her children departed, Walker told Jane to say goodbye to her teacher, get her coat and meet him by the door. Meanwhile, he needed to find Eleanor before she spread more rumors about the two of them. Instead, Eleanor spotted him first, tapping his shoulder from behind. "Is it time for us to go yet?" she whispered into his ear. "Just tell me where you want me to meet you."

He twirled around. "Why did you tell Fern we're courting?"

Eleanor's eyes widened. "She told you I told her? That makes her an even bigger *boubelmoul* than what people accuse me of being! I guess that means I don't have to keep quiet about her and Stephen Hertig, either. Did you know they've reunited?"

Walker already sensed there might have been some interest between Stephen and Fern from the way they were cozying up to each other outside the schoolhouse. Not to mention, she was clearly eager to ride home with him.

"What Fern and Stephen do is none of our business," Walker reminded Eleanor—and himself.

"What I want to know is why you told her *we're* courting."

Eleanor peeked at him from beneath her eyelashes. "I'm sorry. I know how private you are and I shouldn't have mentioned it. But sometimes, *gut* news is worth sharing."

"What are you talking about? We aren't courting. I never said I'd give you a ride home, either!"

"If you didn't want to be my suitor, why did you ask to spend time alone with me?" Eleanor squished her mouth into a pout.

Walker stammered, "I—I—I asked your *bruder* to *kumme* hiking with us, too. I wanted to enjoy hiking in the pleasant weather with friends, that's all."

"Then why did you agree to take me home tonight?"

Walker was adamant. "I *didn't*."

"*Jah*, you did. I remember the exact spot on the trail. I told you about helping my nephew memorize his Bible verses and then I said it would be romantic if you and I could go for a ride after the program and look at all the *Englischers'* homes decorated with lights. And you agreed."

"Did I?" The details of what Eleanor was describing were hazy, but Walker vaguely remembered her talking about the Christmas program. He'd been so preoccupied Sunday afternoon, it was entirely possible he'd mumbled agreement to almost anything she'd said. "I'm sorry. I don't remember saying that."

"Well, you *did*. And I've already told my *fami-*

lye I'd get a ride with one of my friends, so they left without me."

Walker swallowed. "I can take you home, then." Wanting to emphasize that this didn't mean he'd changed his mind about courting her, he added, "As your neighbor, I mean, not as someone who wants to be your suitor."

"Walker Huyard, I wouldn't accept a ride from you if it was forty degrees below and I had to walk home barefoot, much less allow you to be my suitor!" Eleanor ranted. "I don't know what Gloria saw in you, but it certainly wasn't charm or *gut* manners."

Walker didn't defend himself. Regardless of whether Eleanor had misinterpreted his intentions, he was partly to blame. He never should have asked her out for a walk in order to avoid spending time with Fern, and he deserved every irate word Eleanor hurled at him. "I really am sorry," was all he could say before she stomped off.

In the buggy, Jane was uncharacteristically sullen; Walker blamed Fern for souring what should have been a special celebration. When they got home, she went straight to bed, but Walker stayed up, fuming. *Eleanor may have had a reason to be angry at me, but Fern didn't. She ruined my* dochder's *surprise, yet she acted as if she was doing me a favor!*

For the next hour, Walker couldn't stop thinking about Fern riding home with Stephen Hertig and what Eleanor had said about the two of them. Walker was aware Stephen had once courted Fern, but she'd said he wasn't her type. However, it appeared she may have changed her mind. *Fern's emotions are as capricious as ever*, he carped to himself. *I wouldn't be surprised if she changes her mind about selling the* haus, *too, now that she's rekindled her flame with Stephen.*

Walker's ornery thoughts plagued him long into the night, and the next morning he rose with a whopper of a headache. He retrieved two aspirin from the medicine cabinet and shuffled into the kitchen for a glass of water. Jane was already at the table, glumly pushing her cereal around in the bowl.

"Do you have a *bauchweh*?" he asked, figuring her tummy hurt from all the treats she'd eaten the evening before.

"Neh," she said, dragging her fingers across her eyes. "I'm sad."

Walker's chest tightened with renewed anger at Fern. Trying to temper it, he took a swallow of water before asking, "Because you didn't get to show Patience and Phillip the *haus* last night?"

"Neh." Jane could hardly utter the word.

"Then what is it, Jane?"

"You didn't say anything about the pencil case I made for you," she burst out. "Don't you like it?"

Walker smacked his forehead. He'd been so consumed with Fern for being thoughtless and hurting his daughter's feelings he'd forgotten all about the gift. "Ach! Jane—I'm sorry. I tucked it into my coat for safekeeping and I never even opened it. Let me take a look now."

Never one to hold a grudge, Jane leaped from her chair and bounded toward the mudroom. "I'll get it!"

After Walker carefully unwrapped his present, he examined it carefully, complimenting Jane's handiwork as he slid the top open and shut and turned the case over to admire how she'd carved his initials on the bottom.

"I've never had such a handy pencil case. I'll treasure it always," he said, kissing her cheek. "Now, we'd better eat our breakfast or I'll be late for work."

On the way to Roman's house, Jane asked, "Since we didn't get to show everybody the *Englisch haus* last night, can we go tonight, *Daed*?"

"Oh, I don't think that will work out." Given the tension between him and Fern, he was dreading even seeing her briefly this morning. "I'll probably finish working in the yard by four o'clock and the *Englischers'* lights don't *kumme* on until six o'clock."

"We could stay at *Groossdaadi's haus* and eat supper with them until it's time for the lights to *kumme* on," Jane proposed.

"It's not polite to invite ourselves to supper. Fern might not have enough food for us."

Jane had a solution for that, too. "You could let her take our buggy to the grocery store while you're working in the yard with Phillip. Patience and I can help her make supper."

"Jane, I said *neh*."

She paused before timidly questioning, "*Daed*, are you mad Fern and Patience and Phillip rode home with Micah's *onkel* instead of us?"

Walker was shocked his daughter had picked up on his feelings. Was he that transparent? He chose his words carefully. "I was disappointed because I knew how much you wanted to show Phillip and Patience the lights. I didn't want you to be upset."

"I *was* a little upset," Jane confessed. "But now I'm not. My teacher says sometimes people hurt our feelings even when they have *gut* tensions."

"*Gut* tensions?"

"*Jah.* It means they want to do something *gut*, but they end up doing something bad. Like when I made tea to surprise *Groossmammi* and I broke her favorite teacup. Remember?"

"*Jah.*" Walker marveled at his daughter's comprehension.

"My teacher says we shouldn't be quick to judge because we can't see what's in someone's heart. Only *Gott* can do that. But Fern told me she didn't want to wear out Daisy's legs, and Micah's *haus* is closer to *Groossdaadi*'s *haus* than ours is. So I think her heart has *gut* tensions in it."

Walker was stunned silent. His daughter had just unwittingly described what had happened between him and Fern eight years ago: his intentions in marrying Gloria had been good, but he'd caused Fern incredible pain. In light of that, Walker realized how hypocritical it was for him to harbor resentment toward her over something as minor as changing their transportation arrangements, especially since she did it to help him out.

"Your teacher is very wise," he said. "I'm *hallich* you're taking her lessons to heart."

Proving she was still a child despite her momentary insightfulness, Jane wheedled, "Could we invite Fern and Patience and Phillip to go out for pizza at Mario's? We could take them to see the lights after we eat. Please, *Daed*?"

"*Jah*, okay, if they want to go," he relented. *And if their mamm forgives me for behaving like a* dummkopf.

So when Fern came to the door, Walker asked if he could speak with her in private. She welcomed Jane into the house and stepped onto the porch, tugging the door shut behind her. Folding her arms across her chest, she raised an eyebrow at him. "Whatever you have to say, please make it quick. I'm cold."

Walker cleared his throat. "I, uh, wanted to apologize for how I spoke to you last night. I was disappointed Jane's plans were ruined and I was upset about the situation with Eleanor. But I shouldn't have spoken so rudely to you, especially since you were trying to spare me from conflict with Eleanor." He chuckled self-deprecatingly. "Not that it helped—she was awfully mad at me."

"It's nothing to be *glib* about. You hurt her feelings. She thought you cared about her. She probably thought she had a future with you." Fern shook her head and looked away. Were those tears glinting in her eyes?

"I wasn't being glib. I felt *baremlich* about the miscommunication," Walker contended. "But Eleanor *shouldn't* have assumed we had a future together. I never told her I wanted one."

"What was she supposed to think? You took her out alone on *Sunndaag.*"

Walker held up his hands. "I invited her to go hiking, *jah*, but I invited her *bruder* to *kumme*, too. But I wouldn't have even asked him if I weren't so desperate to get out of the *haus* when—" Walker closed his mouth but it was too late.

"When I was visiting your *mamm*?" Fern huffed.

He rubbed his gloved hand over his eyes. "It—it seemed as if you didn't want me around…" Walker's cheeks were scorched with humiliation.

Fern sighed. "You're right. I wasn't very *freindlich* to you at the attorney's office. I was…overwhelmed that morning."

Walker knew there was more to their reasons for avoiding each other on Sunday than that, but he let it go. Daring to look at her again, he asked, "Will you please forgive me for how I acted last night?"

"*Jah*, if you'll forgive me for being so standoffish at Anthony's office and in *kurrich* on *Sunndaag*," she agreed. "And I *am* sorry I spoiled Jane's surprise."

Grinning, Walker said, "As it happens, I talked to her about it and we wondered if you'd want to go see the *Englischers*' lights tonight. They don't turn them on until six, but I'd like to treat you all to supper at Mario's pizzeria first." *Unless you made plans with Stephen already?*

Walker held his breath until a smile widened

Fern's rosy cheeks and she replied, "*Denki*. That would be *wunderbaar*."

A few minutes later, as Walker's horse clip-clopped along the road to the Christmas tree farm, he reflected on his conversation with Fern. Although he was relieved she'd forgiven him for behaving like a dolt the evening before, he caught himself wishing he could tell her why he'd married Gloria. There had been plenty of other times over the years when Walker longed to confide in her, but he'd never felt as tempted as he did right now.

It wasn't just that he wanted to absolve himself in her eyes—although that definitely would have been part of his motivation. It was also that he wanted to release Fern from the pain he recognized she still carried. He'd just seen it in her eyes and heard it in her voice when she'd rebuked Walker for hurting Eleanor's feelings. *It was as if she'd been talking about what happened with me and her, not with me and Eleanor.*

But Walker had made a promise, for Jane's sake, and no matter how much he wanted to ease Fern's burden, he couldn't give in to the desire to tell her why he'd really married Gloria. *In a couple of days, she'll be gone and the feeling will pass*, he told himself.

The startling thing was, he didn't know if he wanted it to.

Chapter Eight

After Walker left, Fern went upstairs to where the children were playing a card game Jane had brought with her. When she asked Jane if she could speak to her alone, the three of them exchanged furtive glances, but the young girl followed Fern back down to the living room. Fern sat on the sofa and Jane stood a few feet in front of her with her head tipped downward, as if she was concerned she was about to receive a scolding.

"Your *daed* told me about the surprise you had planned for last night. I'm sorry we didn't get to see the lights, but he asked me if we could go see them tonight and I said *jah*." Fern thought this would bring a smile to Jane's chubby face, but the girl furrowed her forehead.

"Didn't he ask you to *kumme* to Mario's with us, too?"

"Oh, *jah*! I think that's a *wunderbaar* idea."

Jane beamed, exposing something brown stuck to her teeth. "*I* thought of it."

Fern experienced a flash of disappointment that the idea had come from Jane instead of from Walker. *That's* lappich, she told herself. *It's not as if it's a date...* Rather than reminding Jane it was prideful to boast, Fern said, "I'm glad you did. Now, do you want to tell Phillip and Patience about it or do you still want to keep it a secret until we get there?"

"Oh, I'd better tell them. It's too hard to keep a secret for even one day and I already kept this for one-and-a-half days."

Chuckling, Fern agreed, "You're right about that. But before you go tell Phillip and Patience our plans, how about if I brush your hair for you?" Fern didn't want to hurt Jane's feelings, but she noticed her hair was coming out of its bun and she suspected Walker had forgotten to help her with it. She also figured he'd forgotten to remind her to brush her teeth.

"Okay. I usually brush the snarls out and then *Groossmammi* helps me pin it, but today I did it by myself and it feels all slippery," Jane said, clearly not at all embarrassed by Fern's offer.

Fern went to get a brush. When she returned, the young girl had released her hair from its elastic, and it flowed down past her shoulders in subtle waves. She stood with her back to Fern, who told her, "Your *mamm* had a pretty natural wave to her hair like you do, you know that?"

"Really?"

"*Jah*. Didn't your *daed* ever tell you that?"

"*Neh.* But he told me she had brown hair."

Brown? Gloria's hair was caramel-colored and accented with strands of honey from the summer sun. *Walker told me my eyes were the color of stars, yet he couldn't describe Gloria's beautiful hair other than to say it was brown?* Trying to convince herself she wasn't being nosy, she only wanted to find out so she could add to Jane's knowledge about Gloria, Fern asked, "What else did your *daed* say about your *mamm*?"

Jane shrugged. "He said *mamm* didn't need to have any more *bobblin* because she loved me so much that one *bobble* was enough. That's why I don't have any *breider* or *schwesdere.*"

And because Gloria passed away before she could have more kinner, Fern thought sadly. She pinned Jane's prayer *kapp* on over her tidy bun and then drew the child backward for a hug. "That's true, she did love you very, very much."

"You knew me when I was little?" Jane asked, snuggling closer, just like Patience always did.

"*Neh*, but your *mamm* often talked to me about how much she wanted to have a *dochder* one day." Actually, Gloria used to claim she wanted four daughters and four sons. Fern sniffed away a tear and when she did, she caught a whiff of chocolate. She turned Jane to face her and asked, "Did you have candy for breakfast?"

Jane clasped her hands over her mouth, her voice muffled as she explained, "It's from my teacher.

All the scholars get a box of special candy after the *Grischtdaag* program."

"And you were eating it upstairs with Phillip and Patience?"

Jane ducked her head. *"Jah."*

Fern lifted Jane's chin with a finger so she had to look into Fern's eyes. "Do you know the one thing that's even harder to keep to yourself for two days than a secret?" she asked and Jane shook her head. "A box of candy."

The young girl giggled, and now Fern could see it was chocolate dimming her teeth. She suggested Jane go rinse her mouth and then she accompanied her upstairs. Phillip and Patience wore guilty expressions as Jane bent to slide the box of candy from where they'd hidden it beneath the bed and handed it over to Fern. "I'll put it away for you so you don't get a *bauchweh*. You wouldn't want to be too sick to go you-know-where."

"Where?" Phillip and Patience asked at the same time. Jane barely had the answer out of her mouth before they sprang to their feet in excitement.

When they settled down, Fern instructed her children to brush their teeth again, and then she sent all three of them outside to burn off their chocolate-induced hyperactivity. She wished she had their energy; last night she'd stayed awake stewing over Walker's behavior until almost midnight. Yawning as she went about her morning chores, she reflected on his apology. They'd rarely argued while they were courting, but after they did, his entire body, face and voice would seem weighed down with contrition, just as it had today. Except this morning his frown was even more pronounced because his mustache dragged at the corners, too.

Thinking about Walker's mustache made Fern wonder why he hadn't remarried. When he was her suitor and they discussed their dreams about having a family, he always said he hoped the Lord blessed him with between four and six children. Given how pushy Louisa was, Fern imagined in the five years since Gloria died, Walker's mother must have tried to match him with one of the unmarried women in Serenity Ridge or Unity. Yet here he was, still unmarried and with only one child.

It occurred to Fern maybe Walker didn't want to marry again because he was so anguished over Gloria's death that he still hadn't recovered from the loss. Perhaps in his mind, no one would ever compare to her. Fern felt a jolt of envy at the possibility. She'd once longed to love and be loved like that. In fact, she'd once thought she *had* loved and been loved like that…

I shouldn't be entertaining thoughts that will only lead to resentment and I shouldn't be speculating about Walker's relationship with Gloria, either. Fern wrung the rag she'd been using under the faucet. *For now, I'm just glad that Walker and I aren't at odds with each other anymore.*

But if she was really so glad, why did she feel like weeping?

* * *

Usually Fridays and Saturdays were the busiest days on the Christmas tree farm, but on Thursday morning, the place was bustling with procrastinators and with those people whose tradition it was to wait until Christmas Eve to buy a tree. According to the owner, Levi Swarey, the *Englischers* were nervous about the storm that was forecast to potentially begin the next afternoon and continue into Saturday, so they'd swarmed the farm to get their trees while they could.

It was almost two o'clock by the time Walker left, and on the way to Roman's house, he hastily took a few bites of the sandwich he'd made. Patience, Phillip and Jane were perched on the fence bordering Roman's front yard when Walker arrived. He waved and they raced through the yard to beat him to the barn.

"Fern said *jah*!" Jane announced as soon as he stepped out of the carriage, even though Walker already knew Fern agreed to go out that evening. "Guess how many hours there are until the *Englischers* turn on their lights, *Daed*."

"Eighteen?" Walker kidded her.

"*Neh*. There were only four hours the last time we asked Fern. It's even less now."

As Jane and her cousins took off to race up the hill, Walker thought, *Poor Fern. Jane's so excited she's probably been asking her what time it is every half hour.*

But Fern seemed unruffled when she beckoned him from the porch. "I was just going to put the kettle on for tea. You're *wilkom* to *kumme* in if you'd like to sit down for a few minutes."

Walker approached so he wouldn't have to shout. "*Denki*, but I'd better get to work right away. Supposedly the nor'easter they predicted last week might start tomorrow afternoon. Its path is still uncertain, but if it does hit, it should continue snowing right into *Samschdaag* morning. So I want to make as much progress as I can on the trees today."

Fern's expression was pinched. "Ach. I hope the snow doesn't interfere with our travel plans." She asked if they could stop at the phone shanty that evening so she could touch base with the van driver, and Walker agreed. Before going indoors again, she offered to call Phillip over to give a hand with the logs.

"Don't do that—let him play."

"I think he needs a separation from the *meed* and they need one from him, too."

"Really? They've been getting along so well."

"*Jah*. Even better than we have," Fern remarked, impishly tilting her chin up at him. "But if Phillip really is more of a help than a hindrance, I'd appreciate it if he could work with you as often as possible while we're still here. He's learning so much from you. He quotes nearly everything you say."

Walker's face warmed. "I enjoy being around him, too—and not just because he's closer to the ground than I am so he can pick up all the debris I'm too stiff to bend over and get." Then he asked, "Has Jane been pestering you all day about the time?"

"Only every ten minutes." Walker groaned but

Fern just laughed. "I think it's *wunderbaar* she's so excited about sharing something special with her *gschwischderkinner*. Gloria was the same way—I remember how eager she was to take me to Serenity Lake for the first time. Or to Brubaker's. Not that Jane was old enough to have learned it from her, but it's amusing to see that the two of them are alike in that regard."

Walker tried hard to remember Gloria ever being enthusiastic in the same way Jane was, but he couldn't. After Jordan's death he'd been in such a fog, and once Jane was born, most of Walker's attention was focused on her, not on Gloria. Walker realized he probably hadn't noticed a lot of other qualities in his wife, either. While he strove to be the best father he could be to Jane, he realized he hadn't been much of a husband to Gloria. He'd thought he'd at least been a good friend, but in retrospect, he had his doubts. It couldn't have been easy for Gloria to live with him—not because he was mean, but because he was distant. He was *absent*. Thinking about it now made him wince.

"I'm sorry," Fern said. "I won't talk about Gloria anymore if it makes you miss her too much."

"That's okay." Walker understood Fern's need to reminisce about her cousin, especially now that she was surrounded by memories of living with her in Serenity Ridge. "It—it's just there are things I can't recall very well about her."

Fern touched his arm. "Sometimes it seems like I can't recall the things I want to remember and I can only remember the things I want to forget," she empathized.

"*Jah.* That's exactly how it is with me, too," he admitted, locking his gaze with hers until Phillip came tearing around the house. Fern quickly dropped her hand and stepped backward. When the boy came stomping up the stairs and halted right between them, Walker said, "I hope you've *kumme* to help me."

"*Jah.* I need to work up my appetite again because you're taking us out to a restaurant for pizza. We hardly ever get to go to a restaurant."

"Phillip, we don't want to take advantage of Walker's generosity to us," Fern scolded him.

"It's okay. I only ate half my sandwich today so my *bauch* will have room for lots of pizza, too," Walker said. "C'mon, Phillip, it's your turn to get the wheelbarrow and tarp. I'll carry the ax and saws."

By the time it was dusk and Fern called Phillip in to wash up, Walker only had a small pile of logs to split. He figured it wouldn't take him more than ninety minutes to finish everything the next day, including replacing the shingles on the roof. After he'd put away their supplies and tools, Walker went inside to wash his hands and face before heading back out to hitch the buggy.

"At this pizza place, they give *kinner* a loopy straw and you can take it home," Jane informed her cousins on the way into town. "I have a red one, a green one and a blue one but not a yellow one."

"If I get a yellow one, we can trade," Patience offered.

Phillip surmised admiringly, "You must get to eat out a lot if you already have three loopy straws."

To the children's delight, there was a toy train running around a large Christmas tree in the corner of the restaurant. They went over to watch it while Fern and Walker placed their order and chose a table. Walker seated himself across from Fern. Her eyes shimmered and her voice warbled as she relayed the story of how she'd discovered the children had been eating chocolate in Patience's room that morning. Walker cracked up when she said she'd noticed how dingy Jane's teeth looked and she thought he'd forgotten to tell her to brush them.

"Actually," he confessed, "I *did* forget to tell her to brush them, but she's usually pretty consistent about doing that without a reminder. I forgot to tell her to brush her hair, too, but I can see you must have helped her out with that."

"It's so thick and wavy, it's no wonder she has a hard time pinning it," Fern replied as a customer holding a boxed pizza stopped at their table. Because he was wearing jeans and a flannel jacket instead of a suit and tie, it took a moment for Walker to recognize who the man was.

"Hi, Anthony," Walker and Fern both greeted him at the same time.

"Hello, Fern and Walker. What a nice surprise to see you together," he said. "I—I mean both at once. I was going to stop by Roman's house tomorrow but it might snow, so I'm glad I caught you here. Have you made any decisions about whether you want any of Roman's possessions?"

"We've been having so much fun, I actually forgot all about doing that," Fern exclaimed. "There might be a tool or two I'd like to take, and one of the quilts my *ant* made—I want the *kinner* to have something useful from their great *ant* and *onkel*. Otherwise, as I mentioned, I think we should give Roman's belongings away or sell them with the house." She added, "If Walker doesn't mind, that is."

Happy that Fern had enjoyed their time together, despite their squabble, he agreed with her. Anthony chatted with Walker about his progress on the trees and Walker assured him he'd have everything cleaned up by the next day. Since the following Monday was Christmas, Anthony said he'd wait until after the holiday to talk to his real estate contact.

"We might not be able to officially get the ball rolling until after the first of the year, but just as soon as I have more information, I'll let you both know," the attorney promised. "Unless you change your mind about leaving, Fern."

Walker scrutinized her face, trying to read her reaction. Fern smiled slightly before replying, "I don't think that's going to happen, but I'll let you know if it does."

"I don't think that's going to happen" isn't the same as saying she wants to stay, but it's a far cry from a few days ago when she said she had no intention of ever living in Maine again, Walker noticed. *What changed?* He wondered if it was because she

really *did* have hopes of developing a relationship with Stephen. Then he noticed the children had approached the table and were standing behind Anthony; Fern probably didn't want to give the lawyer a flat-out *no* in front of the three of them, especially Patience.

"Okay, well, I wish you safe travels—and don't hesitate to get in touch if there's anything I can do." Anthony rapped his knuckle on the table twice and turned to leave, almost stumbling over the children on his way.

A moment after he left, the server arrived with their pizza and drinks. As soon as everyone lifted their heads after saying grace, Jane pointed out, "Look, I got a purple loopy straw. That's even better than a yellow one!"

Since they were all ravenous, they ate in relative silence. Phillip and Walker polished off a pepperoni and sausage pizza between them, while Fern and the girls shared the other, since they preferred to only have cheese on theirs.

When the server brought Walker the check, she commented to Fern, "If you don't mind me saying, you have such a nice family. I wish my children were as well behaved as the three of yours."

"Did you hear that?" Patience remarked to Jane once the woman went back behind the counter. "She thinks we're *schweschdere.*"

"That's probably because you're wearing one of my dresses."

Smiling ear to ear, Patience added, "And because we look a lot alike."

Walker had to bite down on his tongue to keep from laughing out loud; the two girls were as different as night and day. *As different as Gloria and Fern.*

"That lady must think *Mamm* is married to you, Walker," Phillip deducted. "She doesn't know you aren't any relation to us."

Logically, Walker understood the boy was only repeating what he'd had impressed upon him by Fern—which was partly why it was so painful to hear—but he felt as if he'd been whacked in the chest with a sledgehammer. Reeling, he couldn't reply.

Fern noticed the shadow that crossed Walker's face and the way his posture went slack. Trying to compensate for Phillip's remark—a remark *she* never should have stated so adamantly to him in the first place—Fern said, "*Denki* for the *appenditlich* supper, Walker. It was a real treat and we enjoyed it. Didn't we, Patience and Phillip?"

Phillip stopped slurping the last of his milk with his straw to raise his head. "*Jah*, it was the best pizza I ever ate. And the most. *Denki*."

Fern glanced at Patience to prompt her to thank Walker, too. Astonishingly, the girl bounced up from her chair, scuffed around the table to where Walker was sitting and threw her arms around his neck. "*Denki*, Walker." Before letting go, she whispered something into his ear that returned the sparkle to his eyes.

My dear, sweet, sensitive dochder, Fern thought as she crossed the room to the coatrack. She reached for her coat, but it snagged on the hook and she nearly pulled the entire rack forward on top of herself.

"Here, let me," Walker offered, reaching over her to steady the coatrack. He lifted hers and held it behind her so she could slide her arms through her sleeves. And tonight he held the door for her, too, just like he used to do when they were courting. It seemed like such a small thing, but Fern missed having a man extend courtesies like these.

Despite the children's protests, they stopped at the phone shanty first, since it was on the way to the *Englischer*'s house. Using Walker's flashlight so she could see to dial, Fern called the van driver, who was scheduled to take her and the children to the bus station in Waterville. He indicated if the nor'easter hit, it would be a doozy, and he suggested Fern ought to consider leaving the next morning to beat the snow.

"Since it's not coming from the west, it won't affect states like New York and Ohio, so you'll be fine if you catch the morning bus tomorrow," he surmised. "But if you take a chance and wait until Saturday and it *does* snow as much as they say it might, you probably won't be able to dig out until late Sunday. Which means you won't make it out of Maine until Tuesday, since Monday is Christmas and the buses aren't running."

Fern dithered. She supposed she could call the station and change her travel date, but she'd given her word to Walker that she'd watch Jane tomorrow morning while he was at work. Of course, he'd understand why she needed to leave early, but the children would be terribly disappointed. Especially Patience, who was already dragging her feet. So Fern told the driver she wasn't prepared to leave until Saturday.

"Okay, but if you don't see me by five thirty a.m., it's because I'm snowed in," the driver cautioned. "Although I suppose if I'm snowed in, the bus will be snowed in, too, so it won't matter if I don't show up."

Next Fern called and left a voice-mail message at the phone shanty nearest Adam's house, indicating that she might be delayed by the snowstorm and she'd call if she was still on schedule to arrive in Ohio late Saturday evening. She figured calling them if she *was* returning on time would be much easier than calling if she *wasn't*.

"Is everything all set?" Walker asked her when she got back into the buggy.

"Jah," she said, not telling him she'd passed up the opportunity to leave a full day earlier. She didn't want him to feel guilty if she stayed in order to watch Jane, nor did she want him to try to convince her it was okay to go.

They saw the glow of the lights even before they rounded the corner to the lavishly decorated house. Walker pulled off to the side of the road so everyone could get out for a better look. Unlike many other *Englischers'* yards, this one contained no lawn ornaments or other types of decorations, except for lights. A rainbow of colors outlined the house and garage, wound around the fence, spiraled up the tree trunks and dripped from the branches. There must have been a hundred lights on the mailbox alone. The display was probably even considered garish by *Englisch* standards, but something about it was mesmerizing.

"I don't know which is brighter—the lights or the expressions on the *kinners'* faces," Fern murmured as she watched Jane, Patience and Phillip taking in the spectacle.

"What did you say?" Walker leaned toward her. As she repeated it into his ear, she noticed the soft fullness of his beard, which looked more coppery than chestnut beneath the multicolor lights. She hadn't been this close to him since—

"Mamm!" Phillip pulled her hand. "Look at that star at the top of the pine tree!"

Walker straightened his posture and Fern did, too. "I see it," she said. "I wonder how they got it up there."

"Too bad they didn't ask Walker to do it. He's the best ladder climber I've ever seen."

"Neh, not me," Walker answered modestly, but Fern could tell he was touched by Phillip's admiration. Sometimes her boy's bluntness made Fern cringe, but other times he would come out with a compliment that made a person grin from ear to ear, the way Walker was doing as he replied, "Whoever hung that star probably used a bucket truck to get up there."

"How could a person fit in a bucket?" Phillip wanted to know.

As Walker described the kind of truck he had referenced, Fern and the girls silently marveled at the lights. After a few more minutes, they all returned to the buggy. When they were seated again, Patience said with a sigh, "I wish this night would never end."

"If your *mamm* says it's okay, it doesn't have to end yet," Walker announced. "I've got a surprise up my sleeve."

"Is it up your shirtsleeve or your coat sleeve?" Phillip was seriously trying to figure out what kind of surprise he could have hidden in his clothing, and Fern hoped his question didn't seem insolent to Walker.

But Walker just patiently replied, "It's not up my *actual* sleeve. The surprise is a place." Once Fern agreed they could extend their outing a little longer, he commanded, "Everybody sit back in your seats, and no fair peeking, Jane. You either, Fern."

Fern promptly closed her eyes, and the children started guessing where Walker was taking them. Jane thought they were going to the bowling alley and Phillip guessed they were going ice skating. Patience supposed the library was their destination.

"I'll give you a hint. It's someplace we wouldn't normally go in the winter."

"I know—Serenity Lake!" Fern exclaimed, opening her eyes.

"Hey, I said no peeking!" Walker extended his arm straight out to shield her face, but she pushed his hand down. So he crooked his arm around her head from behind and covered her eyes with his gloved fingers, drawing her toward him. "You'll find out when we get there," he promised in a voice that was husky and low and made Fern's heart quiver.

She knew she ought to try to wriggle out of Walker's grasp—if the children peeked, they might have seen—but she couldn't make herself move a muscle. Did being so close make him feel as breathless as she felt? Did it make him want to stop time—or to turn it back to when they used to embrace for real, not as part of a guessing game?

"Okay, on the count of three, you can all open your eyes again," Walker directed everyone a few minutes later, releasing his hold on Fern.

"One, two—"

"Foster's Creamery!" Jane shouted.

"*Jah*. Should we go inside or do we want to take our orders to go?" Walker teased.

"Inside!" the children and Fern answered in unison.

Walker and Fern secured a small booth for the two of them, but the children perched atop the swivel stools at the counter. The girls ordered junior hot-fudge sundaes. Phillip wanted to imitate Walker and get a regular-sized banana split, but Fern would only let him order the smaller size because a swivel stool and a large banana split seemed like a precarious combination for his stomach. Fern ordered a single scoop of white chocolate and raspberry.

Having downed his banana split before Fern

had eaten half of her cone, Walker studied her as she licked the white-and-pink dessert. Self-conscious, she shivered noticeably, which made her feel even more diffident. "Ice cream always makes me shiver—even in the summer."

"I remember."

He remembers? Fern shivered again and quickly finished the rest of her cone.

By the time Walker brought Fern, Patience and Phillip home, Patience was so tired she practically sleepwalked into the house and up the stairs.

"This was my favorite day," she murmured drowsily as Fern tucked her in. *"Gut nacht, Mamm."*

When she went into Phillip's room, he said, "I wish it would snow for a whole week. Then we wouldn't have to leave until after *Grischtdaag*, and Jane and all Jaala's *groosskinner* could *kumme* over and go sledding with us every day."

"Maybe it will snow enough for them to *kumme* over tomorrow," Fern replied before kissing him on the forehead.

Within minutes, she was snuggled in bed, too, contemplating whether she was doing the right thing by selling Roman's house instead of continuing to live in it with the children. Obviously, Phillip and Patience loved being there. And the main reason Fern had initially been so eager to leave was that she didn't want to live anywhere near Walker. But now that their discord appeared to be resolved, Fern could picture rebuilding a friendship with him.

Actually, if she was being completely honest with

herself, she could almost envision rebuilding a romantic relationship with Walker, too. Recalling how she felt when he'd pulled her close in the buggy, Fern shivered for the third time that evening. But whether Walker had felt the same flicker of attraction or not, Fern knew better than to trust a fleeting emotion. And she certainly knew better than to trust *Walker*.

But she *could* trust the Lord. Realizing she'd never prayed about her decision to sell the house, Fern sat up, pulled her prayer *kapp* from the bedpost, covered her head and said, "*Gott*, You've given me this provision and I want to use it wisely, especially for the sake of my *kinner*. Please make Your will about it abundantly clear to me. And please help me to know whether to guard my heart or open it concerning Walker, too. *Denki*, Lord." Fern was about to say amen and slide beneath the quilt, when she added, "If You're willing, please let it snow enough for the *kinner* to go sledding tomorrow."

Jane was sleeping by the time they got home, so instead of waking her, Walker carried her into the house and upstairs to her bed. Allowing her to sleep in her clothes, he removed her shoes and piled two quilts on top of her before tiptoeing to his own room.

Once in bed, he pressed his hands against his belly in an attempt to soothe its agitation. *I shouldn't have eaten so much*, he thought, even though he knew that wasn't really why his stomach was in knots. It was his feelings about Fern that were wreaking havoc on his insides. Being with her tonight reminded him of the past they'd once shared. And thinking about their past stirred a yearning to share a future with her, too.

But that was crazy. Even if Fern felt the same inclination toward him, Walker was only too aware that he could never tell her why he married Gloria. Nor could he ever keep a secret about something as important as that from a woman he seriously courted. Just as importantly, Fern had a history of quickly redirecting her affections. *How could I be sure she wouldn't do that again? What if I told her my secret and gave her my heart again and she suddenly decided she preferred Stephen as a suitor?*

Reining in his wild imagination, Walker reminded himself his emotions would be easier to manage after Fern was gone. He'd only have to see her one more time before she left Serenity Ridge, and now that Roman had died, there was no reason she'd ever need to return again. The thought should have calmed him, but Walker's stomach was gripped with a spasm. He moaned as he rolled onto his side, recalling what Patience had whispered into his ear at the pizza parlor.

"If I had a *daed*, I'd want him to be just like you," she'd said. Walker understood her wistfulness, because deep down, in spite of everything, if he had a wife, he'd *still* want her to be just like Fern.

Chapter Nine

It was flurrying when Fern and the children woke up. Phillip gobbled up his eggs on toast and Patience finished hers almost as quickly so they could be dressed—this time Fern insisted Phillip wear his hat—and waiting outside for their cousin to arrive. Fern came outside with them, as she wanted to determine whether it was too cold to hang the clothes she'd washed on the line. There was a breeze, so they might dry if she hung them out here, but they also might freeze. If she hung them in the basement, they might still be damp by the time they left tomorrow—if they left tomorrow.

While she stood there trying to make up her mind, Walker's buggy approached, and Patience and Phillip zoomed across the lawn to greet them. Walker brought the horse to a halt and helped Jane down from the carriage before retrieving a red plastic sled from the back, which he handed to her.

"Look what I brought!" Jane announced, pulling the sled by its rope.

"Oh, *gut*, now we don't have to use a bin cover," Patience said. She'd been apprehensive ever since Fern told her that's how she and Gloria used to go sledding when they were teenagers.

"I'm still going to use a bin cover," Phillip declared. "I want to spin on my way down the hill."

"You're not going to get very far on the sled yet— the ground is barely coated," Fern cautioned, but the three children optimistically dashed off to take a trial run down the big hill behind the house.

As Walker came nearer, a tickle rippled down Fern's spine, just as it had the previous evening. How was it the very sight of him coming toward her with his long, determined stride could make her feel this way when last Saturday she hadn't been able to glance sideways at him? Studying him now, she noticed his face was blanched despite the brisk air. "You look like you could use some tea, Walker. Would you like to *kumme* in?"

He chortled. "Is that your way of telling me I look tired?"

"Frankly, I actually think you look nauseated," Fern said, not unkindly. "Tea always settles my *bauch*."

"*Denki*, but I'll be all right." He patted his stomach. "I admit my eyes were bigger than my *bauch* last night, but I couldn't let Phillip show me up."

"Oh, then your eyes were bigger than *Phillip's* stomach," Fern jested, and Walker chuckled. She had always liked making him laugh. When they were courting she claimed it made his eyes greener, which made him laugh even louder. "*Denki* again for a memorable evening. I'm so glad we didn't miss looking at the lights together. I haven't had that much fun since..." Fern couldn't remember the last time she'd had that much fun. It was probably one of the last times she went out with Walker before she left Serenity Ridge. But she couldn't say that, so she said, "Since Jane's *Grischtdaag* program." *At least, it was* schpass *up until our argument.*

"I enjoyed it, too. A lot," Walker emphasized, pushing the brim of his wool hat upward so he could peer into her eyes. Or so she could peer into his. *Sea green*, she once called them, even though she'd never seen the sea. One of the girls squealed in the backyard and Walker broke off his gaze and tipped his head toward the sky. "I haven't spoken to anyone about the forecast yet, but if this keeps up, I have a hunch you won't be leaving tomorrow."

"I know two *kinner*—no, make that *three kinner* who would be very *hallich* about that, especially if it meant we had to stay into next week."

"I know one adult who'd be *hallich* about that, too," Walker said. Fern's heart skittered. What did he mean by that? It seemed forever before he added, "Jane is going to be very weepy when you go and right now, I'm on my own to console her. So the longer you stay, the better."

Fern's hope melted as quickly as the snowflakes that landed on Walker's beard. She surprised herself by thinking, *I might be weepy when we go, too.* "I think I have it worse," she joked. "I'm on my own to console *two* sad *kinner.*"

"No one's forcing you to leave so soon," he said, grinning. Was he indicating he wanted her to stay, or was he just reminding her it didn't matter to him whether they sold the house or she lived in it for a while?

Fern vaguely responded, "I wonder what the policy is for changing my bus tickets in the event of a storm."

"If you'd like, I can take you to the phone shanty this afternoon so you can call to find out."

"*Denki*, I'd appreciate that." Walker was so helpful; Fern was going to miss that. Adam was helpful, too, but in a general way. When Walker offered to help with something, Fern felt as if he really wanted to do it, and he wanted to do it specifically for her. It made her feel…well, it made her feel special.

After he left, Fern realized since it was snowing harder now, if she hung the clothes on the line, they'd get wet as well as frozen, and they'd have virtually no chance of drying. If she hung them in the basement, they probably wouldn't dry, but at least they'd be less damp than they were now. So she set the basket back on the porch, thinking, *I wish my decision about selling the* haus *was that easy to make.*

Before going inside, she ambled around to the backyard to check on the children. There were several stripes of brown earth stretching down the hill from where they'd worn a path through the snow to the ground. Jane and Patience were together on the sled, and the snow was so sparse they kept getting stuck and had to nudge themselves forward with their hands. Although the incline was relatively steep, there was a long, flat stretch of yard at the bottom, which meant that even if they picked up speed on their descent, the girls would come to a gradual stop at the end of their ride. Fern decided it would be safe for the children to sled alone while she did the breakfast dishes, since she could see them from the kitchen window.

She was turning to leave when Phillip warned the girls to get out of his way. Fern glanced back and saw him beginning to descend the hill while standing on the trash bin lid.

"Absatz!" she shouted, and he immediately hopped off the lid. "I don't want you standing on that to go down the hill. You could break a bone!" Then, so there'd be no question about her instructions, she added, "I don't want you standing up on the sled, either. You can go on your bottom only."

"Can't I go on my knees?" the boy bargained.

"Jah, but only face forward," she allowed.

"What if I start out going face forward but I spin around and end up going face backward? Should I roll off?"

"Neh, if that happens, don't roll off. Hang on for dear life!" On second thought, Fern wondered if she ought to forbid Phillip to go down the hill on his knees. As Walker said, he was athletic, so she didn't want to hinder his abilities by being overly protec-

tive. Nor did she want him to get hurt. She wished that Walker hadn't left yet; he would have had a better sense of what kind of limits to put on Phillip's rambunctious stunts.

After an additional warning to the children to be careful, Fern went inside and washed, dried and put away the dishes, monitoring the trio from the window. By the time she finished tidying the kitchen, they'd moved on to making patterns in the snow with their boots.

Fern darted downstairs to clip the clothes to the line strung from one beam of the ceiling to the other. The rope was so frayed she didn't know if it would hold. *Roman has probably been using the same clothesline since I lived here.* She couldn't imagine him doing his own laundry, yet at the far end of the line hung a shirt and a pair of Roman's trousers. Whether he or one of the women who'd cleaned the house pinned them there, Fern didn't know, but she hadn't been able to make herself take them down.

Roman had been a difficult man in many regards; he was exacting, sanctimonious and frugal to an extreme. He never once expressed gratitude for Fern's help when he was alive, which was why it was so surprising he bequeathed the house to her, and not solely to Jane. *He must have appreciated and cared about me after all. Maybe he knew how much I was struggling financially, but for whatever reason, it seems he really wanted me to* live *here.* As she contemplated her uncle's uncharacteristic generosity,

Fern again questioned whether she was doing the right thing by selling the house.

Footsteps overhead interrupted her thoughts. She pinned Phillip's last sock to the line and scurried upstairs to make sure that whatever child had just come in had taken off their boots. *I guess there's a little of Roman in me, too,* she mused, chuckling to herself.

It was actually Jaala who was standing in the living room, saying she knocked but Fern didn't answer so she had to let herself in before she turned into an icicle. The older woman told Fern that Abram had dropped her and her three eldest grandchildren there on his way to a doctor's appointment. "We came by last night but you weren't here and I was afraid you'd left ahead of the storm. I would have been sorry if I'd missed you."

"I would have been sorry, too, although I'm concerned about all of you traveling in this weather. How are the roads?"

"It's barely starting to stick, so we'll make it home just fine, *Gott* willing." Jaala extended a rectangular container to Fern. "A few slices for your journey—or for dessert tonight, if your travel plans are delayed."

"Oh, *denki*!" Fern didn't have to lift the lid to know Jaala's scrumptious spice cake with cream cheese frosting was inside. "That was so thoughtful of you. Would you like a piece of it with tea? I'm afraid my cupboards are bare, since I thought we'd be leaving."

"*Neh*, save the cake for you and the *kinner*. But I would like tea." Jaala hung her coat, scarf and winter bonnet on an empty peg on the wall. "When Abram returns, he can take you to the store and then *kumme* back for us. I'll stay with the *kinner*. Otherwise, you might be stuck here without anything to eat but cake."

"Phillip would love that!" Fern laughed. "But you don't need to take me to the store. You live so far away and I don't want to keep you from getting home as soon as you can. Walker is returning shortly for Jane and he's bringing me to the phone shanty, so it's not that much farther for us to go into town from there." *I just hope I brought enough money to purchase food for the few extra days...*

Jaala reluctantly accepted Fern's decision. "If the storm prevents you from leaving before *Grischtdaag*, you must spend the holiday with us. We'll *kumme* get you. As I said, the more the merrier. Which reminds me, I heard Louisa had to leave because Willa and her *kinner* were sick. I must be sure to invite Walker and Jane for *Grischtdaag*, too."

Oh, that would be schpass! Fern briskly retreated to the kitchen so Jaala wouldn't see her lips dancing upward with giddy hopefulness. After the tea was ready, the two women chatted for another hour, and Jaala graciously agreed to help Walker organize an estate sale if the agent or home buyer didn't want to acquire Roman's possessions.

"You and Abram should take whatever items you want, first," Fern told her. The deacon and his wife unfailingly shared everything they had with those in need, including Fern, so it was a pleasure to be able to give back to them for once.

When they heard heavy footsteps on the porch, Fern's pulse quickened, wondering whether it was Abram or if Walker had returned early. To her dismay, it turned out to be Stephen.

"I brought two of my nephews over to go sledding," he explained after Fern grudgingly invited him in. He greeted Jaala before continuing, "I also wanted to see if there's anything you need before the storm sets in. This morning an *Englischer* in town told me we're going to get up to twenty inches overnight and it's already awfully slick out there."

Twenty inches! Fern swallowed a gasp. There wasn't any possibility they'd be leaving Serenity Ridge tomorrow and it might be days before the roads were navigable. She knew she couldn't make a box of chocolates, two slices of leftover pizza and a quarter of a spice cake last for that long. Fern glanced out the window; it was snowing much heavier now. While she'd rather go to the market with Walker, she didn't want to put him and Jane in jeopardy by delaying their trip home.

Before Fern could come to a decision, Jaala answered for her. "Fern's pantry is empty. She needs a ride to the market before the roads get too bad. I'll stay here with the *kinner*. If Abram returns meanwhile, he'll wait with me until you two get back."

Fern didn't even have a chance to refuse; Stephen was practically out the door before Jaala finished speaking. She realized she should be grateful for his willingness to help. No matter how uncomfortable she felt about going with him alone to the market, Fern would feel even worse if the children were housebound without anything to eat. So she reluctantly bundled into her coat and bonnet and followed Stephen's footprints through the snow to his buggy.

Although the road Roman lived on was coated with two to three inches of snow, the main road was comparatively clean, since the passing vehicles had melted wide paths on the pavement. *It would have been fine if I had waited until Walker came back*, Fern grumbled to herself. Suspecting Stephen may have exaggerated the magnitude of the storm in order to have an excuse to stop by Roman's house, she balled her gloved fingers on her lap.

"Don't worry, I won't let anything happen to you." Stephen apparently thought she was nervous, which only irritated Fern more.

She asked him to stop at the phone shanty on the way so she could change her bus tickets. To her relief, because of the impending nor'easter, the transportation company rescheduled her tickets without charging any additional fees, as long as she left on Tuesday's bus. "I tried to warn you to leave this morning," the van driver said when Fern called him. But Fern didn't care; she wouldn't have left this morning no matter what. She hadn't felt ready. She didn't even know if she'd feel ready by Tuesday.

"What's your new departure date?" Stephen asked before she was even seated again.

Fern supposed he was just making friendly conversation, but she resented him asking about her schedule and she replied tersely, "Tuesday morning."

"That means you'll be here on *Grischtdaag*. You're *wilkom* to join us at my *bruder*'s *haus* if you have nowhere else to go."

"*Denki*, but if the roads are passable, I've already told Jaala I'd spend *Grischtdaag* with her *familye*." *And with Walker,* Gott *willing.*

Then it dawned on Fern that even if the roads *were* passable, there was a good chance Walker and Jane would go to Willa's, not to Jaala's, provided Willa's family had recovered. *Unless the Lord gives me a clear indication I shouldn't sell the haus, I probably won't see Walker again after he picks Jane up this afternoon.* Fern's chest tightened when she realized she might not even see him *then*. It was possible Walker would return to Roman's house while she was at the market and he'd need to leave for his own home before the roads worsened. *Please* Gott, *don't let that happen*, she silently pleaded.

"I've already sent everyone else home. You ought to leave, too," Levi Swarey told Walker shortly before noon, even though the tree farm was hopping with frantic customers. As the owner of the tree business, Levi lived on the property, so at the end of the day all he had to do was stroll up the driveway to his house. He said he'd be closing the farm shortly anyway, since the roads were getting too bad for the *Englischers* to travel on them.

"But you've got a dozen customers in line to have

their trees baled, and who knows how many more are still out in the aisles searching for their trees," Walker argued.

"Otto will help me take care of them." Levi was referring to his brother-in-law, who also worked for him and lived within walking distance. "Go ahead. Be safe and *Frehlicher Grischtdaag.*"

On the way to Fern's house, Walker took a slight detour to stop at the phone shanty closest to Levi's farm, since that was the one Walker and his mother always used, to see if there were any messages for him. Even though he and his mother had arranged to speak the following morning, Walker figured she might have heard the weather report and decided to give him an update while she still could.

His intuition proved right; someone had scrawled a lengthy message from Louisa on the whiteboard. It was marked with today's date and indicated everyone in Willa's family had recovered and was looking forward to seeing Walker and Jane, but Louisa hoped they wouldn't take any chances journeying in inclement weather. The note also mentioned she said he ought to purchase enough food to last him and Jane three days. Walker chuckled at his mother's ability to treat him like a child even long distance. In turn, he left a message for her at the phone shanty in Unity, obediently promising to wait until the roads were safe before going to Unity, and informing her there were enough leftovers in the fridge to keep him and Jane alive for a week.

As he continued toward Fern's house, Walker

kept a tight rein on Daisy. Some of the roads had either been sanded or plowed, while others hadn't. It wasn't that the snow was too deep yet—maybe four inches—but the flakes were big and they were falling fast. Every once in a while a gust of wind would blow the precipitation sideways, diminishing Walker's visibility and unsettling Daisy. While he imagined the conditions were going to be even more hazardous by the time he took Fern and the *kinner* to the phone shanty, he hesitated to push his horse faster than she was already moving. *Lord, please protect everyone on the road today and deliver me quickly to Fern's haus,* he prayed without closing his eyes.

Then he realized he'd been thinking of Roman's house as Fern's, even though she apparently had no intention of making it hers. That morning he'd told her how much he enjoyed being with her again. And, despite being fully aware of all the reasons it would be better for both of them if she left, he even hinted that she should reconsider staying, but she'd acted as if she hadn't heard. *I suppose I ought to be glad—at least that means she isn't interested in staying here to pursue a courtship with Stephen.*

Or so he thought, until he arrived at Fern's house and learned from Jaala and Abram that Stephen had stopped by with his nephews and he'd taken Fern to the phone shanty and market so she could stock up on groceries before the storm.

"We expected them back some time ago," Jaala said, her forehead stitched with lines.

Abram placed his hand over his wife's. "I think

they're fine, but let's ask *Gott* to protect them and all the other people out on the road."

The three of them had just finished praying together when the children clamored onto the porch.

"*Kumme* watch us sledding, *Daed*," Jane pleaded when Walker opened the door. Her skin around her mouth was bright red; she'd been licking her mittens again.

"I'm cold," one of Jaala's grandchildren whined. "And *hungerich*."

"You should take your *groosskinner* home. You live farther away than I do," Walker insisted to Jaala and Abram. "I'll stay with the other *kinner*."

It took some persuading, but Jaala eventually relented. Before she left, she told Walker, "You and Jane are invited to spend *Grischtdaag* with us if you don't head off to Unity. And please remind Fern now that she's staying, I expect her for *Grischtdaag*. Abram will *kumme* get her in the morning, won't you, Abram?"

"Of course." The deacon nodded and clapped Walker on the shoulder. "If we don't see you on the twenty-fifth, have a *Frehlicher Grischtdaag* with your *familye*."

Walker followed Abram and Jaala out onto the porch. Abram apparently had cleared the drive at least once because there was only a dusting of snow on it and his buggy rolled along with ease. After the couple departed, Walker went around to the backyard and watched and waved as the children took turns sailing down the hill on an assortment of sleds. Although he occasionally clapped and cheered them on, his mind was on Fern and Stephen.

Once again, she'd opted to go with him when she'd made plans to go with Walker. But this time, he knew he had no reason to be angry. Fern likely had chosen to go with Stephen because the weather was getting worse, and she thought it would be too risky to wait until Walker returned before heading out in it. Jaala was there to watch the children, so the timing must have seemed perfect. Fern's decision to ride with Stephen likely had nothing to do with her having a romantic interest in him.

Yet in spite of logically understanding Fern's motives, Walker still felt utterly deflated because he kept circling back to the same conclusion: as much fun as he'd had with Fern and hoped she'd stay in Serenity Ridge, Walker could never tell her about Jane. He could never marry her. The closest he'd ever come to being her husband—or even her suitor— was taking her out to an ice cream parlor or sharing supper with their children. That wasn't enough for him. And if she felt any romantic inclination for him, it wouldn't be enough for her, either. No, it was better if she left.

And it was better if he put his mind on other things. Telling the children he'd be in the front yard, Walker retrieved the ax from the barn. The logs were covered in snow and the chopping block was slippery, so he gave up after only a few attempts. *I hope Fern and Stephen are okay*, he thought as he went back to the barn to put the ax away.

When he emerged, he saw them slogging from Stephen's parked buggy toward the house, each hugging a paper bag of groceries, their heads bent against the wind and snow. Stephen noticed Walker first and gave him a wave. Then Fern lifted her head.

"Walker!" she exclaimed. "I'm so sorry you had to wait for us. There was an accident on Laurel Lane and we waited forever for traffic to clear, only to be detoured to the other side of town because they closed Grove Street completely. I feel *baremlich* you've had to stay here with the *kinner*. When did Jaala and Abram leave?"

"A while ago, but it's okay, I don't mind. I'm just glad the two of you are all right," Walker answered, feeling guilty she was so distressed. *After how I reacted last time she got a ride from Stephen, it's no wonder.* Taking the bag from her arms and motioning for Stephen to give him the other one, he added, "I'll place these inside the door and then I should be on my way."

"So should I." Stephen started around toward the back of the house to call his nephews, but Fern hung back, waiting for Walker to set the groceries inside before heading for the backyard. Stephen had already summoned his nephews and they were running toward him, dragging their sleds behind them. He directed the children to say goodbye to Fern and Walker, and then he touched Fern's shoulder. "I hope this isn't the last time I get to see you."

"Goodbye, Stephen," was Fern's simple reply, but Walker noticed she took a step backward, closer to him than to Stephen. Once they left, Walker beckoned to Jane, too.

"We have to go already?" she whined loudly from the top of the hill.

"*Jah*, the roads are getting dangerous. We need to skedaddle."

"Aww," Jane grumbled. She appeared to be on the brink of tears. "Can't we just go down three more times? Please, *Daed*?"

"Okay," he relented. "Three more times if you go together. Or one more time each if you go separately."

They chose to go together, so they'd each get three more turns. The snow was packed down where they'd been sledding and their combined weight increased their momentum, so they whizzed down the hill. Since Phillip was in front, a spray of snow coated his face, and when they came to a stop a few yards in front of where Walker and Fern were standing, he rolled off the sled and mugged. "Look, I've got a beard like you'll have when you're an old man, Walker."

Walker doubled over and Fern did, too. By the time they'd stopped laughing, the children had plodded to the top of the hill again. This time it was Jane's turn in the front. Watching them position themselves on the sled, Fern remarked, "Jaala said we're invited for *Grischtdaag* if we're both stuck in town."

"*Jah*, she told me that, too. She said Abram's picking you up in the morning. But I stopped at the phone shanty and my *mamm* left a message that Willa's *familye* is well again. So as soon as the roads are travelable, we'll leave for Unity."

"Oh, well, I'm glad your *schwesder* and her *kinner* feel better." Fern wrapped her arms around herself. "Jaala also said she'd help organize an estate sale for Roman's belongings."

"I'd appreciate that. My *mamm* will help too, I'm sure. And I'll finish the shingles on the roof and clean up the rest of the yard after *Grischtdaag*."

"I can't tell you how much I appreciate all you've done for me—for all three of us," Fern said, a catch in her voice.

Walker couldn't look at her for fear he'd choke up. "I was glad to do it."

"The *kinner* will want to write each other, and who knows, maybe we'll visit Serenity Ridge some time and they'll see each other then."

"Or we'll have a reason to go to Ohio and our paths will cross there," Walker said, although he knew neither scenario was likely.

For the children's final run down the hill, Patience was supposed to sit in the front, but she must have opted out, because Phillip was first and it looked like Jane's arms that were wrapped around his torso from behind. Patience was obscured behind her. The children whooped the entire way down the hill. Hearing their elation, it occurred to Walker that was how exhilarating the past week was, too—and how soon it was over.

All five of them trudged to the barn together, with Phillip carrying the sled upside down on his head.

Walker had wheeled the buggy inside so he could hitch Daisy to it without the animal being unnerved by the swirling snow.

When he was finished, he took the sled from Phillip, and Fern said, "We'll send you our address when we get to Ohio so you can write to us, Jane."

"But how can we leave when it's snowing so much?" Phillip questioned.

"We aren't leaving today, but this is the last time we'll see Jane and Walker," Fern explained. "They're going to Unity for *Grischtdaag*. Jane's other *gschwischderkinner* are excited they get to see her."

"*I'm* excited *I* get to see her, too," Phillip groused.

"I know, but *Gott* gave us a blessing by allowing us to spend this week together, and instead of asking for more, we ought to be grateful for the *schpass* we had," Fern exhorted her son, and Walker glumly supposed he ought to take her admonishment to heart, too. "It's time to say goodbye so Walker and Jane can get home safely."

Phillip wrapped his arms around his cousin's waist so tightly he practically lifted her off the ground. When he let go, Jane hugged Patience, who, oddly, was the only child smiling. "*Denki* for sharing your sled, Jane," she said. "Next time, I might try going in the front."

Fern bent over and kissed Jane on the cheek before embracing her tightly, and Walker also crouched down to give Phillip and Patience a hug. When he straightened, he and Fern looked at each other, as if not sure what to do. They both stretched out their arms at the same time and moved forward for a quick embrace, but Walker bumped his chin against the stiff brim of Fern's bonnet and he jerked backward, so then they just squeezed each other's hands instead.

"Goodbye, Walker." Although a scarf covered Fern's eyes and nose, Walker saw that her sterling-colored eyes were blurred with tears, whether from the cold or from emotion, he wasn't sure.

His voice gravelly, Walker uttered, "Goodbye, Fern."

Then he and Jane climbed into the buggy and started down the driveway. Although he'd given her the option of sitting up front with him, she wanted to sit in the back, and Walker could hear that she was trying to stifle her sobs, just as he was trying to keep his own emotions in check.

It might have been better if they had never kumme, *rather than to see Fern again and have Jane meet the* kinner *and then go through the pain of separation. And the knowledge of what we're missing,* he thought as he journeyed homeward. Since Fern indicated Grove Street was closed, Walker had to take a side road that was straighter but less heavily trafficked than the main road.

As soon as he turned onto it, he realized a plow was headed in their direction. Walker didn't have time to bring the animal to a stop, so he directed Daisy to the side of the road, but it was no use: the plow's flashing lights and rumbling sound spooked her and she bolted.

"Daed!" Jane exclaimed, but Walker couldn't

comfort her. He had to focus on halting the horse. In the blowing snow, he could hardly tell which way was up and which way was down, much less which side of the road they were on. But when the buggy began to jostle so hard he lost his hat, Walker knew they were no longer on the pavement at all.

"Daed!" Jane screamed again, louder this time. "Make her stop!"

Chapter Ten

Once Fern put away the groceries, she made hot chocolate—she'd purchased a canister of cocoa as a Christmas treat—and carried three mugs on a tray into the living room, where the children were snuggled under quilts on the sofa.

"We get to drink that in here?" Patience asked.

"*Jah*, we'll be careful," Fern said as she situated herself in between the two children and handed them each a mug and a napkin. Usually Fern made them sit at the kitchen table to eat or drink anything, but after the children had spent so much time outdoors, they were chilled to the bone. "I want to keep you as close to the woodstove as possible so you won't catch colds. The last thing I want is for you to have to travel on Tuesday when you're sick."

"I don't want to have to travel at *all*," Phillip complained. "I like it here."

Rather than reminding her son a second time that it wasn't appreciative to ask the Lord to give them more time in Serenity Ridge than He'd already given them, Fern admitted, "I like it here, too."

"Then why do we have to leave?"

Because that's what I believe is Gott's best for *us*, Fern thought. But she still wasn't positive. "I've already paid for our bus tickets." Her answer rang hollow, so she added, "And there might be a surprise for us in Ohio, but unless we go back we can't find out what it is."

"What kind of a surprise? Is it a *Grischtdaag* present?" Patience asked.

Fern had actually been alluding to securing a home of their own, but Patience's question caused her to remember she'd left the children's modest presents at Adam's house, since she thought they'd return by Christmas. "*Jah*, your *Grischtdaag* presents are in Ohio. There might be something else there for you, too."

Phillip didn't seem the least bit curious. Nor was he interested in his hot chocolate. Setting the cup on the surface of the rolling lamp table next to Roman's Bible, he sighed. "I'm too sad to drink my cocoa."

"Don't be sad, Phillip." Patience tipped her head backward to slurp down the rest of her drink. When she finished, she had a brown mustache above her lip. "*Mamm* said I could ask *Gott* to let us use this *haus*. I think He will say *jah*, so we're not going to have to leave."

Now Fern understood why Patience hadn't been at all dismayed about saying goodbye to Jane and Walker; the child had full faith it wasn't the last time they'd see each other. Fern gently tried to disavow her of the notion, saying, "I don't think you should count on that, Patience. But the Lord has given us almost three more days here than we would have gotten if it hadn't snowed. So we ought to show that we're grateful. How would you like to worship in preparation for *Grischtdaag*?"

"I know!" Patience's eyes glimmered. "Let's light the candles and read the verses about Jesus being borned. The ones Jane said at her *Grischtdaag* program."

This got Phillip's attention. He pulled the Bible from the table and handed it to Fern, and then both children cuddled up close to her. She read aloud until she got to the verses Jane had recited at the school and Phillip interrupted, "*Neh*, let me say that part, *Mamm*."

He quoted the verses word for word, amazing Fern, who hadn't realized Jane had had such a positive influence on him, as well as on Patience. After completing the passage, Fern got up and lit the candles, and then they sang four Christmas carols before Phillip announced his stomach was rumbling.

Glad to see he was feeling more like his usual self, Fern said she'd go start supper while they put away their mittens, scarves and socks that had dried in front of the fire. As she measured water into a pot— she was back to serving rice and beans for supper— Fern overheard Phillip ask his sister, "Remember when Walker said Jane's feet *schtinke*?"

"*Jah*, that was *voll schpass*," Patience said with a giggle.

"Smell these."

After a pause, Patience squealed, "Eww! Why do they smell like that?"

"It's because I'm a man and men sweat a lot on their heads and feet. Walker sweats a lot, too."

Fern made a noise that was neither a chuckle nor a sob as she realized this was a trip her children would never forget. *And neither will I*, she thought.

When the meal was nearly prepared, she turned down the flame beneath the pot of rice and called the children, who by then had gone upstairs to play the card game Jane had forgotten. They sounded like a herd of cattle clamoring down the stairs, so Fern rushed to the living room to see if one of them had taken a tumble. Instead of her children she was startled to find the front door open and Walker standing on the threshold, literally coated in snow, with Jane in his arms. She was wrapped in a blanket and shivering, her eyes closed and her plump cheeks nearly scarlet from the cold.

"Help," he implored. "We went off the road. Jane hit her head on the buggy seat."

That was all the information Fern needed for now. "*Kumme* lay her on the bed. Be very gentle," she directed Walker and led him to Roman's old bedroom. Then she told him to go put a kettle of water on the stove. As she exchanged Jane's wet clothing for one of her own dresses, Fern checked her for any bleeding or additional injuries. All the while, she asked the child questions to assess whether she was having nausea or vision problems. Although Jane's teeth chattered and a large egg had formed on her scalp just above her forehead, to Fern's relief she was cognizant of her surroundings, and it appeared she'd be fine once she warmed up.

"Walker!" she cried, and he was through the door in an instant. "Let's get her onto the sofa by the woodstove."

Walker picked Jane up again, and Fern whisked the quilt and wool blanket from her bed. In the living room, she told Patience and Phillip to fetch their quilts from upstairs. Fern layered those on top of Jane, too, assuring Walker, "She's okay. She's going to be just fine."

He just hovered over his daughter, completely speechless, a grimace distorting his features.

"D-d-daed." Jane's teeth knocked together as she stammered, "Your b-beard is d-d-dripping on me."

Fern chuckled and dabbed the water from Jane's forehead with a corner of the blanket, but Walker still didn't utter a sound. Growing more concerned about him than she was about his daughter, Fern touched his shoulder. *"Kumme,* you're soaking wet. Take off your coat and sit in the rocker by the fire. I saw a pair of my *onkel*'s work clothes in the basement. I'll go get them."

"I—I—I have to put Daisy in the b-b-barn first. Sh-she's tethered to the fence and she's ag-agitated from the snow."

Fern didn't want Walker to go back outside alone

in the state he was in; neither did she want to leave Jane just yet. "Phillip can go with you," she said, shooting Phillip a meaningful look. Her young, courageous son gave her a nod, acknowledging he understood.

"Neh—" Walker began to object but Phillip cut in.

"I can hold the flashlight," he volunteered, scrambling to put his boots and coat on.

By the time the two went out and came back, Patience had brought Jane a sweater and had managed to put dry wool socks on her feet for her. Jane was sitting upright, sipping the hot chocolate Fern made with the water she'd asked Walker to boil. After Walker had dried off and changed into Roman's old clothes, Fern gave him a cup of tea, but he set it aside and picked up his daughter, settling into the rocking chair with her.

Jane's legs dangled over the arm of the chair and as Fern covered them with the quilt, she noticed the tempestuous look in Walker's eyes. She'd seen that same look only once before, after he'd rescued Phillip from the tree branch. Whatever happened on the road had frightened Walker gravely, but she dared not question him about it. He wasn't ready to talk and she didn't want to upset him further by pushing him. Her children seemed to pick up on her cue— they sat beside Fern in silence as Walker rocked Jane back and forth.

Without realizing she was doing it, Fern began to softly hum. First, a song from the *Ausbund*. Then, a Christmas carol. And another and another until in the middle of the fourth one, Jane announced, "Something smells *gut*. I'm *hungerich*."

"It's supper," Fern announced brightly. "But I don't think you should eat very much until we're sure your *bauch* is all right. Maybe you can have a little rice, but no beans."

"Aw, I wish I didn't have to eat any of those beans, either," Phillip grumbled, since black beans were one of the few foods he disliked. To Fern's relief, his comment seemed to pull Walker back into the present. He stood Jane upright in front of him and then they all moved into the kitchen.

Although Fern was worried she wouldn't have enough food to satisfy everyone, Walker hardly ate a bite anyway. He still looked stunned but he told the story, little by little, of how the lights from a snow plow had frightened Daisy and the animal took off into a field, throwing Jane from the seat and nearly tipping the buggy in the process. Walker blindly managed to guide the horse in big circles, so eventually she tired out and wound to a halt. Since the road was infrequently traveled, it was already getting dark and the horse had run herself ragged, Walker unhitched the buggy. Then he pulled Jane on the sled with one hand and led Daisy to Roman's house—the nearest residence—with the other.

When he was done speaking, he tugged at the hair on his chin. His face slipped into a faraway expression again, as if he was literally lost in thought, until Patience patted his shoulder. "I'm *hallich* you and Jane and Daisy are okay," she said. "You must have been sore afraid."

For a moment, Walker just stared blankly at the little girl, so she added, "That's really, really afraid. So afraid it makes you sore. Like the shepherds in the field with their flocks, except you were in a field with Jane and you didn't see an angel, did you?"

Fern held her breath, half anticipating an emotional outburst from Walker. But he cupped his hand behind Patience's head and drew her toward him to kiss her forehead. "*Neh.* I didn't see an angel, but *Gott* protected us and I'm *hallich* about that, too." He picked up his fork and began eating his rice.

"And I'm *hallich* you get to stay overnight." Phillip pushed a bean to the side of his plate. "You can sleep with me in my room, Walker."

"*Denki*, but I'll sleep in the workshop," Walker asserted and Fern didn't argue with him. She figured he might need space for himself and besides, it didn't seem proper for them to stay overnight in the house without any other adults there. When they were courting he was as committed to maintaining their reputations and protecting their modesty as she was, and she was relieved he hadn't changed in that regard.

The children were so tired from sledding that they went to bed almost immediately after Fern and Patience washed, dried and put away the supper dishes.

"If you hear something hitting the roof, that's the tree," Patience told her roommate before they headed toward the stairs. "Your *daed* sawed off the branch that used to tap every night but there's a new one that hangs down because it's got heavy snow on it."

"Really?" Fern was surprised. Patience must have noticed the branch rapping against her side of the house that afternoon but she hadn't complained about it.

"*Jah*, but it's okay. Walker said it's just the tree waving its arms to get my attention. It's too sturdy to fall."

Fern caught Walker's eye. "Well, he knows more about trees than anyone I know," she said with a wink before following the children upstairs to tuck them into bed. When she returned with a stack of blankets, Walker was stoking the fire and he'd filled the wood bin, too. Fern thanked him and asked if he wanted tea. "I plan to bake dessert tomorrow, but for now I can offer you a piece of *kuche* from Jaala. Or one of the chocolates I confiscated from Jane."

Walker's smile belied the sadness in his eyes. Or maybe he was merely exhausted as he said, "I'd better go check on Daisy and then get a fire started in the workshop. So I'll say good-night now."

While he put on his boots and coat, Fern retrieved a couple extra blankets for the horse and a pillow for Walker. She divided the bedding between two over-size canvas bags she'd also found in the linen closet so they'd be easier for him to carry.

Walker reached to take them from her but she wouldn't let go of the handles, forcing him to look her in the eyes. She wasn't sure what she wanted to say. She only knew she didn't want him to leave without expressing how relieved she was that he and Jane were okay. He raised an eyebrow, waiting. Fern opened her mouth but she was still at a loss for words, so she released the handles.

The next thing she knew, Walker had set the bags back down and drew her toward himself so that her cheek pressed into his damp, scratchy wool coat. He hugged her tightly, just as Phillip had embraced his cousin a few hours earlier, nearly lifting her from the floor. And Fern held on just as tightly for what seemed like a long time, but not nearly long enough.

When he let her go, his eyes were misty. "*Denki*, Fern," he said before turning to leave. "Sleep well."

But sleep eluded her, in part because she was vigilant about checking on Jane. But also because Walker's reaction to another near accident emphasized to her how traumatized he must have been by Jordan's death. She again thought of Louisa telling her that Walker hadn't been in his right mind afterward. That he hadn't been in his right mind when he married Gloria, either.

Is this the Lord's way of telling me to keep an open heart toward Walker after all? she wondered. But even if God was showing her that she ought to be more understanding of Walker, that didn't necessarily mean the Lord was guiding her to stay in Maine. Nor did it mean she was meant to have a romantic relationship with Walker, especially since he hadn't directly expressed an interest in her. Not with words anyway. But was the way he embraced her an indication of his feelings for her? Or was it only another reaction to the trauma of the day's events? Fern had no way of knowing, so again she asked the Lord for guidance.

This time she prayed, "*Gott*, if it's Your will for Walker and me to be in a romantic relationship, please have him show me plainly. And if it's not, please let him show me that in a way that's unmistakable, too. *Denki* for keeping him and Jane safe and *denki* for bringing them back for one more day."

With the woodstove burning, Roman's orderly little workshop was actually warmer than Fern's house, which was fortunate because it meant Walker could use most of the blankets as padding beneath him rather than as a covering over him. After he'd fashioned himself a bed, he turned off the flashlight and lay in the dark. His thoughts whirled through his mind just like the wind whistled through the trees.

He couldn't stop thinking about how comforted he'd been by Fern's presence tonight. Not only had she known exactly how to care for Jane—no doubt because she'd tended to so many relatives with various health conditions over the years—but she'd also calmed his frazzled nerves. Just by being at his side, humming as he gathered his thoughts, Fern had helped quiet the pandemonium in his head and slow his sprinting pulse.

Walker's stomach growled. He would have enjoyed having a piece of dessert with Fern, but he didn't trust himself to be alone with her. The way he was feeling tonight, he was only half a sentence away from breaking down and telling her about Jane. About Gloria. About *every*thing. He'd nearly done it, too, when they were standing near the door and she was looking at him like that… Instead, at the last minute, he'd hugged her, which may have been inappropriate, but she didn't seem to mind. She probably attributed the embrace to his being in shock, and maybe it was.

For several harrowing minutes as Daisy ran pell-mell through the snowy expanse, Walker was certain the buggy was about to overturn and he'd lose his life, or worse—his daughter would lose hers. So it was only natural if he wasn't quite himself tonight. But having acted in haste after Jordan's death, Walker didn't want to do something he'd regret now, like telling Fern about Gloria's pregnancy. He was aware he needed time to recover emotionally from the fright of what had almost happened.

And because of God's grace, he *had* time to recover. He had more time to spend with Fern and her children, too, and he was determined to make the most of it.

Walker slept through the night and to his relief, he didn't even dream, much less suffer any nightmares. A glance out the window told him it was still snowing. Or maybe it had stopped and started again. Walker shuddered; the fire had died out overnight and he couldn't wait to get back inside the house, but first he wanted to check on Daisy. Fortunately, the Fry boys hadn't taken all of the hay from the barn when they took Roman's horse to their house, so there was plenty for the animal to eat, but Walker was concerned her water might have frozen over.

When he opened the door to go outside, he discovered the snow was over two feet high, which made for a laborious trek to the barn. After tending to the horse, he took Roman's snow shovel from the stand where it was neatly positioned with the other types of shovels and rakes. Walker intended to clear paths from the barn to the workshop and from the workshop to the house. But first, he wanted to get inside and have a cup of coffee. Although the snow was fine and powdery, it was deep, so rather than wading through it, Walker had to pick his way across it by lifting each leg high and extending it forward as far as possible with every step. It took him three times as long as usual to reach the house.

"Guder mariye," Fern greeted him with a mug of coffee. Her eyes were as luminous as her smile this morning. "I'm making oatmeal. Go sit by the stove—you must be freezing."

"I was toasty warm until the fire died out." Instead of sitting in the rocking chair by the woodstove, once he removed his boots, Walker followed Fern into the kitchen and took a seat. Just as he was about to ask how Jane was, his daughter joined him at the table.

"Hi, *Daed*!" she greeted him, as vibrant as ever. "Did you see all the snow?"

"*See* it? I had to *swim* through it."

"You did?" Phillip had come into the room from

down the hall. "How does somebody swim through snow?"

"As quickly as they can. It's really cold!" Walker joked.

Patience was the last one to take a place at the table. *"Guder mariye,"* she mumbled, rubbing her eyes.

Everyone wished her a good morning, too. "You look sleepy." Walker added sympathetically, "It's not easy sharing a bed, is it? I'm glad I've never had to do that."

"I share a bed with my *gschwischderkind* in Ohio, so I like it. And Jane kept me nice and warm," Patience said with a yawn. "But in Ohio *Mamm* doesn't *kumme* into our room and wake us up with a flashlight to ask us questions."

"I wasn't asking you—I was asking Jane. I wanted to be sure the bump on her head didn't affect her thinking," Fern told her daughter before sitting down and asking Walker to say grace. When he was done thanking the Lord for their food, Fern apologized, "I'm afraid there's not a lot of toast because I need to conserve the flour in case we're snowed in through Monday, but everyone can have as much oatmeal as you want. Phillip, I heated the two leftover slices of pizza for you."

"I get to eat pizza for breakfast?" Phillip marveled. "I wish we had snowstorms every day!"

"You might not wish that after you're done helping me shovel," Walker joked. He didn't really intend to put the boy to work, but Phillip was dejected after breakfast when Walker said he couldn't help because there was only one shovel. So Walker ended up giving him the same handy plastic bin cover he'd used as a sled to use as a scoop. In the yard the snow came up past Phillip's stomach, and in some places the drifts were so deep he all but disappeared when he hopped into them, yet the sky showed no signs of stopping.

Because of the bump on Jane's head, Fern didn't want her to overexert herself, so she kept both girls inside. After a couple of hours, Walker sent Phillip inside, too, but he continued to work until lunchtime, carving paths to the barn and workshop and clearing half of the driveway, as well.

A delicious aroma filled his nostrils when he opened the door. "That smells *appenditlich*."

"It's chocolate *kuche*," Jane told him. "Fern did something secret while she was making them."

"I know what the secret is," Phillip taunted. "*Mamm* warmed the cookie sheets."

Patience set her brother straight, jeering, "*Neh*, that's not it. She made them with love."

"Patience, you just told the secret!" Jane's exasperation caused Patience's cheeks to redden.

"It's okay, Patience," Walker comforted her. "Anyone who knows your *mamm* knows she puts love into everything she does."

Now *Fern's* cheeks went pink and Walker regretted his comment. It was truly how he felt about her, but he hadn't meant to voice the thought. She addressed the children instead of him, but there was a lilt in her voice as she said, "It's easy to put love into something you're making for people you care about so much."

Walker blushed so hard he could practically feel the snow evaporating from his damp hair and beard. Was she flirting with him? Even if she had been, Walker understood nothing would come of it, but he liked imagining on some level they still shared a mutual attraction. After lunch he whistled as he ambled back outside and got to work again.

By the time he'd come in for the evening, it was barely flurrying. Inside, he found the children somberly sitting on the sofa, three in a row, like birds on a wire. "Where's your *mamm*?"

"In the bedroom. She's crying."

Walker's heartbeat quickened. "Crying? Why?"

"Phillip broke her teacup," Jane tattled.

"I didn't break it—you and Patience broke it when you pulled the box away. *I* was the one who found it."

"We wanted to see it, too. You should have shared," Patience argued.

Walker gave them each a turn to tell him what happened. He learned that Phillip found a box hidden beneath a floorboard in Gloria's old room. The box contained two teacups wrapped in packing paper but when the children scuffled over their find, one of the teacups dropped to the floor and the handle broke off. Fern came in and when she saw the broken china, she burst into tears—big, loud tears, according to Patience—and grabbed the teacup and box and ran downstairs. The children followed her but she told them she needed to be alone.

Realizing the teacups must have been the same ones Fern had given Gloria when they were young, Walker groaned and sank into the armchair as the children continued to quibble over who was at fault. Finally, he held up his hand and raised his voice. "It doesn't matter who did what or how the teacup was broken. It was an accident. Nobody meant for it to happen. What's important is that Phillip and Patience's *mamm* is sad right now. Those teacups were very special to her. Sometimes, when you make someone sad, instead of saying how or why something happened, the best thing you can do is say you're sorry and ask for their forgiveness."

Walker hadn't noticed Fern had crept into the room until Phillip glanced toward the doorway. Walker immediately jumped to his feet in concern. Her eyes were pink-rimmed and her nostrils were, too, but she gave him a weak smile.

"I'm sorry, *Mamm*," Patience said, sniffling.

"Me, too." The knob on Jane's forehead was even more pronounced because she was crimping her brow.

"I'm *very* sorry." Phillip shook his head remorsefully. "I wish I'd never found those teacups."

"Will you forgive us, *Mamm*? Please?" Patience wailed.

Fern swept across the room and crouched in front of the children, her hands on Patience's knees. "Of course I forgive you. *All* of you. And do you know why?" she asked. When they didn't answer, she told them, "Because if you really love someone, you forgive them when they ask you to, just as *Gott* forgives us. Forgiveness is a very important way of showing love."

Phillip jumped up and flung his arms around his mother's stomach, knocking her off balance. She caught herself on her palms, and then Patience and Jane knelt to embrace from both sides and she fell the rest of the way onto her bottom. Fern laughed and tipped her head backward to grin up at Walker. "Hugs are an important way to show forgiveness, too," she quipped.

"C'mon, *kinner*, give Fern some air," Walker ordered after a couple minutes, and the children released their grip on her. He reached to help Fern into a standing position but she was so light that when he pulled her up she lost her balance. As he grasped her other shoulder to steady her, their eyes met. He could have stood there with one hand holding hers, the other resting on her upper arm, until Christmas if it weren't that the children were standing there watching them.

Fern blinked twice before slowly stepping away and announcing it was time for supper. Although she apologized again for the modest portions of carrots and macaroni and cheese for the main meal, she said there were plenty of cookies and Jaala's spice cake for dessert.

As they were eating their sweets, Walker broke the news to the children that the next morning after they held their Sunday worship services together, he was going to take Daisy back to the field where he'd abandoned the buggy, so he could shovel it out and then return to Roman's house to pick up Jane.

As expected, the children bellyached about not being able to celebrate Christmas with each other. But Fern came up with an idea to distract them; she suggested they could all make gifts for each other to open on Christmas morning. "It will make us feel like we're still together."

"How can we make gifts? We don't have enough supplies," Phillip countered.

"We won't make *actual* gifts," Fern explained. "See, with gifts it's the thought that counts. So we'll think about what we'd give each other if we could give anything in the world. Then we'll write down what that is—or we'll draw a picture of it—on a piece of paper."

Patience was all for the idea. "We can fold them up and tie them with a ribbon, just like a present."

Delighted with the idea, the children claimed separate parts of the room where they could work on their gifts without anyone else seeing them. Fern cut a couple paper bags into sections and distributed them along with pencils and some lengths of twine she'd found in a drawer in the kitchen. Walker was surprised when she handed him four pieces of paper and as many pieces of string. He hadn't expected the adults would play this game, too, but it was fun trying to think of the gifts he'd most like to give to everyone.

Choosing Phillip's present was easy: a very fast horse. He'd give Patience a dress that wasn't a hand-me-down, although Walker suspected she genuinely preferred clothing that belonged to someone else first. Jane had nearly outgrown her yellow scooter, but he'd actually gotten her a new one this Christmas and didn't want to repeat himself, so he drew a box of loopy straws.

Walker studied Fern as she chewed on the eraser of her pencil. She was always so thoughtful about others, even when playing a game. It was one of the many qualities he'd always valued in her. In that instant, Walker knew exactly what he would give her if he could: the truth. It took all of his willpower to suppress the impulse to write, "I never loved Gloria—or any other woman. I've only ever loved you. I still do. Even though you didn't truly love me as much as you said you did. And even though you didn't love me as much as I loved you." Instead he jotted, *A half gallon of ice cream from Brubaker's.* Then he sighed and Fern glanced up, first at him and then at the clock.

"It's almost bedtime," she told the children. They pleaded with her for a few more minutes to finish with their gift ideas, and then she and Walker both helped them fold and tie the papers. Then they used clothespins to fasten their "gifts" to the twine Fern looped around the staircase until it was time for Walker and Jane to take theirs home with them.

While the children were putting on their pajamas, Fern offered to make tea. This time, Walker didn't refuse, rationalizing that it was his last night with Fern and he'd made it this long without divulging his secret—or his secret feelings—so he could last a couple more hours.

"It's my turn to tuck in the *kinner*," he said, as if taking turns putting the children to bed was part of a long-established domestic routine.

When Walker turned off the lamp in Phillip's room, the boy said, "Maybe tomorrow when you get back, I can show you how to go down the hill on the trash bin cover. It's a lot of *schpass*."

"I'd like that. *Gut nacht*, Phillip. *Denki* for your help today."

Walker paused outside the girls' room. He thought they were already asleep until he heard Jane say, "I wish my *daed* would marry your *mamm*."

Walker caught his breath to hear his daughter express the longing he'd been wrestling with for the past few days. He stood perfectly still, straining to hear Patience's response.

"Shh!" she cautioned and for a moment, Walker thought she'd sensed he was in the hallway listening to them. Then she explained, "My *mamm* said not to talk like that."

"Why not?"

"She said it's nonsense because two people have to love each other specially to get married." There was a pause before Patience sleepily added, "But your *daed* is our friend."

Utterly dejected, Walker edged toward the staircase. It *was* nonsense to imagine Fern had any romantic feelings toward him. And it was past time for him to put the notion—and himself—to bed.

Chapter Eleven

Fern didn't understand why Walker suddenly changed his mind about staying for tea, but now that he'd left, she didn't feel like having any, either. She removed the kettle from the burner, turned the burner off and went to her room. After she'd put on her nightgown, she settled into a sitting position on her bed and pulled the box from her nightstand onto her lap. She opened it and gently removed the teacup with the broken handle. This was the one she had always used; it was adorned with red tulips. Gloria's tulips were yellow.

Fern had assumed when Gloria got married and moved into Walker's house, she had taken all of her possessions with her. So she was shocked to learn Phillip had found the china beneath a floorboard under the carpet where Gloria used to hide the things she didn't want Roman to find when she lived here. When Fern had realized the handle was broken, she'd burst into sobs as if her heart had fragmented, too, and shut herself up in her room, no doubt frightening the children with her uncharacteristic behavior. But when she'd regained control of her emotions, Fern examined the cup and saw it could be repaired with a little glue. As she was gingerly replacing the china within its bed of packing paper, Fern had found a note and she'd realized prior to marrying Walker, her cousin must have intended to send her the cups, but she'd either forgotten about them or changed her mind.

Now, Fern unfolded the message to read it again.

Dear Fern,
I can imagine it will be very hurtful for you to find out I'm marrying Walker and I'm so sorry about causing you pain.

You told me once there was nothing that could separate us from the love of God in Christ and there was nothing I could do that would be so awful He wouldn't forgive me. I believe that but it doesn't mean I'm not ashamed.

And it doesn't mean you shouldn't be angry with me, either, because you have every right to be. In time, I hope you'll come to forgive me. Knowing you like I do, I think you will. It's my fondest dream our children might share a little bit of the closeness we shared as cousins. As friends.

But even if you stay angry at me forever, I will never stop loving you.
Your Gloria

When she'd first read the letter, Fern felt stung that Gloria expressed regret about hurting her, without actually saying she was sorry for marrying Walker. If she had been so ashamed, why did she go ahead and do it anyway? But upon a second and third reading, Fern's resentment dissipated and in its place, a profound sense of remorse filled her heart. She realized that while God had enabled her to let go of much of the bitterness she'd harbored toward Gloria and Walker, she was stubbornly clinging to a little shred of it. If she'd really loved her cousin and her former suitor—and if she really loved *Gott*—as much as she claimed to love them, it was time for her to show it. It was time for her to entirely forgive them for what they'd done in the past.

Surely, this is Gott's *prompting*, Fern thought. She was less certain about what God's answers were to her other questions, the ones about whether she ought to stay in Maine or if she and Walker had a romantic future together. That's why she was so delighted when he said he'd stay for tea—she'd desperately wanted to talk to him. But then he'd changed his mind and went back to the workshop. Time was running out; if Fern was going to stop Anthony from putting the house up for sale, she'd have to act soon.

Dear Lord, she prayed, *please give me the opportunity to speak privately with Walker tomorrow.* She removed her prayer *kapp*, slid the box under her bed and pulled the quilt up to her chin, wondering how she'd broach the topic of courtship. She had just about drifted to sleep when inspiration struck. Fern got out of bed and tiptoed to the staircase to retrieve the Christmas "gift" she'd made for Walker. She had written that she'd like to give him an extra large container of peanut brittle. She took a new piece of paper and wrote, "If I could give you anything in the world, I'd give you my heart, but I can't because it's already yours and only yours." After folding the note and tying a bow around it with twine, she brought it to her room, so she could give it to him in person if it seemed appropriate once they began talking.

But the next morning immediately after they'd worshipped together and enjoyed a light brunch, Walker announced he needed to head out to get the buggy. Fern didn't understand why he was so eager to leave; he and Jane wouldn't travel to Unity until tomorrow anyway, since today was the Sabbath.

Phillip asked if he could go with him, but Walker curtly said it was too far and he didn't want Phillip to slow him down. He must have caught the disappointment clouding Phillip's face, because he added, "The *meed* need your help navigating through the backyard, since you know where the biggest snowdrifts are."

Because she was still concerned about the bump on Jane's head and wanted to keep an eye on her, Fern followed the children outside. They shuffled through the snow to the top of the hill, using their legs to etch a rough path, and then Fern shuffled back down the same way she came, to clear away even more of the fine white powder.

After watching them sled—and, in Phillip's case,

roll—down the hill for well over an hour, Fern heard someone near the side of the house call her name. *That can't be Walker already,* she thought, just as Stephen clumped into view.

After Fern greeted him he said, "I came to clear your driveway for you but it looks as if someone beat me to it."

"*Jah*, Walker did it." She gestured toward Jane on the hill. "He and Jane went off the road on Friday night and their *gaul* was so tired and spooked they had to leave the buggy in a field and trek all the way back during the storm. Walker is out retrieving it now."

"Walker stayed here overnight?" Stephen raised his brows.

"*Jah*. Both Walker and Jane."

Stephen shook his head, clucking his tongue against his teeth. "I'm surprised at you, Fern—not at Walker, but at you."

Fern lowered her voice so it wouldn't carry up the hill to the children. "What is *that* supposed to mean?" But she knew exactly what he meant, so before he could respond she growled, "For your information, Walker slept in the workshop."

Stephen shrugged. "I believe you, but, you know, given what happened with Gloria, you should guard your reputation better."

What happened with Gloria? "I have no idea what you're talking about."

"Oh, that's right. You weren't here when her baby was born. Her eight-and-a-half-pound premature baby. They never made a confession to the *kurrich*, but…" Stephen let his implication hang in the air.

For a moment Fern thought she'd gone blind with rage at Stephen, but once she blinked she realized it was just the effect of the sun against the snow. Using all her concentration to temper her response, she intoned, "I'd like you to leave. And don't *kumme* back until you can talk like a gentleman."

Storming away, she shouted to the children, telling them she needed to go warm up for a few minutes. Once inside the house, she filled a glass at the kitchen sink but her hand was trembling too severely to lift it to her mouth. *I don't believe it. Walker wouldn't do something like that and neither would Gloria.* But the more she thought about her cousin's note, the more Fern suspected maybe *this* was what Gloria had been ashamed of doing. Suddenly, everything made sense and nothing made sense at all. *How can this be?*

Fern didn't know how long she stood like that, staring out the window but not really seeing the children fly down the hill on their sleds. When the front door opened and Walker came into the kitchen, she was still wearing her coat and clutching the water glass. He told her Abram happened to be passing as he was shoveling the buggy out of the field.

"He said to let you know he'd pick you and the *kinner* up tomorrow morning at ten o'clock." When Fern only nodded in response, Walker continued, "I want to get to the phone shanty as soon as possible to call my *mamm*, so I'm going to go round up Jane now."

Fern clapped the glass down, twirled around and blurted out, "Was Gloria with child before you married her?"

"Wh-what? Who told you that?" Walker didn't look nearly as appalled as Fern expected him to look. It must not have been the first time he'd heard the rumor.

"Stephen said Jane was too big to be premature. Was Gloria with child before you married her?" she repeated. The Amish rarely used the word *pregnant*, but even saying "with child" seemed immodest to Fern, given the context of what she was asking.

"Stephen doesn't know what he's talking about," Walker replied scornfully. But that wasn't the same as saying no.

Fern enunciated deliberately, replying, "I asked you a direct question. For the third time, was Gloria with child before you married her?"

"It's not what you think, Fern." Walker's mustache quivered as he replied. Oh, how Fern loathed the sight of that mustache now.

"You're right—it's *not* what I think. I never would have thought you'd do such a thing. *Neh*, stupid me, I actually started to believe you'd married Gloria because you were so distraught over Jordan's death that you weren't in your right mind! For the life of me, I couldn't comprehend any other reason for it! And now I know. But what I don't understand—what I'll *never* understand—is why you acted as if you loved me. If you and Gloria wanted to…to *court*, why did you claim your abiding love for me? Why would you deliberately trample on my heart like that? It was just plain *cruel*."

"Ha!" Walker sneered. "Quit acting so wounded, Fern. Because for someone who claimed she'd never loved anyone the way she loved me, you sure got over me pretty fast. It took what, a couple of months for you to marry Marshall? I wanted you to marry me when we were nineteen and you made me wait for two more years. But you didn't even wait six more months until *hochzich* season to marry him."

"How dare you talk to me about waiting! You and Gloria didn't even wait until your wedding—" Fern stopped short, unable to complete the thought. She shoved past Walker and went into the living room, yanked one of the paper gifts from the twine around the staircase and returned to hold it up in front of his face. "You want to know why I married Marshall so quickly? *This* is why. Because I was so destitute I couldn't even afford to give anyone a *paper Grischtdaag* present!"

"So you married him for his money?" Walker shot back at her. "At least I married Gloria for a noble reason!"

"Noble? There was nothing noble about what the two of you did. You *had* to marry Gloria!" Fern couldn't stand to look at Walker. She turned her back toward him and peered out the window again. Gripping the edge of the sink, she said, "You can send Jane in to collect her things and say goodbye, but you are not *wilkom* to cross that threshold as long as I'm in this *haus*."

"You don't have to worry about that!" Walker barked. A few seconds later the door slammed behind him.

Fern worried she was about to be sick, but she fought the feeling and managed to catch her breath again before Jane came in. "*Daed* says we have to leave now."

"*Jah.*" Fern couldn't say anything else without weeping and she didn't want Jane's last memory of her to be a sad one.

"I'm going to leave my card game upstairs for Phillip and Patience to keep and my chocolates for you. But I can't forget my presents." Jane plucked the papers from the twine then hugged Fern so hard her stomach hurt. "I love you," the little girl said, which made Fern's stomach hurt even more.

"I love you, too."

By the time Patience and Phillip came in, Fern had hung her coat up and washed her face, but Patience still noticed something was amiss. "Don't be sad, *Mamm. Gott* might still let us live in this *haus* and then we'll be able to see Jane and Walker again."

Neh, I'm quite certain the Lord doesn't want us to live in this haus. *And neither do I*, Fern thought. She couldn't fathom the idea of living anywhere near Walker now. It was one thing if he'd married Gloria because he'd been suffering from some kind of emotional upheaval after the accident. But to behave as he and Gloria had behaved? Fern saw no way to justify that, especially since he'd made a commitment to God and to the Amish way of life. Even more importantly, he'd never repented; if he had, he would have confessed his wrongdoing to the church and they would have accepted his apology. But Stephen made it clear no such thing had happened.

For the rest of the afternoon and into the evening, Fern seethed about how Walker acted as if *she'd* done something wrong by marrying Marshall! She was so upset she could hardly eat supper, and she was glad when the children didn't ask her to light the candles or sing carols, as she was in no mood for festivity. "Let's all go to bed early tonight, since the *Sabbat* is a day of rest," she suggested. "Tomorrow we'll celebrate with Jaala's *familye* and you'll need lots of energy since her *groosskinner* will probably want to build a snowman with you."

She tucked Patience in first. No sooner had the girl rested her head against the pillow than she popped upright again. "*Mamm*, Jane forgot her dress and took yours instead!" Fern realized her daughter was right; after the accident she'd hung Jane's dress in the basement to dry and Jane had been wearing Fern's dress—with a pinned-up hem—for the past two days. She wished one of them would have thought of this sooner, especially since Fern only owned three dresses instead of four, as was customary. "Can we bring it to her?"

"*Neh*, we'll leave it here and her *groossmammi* can pick it up when they get home from Unity," Fern answered.

When she walked into Phillip's room, she stubbed her foot on something. Peeling back the small braided rug, she noticed one of the boards was off center. "What happened to the floor?"

"That's where we found the teacups. I couldn't make the board fit again."

Fern lifted up the plank, telling him he'd put it back upside down. When she did, she saw a dusty, leather-covered book in the little open compartment beneath it. She reached in and pulled it out. It must have been Gloria's journal. *It probably contains a lot of other secrets she literally swept under the carpet*, she thought bitingly and carried the diary downstairs.

Fern had no interest in perusing it, nor did she want anyone else to read it, so she opened it to tear out the pages for burning in the woodstove. Her eye caught on the phrase, "I don't want to marry Walker and I certainly don't love him."

It made Fern furious that her cousin hadn't even *wanted* to marry the man Fern had loved with her whole heart. She read on:

He doesn't love me, either. He said the only way he'd marry me is if we live as brother and sister, not as husband and wife. For the sake of the baby, we've also agreed to never, ever tell another soul why we got married.

I don't understand... Fern flipped back several pages to read, "If my father ever finds out I'm with child and the father was an *Englischer*, I don't know what he'll do."

Gasping, Fern collapsed onto the sofa. Jane's father was an *Englischer*? Then why did Walker marry Gloria? Fern turned back further in the journal until she found her answer. "I can't believe Jordan is gone. I am so scared. So alone."

Jordan. Jordan was Jane's daed*!* Fern scanned the diary greedily, unable to take in the information quickly enough. According to what her cousin had written, Gloria had been planning to leave the Amish in order to marry Jordan, even before she realized she was pregnant. Fern gathered that she was devastated by Jordan's sudden death and terrified Roman would send her out of his home if he found out. Knowing she couldn't make it on her own in the *Englisch* world, Gloria had confessed her dilemma to Walker on the day of Jordan's funeral.

"When I told Walker, I never expected him to say we should get married," Gloria had scrawled. Some of the ink was smeared across the page. "But he insists he can't allow the baby to grow up fatherless and homeless, not after Jordan gave his life to save Walker's. If I could think of any other way to help my baby without hurting Fern, I would do it…"

Fern dropped the book to the floor and pressed the heel of her hand against her mouth to keep the sobs from escaping her lips and waking the children. As she rocked back and forth, reflecting on Gloria's predicament and Walker's sacrifice, Fern cried and cried.

In retrospect, so many things he'd said to her since she returned to Serenity Ridge took on a new meaning. Like when he'd insisted, "I wouldn't tell you something unless I meant it." *He was referring to the past. He was saying he hadn't lied, that I really was the only woman he ever wanted for a wife.* Similarly, it had seemed so hypocritical that he'd been angry at her for marrying Marshall after he'd married Gloria first, but now Fern understood. She nearly wept herself sick, thinking about it.

By the time the sun came up, she hadn't been to bed at all. Fern climbed the stairs, declaring, *"Frehlicher Grischtdaag,"* in a loud voice.

Phillip was the first to rouse. *"Frehlicher Grischtdaag,"* he said. "Is it time to open our presents?"

Fern was confused. "I left your presents in Ohio, remember?"

"I mean the presents we made for each other downstairs."

"Oh, *jah*, we can open those. But instead of opening them now, I have a better idea."

"What is it, *Mamm*?" Patience asked from the hall.

Fern explained how it's always more fun to watch someone open a present you give them in person, so she suggested they ought to visit Jane and Walker at their house. "We can bring Jane's dress back, too. But it's a very long walk. Do you think you can make it?"

"Jah!" they cried together.

"Then let's hurry. We need to get there before they leave for their *ant* Willa's *haus*."

Within a few minutes, they'd set out. Frosted in white, tall pines glistened with touches of sunshine along both sides of the quiet country road. "Isn't this the perfect *Grischtdaag*?" Phillip asked Patience. The two of them skipped hand-in-hand in front of Fern until a buggy crested the hill in their direction and Fern urged them to move to the side of the street so it could safely pass.

But the buggy slowed to a stop and a man got out. *"Frehlicher Grischtdaag!"* he shouted, and it took a moment for Fern to recognize it was Stephen. She repeated the greeting and tried to walk around him but he blocked her way. "Can I speak with you a second?"

Since Fern had a word or two to get off her chest, as well, she told the children to wait by Stephen's buggy at the side of the road. Fern couldn't honestly defend Gloria, but she figured she could at least tell Stephen he was wrong about Walker, without betraying any confidences.

But before she could speak her piece, Stephen apologized. "I'm very sorry I said what I said about Walker yesterday. You were right. It wasn't gentlemanly. Nor was it fair of me to make assumptions or spread rumors."

Hearing the sincere penitence in his voice, Fern replied, "It's okay. I've been guilty of doing the same thing. Let's not mention it again, agreed?"

"Agreed." For some reason, Stephen wasn't wearing gloves, and he rubbed his hands together and then blew on his fingers. "What are you doing out walking so early this morning?"

When she told him she was returning Jane's dress before they left, Stephen offered to take Fern and the children to Walker's house.

"That would be *wunderbaar*. But weren't you going somewhere in the opposite direction?"

"*Jah*. I was going to apologize to you," he admitted sheepishly. "I didn't want you to leave Serenity Ridge without reconciling."

Gott *willing, I won't be leaving*, Fern thought. "I can't think of a better way to celebrate *Grischtdaag* than reconciling with a friend," she said.

Since the previous day was the Sabbath and unnecessary work was prohibited, Walker hadn't cleared his driveway. But this morning he funneled all of his anger at Fern into shoveling snow. *I could understand why Stephen Hertig would think Gloria and I had to get married, but Fern knows me better than to ask me a question like that! I courted her for almost three years—she knows that's not what I was like!*

Of course, it wasn't lost on Walker that he hadn't been able to deny that Gloria was with child when he married her, but he considered that to be beside the point. In his mind, Fern never should have questioned him in the first place. As for her reason for marrying Marshall so quickly? Walker didn't believe it for a second. If she had been that impoverished, she could have found a relative to live with. She could have gone to the church and asked for help. No, she was just making excuses. Making herself look like the injured party. She was so self-righteous...

Completely absorbed by his thoughts, Walker didn't notice that a buggy had pulled up in front of his house until the front door opened and Jane hollered, *"Frehlicher Grischtdaag!"* from the porch.

Of all people, it was Stephen who got out of the carriage, along with *Fern*. Then Patience and Phillip spilled out, too. *What's this about?* Walker jammed his shovel upright in the snow and turned to go check on Daisy in the stable. He had nothing to say to Fern and even less than nothing to say to Stephen.

But he couldn't ignore Phillip and Patience, who tore up the driveway, yelling that they'd brought Jane's dress back and they'd come to open their paper gifts with her. She held the door open and the three of them disappeared into the house before Walker could protest. Stephen waved before getting into his buggy and pulling away.

As Fern slowly approached him, Walker picked up the shovel again and started flinging snow to the side of the driveway. "You should have told Stephen to wait for the *kinner* to finish opening their gifts together." *Because I'm not giving you a ride.*

"That's okay. We can walk to Jaala's *haus* from here," Fern said. She stood off to his right and he nearly tossed a heap of snow onto her boots by accident.

"Could you move out of the way, please?"

"*Neh.* Could you stop shoveling, please?" When

he didn't stop, Fern insisted, "Walker, I have something important to tell you and I don't want to have to shout."

If Fern was going to say something else about Gloria or Jane, Walker didn't want to hear it. But neither did he want the children to hear it, so he chucked one last scoopful of snow. "Make it quick," he allowed, but instead of giving her his full attention, he surveyed the driveway, trying to figure out how long it would take him to complete his task.

"I—I found a journal of Gloria's," she confessed. "I know about… Jordan and Jane. I know you and Gloria were never…"

Walker couldn't bear to talk about this subject. He winced and said, "That was a long time ago. It doesn't matter now."

"*Jah*, it does." Fern sidled closer. "It matters to me. It matters a *lot* to me."

Walker guffawed, unable to look at her, even though she was standing inches from him, for once not folding into herself but forcing herself into his space. She continued to speak. "You said I got over you quickly, but you're wrong. I've *never* gotten over you. I never loved Marshall the way I loved you."

"You married him." He squinted down at her. "You had two *kinner* with him."

"*Jah*, and I'll never say I regret having Phillip and Patience. Just like I know you'll never say you regret being Jane's *daed*," she countered, and she was right, but that didn't make Walker feel any better. "Even if you married Gloria for what you thought were very *gut* reasons, it still broke my heart, but I forgive you. Please, forgive me for breaking yours."

Walker wouldn't budge. After a few seconds of his stony silence, Fern said, "You were traumatized when you married Gloria, Walker. I married Marshall because I'd been traumatized, too. It was to a much lesser extent than when Jordan died, but when you married Gloria instead of me..." Fern swiped at her cheek. "I felt as if *you'd* died a sudden and unexpected death. And I did something desperate in response, just like you did. I didn't trust the Lord with my future—I didn't even ask Him what to do. I should have, but I didn't."

Every word Fern spoke resonated with truth, but Walker couldn't allow himself to believe she loved him. He glanced down the street. The van would arrive soon and he needed to change his clothes.

Apparently, Fern had more to say. "I want to stay in Maine. I want to live here for *gut*. But I can't if my living here is going to upset you. But whether I live here or in Ohio or anywhere else, you should know that I'll never stop loving you."

"But not the way a wife loves a husband." The words tasted bilious as Walker spoke them.

"What?"

"Patience told Jane you said it was nonsense to think you could love me the way a wife loves a husband."

It took a moment but Walker could practically see recollection dawn across Fern's face. "Oh, that," she said, rolling her eyes, but Walker wasn't amused. Glowering, he lifted his shovel again, but Fern grabbed it from him with a fierceness he hadn't seen in her before now. "Patience is a *kind*, Walker. Earlier in the week she told me she wanted you to… to ask me to marry you. I was afraid she'd start saying the same thing to Jane or to you and I didn't want you to feel uncomfortable. I didn't want you to think *I* was suggesting we get married."

"No chance I'd ever think that," Walker muttered, pushing his hat farther down on his head.

Fern's lower lip trembled as she gazed up at him, her eyes awash with tears. Without breaking eye contact, she pulled off her glove and removed a square of folded paper from her palm. "This is for you. And for what it matters, I wrote it before I found Gloria's journal," she said, pressing it against his chest so he had to take it. "I'll go get the *kinner* now."

As she walked toward the house, Walker unfolded the paper and read, "If I could give you anything in the world, I'd give you my heart, but I can't because it's already yours and only yours."

Walker let the shovel clatter against the pavement. Charging toward Fern, he called her name. She had just reached the second porch step and she turned toward him, so that her beautiful silver eyes were level with his. He took hold of her hands and pulled her forward. After a long kiss, he murmured, "*Denki* for my *Grischtdaag* gift. It's exactly what I've always wanted."

Epilogue

❧

"I'm *hallich Gott* let us live in *Onkel* Roman's *haus* for a whole year," Patience said as she climbed into the back of the buggy with Phillip and Jane. "But I'm *hallich* we got to move into a new *haus*, too."

Before marrying Fern, Walker had built a house for their family, with the help of the men in the district. Fern had told him she didn't need a new house, but Walker insisted on fulfilling the promise he'd made to her the first time he'd asked her to marry him.

"I'm *hallich* I get to have your *daed* for my second *daed*," Phillip announced.

"And I'm *hallich* I get to have your *mamm* for my second *mamm*," Jane copied.

Sitting in the front of the buggy, Walker and Fern exchanged glances. They'd talked about allowing Jane to read some of Gloria's diary once she was a little older so she could learn about Jordan. Walker still wasn't convinced this wasn't a violation of the agreement he'd made with Gloria, but Fern trusted that if they prayed about it first, God would help them make a wise decision.

As soon as they pulled out of the parking lot of Foster's Creamery after their second annual pre-Christmas treat, Fern shivered.

"Are you still cold from eating an ice cream cone?" Walker asked.

"*Jah.* A little bit."

He brought the horse to a halt so he could spread a blanket over Fern's lap. "Warm enough?" he asked.

"Not yet."

He unfolded a second blanket over her legs and inched closer. "*Now* are you warm enough?"

"*Neh*, not yet," she replied, so he slid close enough to wrap his arm around her from the side and she snuggled against him. "There. *Now* I'm warm enough."

Now I'm home.

* * * * *

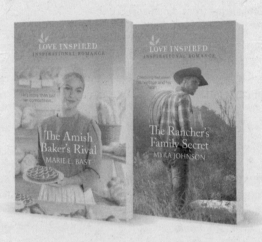

LOVE INSPIRED
INSPIRATIONAL ROMANCE

He needs a housekeeper. She needs a job.
This holiday season, will they join forces—
and find true love?

Read on for a sneak preview of
Her Christmas Dilemma *by Brenda Minton.*

"We need a housekeeper because I can't chase you down every other—" Tucker suddenly remembered they had an audience. "We can talk about this at home."

Nan, spritely at seventy with short silvery hair, grinned big and inclined her head toward the other woman.

"Clara needs a job," she said.

"I don't think so," Clara shot back.

"You need something to do," Nan insisted.

"She doesn't want the job." Tucker winked at the woman and watched her cheeks turn rosy.

Flirting was an art he'd learned late in life, and he still wasn't too accomplished at it. He'd never been a ladies' man.

"No, I really don't," she answered. "I'm only here temporarily."

Should he feel relieved or let down?

"You should introduce us," he told Nan.

"Tucker Church, I'd like you to meet Clara Fisher," Nan said. "She's one of my kids."

One of Nan's foster daughters. She'd had a dozen or more over the years. He held a hand out. "Clara, nice to meet you."

It was a long moment before Clara slid her hand into his. Then she stepped back, putting space between them.

"Nice to meet you, too. But I'm afraid I'm not interested in a job." She gave his niece a genuine smile, then her gaze lifted to meet his. "I think that we probably met in school, but you were a senior and I was just a freshman."

He couldn't imagine forgetting Clara Fisher, with her dark brown eyes that held secrets and a smile that was captivating. He found himself wishing he could make her smile again.

Shay elbowed him. "She doesn't want the job," she whispered. "Can we go home now?"

"Of course she doesn't want to work for us. She's probably heard the stories about you running off two housekeepers." He gave Clara a pleading look.

"Would you take my number? In case you change your mind?"

"I won't change my mind," she insisted.

He had no right to feel disappointed. She was a stranger. And yet, he was.

"Well, we should go," he said as he walked Shay toward the door.

"I bet she can't even clean," Shay said under her breath.

He didn't disagree. But Clara looked like a woman who was trying to put herself back together. He needed someone strong who could stand up to Shay.

The woman who replaced Mrs. Jenkins couldn't have soulful brown eyes and a smile that made him want to take chances.

Don't miss
Her Christmas Dilemma *by Brenda Minton,*
available December 2021 wherever
Love Inspired books and ebooks are sold.

LoveInspired.com

LOVE INSPIRED

Stories to uplift and inspire

Fall in love with Love Inspired—
inspirational and uplifting stories of faith
and hope. Find strength and comfort in
the bonds of friendship and community.
Revel in the warmth of possibility and the
promise of new beginnings.

Sign up for the Love Inspired newsletter
at **LoveInspired.com** to be the first
to find out about upcoming titles,
special promotions and exclusive content.

CONNECT WITH US AT:

Facebook.com/LoveInspiredBooks

Twitter.com/LoveInspiredBks